Praise for
A FATAL INVERSION

"This simply superlative piece of storytelling should convince the last doubter that Ruth Rendell is the English-speaking world's finest writer of psychological suspense novels. . . . Flawlessly crafted, cunningly narrated, it is deceptively low-key, yet cumulatively powerful. . . . The author's uncanny ability to slip inside each character's internal torment is awesome. . . . Unexpected revelations continue to stun, even on the final page."
—*Buffalo News*

"*A Fatal Inversion* transcends the genre . . . beautifully ambient writing . . . [Rendell] virtually defies one to pause between incidents in the exquisitely controlled developments that peak in a marvel of irony that no reader could foresee."
—*Publishers Weekly*

"Nothing in [Rendell's] story of inverted passions happens predictably, and the ending is a quiet shocker. . . . Rendell has a surgeon's disenchanted but not unkindly eye for the lives she is dissecting."
—*San Francisco Chronicle*

"[Rendell's] reputation for creating teasing tension from first page to last will be sustained by this riveting novel, which effectively bridges the gap between her detective stories and her psychological suspense novels. . . . The plot works like quicksand, drawing the reader relentlessly in."
—*Booklist*

"[Rendell] has the gift of devising an ingenious plot, and of maintaining interest by driving along the narrative with zest and cunning. . . . [Her work] says as much about the habits, manners, talk and behavior of people in contemporary Britain, as those of Kingsley Amis, Iris Murdoch or any other novelist in current practice."
—*The Washington Post*

"The character psychology is astonishingly incisive, as [Rendell] advances her ruthlessly meticulous investigation into those closed, terrified minds."
—*Cleveland Plain Dealer*

P9-CFD-592

Bantam offers the finest in classic and modern British murder mysteries. Ask your bookseller for the books you have missed.

Agatha Christie

Death on the Nile
A Holiday for Murder
The Mousetrap and Other Plays
The Mysterious Affair at Styles
Poirot Investigates
Postern of Fate
The Secret Adversary
The Seven Dials Mystery
Sleeping Murder

Dorothy Simpson

Last Seen Alive
The Night She Died
Puppet for a Corpse
Six Feet Under
Close Her Eyes

Sheila Radley

The Chief Inspector's Daughter
Death in the Morning
Fate Worse Than Death
Coming Soon: Who Saw Him Die?

Elizabeth George

A Great Deliverance

Colin Dexter

The Riddle of the Third Mile
The Lost World of Nicholas Quinn
Service of All the Dead
The Dead of Jericho
Coming Soon: The Secret of Annexe 3

John Greenwood

The Mind of Mr. Mosley
The Missing Mr. Mosley
Mosley By Moonlight
Murder, Mr. Mosley
Mists Over Mosley
Coming Soon: What, Me, Mr. Mosley

Ruth Rendell

The Face of Trespass
The Lake of Darkness
No More Dying Then
One Across, Two Down
Shake Hands Forever
A Sleeping Life
A Dark-Adapted Eye
       (writing as Barbara Vine)
A Fatal Inversion
       (writing as Barbara Vine)

Marian Babson

Death in Fashion
Reel Murder
Murder, Murder Little Star
Coming Soon: Murder On a Mystery Tour

Christianna Brand

Suddenly at His Residence
Heads You Lose

Dorothy Cannell

The Widows Club
Coming Soon: Down the Garden Path

A
FATAL
INVERSION

BARBARA VINE

BANTAM BOOKS
TORONTO • NEW YORK • LONDON • SYDNEY • AUCKLAND

A FATAL INVERSION

A Bantam Book
Bantam hardcover edition / September 1987
Bantam paperback edition / October 1988

Library of Congress Cataloging-in-Publication Data

Rendell, Ruth, 1930–
  A fatal inversion.

  I. Title.
PR6068.E63F35 1987   823'.914   87-47556
ISBN 0-553-27249-7

Bantam Books are published by Bantam Books, a division of Bantam Doubleday Dell Publishing Group, Inc. Its trademark, consisting of the words "Bantam Books" and the portrayal of a rooster, is Registered in U.S. Patent and Trademark Office and in other countries. Marca Registrada. Bantam Books, 666 Fifth Avenue, New York, New York 10103.

PRINTED IN THE UNITED STATES OF AMERICA

O   0 9 8 7 6 5 4 3 2 1

1

The body lay on a small square of carpet in the middle of the gun room floor. Alec Chipstead looked around for something to put over it. He unhooked a raincoat from one of the pegs and, covering the body, reflected too late that he would never wear that again.

He went outside to see the vet off.

"I'm glad that's all over."

"Extraordinary how painful these things can be," said the vet. "You'll get another dog, I suppose?"

"I expect so. That's really up to Meg."

The vet nodded. He got into his car, put his head out of the window, and asked Alec if he was sure he didn't want the body taken away. Alec said no, thanks, really, he'd see to all that. He watched the car move off up the long, sloping lane that in those parts was called a drift, under the overhanging branches of the trees, and disappear around the bend where the pinewood began. The sky was a pale silvery blue, the trees still green but touched here and there with yellow. September had been a wet month, and the lawns that ran gently to meet the wood were green too. On the edge of the grass, where a strip of flower border separated it from the paved drive, lay a rubber ball dented with toothmarks. How long had that been there? Months, probably. It was a long time since Fred had been up to playing with a ball. Alec put it into his pocket. He walked around the house, up the stone steps onto the terrace, and in by the french windows.

Meg was sitting in the drawing room, pretending to read *Country Life*.

"He didn't know a thing," Alec said. "He just went to sleep."

"What fools we are."

"I held him on my lap and he went to sleep and the vet gave him the injection and he—died."

"We couldn't have kept him any longer. Not with that chorea. It was too painful to watch and it must have been hell for him."

"I know. I suppose if we'd had a family, love—I mean, Fred was just a dog and people go through this with kids. Can you imagine?"

Meg, who was made sharp-tongued by distress, said, "I've yet to hear of parents calling in the doctor to put their sick children down."

Alec didn't say any more. He went back through the house, across the large, finely proportioned hall, with its pretty, curved staircase, under the wide arch to the kitchen area, and then to the gun room. The front kitchen and the back kitchen had been converted into one, lined with the latest in cupboards and gadgets. You wouldn't have imagined, while in there, that the house was two hundred years old. It was the real estate agent who had called the place where the freezer lived and where they hung their coats the gun room. No guns were kept there now. No doubt there had been in the Berelands' time, and some old Bereland squire had sat in here in a windsor chair at a deal table, cleaning them. . . .

He twitched the corner of the raincoat and had a last look at the dead beagle. Meg had come up behind him and was standing there. Sentimentally he thought, though did not say aloud, that the white and tan forehead was still at last, would suffer no more brutal spasms.

"His was a good life."

"Yes. Where are we going to bury him?"

"On the other side of the lake, I thought, in the Little Wood."

Alec wrapped the body up in his raincoat, wrapped it like a parcel. The raincoat had seen better days, but it had come originally from Aquascutum, an expensive shroud. Alec had an obscure feeling that he owed this last sacrifice to Fred, this final tribute.

"I've got a better idea," Meg said, putting on her parka. "The Bereland graveyard. Why the Little Wood when we've already got an animal cemetery? Oh, do let's, Alec. It seems so *right*. It's been a traditional burying place for pets for so long. I'd like Fred to be there, I really would."

"Why not?"

"I know I'm a fool. I'm a sentimental idiot, but I'd sort of like to think of him with those others. With Alexander and Pinto and Blaze. I am a fool, aren't I?"

"That makes two of us," said Alec.

He went across to the old stable block, where they kept the tractor and the wood stacked for winter, and came back with a wheelbarrow and a couple of spades.

"We'll mark the grave with a wooden plaque, I think. I could make one out of a sycamore log, that's a nice white wood, and you could do the lettering on it."

"All right. But we'll do that later." Meg bent to lift up the parcel but recoiled at the last moment, straightening up again and shaking her head. It was Alec who put the dog into the barrow. They set off up the drift.

There were two woods, three if you counted the one below the lake. The lawn in front of the house in which a great black cedar grew ended at the old wood, five or six acres of deciduous trees, and beyond that, as the ground rose, a green ride of turf separated it from the pinewood. This was a plantation, rows of cluster and knobcone pines, set rather too close together and now forming a dense reforestation. It was larger than the deciduous wood, nearly twice the size of it, and forming a windbreak between it and Nunes Road, across which, since the uprooting of hedges, gales swept unchecked from the prairielike fields.

Impenetrable the pinewood seemed to be from the drift and Nunes Road. But on the southern side an offshoot from the green ride led in between the ranked trees, led into the center, where it broadened out into a rough circular shape. Here both the Chipsteads had penetrated on one previous occasion, on a Sunday of exploration not long after they bought the house and land. If you have twenty acres of land it takes you a little time to learn exactly what your possession consists of. They had been a little moved by what they saw, gently derisive, too, to conceal their sentimentality even from the other.

"This could only be in England," Meg had said.

This time they knew exactly where they were going and what they would find. They left the drift by the green ride that was rather like a tunnel between the two kinds of wood and which at its distant end showed a little vista of green meadows piled in lozenge shapes, scraps of darker copse, a church tower. Underfoot, where the grass ended, was a slippery floor of pine needles. The air smelled of resin.

Turf covered the circular place, but here it was raised into a dozen or so small hummocks, shallow hills, grassy knolls. The monuments were mostly of wood, oak, of course, or it would not have lasted so long, but even some of these had fallen and rotted. The rest were greened with lichen. Among them was the rare stone: a block of slate, a slab of pink granite, a curb of bright white Iceland spar. On this last was engraved the name Alexander and the dates: 1901–1909.

What writing there might have been on the wooden crosses had been obscured by time and weather. But the inscription on the pink granite remained sharp and clear. *Blaze* was printed there in capital letters, and under it:

> *They do not sweat and whine about their condition;*
> *They do not lie awake in the dark and weep for their*
>   *sins . . .*
> *Not one is respectable or unhappy over the whole earth.*

Meg stooped down to look at brushstrokes almost obliterated by yellow mold. "'By what eternal streams, Pinto . . .'" she read. "'Gone from us after three years.' Do you think Pinto was a water spaniel?"

"Or a pet otter." Alec lifted out Fred's shrouded body and laid it on the grass. "I can remember doing this sort of thing when I was a kid. Only it was a rabbit we were burying. My brother and I had a rabbit funeral."

"I bet you didn't have a ready-made cemetery."

"No. It had to be the back of a flower bed."

"Where shall we put him?"

Alec picked up the spade. "Over here, I should think. Next to

Blaze. It seems the obvious place. I should think Blaze was the last to be buried here, the date's 1957. Presumably succeeding occupants didn't have pets."

Meg walked around, eyeing the graves, trying to calculate the order in which the plots had been used. It was hard to tell because of the collapse of so many of the wooden monuments, but certainly it seemed as if Blaze had been the last animal laid here, there being two rows of seven hummocks each behind his grave and three hummocks to the left of it.

"Put him on the right side of Blaze," she said.

Now that Alec had begun to dig, Meg would have liked to get it over with as soon as possible. It was all folly; it was beneath their dignity as middle-aged, presumably intelligent people; it was what children did. Alec's recounting his pet rabbit's funeral brought this home to her. Why, at one moment she had almost been going to suggest uttering a few farewell words as Fred was laid to rest. They must bury him, they must replace the turf over him, forget all that nonsense about a memorial. White sycamore indeed! Meg seized the other spade and began digging rapidly, turning up the soft, needle-filled leafmold. Once the turf was penetrated, the ground yielded to the spade as easily as the sand on a beach above the water line.

"Easy does it," Alec said. "It's Fred we're burying, not a coffin six feet under."

These were unfortunate words that he was to remember in the days to come with a squeeze of the stomach, a wrinkling of the nose. His spade struck what he thought was a stone, a long flint. He dug around it and cleared a blade-shaped bone. There was an animal buried here already then. . . . Something that had a very big rib cage, he thought. He wasn't going to say anything to Meg but just cover up that rib cage and that collarbone quickly and start afresh up where she was digging.

Alec was aware of a crow cawing somewhere. Down in the tall limes of the deciduous wood, probably. The thought came unpleasantly to him that crows were carrion birds. He plunged the spade in once more, slicing into the firm dry turf. As he did so he saw that Meg was holding out her spade to him. On it lay what looked like the bones, the fan splay of metatarsals, of a very small foot.

"A monkey?" Meg said in a faint, faltering voice.

"It must be."

"Why hasn't it got a headstone?"

He didn't answer. He dug down, lifting out spadeloads of resin-scented earth. Meg was digging up bones; she had a pile of them.

"We'll put them in a box or something. We'll rebury them."

"No," he said. "No, we can't do that. Meg . . . ?"

"What is it? What's the matter?"

"Look," he said, and he lifted it up to show her. "That's not a dog's skull, is it? That's not a monkey's?"

2

The things that had happened at Ecalpemos, Adam resisted thinking about. He dreamed of them, he could not expel them from his unconscious mind and they also came back to him by association, but he never allowed himself to dwell on them, to operate any random access techniques or eye for long the mental screen where options appeared. When the process began, when association started an entering procedure—at, for instance, the sound of a Greek or Spanish place name, the taste of raspberries, the sight of candles out of doors—he had taught himself to touch an escape key, rather like that on the computers he sold.

There had never been, over the years, more than an associative reminder. He had been lucky. On that last day they had all agreed not only never to meet again, that went without saying, but also if a chance encounter should occur, not to seem to notice the other, to pass without recognition. It was a long time since Adam had ceased to speculate as to what had become of them, where their lives had led them. He had made no attempt to follow careers and had had no recourse to the phone book. If asked by an inner inquisitor and required to be honest, he might have said he would have felt most comfortable if he knew they were all dead.

His dreams were another story, a different area. They visited him there. The setting of the dream would always be Ecalpemos, where, alone at night or on some hot, still afternoon, entering the walled garden or turning the corner to the back stairs, where Zosie had seen the ghosts of Hilbert and of Blaze, he would meet one of them coming toward him. Vivien in her bright blue dress, it had once been, and at another time Rufus, white-coated and with blood on his hands. After that particular one he had been afraid to go to sleep at night. He had lain awake purposely for fear of having another dream like that. Soon after that the baby had been born and this had been an excuse for him to have restless, disturbed nights, to resist sleep until he was too tired to dream. It was his misfortune really that Abigail was such a good baby and slept seven and eight hours at a stretch.

This not only prevented him from putting forward the excuse of having to stay awake to nurse her but also had its own power to frighten. She slept so peacefully, she was so quiet and still. He had gotten into the habit of getting up five or six times a night and going into her room to see if she was all right. An anxiety so acute was not natural, Anne said, and he ought to see a psychiatrist if he was going to go on like that. She, the mother, slept dreamlessly, thankfully. Adam did see a psychiatrist and received some therapy, which was not much use since it was impossible for him to be open and tell the truth about the past. When he told the therapist he was afraid of going into the room and finding his child dead, he was offered tranquilizers.

Abigail was now six months old and still very much alive, a placid child, large and bland-looking, who at lunchtime on a Thursday in late September took an incurious look at the check-in line in which she found herself, laid her head back on the stroller pillow, and closed her eyes. A Spanish woman, going home, who had been watching her, gave a sentimental sigh, while an American with a backpack, irked by the slowness of the service, opined that Abigail had the right idea. Adam and Anne and Abigail—if they ever had a son they intended to call him Aaron—were on their way to Tenerife with Iberia Air Lines, a ten-day vacation carefully planned for when Abigail was too old to be endangered by climatic and environmental changes and young enough still to be dependent on her mother's milk.

Heathrow was densely crowded—when was it not?—thought sophisticated Adam, a frequent traveler for his firm—a milling mass of strangely dressed people. You could always tell the seasoned ones by their jeans and shirts, invulnerable garb, sweaters to roll up and stuff into the overhead locker, from the tyros in smart linen suits and Italian glitter and skin, boots that might have to be sliced open to release swollen feet at the other end.

"I'd prefer window to aisle," said Adam, handing over their tickets. "Oh, and nonsmoking."

"Smoking," said Anne, who had given it up when she was pregnant. "Unless you're going to sit by yourself."

"All right. Smoking."

It so happened that there was no room left in smoking and only aisle seats. Adam put their two big suitcases, one stuffed with disposable diapers in case these were not easily obtainable in the Canary Islands, onto the weighing machine. He kept his eye on them as they passed through to see that the correct label went on the handles. Twice last year, going to Stockholm and Frankfurt, his baggage had been mislaid.

"I'd better change Abigail," Anne said. "And then we could go straight through and have some coffee in the departure place."

"I'll have to find a bank first."

Giggling, Anne pointed to the international sign indicating the mothers' room. "Why a feeding bottle? Why not a breast?"

Adam nodded, absently acknowledging this. "You have your coffee and I'll join you." He had once had a sense of humor, but it was all gone now. The dreams and the subtext of anxiety that underwrote his actions and speech had eroded it. "And don't have more than one Danish pastry," he said. "Having a baby doesn't just make you eat more, you know. It alters the metabolism. You need a whole lot less food to put on weight." Whether or not this was true he wasn't sure, but he had gotten back at her for wanting to sit in smoking.

Abigail opened her eyes and smiled at him. When she looked at him like that it made him think, with infinite pain and terror, of what losing her would be like, how he would instantly and without a thought kill anyone who harmed her, how gladly and easily he would die for her. But how much harder it is, thought Adam, to live with people than to die for them. The associative process brought another father to mind. Had he felt like that about his child, his baby? And had he recovered by now; did you ever recover? Adam touched the canceling switch, experienced very briefly a frightening blankness, made his way with an empty mind across the check-in area toward the escalator.

Empty minds are abhorred by thought as vacuums are by nature, and Adam's was quickly filled again by the small speculations and stresses that were attached to banks and exchange rates. The crowd upstairs was even greater than that down below, augmented by two planeloads, one from Paris and one from Salzburg, which had taken their baggage from adjoining carousels and surged simultaneously through Customs. In the far distance Adam could see the illuminated turquoise blue sign for Barclays Bank. It was a color he deeply disliked, had almost an antipathy for, but some interior warning voice always stopped him inquiring of himself why this should be. Only reason, or reasonableness, had stopped him changing his bank on this account. He began battling toward this band of blue light past ticket desks, apologized perfunctorily for sticking his elbow into the ribs of a woman in tyrolean hat and *Trachtenkleid*—and through a turbulent sea of faces looked into the face of the man he always thought of as the Indian.

His first name was Shiva, for the second god of the Hindu trinity. What his surname was Adam could not remember, though he supposed he must have known it once. The ten years that had gone by had not done much to Shiva's face, unless it was a little more set, carrying within it now the foreshadowing of a gauntness to come, an inborn racial sorrow. The skin was darkly polished, the color of a horse chestnut fruit, a conker, the eyes a bluish–dark brown, as if the pupils floated in ink-stained water. It was a handsome face, more intensely Caucasian than any Englishman's, the features more Aryan than any Nazi ideal or prototype, sharply cut and overchiseled except for the mouth, which was full and curved and delicately voluptuous and was now shyly, hesitantly, parting in the beginnings of a smile.

The eyes of each of them held the other's for no more than a matter of seconds, an instant of time in which Adam felt his own features screw into a scowl, prohibiting, repelling, brought on by terror, while the smile on Shiva's face shrank and cooled and died away. Adam turned his head sharply. He pushed through the crowd, gained a freer space, hastened, almost running. There were too many people for running to be possible. He reached the bank where there was a line and stood there breathing fast, momentarily closing his eyes, wondering what he would do, what he could possibly do or say if Shiva were to pursue him, declare himself, *touch* him even. Adam thought he might actually faint or be sick if Shiva were to touch him.

He had come to the bank because it had occurred to him, while bound for Heathrow in a taxi, that though in possession of traveler's checks and credit cards, he had no actual pesetas in cash. In Tenerife there would be another taxi driver to pay and at the hotel a porter to tip. Adam turned over to the bank cashier half of what he had in his wallet, two ten-pound notes, and asked, in a voice so cracked that he had to clear his throat and cough to make it audible, for these to be converted into Spanish currency. When his money had been given to him he had to turn around to give way to the next person in the line, there was nothing else to do. With a considerable effort of will he forced himself to lift his head and look ahead, down the long length of the arrivals area, at the milling host of travelers. He began to walk back. The crowd had cleared a little, to swell again no doubt in a minute or two when the planeload arriving from Rome came through. He could make out several dark-skinned people, men and women of African, West Indian, and Indian origin. Adam had not always been a racist, but he was one now. He thought how remarkable it was that these people could *afford* to travel around Europe.

"Europe, mark you," as he had said to Anne when first they got there and in answer to his scathing comment she had suggested that the black people might have been going home or arriving from lands of their own or ancestral origin. "This is Terminal Two," he said. "You don't go to Jamaica or Calcutta from here."

"I suppose we should be pleased," she said. "It says something for their living standards."

"Hah," said Adam.

He started looking for Shiva. His eye lighted on an Indian man who was evidently an airport employee, for he wore overalls and carried some kind of cleaning equipment. Could it have been this man he had previously seen? Or even the sleekly dressed businessman, passing him now, on whose luggage label was the name D. K. Patel? One Indian, Adam thought, looks very much like another. No doubt, to them, one white man looked very like another, but this was an aspect of things Adam felt to be far less significant. The important thing was that it might not have been Shiva he had glimpsed so briefly among the faces of the crowd. It might be that his mind, in general so prudently policed, had been allowed to get a little out of hand, to run amok as a result of the previous night's dreams, of his anxiety over Abigail, of the sight of that baggage label, and had thus become receptive to fears and fancies. Recognition there had seemed to be on the Indian's part, but could he, Adam, not have been mistaken there? These people were often ingratiating and a scowl evoked in them a smile of hope, of defensiveness. .   .

Shiva would not have smiled at him, Adam now thought, for he would surely have been as eager to avoid a meeting as Adam was. They had done different things at Ecalpemos, he and Shiva—indeed all five of them had had different roles to play—but the actions they had taken, the dreadful and irrevocable steps, would have lived equally in the memory of each. Ten years afterward they were not of a sort to raise a smile. And in some ways it might have been said that Shiva had been closer to the heart and core of it, though only in some ways.

"If I were he," Adam found himself saying not quite aloud though his lips moved, "I would have gone back to India. Give me half a chance." He bit his lips to still them. Had Shiva been born here or in Delhi? He could not remember. I won't think of him or any of them, he said inwardly, silently. I will switch off.

How could he hope to enjoy his vacation with something like that on his mind? And he intended to enjoy his vacation. Not least among the blessings it would confer was sharing their bedroom with Abigail, whose crib would be (he would see to that) on his side of their bed so that he could keep his eye on her asleep through the long watches of the night. Now he could see Anne standing waiting for him outside the entrance to the departure halls. She had obeyed him and avoided food but, strangely, this made him feel more irritable toward her. She had taken Abigail out of the stroller and was holding her in that fashion which is possible to women because they have well-defined hips and the sight of which therefore angered Adam. Abigail sat on Anne's right hip with legs astride, her body snuggled into Anne's arm.

"You were so long," Anne said, "we thought you had been kidnapped."

"Don't put your words into her mouth."

He hated that. "We thought," "Abigail thinks"—how did *she* know? Of course he had never told Anne anything about Ecalpemos, only that a legacy from a great-uncle had helped set him up in business, put him where he was today. In the days when he was "in love" with Anne instead of just loving her (as he told himself one inevitably feels toward a wife of three years standing) he had been tempted to pour it all out. There had been a time, a few weeks, perhaps two months in all, when they had been very close. They seemed to think each other's thoughts and to be shedding into each other's keeping all their secrets.

"What wouldn't you forgive?" she had asked him. They were in bed, in a cottage they had rented in Cornwall for a spring vacation.

"I don't know that it's for me to *forgive* anything, is it? I mean, I wouldn't think things you'd done my business."

"Heine is supposed to have said on his deathbed, '*Le bon Dieu me pardonnera. C'est son métier.*'"

She had to translate because his French was so bad. "Okay then, let's leave it to God, it's his job. And, Anne, let's not talk about it. Right?"

"There's nothing I wouldn't forgive you," she said.

He took a deep breath, turned over, looked at the ceiling on which the irregular plaster between the dark-stained beams showed strange patterns and silhouettes, a naked woman with arms upraised, the head of a dog, an island shaped like Crete, long and beaky, a skeleton wing.

"Not—molesting kids?" he said. "Not kidnap? Not murder?"

She laughed. "We're talking about things you're *likely* to have done, aren't we?"

A distance yawned between them now so great as to make their relationship a mockery of what it had been during those days, during that time in Cornwall and a bit before and a bit after. If I had told her, he sometimes thought, when opportunity came and held open that door, if I had told her then we would either have parted for good or else moved toward a real marriage. But it was a long time since he had thought like this, since thinking like this was always handled by the escape key. Irritable shades of it crossed his consciousness now. He would have liked to carry Abigail through passport control, but she was on Anne's passport and it was in Anne's arms that she sat as the official looked at her, and at her name written there, and back again at her and smiled.

If it was Shiva, he thought, at least it was in *arrivals* that he had seen him, not *departures*. That meant Shiva was going home—wherever that might be, some ghetto in the north or east, some white no-go place—while he was going away. There was therefore no possibility of his encountering Shiva again. And what harm, after all, could come of this chance sighting, if sighting it had been, if Shiva it had been? It was not as if he had seriously believed Shiva to be dead any more than the rest of them were dead. Nor was it likely that he could hope to pass through life without ever seeing any of them again. Until now there had not been so much as a mention in a newspaper or word-of-mouth news. He had been lucky. He *was* lucky, for sighting Shiva had made no difference to things, had made them neither better than they had been before nor worse. Life would go on as it had been going on with Anne and Abigail, the business on a gradual ascent, their existence steadily upwardly mobile, exchanging their house next year perhaps for a rather better one, conceiving and bringing into being Aaron their son, the associative procedure retrieving Ecalpemos from among the stored files and the escape key banishing it.

Life would go on more or less in tranquility, and time, a day or two in Tenerife, would dim the memory of that brown and shining face glimpsed between pale, anxious, stressful faces. Most probably it had not even been Shiva. In the neighborhood where Adam lived he seldom saw any but white people, so naturally he confused one dark-skinned person with another. Wasn't it natural, too, that whenever he saw an Indian face he should retrieve Shiva from his memory? It had happened before in shops, in post offices. And it hardly mattered anyway, for Shiva was gone now, gone for another ten years. . . .

He humped their hand luggage off the baggage cart, passed

Anne her handbag, and had recourse to a therapy he sometimes employed for turning away the rage he felt toward her. This was with a false niceness.

"Come on," he said, "we've time to get you some perfume in the duty-free."

3

Evil was a stupid word. It had the same sort of sense, largely meaningless, amorphous, diffuse, woolly, as applied to "love." Everyone had a vague idea of what it meant but none could precisely have defined it. It seemed, in a way, to imply something supernatural. These thoughts had been inspired in her husband's mind by a sentence from a review on the cover of a paperback novel Lili Manjusri had bought at the Salzburg airport. "A brooding cloud of evil," the commentator had written, "hovers over this dark and magnificent saga from the first page to the astonishing dénouement." Lili had bought it because it was the only work in English she could find at the bookstall.

Whenever Shiva considered the word, he saw in his mind's eye a grinning Mephistopheles with small, curly rams' horns, capering in a frock coat. Events in his own past he never thought of as evil but rather as mistaken, immensely regrettable, brought about by fear and greed. Shiva thought most of the folly of the world was brought about by fear and greed, and to call this evil, as if it were the result of purposeful calculation and deliberate wrongdoing, was to show ignorance of human psychology. It was in this way that he was thinking when, with Lili by his side and their suitcases on a trolley he would abandon at the tube station entrance, he looked up and met the eyes of Adam Verne-Smith.

Shiva had no doubt it was Adam he saw. To him Europeans did not specially all look alike. Adam and Rufus Fletcher, for instance, though both white, Caucasian, and of more or less Anglo-Saxon-Celtic-Norse-Norman ancestry, were very dissimilar in appearance, Adam being slight and white-skinned with a lot of bushy (now receding) dark hair, while Rufus was burly and fair, with curiously sharp-pointed features for so fleshy a man. Shiva had seen Rufus some years before, though he was absolutely certain Rufus had either not seen or not recognized him, while he was equally sure Adam knew perfectly well who he was. He began to smile from exactly the motive Adam had attributed to him, a desire to ingratiate and to defend himself, to turn away wrath. He had been born in England, had never seen India, spoke English as his cradle tongue, and had forgotten all the Hindi he had ever learned but he had all the immigrant's protective reactions and all his self-consciousness. Indeed, he had *more,* he thought, since the events at Ecalpemos. Things had gotten worse since then. There had been a gradual slow decline in his fortunes, his fate, his happiness, and his prosperity, or prospect of prosperity.

Adam glared back at him and looked away. Of course he would not want to know me, Shiva thought.

Lili asked him what he was looking at.

"A chap I used to know years ago." Shiva used words like "chap" now and "pal" and "kiddy," words used by Indians wanting to sound like true Brits, though he would not have done this once.

"Do you want to go and say hello to him?"

"Alas and alack, he doesn't want to know me. I am a poor Indian. He is not the kind of bloke who wishes to know his colored brethren."

"Don't talk like that," said Lili.

Shiva smiled sadly and asked why not, but he knew he was being unfair to Adam as well as to himself. Had they not all agreed when they left Ecalpemos and went their separate ways that it was to be as if they had never met, known each other, lived together, but that in future they must be strangers and more than strangers? Adam, no doubt, adhered to this. So, probably, did Rufus and the girl. There was something, some quality, more fatalistic, more resigned, in Shiva. He might deceive others, but he was incapable of deceiving himself, of pretending, of denying thoughts. It would not have occurred to him to attempt forgetfulness by inhibiting memories of Ecalpemos. He remembered it every day.

"It was at that place I told you about that I knew him," he said to Lili. "He was one of the group of us there. Well, he was *the* one, it was his place."

"All the better not to know him then," said Lili.

She bought their tickets. Adam had been right, it was in an East London near ghetto that Shiva lived. Lili tucked the two slips of green cardboard into a fold of her sari. She was only half Indian, her mother being a Viennese woman who had come to England as an au pair and married a doctor from Darjeeling, a surgical registrar in a Bradford hospital. When Lili grew up and the doctor died, her mother went home and settled in Salzburg selling Glockenturm beer mugs in a souvenir shop. It was there that they went each summer, during Shiva's holidays, their fares paid by Sabine Schnitzler who, having reverted to her maiden name and largely to her native tongue, sometimes wore a surprised, even bewildered look at being surrounded, as she put it, by "all those Indians." For Lili, whose skin was nearly as white as Adam Verne-Smith's, was more Indian than true Indians, wore the sari, grew her curly brown Austrian hair down to her waist, and took language lessons from a Bengali neighbor of theirs. In her voice were hints of the singsong tone, Welsh in its rhythms, so characteristic of the Indian speaking English. Shiva thought he should be grateful for all this, though he was not. How would he have felt, he sometimes asked himself, if he had married a woman who set herself against his ethnic origins?

He had told Lili about Ecalpemos before they married. It would not have been in his nature, nor would he have been inclined, to do otherwise. . . . But he had not gone into details, giving only the bare outline, the facts, and Lili had asked few questions. He bore in mind that the time might come when he would have to tell her everything.

"It wasn't your fault," she had finally said.

"It's true that they never consulted me. If I had given my advice, it would have been ignored."

"Well, then."

He began haltingly to explain but stopped himself. He could

tell the truth but not all the truth. Openness did not demand that he tell her he had suggested it.

"You should try to forget," she said.

"I suppose I feel that would be wrong. I ought never to forget about the kiddy."

And it was perhaps inevitable that he should see the death of his own child, his and Lili's, as retribution, as a just punishment. Yet he was not a Christian to look at things in this light. He was not really a Hindu either. His parents had neglected this aspect of his upbringing, having largely abandoned their religion but for a few outer forms before he was born. Some lingering race memory remained though, some pervading conviction common to all Orientals, that this life was but one of many on the great wheel of existence and that reincarnation as someone better endowed or worse (in his case surely worse) awaited him. He saw himself returning as a beggar with limbs deliberately deformed whining for alms on the seafront at Bombay. The incongruity was that at the same time he was convinced of retribution in this world. He saw the death of his son, a placenta previa child who died during Lili's labor, as direct vengeance, though he could not have said who was exacting it.

Crossing the hospital courtyard that divided the maternity wing from the general wards and administration building, hearing over and over in his head the words they had gently but coldly told him, the announcement of his son's death, leaving Lili asleep, carefully sedated, he had lifted his eyes and seen Rufus Fletcher. Rufus was wearing a white coat and had a stethoscope hanging around his neck. He was walking very rapidly, far faster than Shiva was going in the opposite direction, from a building with long windows and white-uniformed men and girls behind them that looked like a lab, toward the main block. He turned his head to look at Shiva, cast on him an indifferent glance, and turned away. Rufus had simply not known who he was, Shiva was sure of that, had not recognized him as one of the other two male members of the little community in which they had all lived in such close contiguity for something like two months. Shiva was astonished to find that Rufus had in fact finished his studies and become a doctor. Of course he had known Rufus had this in mind, was three years through his time at medical school, had already considerable knowledge and *nous*—who could forget *that*?—but somehow he had imagined that the same fate would have overtaken the others as had overtaken him, a deathly stultifying, an inhibition on all that was ambitious and of ascendant character, a remorseful withdrawing into the shade. Only if they did not show their faces, only if they kept their heads low and lived in obscure corners could they hope to pass at least in physical safety through life. So he had thought. But the others evidently had not, or Rufus had not, walking jauntily and with swinging stride across the road, his stethoscope bobbing up and down, letting himself into the main hospital block, Shiva later saw, by a door marked Private, which he slammed behind him with a fine disregard for the notices exhorting all to silence.

Lili had had no more babies. Perhaps they would have another child one day. Lili was still under thirty and there was no reason, the hospital staff had said, why such an unfortunate thing as a placenta previa should occur again, or if it did, they would be ready for it. Shiva was not too keen. The area in which they lived was overcrowded and unsalubrious, and if there was rather less unemployment than in the north of England, that was about all that could be said for it.

The name of their street was Fifth Avenue. It is not the custom in English cities to name streets by numbers, but it has happened. There are, for instance, no less than fourteen First Avenues in the London area, twelve Second Avenues, nine Third Avenues, and three Fourth Avenues. The only other Fifth Avenues are in West Kilburn and Manor Park, which also possess a Sixth, while the latter possesses a Seventh. Shiva's Fifth Avenue was a long, curving treeless street that dipped steeply down and switchbacked up again, though the neighborhood was not in general a particularly hilly place. At the end nearest the tube station was a block of shops containing a small supermarket run by Pakistanis, a Greek restaurant run by Cypriots, a triple-fronted emporium given over to the sale of motorcycle spare parts and equipment, and a newspaper shop run by people who when asked where they came from ingenuously replied that they were Cape coloreds. In the middle of Fifth Avenue, where Pevsner Road crossed it, was another small grocer's and a pub called The Boxer, and at the far end, opposite each other, a unisex hairdresser's and a betting shop. These were linked by belts of houses in infrequently broken blocks, composed of bricks in a dull purplish-red or khaki yellow, and all now between ninety-seven and ninety-nine years old. A double line of parked cars ran parallel to the sidewalks from the newspaper shop to the pub and the grocer's to the hairdresser's. If you half-closed your eyes and looked at it, you might have likened it to a string of colored beads.

Shiva went into the newspaper shop. There were two Jamaican boys in there and they made a point of crowding the counter, holding their elbows akimbo, so that Shiva was unable to pick up his paper from the pile in front of them. Quietly he asked for the *Standard* and handed across his money between the jutting arms; he didn't want any trouble. It was the Indians they hated down here, not the whites. Well, there were few whites left except for very old people who couldn't have moved if they had wanted to.

Lili was waiting outside, standing between their cases. She was very brave, he thought, to wear the sari and shop in the Indian shops and have her Bengali lessons when all these things drew attention to her. It would have been easy for her to pass for a white girl. Only her eyes, that distinctive dark bluish-brown and with somewhat protuberant bluish whites, betrayed her. But people were not that perceptive and for God's sake this was London, not Johannesburg in the fifties. She could have gotten away with it, and he had more than once suggested she should, begged her almost. But it was her identity, she said, it was all she had, and she went on putting a caste mark which she had no right to on her forehead and wearing all her gold bracelets and cooking sag ghosht and dal instead of the defrosted hamburgers and chips that most people around there ate. He picked up the suitcases and she took their hand luggage and they walked home, passing three separate black people who looked at them with silent hostility and two elderly white women who did not look at them at all.

Lili would start unpacking at once. She would put all the light clothes into one bag and all the dark into another and take them to the launderette in Pevsner Road. He knew it would be useless to try to hinder this; she would be fidgety and fretful if there were dirty clothes around. So long as she wasn't out after dark, he supposed it would be all right. Nothing much could happen to her on a sunny September afternoon between here and the launderette, and Mrs. Barakhda, who ran it, was a friend of hers, or the nearest Lili had to a friend.

He made her a cup of tea while she sorted the washing, closed up the valises, and pushed them into the closet under the stairs. At least they had a whole house with three bedrooms. Most of the houses down here were divided into two flats, two front doors squeezed in under the tiny porch. He offered to carry the bags for her but she wouldn't hear of it. In her reactionary way—for Lili had been brought up by an independent feminist mother—she thought it all right for men to carry suitcases but not bags of wash.

With his second cup of tea in front of him, he sat down to look at the newspaper.

There was a big picture of the Princess of Wales visiting a home for handicapped children. The main story was about trouble in the Middle East and a subsidiary one about racial trouble in West London, street fighting mainly and breaking shop windows. Shiva's eye traveled down the page. At the foot of one of the left-hand columns he read a headline. For the amount of text underneath it, a mere paragraph, it was a disproportionately large headline. It even rather spoiled the symmetry of the page.

The headline said: *Skeleton Found in Woodland Grave* and the story beneath it ran: *While digging a grave for his pet dog, a Suffolk landowner with a home near Hadleigh unearthed a human skeleton. The remains appear to be those of a young woman. Police declined to comment further at this stage and Mr. Alec Chipstead, a chartered surveyor, was not available for questioning.*

Shiva read it twice. It was rather strangely put, he thought. He felt this about most articles in newspapers. They didn't know much but they told you what they did know in the most cryptic way possible to whet your appetite and make you speculate. For instance, they didn't tell you if the landowner and Mr. Alec Chipstead were one and the same person, though you could tell that was what they meant.

He could feel sweat standing on his face, on his upper lip, and forehead. Wiping it away with his handkerchief, he closed his eyes, opened them, and looked around the room, then back at the newsprint in front of him, as if he might have been dreaming or have imagined it. The paragraph, of course, was still there.

There was no reason, Shiva thought after the first shock had subsided, to suppose any connection between this find and Ecalpemos. Suffolk was the only link, and he could remember quite distinctly, on first going to Nunes, how there had been some dispute as to whether it was in Suffolk or Essex. The blurring of boundaries, which took place at about that time, had created such anomalies as a householder having an Essex postal address while paying his taxes to the Suffolk County Council. This, surely, was what had actually happened to Adam Verne-Smith.

It was not quite true that this was the only connecting link. The other, of course, was the body, the young woman's body. Shiva thought, I must wait for more news, I must bear it and wait.

His patient was close to fifty, a handsome, tall woman, very well-dressed. Her expensive clothes—Jasper Conran, he guessed—she had put on again and, while behind the screen, a little more lipstick. He had just done a smear test on her.

"You have a very nice inside," he told her, smiling.

The nurse smiled too. She could afford to, being twenty years younger and with her gynecological problems, if any, taken care of by Dr. Fletcher for free.

Mrs. Strawson said she was very glad to hear it. She looked happy and relaxed. Rufus gave her a cigarette. One of the many aspects of his personality which endeared him to his patients—the others being good looks, charm, youth, boyishness, and treating them like equals—was his inability to give up smoking.

"I am that monstrous sinner," he would say to them, "the doctor that smokes. Each one of us is said to be worth fifty thousand pounds of advertising per year to the tobacco companies."

And the patient, especially if she didn't smoke, would feel empathy for him and maternal toward him. Poor boy, with all that stress, he works so hard, it's only natural he needs something to keep him going. Mrs. Strawson inhaled gratefully. This was her first visit to Rufus Fletcher in Wimpole Street, and she was already delighted to have taken up her friend's recommendation.

"Now, how about contraception? Do you mind telling me what method you're using?"

After that implication that she was still in the prime of her fertile years, Mrs. Strawson wouldn't have minded telling him anything. An account of an ancient intrauterine device, implanted twenty years before and never since then disturbed, made them all laugh once more. Rufus, however, suggested he should take a look, just to be on the safe side.

The Jasper Conran dress removed once more, Mrs. Strawson got back on the table. Rufus had a probe around. It was impossible to tell whether the thing that she had surprisingly described as being shaped like a Greek alpha was still there or not. His thoughts wandered to the *Standard,* which he had folded up and stuffed into the top drawer of his desk when Mrs. Strawson was announced. It could not refer to the events of ten years past, of course it couldn't. If it had been *the* house and *the* body, it would surely have referred not to digging a woodland grave but to digging in an animal cemetery. They would not have gotten that wrong. Rufus had forgotten how often he castigated the press for inaccuracy, how constantly he said to Marigold that you couldn't believe a word you read. He told—or, rather, politely asked— Mrs. Strawson to get dressed again.

"If we attempted to remove it," he said to her, "it would have to be done under anaesthetic. I don't suppose you want that, do you? It's not harming you. Rather the reverse, I should say. It seems to have done you proud. Why not let it continue with the good work?"

He sometimes thought how astonished, how appalled indeed, many of these women would be if they knew that these intrauterine devices were not in fact contraceptives but abortifacients. Before the IUD could do its work, conception must already have taken place, egg and sperm having fused in a fallopian tube and the multiplying cells traveled down to the womb to seek a place of anchorage, a home which the alpha-shaped loop by its very presence denied them, causing the minute beginnings of an embryo to swim in vain and ultimately be shed. Rufus did not in the least care about the moral issue, but the subject itself interested him. He had long ago decided never to say a word about it to any of his patients. Marigold, his wife, he would not of course have permitted to give womb room to such a foreign body or to take the pill or consider any so-called reversible tube-tyings. In his own bed in Mill Hill Rufus used a condom or practiced coitus interruptus, which he prided himself on being rather good at.

He said that was all, thank you, to Mrs. Strawson, he would let her know the result of the smear, and he walked all the way back to the reception desk with her, where her forty-pound fee was taken from her. They shook hands and Rufus wished her a pleasant journey home to Sevenoaks, she would just be in time to avoid the rush. He was aware of the accusation frequently leveled at doctors of his sort, that they are charming to their private patients who pay them, while treating like so many malfunctioning machines their National Health patients who merely pay the state. He was aware of this and in principle disliked it, attempting when he first set up in private practice, to resist it, but he had not been able to. In this land of two nations he was not big enough to be one of the just. At the hospital with its crowd of outpatients and wards full of inpatients he was so busy, so plagued and hassled and rushed off his feet, and the women so submissive and ignorant or merely sullen, that he forgot about principles. Nor did they speak nicely or carry handbags from Etienne Aigner in which reposed American Express Gold Cards. These two sorts of women seemed to belong to different species, being sisters only under their panties whether these came from Janet Reger or the British Home Stores. The treatment Rufus meted out to them was, after all, the same.

She was his last patient of the day. At this particular time he liked to begin the unwinding process. Whatever shamefaced and boyish confessions he might make to his patients, he kept control over his smoking, rationing himself to between ten and fifteen cigarettes a day. But in the afternoons he always smoked two after the last patient had gone. He sat smoking his cigarettes and reading the evening paper for the half hour it took to accomplish these combined exercises before leaving and getting into the tube at Bond Street.

Today this usually pleasurable half hour was spoiled by the paragraph he had read prior to the arrival of Mrs. Strawson. His nurse had brought the paper back at lunchtime and left it lying on the low coffee table during his appointments with his two previous patients. It was because Mrs. Strawson was five minutes late—behavior he made no demur at, though he would have refused to see a National Health patient who failed to turn up on time—that he had picked up the *Standard* and seen that paragraph.

The half hour was spoiled, but Rufus, just the same, was a disciplined man. He had not gotten where he was at the age of thirty-three by giving way to pointless speculation and neurotic inner inquiry. To have recovered as he had done, so successfully, so brilliantly, after such a traumatic experience had been a considerable feat. He had subjected himself to his own personal therapy, requiring himself to sit alone in a hospital room and speak of those happenings aloud. He had been therapist and client both, had asked the questions and supplied the answers, aiming at total frankness, keeping nothing back, expressing to those bare walls, that metal table and black leather swivel chair, that window, with its half-drawn dark blue blind, the crawling distastes and shames, the self-disgust, the shrinking from light and the fear which seemed sometimes to beat with frenzied wings against bars in his brain.

It had worked—up to a point. This stuff (as he put it to himself) often does work up to a point. The point, though, is on a rather low threshold. Getting it all out and so getting rid of it—well, yes. Nobody tells you how it comes back again. With Rufus it did to some extent come back again, and all he could do was grind it down and soldier on. Time, the best of all doctors, though it kills you in the end, had done more than therapy could, and now days would pass, weeks, without Rufus thinking of Ecalpemos at all. For quite long periods of time it went away and he forgot it. The associative process did not work with Rufus in quite the same way as it did with his erstwhile friend, Adam Verne-Smith, for Adam was an "arts" person and he a scientist, so that Greek or Spanish names, for instance, evoked none of it. Ecalpemos, after all, was not Greek and did not even sound so to Rufus who, unlike Adam, had not received a classical education. Nor was he neurotically sensitive about babies. It would hardly have done him much good in his professional life, where women were always wanting to know if they were having them or how to stop them or conceive them, if he had been. He had long ago gotten the whole business of Ecalpemos under tight control and lived in high hopes of never having to refer to it again in word or thought—and then there had appeared this paragraph.

If the house they referred to, thought Rufus, had been Wyvis Hall, why had they not said so? Or said "near Nunes" rather than "near Hadleigh"? The place had certainly been nearer Nunes than Hadleigh, three miles nearer, though of course Hadleigh was a town and Nunes merely a small village. There were a great many houses in the vicinity of Hadleigh of the same sort of size as Wyvis Hall, and a newspaper would be likely to describe anyone who possessed a few acres as a "landowner." For all he knew it might not be unusual to unearth human bones in grounds such as these. Possibly they were ancient bones. . . .

The only really hard piece of information the *Standard* gave was the name of the present owner of the house: Alec Chipstead. A chartered surveyor, it said. Rufus stubbed out his second cigarette, put the paper into his briefcase, and slung over his shoulders the marvelous black leather coat from Beltrami he had bought in Florence and which would have made him look like a gangster if he had not been so fair and ruddy-faced and with such blue English eyes.

He said good night to his nurse and to the receptionist and walked off down the street, across Wigmore Street toward Henrietta Place. It occurred to him that he could go into any public library where they kept phone directories for the whole country and look up Alec Chipstead and see if his address was Wyvis Hall. There might well be a public library very near where he was now walking. Rufus told himself now was no time to go hunting for libraries; he would go home first. He would go home and think about what to do. He had an idea it was a rule with libraries to stay open late on Thursday evenings.

Deliberately, he switched his thoughts. Library or no library, he would take Marigold out to dinner. Hampstead somewhere, he thought, and then he might take the opportunity to slip into the big library at Swiss Cottage. . . . No more of that. Over dinner they would talk about moving. Rufus thought he was growing out of Mill Hill and it was time to consider Hampstead. Marigold would have preferred Highgate, he knew, but in spite of the therapy and the control he shied away from Highgate. These places were all villages really, you got to know the neighbors, met people at parties and given that you were a middle-class professional person there was a limited number of like people it was possible to meet. Suppose he were to encounter the Ryemarks or even Robin Tatian? No, it was unthinkable.

A house in Hampstead would mean taking on an astronomical mortgage, but so what? Take what you want, have what you like, he had read somewhere, and drag your income along behind you. He was doing well, anyway, getting more patients each month, would soon have more than he could comfortably cope with.

The means he used for getting home was the Central Line to

Tottenham Court Road and then the Northern Line to Colindale where he had left his car. Rufus just made it into the train before the rush began. Something happened that always pleased him. His wife opened the front door to him just as he was about to put his key into the lock.

Marigold's name suited her. She was tall and generously built and fair, with a high color and a red mouth and white teeth. In other words, she looked a lot like him. If not twins, they might have been taken for brother and sister. Rufus was one of those rare people who admire their own kind of looks better than any other sort and whose partners are chosen because they belong in the same type as themselves. Soon after he met Marigold he had taken her to the opera to see *Die Walküre,* and afterward had said without forethought, "The Brunhilde was all wrong. She should have looked like you."

She had made some preparations for their dinner, but she didn't object to going out. She never did. It wasn't yet five-thirty but not too early, in Rufus's opinion, for a drink. He looked forward to this drink, the first of the day, with a sensuous desire. Any white spirit would do for him, he wasn't fussy, and he poured himself a stiff vodka, some of that Polish stuff they had brought back from their Black Sea summer holiday. It flooded his head, charged it with recklessness, and brought—he could feel it happening—a warm flush to his face.

"We'll go out and drink a lot and get pissed," he said.

He gave her his golden ferocious grin. She knew that grin; it meant something had happened, but she wasn't going to ask what. Let him tell her if he liked. There was a lot of underlying violence in Rufus, and not all that underlying either, a lionlike aggression in times of stress that took the form of a whooping destructive merriment. She didn't mind that, though sometimes she had a prevision that one day when he was a rheumy old lion and she a worn-out weary lioness she might mind it very much.

"Go and put on something beautiful," he said at seven after he had had two overt vodkas, and poured, as was his habit, a single large secret one, and had taken her to bed.

Marigold disappeared into the bathroom. Rufus, sleek with love and ardent spirits, thought with wonder about how he had actually imagined for all of ten minutes that the house they talked about in the *Standard* might be Wyvis Hall. It amused him for a moment to speculate about the others, if they, too, had seen the paragraph and whether they had been astonished and afraid. The five of them, he repeated their names silently: Adam, himself, Shiva, Vivien, and—Zosie.

They would be more discomposed than he. Discomposed, he thought, a word entirely different in meaning (as Adam himself might have pointed out) from its near homophone, *de*composed. There was no point in dwelling on that. He and Adam had been at the same school, though he was a bit older. From the day they had all parted, diverging from Ecalpemos out into the world, he had never seen Adam again but he knew all about him, knew for instance that he had become a partner in a company selling computers that called itself Verne-Smith-Duchini. And old man Verne-Smith and his wife he knew, they lived no more than a mile away, but them he avoided out of simple antipathy. What had the Indian's surname been? He had heard it but not often, it was a strange one and it escaped him. Manresa? No, that was a town in Spain and a street in Chelsea. Malgudi? A place in the novels of R. K. Narayan that Marigold read. Anyway, it was something of that sort. Vivien had been called Goldman, not particularly euphonious or attractive, that. And Zosie? What was Zosie's name?

He got out of bed and put his clothes on, the same clothes but a clean shirt. Marigold was running a bath, stepping into the water. She always made a great splashing. Secrecy was a necessary ingredient of Rufus's life. Even if the things he kept from his wife—had once kept from parents, brother, girlfriends—were very minor, he had to have them, had if need be, to create them. The photograph was one of these. All these years he had had it and kept it for safety's and secrecy's sake inside a boring medical book. Not one of those books on healthy vaginas and wombs which Marigold might easily have looked into but a work on the nasty bacilli which may infest the human reproductive organs after a bungled or septic abortion. Rufus had not looked at the picture for years.

It was still there, though, and looking at it gave him a shock. If it was possible to be surprised by a shock, Rufus was surprised. He had thought he could look at a picture of Wyvis Hall, a photograph he had taken himself with a cheap camera Zosie had stolen, with equanimity and even a rueful amusement, but it appeared he could not. It made him feel chilled and sober as if the love and vodka had never been.

"I will get pissed tonight, by God," he said aloud. "And why not?"

The house stood remote in the middle of nowhere, on the side of a river valley, embowered in trees of many kinds. Woodland, Rufus thought, a woodland grave. It had been built in the late eighteenth century, two stories high, shallow slate roof, red brick, seven windows set in ashlar along the upper floor, six below, and the front door set centrally under a portico and pillared porch. A chimney at each end. Outbuildings, the stable block. In front a broad sweep of gravel, and this side of it, just in the picture, a rolling lawn with a cedar set in it, a huge black ungainly tree that lurched like a galleon at sea when the wind blew. To take the photograph he must have stood on the edge of the wood, under the beech hedge which bounded it perhaps. The sun looked very bright, but when had it not been bright that summer?

Rufus found his heart was beating fast. He even considered fetching his sphygmomanometer and taking his blood pressure, simply out of curiosity. Instead, he turned the photograph face downward. He then picked it up delicately between thumb and forefinger as if he held something highly vulnerable in tweezers. He opened the medical book, placed the photograph inside the chapter on *Clostridium welchii,* a rod-shaped bacterium which decays the body while it is still alive, and went into his living room. On a windowsill, hidden by the curtain hem, was his secret vodka, still half a glass left.

But he was already affected by a euphoria that induced courage and recklessness. His heart had steadied. He wondered why he had considered having recourse to a public library when he had a much simpler means at hand of identifying the house in the newspaper paragraph.

Now that his consciousness was changed, how could he possibly have allowed himself to speculate about its identity, postpone the means of putting his mind at rest and then, ostrichlike, avoid the issue altogether? This was no way to conduct one's life, as he had always maintained. You do not shirk things, was a first principle, you face up to them. One of the reasons he drank a lot was because it made this possible.

He took a mouthful of the secret vodka, savoring it, carried it to the door, listened. The water was running out. She would be ten minutes. Rufus picked up the phone and dialed 192. Directory Enquiries were better about answering these days than they had used to be. Something must have given them a shake-up.

It was a man's voice that said, "What town?"

It was odd that he hadn't thought about that, but immediately it came back to him, the name of the exchange, though Hilbert's phone had been disconnected.

"Colchester," he said.

Rufus finished his vodka, slid a cigarette out of the packet on the shelf in front of him.

"Chipstead," he enunciated carefully, and then he spelled it. "C Charlie, H Harry, I Ivan, P Peter, S sugar, T Tommy, E Edward, A Adam, D David."

"A apple," the voice corrected him.

"Okay, A apple," said Rufus, conscious of his Freudian slip. "Wyvis Hall, Nunes, Colchester."

He waited, anticipating the usually annoying rejoinder that they had no subscriber of that name on record. In this case it would possibly be that they had the name of the subscriber but . . .

The operator interrupted this thought.

"The number is six-two-six-two-oh-one-three."

Rufus put the receiver back, feeling a clutch at his stomach as if a hard hand had made a grab at the muscles.

4

The picture, very like the one Rufus Fletcher had taken in the summer of 1976, occupied the screen for about fifteen seconds. The whole item was allowed no more than four times that in the BBC's Sunday evening news broadcast at 6:30. The other forty-five seconds were taken up by a policeman talking to a reporter about having nothing to say except that there would be an inquest. But Shiva and Lili Manjusri saw the picture and so did Rufus Fletcher. Adam Verne-Smith, unwinding in Puerto de la Cruz, did not, of course, see it. He did not even see an English newspaper. They were expensive to buy and came a day late. He did not want to be reminded of home, and the only paper he even glanced at was the *International Herald Tribune*, a copy of which Anne found on the beach.

His father, at home in Edgware, said to his wife: "Good God, Wyvis Hall, as I live and breathe."

Beryl Verne-Smith peered, but the picture immediately vanished.

"Yes, I suppose it was."

The policeman talked, the reporter trying to jog him into revelations and failing. In the background autumnal trees could be seen and a church on the summit of a low hill. Lewis Verne-Smith sat shaking his head, less as a gesture of denial than of a generalized despair at the state of the world. It was not that unpleasant memories were evoked, for these were always with him, his existence was inseparable from that old bitterness, but that a sight of the house, even the glimpse of a photograph, revived the precise feelings he had had—why, it must be getting on for eleven years ago.

"Ten and a half," said his wife.

"I shall have to get in touch with the police. No two ways about it, I shall have to get in touch with them."

"Not this evening surely?" said Beryl, who wanted to watch *Mastermind*.

Lewis said nothing. The room in which they were sitting underwent the curious shrinking process to which it was subject whenever he was reminded of Wyvis Hall or his uncle Hilbert or even if the county of Suffolk were mentioned. Suddenly it grew small and poky. The brick side wall of his neighbor's house seemed to have moved itself four or five feet farther toward the dividing fence, so that it loomed offensively. Lewis got up and pulled the curtains across with a pettish jerk of his hands.

"Shouldn't you wait until Adam gets back?" Beryl said.

"Why? What would that be in aid of?"

Beryl meant that Adam had been among the previous owners of Wyvis Hall while her husband had not, but she knew better than to point this out.

"There is no one living knows that lovely place better than I."

"That's true."

"I shan't wait till Adam returns," Lewis said in that manner that had once led his daughter to call him the Frog Footman, "but I shall wait until tomorrow."

Men and women do not usually put their baser feelings and intentions into words, not even in the deep recesses of their own minds. So Lewis did not say, even to himself, when he was privately considering trying to get hold of his son in Tenerife, that he disliked Adam and would have been pleased to spoil his holiday. Instead, he rationalized his thoughts and justified himself. Adam probably—indeed, almost certainly—knew nothing about the find in the pinewood, but Adam had once owned the house and thus taken on a responsibility. He could not shed that responsibility just because he had sold the place. Lewis would have agreed with Oscar Wilde that our past is what we are. We cannot rid ourselves of it. Therefore it was Adam's duty to come home and face the music, even though this might be no more than a short blast on a tin whistle.

But he had no precise idea where Adam was and he did not think Adam's travel agent (a personal friend of the young Verne-Smiths) would tell him. Some excuse would be made for not telling him. Lewis's bark, anyway, was always worse than his bite. He had virtually no bite, as he had once overheard Adam say to Bridget, and heard it with helpless chagrin.

"A bloody good thing or our childhood would have been a misery instead of just a bore."

Lewis walked into his local police station in Edgware on Monday morning. They seemed surprised to see him but not astonished. The Suffolk police had begun hunting up previous owners of Wyvis Hall and they had been alerted that a Verne-Smith lived in their area. There were, after all, only two in the London phone directory.

This might be a bonus. He was asked to wait and then shown into a room where a detective sergeant prepared to take a statement from him. With busy pomposity Lewis dictated it to a typist and would have gone on and on had he not been diplomatically restrained.

"Wyvis Hall, Nunes, Suffolk, and the twenty acres of land surrounding it were the property, through his marriage, of my uncle Hilbert Verne-Smith. They came into the possession of my son Hilbert John Adam Verne-Smith under my uncle's will, bypassing myself, though my son was no more than nineteen at the time of my uncle's death. Being an undergraduate at the time, my son naturally never considered actually residing in the house. He was in agreement with my suggestion that the property be sold, and before he returned to college in the autumn of 1976, he took my advice and placed house and lands in the hands of a real estate agent.

"Country properties were not selling well at the time. Forty-five thousand pounds was the asking price, and I was not surprised that the sale, so to speak, hung fire. However, in the spring of 1977 an offer was made which my son accepted. This sale later fell through and it was not until the following August that Wyvis Hall was finally sold to a Mr. and Mrs. Langan for the much improved figure of fifty-one thousand nine hundred ninety-five pounds.

"As far as I know, my son's personal acquaintance with Wyvis Hall was confined to my uncle's lifetime when I, my wife, and son and daughter frequently stayed with him. After my uncle's death in April 1976 he visited Wyvis Hall on perhaps two, or at the most three, separate occasions simply for the purpose of looking it over and reaching a decision about the disposal of furniture and effects.

"I suppose it is possible that squatters or other vagrants took possession of the house between the time of my uncle's death and the sale of the property. Certainly my son never rented it or allowed anyone to occupy it on either a temporary or permanent basis.

"My son is at present on holiday in Tenerife with his wife and daughter. I cannot say precisely when I expect him to return, though I should suppose in about a week from now."

It was all very small and quiet and low key. The snippet in Rufus's Monday morning newspaper measured just an inch in depth. It answered the question he had asked himself and told him that the bones of a very young child had been found as well as those of a young woman. This was not a shock. How could it be otherwise, since this was Wyvis Hall and the pinewood and the animal cemetery?

To photograph the house for the news last night the cameraman must have stood just where he had stood himself, on the edge of the lawn with his back to the cedar tree. A popular massproduced camera he had used but quite a good one. One thing about Zosie's pilfering; she never stole rubbish. He had taken a picture of her after that and one of the animal cemetery.

"Why is the grass always so short up here?" Adam had asked.

"Rabbits, I expect."

"Why can't bloody rabbits come and eat my lawns?"

Adam always referred to "my lawns," "my house," "my furniture." It had got up Rufus's nose a bit, though Adam had a perfect right to do this. It was his, all of it, and it went to his head rather. Nineteen-year-olds seldom inherit country mansions, after all.

It must have been sometime in August when I took those pictures, Rufus thought, and a couple of weeks later it was all

over. Coincidentally, as the community and their lives together
broke up, so did the weather. It was raining intermittently all the
time they were in the cemetery, the pines bowing and shivering in
the wind. Sometimes they had had to stop and take shelter under
the closely planted trees.

If the weather had held and it had still been hot and dry, would
they have dug deeper? Probably not. In spite of the rain, the earth
was still hard as iron. A sheet of rain had come down then, a hard,
gusty shower, while they were laying the squares of turf back in
place, and Adam had said something about the rain making the
grass grow quickly, the rain being on their side.

"We should all go our separate ways as soon as we can,"
Rufus had said. "We should pack up now and go."

The spade and the fork they had hung up among the other tools
in the stables. They had packed and Adam had locked up the
house. At some point Rufus himself had taken the things out of the
fridge and left the door open to defrost it. Adam closed the front
door and stood there for a moment as if he could not wrench
himself away.

So much of its beauty had been stripped from it by the
whipping winds. And by the neglect of the long hot summer. A
sudden gust of rain dashed against the red bricks that were already
stained in patches by water. The house that when he first saw it
had seemed to float on a raft of golden mist now lay in a
wilderness, amid ragged grass and straggling bushes and trees
dead from the heat. Dirty gray clouds tumbled across the sky
above the slate roof, now the only thing that shone, glazed with
rain.

But Rufus admitted to himself that the beauties of nature and
architecture had never meant much to him. It was the heat and
sunshine and privacy he liked. And now he longed only to get
away. They all got into Goblander and he drove away up the drift,
Adam next to him, the others in the back. The drift had become a
tunnel of overgrowth that dripped water onto the roof of the van.
None of them allowed their eyes to turn toward the pinewood. At
the top they came out into uncompromising bright gray light, the
bleak hedgeless lane, the flat meadows where here and there
stunted trees squatted like old men in cloaks. Adam's simile, not
mine, thought Rufus with a grimace.

No one asked where he was taking them. No one spoke. Adam

had Hilbert's old golf bag stuck between his legs and Rufus guessed the gun was inside it. They must have gone a good two miles before they met another car. Rufus overtook a bus going to Colchester and dropped the two in the back so that they could catch it. He took Adam on to Sudbury for him to catch a train there and at that point they parted. Adam got down from Goblander and said, "For ever and forever farewell, Rufus."

Which was probably a quotation from something, though Rufus did not know what and thought fastidiously that it was in bad taste, histrionic, though just like Adam.

"Take care," said Rufus, and not looking back any more than he had done when they returned from the cemetery, drove off around the town he had gotten to know so well, over the Stour bridge, into Essex, heading for Halstead and Dunmow and Ongar and London.

He never had seen any of them again. There had been no need to pretend, to turn aside. Briefly, starting his fifth year in medical school something over thirteen months later, he had wondered if Shiva Manjusri would be one of the incoming freshmen. But no, his intuition had been accurate. At any rate Shiva's face was not among the several brown faces. As for the others, avoiding them had presented no problems.

Would they get in touch with him now?

No contingency plans had been made for this eventuality. So long as there was no hunt for a missing girl they had felt themselves reasonably safe. Their minds had not reached out to the terror of what had in fact happened. None of them had been the kind of people who could have imagined devotion to a pet animal or according to it funerary rites. It was Shiva who had proposed the site. They had congratulated him on his ingenuity.

Ten years . . .

An ovarian cyst, nothing to get upset about, Rufus told Ms. Beauchamp. She was thirty-two, an editor with a distinguished publishing house, married to an investigative journalist. As yet they had no children, but she wanted four, she told Rufus.

"No reason why you shouldn't." He had another glance at her notes. "In fact, a peculiarity about this condition is that it seldom if ever occurs in a woman who's had a baby."

"My God," she said, putting her coat on, "and there was I, making my husband's life a misery, sure I'd got the dreaded C."

They all thought they'd got the dreaded C, poor things. You couldn't blame them. Rufus took her forty pounds off her by the reception desk, having set in motion the arrangements by which she would be admitted to a fashionable West End clinic, Rufus, her surgery and her hospitalization ultimately paid for by some provident association to which she and her husband subscribed. Rufus shook hands. He walked back to his consulting room, dying for a cigarette.

This was unlike him. He could usually get through quite easily until after lunch. He thought, I know what my idea of heaven would be, if by heaven we mean a place of bliss in which to pass eternity: a sanctuary where one might chain-smoke without impairment of breathing, destruction of the lungs, or damage to the heart, light each fresh cigarette from the glowing butt of its predecessor, and drink ice-free but hundred-proof chilled vodka laced with two drops of angostura and a gill of newly opened Perrier endlessly, with increasing euphoria, until a peak of joy and ease was reached but without any subsequent nausea or pain or dehydration or oblivion. . . .

Sitting alone, he lit his cigarette, the first of the day, and there came that faint swimming in the head, a tautening of the gut. He closed his eyes. If it comes to light that I was in that house with Adam and the others, he thought with cold clarity, if someone tells the papers, or the police and then the papers, that I was there during the summer of 1976, living there, it will be all up with me. I will lose my practice and my reputation and everything that I have and can look forward to, if not my liberty. And without the rest I won't care about my liberty. It would be bad enough if I were a GP or an expert in some other branch of medicine, an orthopedic surgeon, for instance, or an ear, nose, and throat man, but I am a *gynecologist*, and it is the bones of a young woman and a baby that have been found there. . . . What worried woman would come to me? What Mrs. Strawson or Ms. Beauchamp? What GP would send her to me?

If I were innocent, thought Rufus, I know very well what I would do. I would pick up the phone and phone my solicitor and ask to come and see him and get his advice. He might advise me to make a statement to the police, which I would, of course, do under his guidance. But I shall not do this because I am not innocent. I shall sit here and wait and sweat it out and look the facts in the face, trying to anticipate the worst that can happen.

5

When he said he did not know the date of Adam's return, Lewis Verne-Smith had not lied to the police. It would have been very unusual for him to have known a fact like that about his son's life and movements. If not exactly estranged, they were not close. Lewis was inclined to say he had "no time for" Adam. He believed his son disliked him and this he thought outrageous. Sometimes he thought about Adam when he was a child and what a dear little boy he had been, affectionate and not troublesome.

"They undergo a complete change when they grow up," he said to Beryl. "Adam, for instance, he might not be the same person."

He had decided to find out when Adam was coming back and drive to Heathrow and meet the plane. Adam lived as far away from the parental home as was possible while still living in North London. Without saying anything to his wife, Lewis drove to Muswell Hill and checked that Adam's car was in its garage. It was. This meant they must have had a hired car to take them to the airport or have gone by tube. Adam's own car was bigger and newer than Lewis's and very clean and well polished, all of which Lewis disliked.

An obscure feeling that he ought to have a key to this house made him resentful. It was something he found hard to understand, though, of course, it must be accepted, this escape of children from the parental bonds so that they could have secrets from you and hiding places you couldn't penetrate, that they were adults and possessed houses and cars which you had had no hand in choosing or buying, that they could lock up those houses as they locked up their thoughts.

He made his way around the side of the house, peering in at the windows, noting that some dishes, though washed, had been left on the drainboard. There were dead flowers in a vase half full of green water. Lewis held simultaneously two opposing views of his son, one that he was a feckless, idle, good-for-nothing layabout and the other that he was a hard, ruthless, astute and already well-off businessman. When the former view of Adam predominated, Lewis felt easier, happier, more justified.

On the way it had occurred to him that he might find the police at Adam's. It would not have surprised him as he walked clockwise around the house to have met a policeman proceeding in the opposite direction. However, there was no one around, not even the neighbors. Lewis stood on the front lawn, looking up at the bedroom windows.

It was a very nice house, bigger than Lewis's own and in a more attractive neighborhood, a neo-Georgian double-fronted detached house, altogether superior to the kind of thing most married men of twenty-nine could afford to live in. Adam could afford it because of the money he got from the sale of Wyvis Hall and later from the sale of the London house he bought with the money from the sale of Wyvis Hall. If things had happened differently, he, Lewis, would be living in a house like this or in a flat in Central London with a cottage in the country as well. And Adam would have what was proper for someone of his age and standing in the world, a terraced cottage in North Finchley or maybe Crouch End, first rung on the slow ladder of upward mobility. Lewis thought bitterly that as it was, the only possible next step up for Adam would be Highgate Village. . . .

He drove home and this time he felt able to phone the travel agent friend of Adam's without fear of a rebuff. And the man was very pleasant, reminding him that they had met at Adam's wedding. He had no objection to telling him when Adam and

Anne were returning: next Tuesday on the Iberia Air Lines flight from Tenerife that got in at 1:30 P.M.

After he had hung up, Lewis considered informing the police; he thought this might be his duty, but on the other hand he did not want the police actually to be there when Adam arrived. He told his wife (and himself) that he was going to meet Adam in order to break the news gently to him that these awful discoveries had been made at Wyvis Hall and that foul play might have taken place while he, Adam, was actually its owner.

"Aren't you getting things out of proportion?" said Beryl.

"How so?"

"There hasn't been anything said about foul play yet."

But even as she said this, as Lewis later rather dramatically told her, the *Standard* was on the streets announcing that police were treating the case as murder. It was only a few lines, it was tucked away, all very low key, but the word *murder* was there to be seen and read.

As he set off for the airport, Lewis remembered that he had told Adam from the first that only trouble could come from a person of his youth and inexperience inheriting a big house and land of the dimensions of Wyvis Hall. And he was right, for trouble had come, if rather tardily. Ten years it had taken, more than ten years. In some ways it seemed longer than that to Lewis and in others only yesterday. On the other hand, he could not remember a time when it had not been taken for granted the Hall would one day be his own.

The Verne-Smiths were minor gentry. Lewis's grandfather had been a parson in a Suffolk village, with nothing but his stipend to live on, and the father of seven children. Two of them had died young, one of Lewis's aunts had married and gone to America, the other two had remained spinsters, living as many unmarried women in the country used to, in tiny cottages in the middle of a village, busy in a mouselike way about parochial matters, having no youth, earning nothing, buried alive. The remaining brothers, his father and his Uncle Hilbert, were much younger. His father also took holy orders while Hilbert, practicing as a solicitor in Ipswich, took care of himself by marrying a rich woman.

The Berelands were wealthy landowners. If a son or daughter married and no suitable home was in the offing, a house would be made available. Lilian Bereland brought Wyvis Hall with her, not as a grace and favor dwelling to revert to her family on her or her husband's death but hers to do absolutely as she liked with. Of course, in her father's estimation, it was not much of a house, a warren of smallish rooms was how he saw it, and set in a damp situation on the side of a river valley. There was not much sale for that kind of thing at the time of Hilbert's marriage.

The parson and his wife and children used to go there for their holidays. Lewis's father's parish was on the outskirts of Manchester and the vicarage was Victorian-Byzantine-Gothic soot-blackened yellow bricks with the pseudo-Romanesque windows picked out in red bricks. Black-leaved ilexes grew in the churchyard and a brassy laburnum had flowers on it for one week out of the year. Wyvis Hall was the most beautiful place the seven-year-old Lewis had ever seen and the countryside was glorious. In those days the fields were still small and surrounded by hedges and the lanes ran deep between lush banks. Wild orchids grew in the fens and monkshood and hemp agrimony on the borders of the little streams where there were caddis flies and water boatmen and dragonflies in gold velvet or silver armor. Clouded Yellow butterflies abounded and Small Coppers and Blues and once the little boy saw a Purple Emperor. A pair of spotted woodpeckers nested in what was known as the Little Wood below the lake, and when the nuts were ripe on the copper cob trees, a nuthatch came up quite close to the house.

That house! How differently did it appear to him from the Berelands' assessment! To him it was grand and spacious. In the drawing room a pair of pink marble pillars supported the embrasure of the windows. The staircase curved up prettily to a gallery. There was a library that Uncle Hilbert used as his study and, even more awe-inspiring, a gun room with stuffed animals and shotguns on the walls. But the interior meant less—though it was not always to be so—than the grounds, the lake, the woods. The place took on a magical quality for Lewis, who had toward it something of that feeling of the Grand Meaulnes for his lost domain. He used to long for his vacations and grow deeply depressed when they drew to an end. It was a glorious victory when he managed to persuade the grown-ups to let him stay on after his parents had gone back to Manchester.

Aunt Lilian had never had any children and she died in 1960, when she was only fifty-five. Uncle Hilbert took the loss of his wife very hard and the only company he seemed to want was Lewis's. It was about this time that he started telling Lewis Wyvis Hall would be his one day.

He also informed Lewis's parents, who got into the habit of saying things like "when all this is yours" and "when you come into your property." Uncle Hilbert, however, was only just sixty, very hale and hearty, still very much in practice as a solicitor, and Lewis could not imagine stepping into his shoes, nor did he in those days think it very nice to anticipate such things. But he went down to Suffolk very often, much more often perhaps than he would have had Wyvis Hall been destined to pass back to the Berelands or on to one of those cousins in the United States.

His feeling for the place underwent many changes. In the nature of things, meadow, grove, and stream no longer appeared to him appareled in celestial light, the glory and the freshness of a dream. He was growing up. He began to see the grounds as a *possession*, the gardens as something to impress others, the orchard and walled fruit garden as places that would produce delicious food. Although he intended to live in the house for at least part of the time, he saw it, too, as salable and the value or price of it (however you liked to put it) going up every year. The pines in the wood where Uncle Hilbert's hunt terrier Blaze was the last creature laid to rest he saw as a useful and lucrative crop. He noticed the pieces with which Wyvis Hall was furnished, took books out of the public library on antiques and porcelain and measured the remembered articles against illustrations, catching his breath sometimes at mounting values. Another thing he did was picture himself and his wife in the drawing room receiving dinner guests. The address on his writing paper would simply be: Wyvis Hall, Nunes-by-Ipswich, Suffolk. It was one of Lewis's ambitions to have an address in which the name of the street might be left out without causing inconvenience to the post office. The house and grounds were marked on the ordnance survey map for that part of Suffolk, and Lewis, when he was feeling low, would get it out and look at it to cheer himself up.

By the 1960s he had married and had two children, a son and a daughter. When his son was born he thought it would be nice, a nice gesture, to name him after Hilbert.

"An old family name," he told his wife, though this was not

true at all, his uncle's being thus christened having been an isolated instance of the use of Hilbert. There had been a fashion in the late nineteenth century for Germanic names, and his uncle, born in 1902, had caught the tail end of it.

"I don't like that at all," his wife had said. "People will think it's really Gilbert or Albert. I don't want him teased, poor baby."

"He will be called by his surname at his public school," said Lewis, who though poor had grand ideas as befitted the future owner of Wyvis Hall and its acres. So he won, or appeared to win, that battle and the child was christened Hilbert John Adam.

Lewis had written to Uncle Hilbert and told him of his intention to name his son after him, inviting him to be the child's godfather. Declining on the grounds that he no longer had any religious faith, Uncle Hilbert sent a silver christening mug, large enough to hold a pint of beer. But the note that accompanied it made no mention of the choice of name and it was rather a cold note. Later on, when Lewis and his wife and the baby went to stay at Wyvis Hall, Hilbert's only comment on his great-nephew's name was: "Poor little devil."

By then, anyway, the baby was always called Adam by everyone.

Lewis, who was no fool, soon saw that in some incomprehensible way he had put his uncle's back up. He set about rectifying matters, attempting to redress the balance. His uncle's birthday was noted; he must always have a Christmas present bought and sent in good time. He was invited to London and all sorts of treats were held out to him as to how he would be entertained on such a visit, trips to the theater and concerts, a specially organized tour of "Swinging London," Carnaby Street, King's Road, and so on. Lewis knew very well he should not do this, that he was sucking up to someone for the sake of inheriting his property. But he could not help himself, he could not do otherwise.

Of course he continued to take his family to Wyvis Hall regularly for their summer holidays. He had a daughter as well now whom he had been tempted to call Lilian but had seen the unwisdom of this in time and named her Bridget. His wife would have liked to go to Cornwall sometimes or even to Majorca but Lewis said it was out of the question, they couldn't afford it. Perhaps what he really meant was that they couldn't afford not to go to Nunes. By 1970 you couldn't buy a derelict cottage in the

Nunes neighborhood for less than 4,000 pounds, and Wyvis Hall would fetch five times that.

One day, soon after he had retired from his legal practice, Hilbert told Lewis he had made a will that was "very much to your advantage." He smiled in a benevolent sort of way when he said this. They were sitting out on the terrace on the low wall of which stood, in pairs, stone figures from classical mythology of a rather embarrassing kind. Under the drawing room window *agapanthus africanus*, the blue lily, was in full flower. Hilbert and Lewis and Beryl sat in old-fashioned deck chairs with striped canvas seats. Hilbert leaned toward Lewis when he told him about the will and gave him a pat on the knee. Lewis said something about being very grateful.

"I finally made up my mind when you named the boy after me," said Hilbert.

Lewis said more grateful things and about naming his son Hilbert being only proper and suitable under the circumstances.

"*In* the circumstances," said Hilbert.

He was in the habit of correcting minor errors of grammar or usage. Adam must have got it from him, Lewis sometimes thought, or perhaps (he much later and very bitterly thought) a similar pedantry in Adam was among the things Hilbert liked about him.

Lewis did not like being corrected, but he had to take it and with a smile. It wouldn't go on forever. The Verne-Smiths were not long livers. Lewis's father had died at sixty and his grandfather at sixty-two. His three aunts were all dead at under seventy. Hilbert would be seventy the following year and Lewis said to his wife that his uncle was beginning to look very frail. He began "running down" to Suffolk at weekends by himself, and that Christmas he had his wife accompany him for four days, taking all the Christmas food with them. The woman who came in to clean and the old boy who saw to the garden had been instructed to call him "Mr." Lewis and he felt very much the heir. His uncle hadn't much money, he supposed, but there would be a little, enough to put central heating in, say, and have the place redecorated. Lewis hadn't made up his mind whether to sell Wyvis Hall after he had smartened it up a bit and with the proceeds buy a bigger and better London house and a country cottage or to keep the Hall and sell off some of the land for agriculture. According to his estimate, the result of perusing real estate agents' windows in Ipswich and Sudbury, Wyvis Hall by the end of 1972 was worth about 23,000 pounds.

It was a continual source of irritation to Lewis that Adam did not show more respect and deference to Hilbert. The boy was offhand and always trying to be clever. He called his great-uncle by his Christian name with no title and did not jump to his feet when the old man entered the room. Lewis pressed Adam to accompany him on those solicitous weekend visits but Adam nearly always said he was too busy or would be bored. There had in fact been only one occasion during those last years that Lewis could remember, and he was sure Adam had only gone because there had been a promise of some shooting. The visit had been far from successful, for Adam had sulked when offered the four-ten, the so-called "lady's gun." Sometimes, since then, Lewis had wondered what would have happened if Adam had obeyed him and been kind and polite to the perverse old man. Would Hilbert have left his property to Bridget perhaps or even to the Law Society?

It was to be three more years before his uncle died, thus becoming the longest-lived Verne-Smith that anyone had heard of. The daily woman found him dead one morning in the April of 1976. He was lying on the floor outside his bedroom at the top of the back stairs. The cause of death was a cerebral hemorrhage. Adam was nineteen and in his first year at college, though at that time at home for the Easter break. After the cremation, while the few mourners were looking gloomily at the flowers, his uncle's solicitor, a partner in the Ipswich practice, spoke to Lewis simply to say that he believed he already knew the contents of the will. Secure as he thought in possession, Lewis brushed this aside as being an unsuitable subject for discussion at such a time. The solicitor nodded and went on his way.

A week later Adam got a letter saying he was the sole beneficiary under the will of his late great-uncle. There was no money, Hilbert having used all he possessed to purchase himself an annuity, but Wyvis Hall and its contents were Adam's absolutely.

There were traffic jams all along the North Circular Road, a particularly long one at Stonebridge Park, and another at Hanger

Lane. Lewis, sensibly, had allowed himself a lot of time. Adam would be very surprised to see him. He would probably think something had happened to his mother and that Lewis was there as the bearer of bad news. Of course in a way he was, though not of that kind. For a moment or two, as he waited in the line behind a truck full of German furniture and a leased moving van, Lewis returned to speculating as to how and why those bones had gotten into the animal cemetery. Frankly, he did not suppose Adam had had anything directly to do with this at all. What seemed likely to him was that Adam had allowed some undesirable person or persons access to the place and it was these vagrants or hippies—there had been a lot of hippies still around then—who were responsible.

Adam himself had never shown any interest in Wyvis Hall, as far as he had noticed. That was part of the unfairness of it. He had seen this unlooked-for inheritance simply as a source of lucre. When the letter came, Lewis had nearly opened it himself. The postmark and the old-fashioned and precise direction (Esquire and the name of the house as well as the street number) told him it was from Hilbert's old firm. And he thought he knew what had happened. They had made a mistake, that was all, and sent it to his son. Or else it might be that Hilbert had left Adam some small memento or keepsake. . . .

Adam was lying late in bed. Lewis would never forget that if he forgot all the rest. And he, for his part, was feeling so euphoric that instead of shouting to his son to get up and stir his stumps, he had actually gone in there and put the envelope on Adam's bedside table. The awful thing was that all this time Lewis had never had any doubts he was himself the new owner of Wyvis Hall.

It must have been a Saturday or else Lewis for some reason or other had the day off from work. Anyway, he was at home that day, home for lunch, and he and Beryl were actually sitting at the table, talking as it happened about going down soon to take a look at the Hall, when Adam came in. He had very long hair at the time and a beard, Lewis remembered, and looked, as they all did, like some kind of weird prophet. To this day Lewis had a picture in his mind of how his son had looked walking into the dining room (or dining area of the living room really) wearing jeans, of course, jeans with ragged hems, and a collarless tunic garment, tie-dyed, with colored inks. Afterward Lewis wished he had said something scathing, alluding perhaps to the lateness of the hour of Adam's appearance. Well, he had alluded to Adam's appearance but in a genial way. He had been feeling cheerful, God help him!

"Just in time for the locusts and honey!"

Adam said, "Something rather fantastic, old Hilbert's left me his house."

"Yes, very funny," Lewis had said. "What *has* he left you? His desk? You always said you liked that."

"No kidding, he's left me his house. Whatsitsname Hall. Unbelievable, isn't it? It was quite a shock. You can see the letter if you like."

Lewis snatched the letter. He had begun to tremble. There it was in black and white: ". . . the property known as Wyvis Hall at Nunes in the county of Suffolk, the lands pertaining thereto . . ." but it must be a mistake.

"They've mistaken you for me, my boy," Lewis said grimly.

Adam smiled. "I doubt that."

"*You* doubt it? You know nothing about it. Of course Wyvis Hall is mine, it's always been a matter of fact it would be mine. This is a simple mixup, a confusion of names, though I must say it amounts to criminal carelessness."

"You could phone them," said Beryl.

"I shall. I shall phone them immediately I've finished my lunch."

But he was not able to finish his lunch. He couldn't eat another mouthful. Adam ate. He ate his way through bread and butter and ham and pickles and drank a half-pint of milk. Lewis went into the hall and phoned Hilbert's solicitors. The one he wanted was still out to lunch. Adam got up from the table and said he thought he might go over to Rufus's.

"You're not going anywhere," said Lewis. "I forbid you to leave this house."

"You what?" said Adam, looking at him and grinning.

Beryl said, "Just wait a few minutes, Adam, till we've got this cleared up."

"Why's he getting his knickers in a twist anyway if he's so sure it's a mistake?"

It was not then but ten minutes afterward when he had spoken to the solicitor and been assured there was no mistake that Lewis began to dislike his son. Adam said: "You can't expect me to be *sorry* he left the place to me and not to you. Obviously, I think he made the right decision."

"Can't you see what an outrage it is?"

Adam was excited. He wanted to go and tell the Fletcher family his good fortune. Lewis was boiling with rage and misery and shock.

"Can I have the car?" said Adam.

"No, you can't! Now or at any other time, and that's final!"

Lewis soon formulated a plan whereby they could all share Wyvis Hall. It was not ideal, it was not what he had anticipated, far from it, but it was better than abandoning it to Adam. After all, Adam would be back at college in a week's time, the will would have to be proved, but by the middle of the summer why shouldn't he and his wife and Bridget use the Hall regularly at weekends? Adam could have it for his long vacation. He, Lewis, was quite prepared to get the place redecorated at his own expense. It was a family house, after all, no doubt Hilbert had intended Adam to share it with the rest of his family. He and Beryl and Bridget could go there on weekends and they could all be there together for Christmas. What did a boy still at university, with no prospects yet of any sort of career, what did someone like that want with a massive country house?

"I want to sell it," Adam said. "I want the money."

"Sell the land," said Lewis.

"I don't want to sell the land. It wouldn't fetch much anyway, agricultural land. And who's going to want to buy it?" It was plain that Adam had gone into this aspect of things. "No, since you ask . . ." Clearly, Adam was only reluctantly willing to share his plans with his parents. "Since you ask, I'm going to go down and take a look at it as soon as I can and then I'm going to put it on the market."

Adam returned to college. That summer Lewis thought perhaps he was on the verge of a nervous breakdown. He made all sorts of wild plans. He would go down to Nunes and take over the house. If necessary he would break in and take possession. The village people would support his cause—didn't they call him Mr. Lewis? Wasn't he the rightful heir? Adam would never try to regain the house by force. By this time his fantasies took on the air of medieval barons' wars. He actually dreamed of himself in a suit of armor opening the big oak front door with a mace in his hand

and Adam riding up on a black colorfully caparisoned horse. More practically, he consulted solicitors of his own in an attempt to have the will disputed. They advised him against trying. He had another go at persuasion and wrote Adam long letters to his college begging for compromises. Adam phoned home and asked his mother to stop his father bothering him when he was in the middle of exams. Lewis's doctor put him on tranquilizers and advised him to go away on holiday.

In the middle of June he suddenly gave up. He washed his hands of Adam and Wyvis Hall and the memory of his Uncle Hilbert. The whole thing disgusted him, he told Beryl, it was beneath his dignity, only he couldn't help feeling utterly disillusioned with human nature. He wouldn't go to Wyvis Hall now if Adam invited him, if he went down on his bended knees.

His exams over, Adam came home. He slept one night at home and then went down to Nunes, taking Rufus Fletcher with him. Or, rather, being taken by Rufus, in whose van they went. Lewis refused to show any interest. He practically ignored Adam for whom he now felt a deep distasteful antipathy. A few months before, if anyone had told him you could feel dislike for your own child, a real aversion from your own flesh and blood, he would not have believed them. But that was how he felt. He couldn't get Adam out of the house fast enough. Two days later he was back. So much for Wyvis Hall. That was how much Adam appreciated the beautiful old house he had had the unheard-of good fortune to inherit at the age of nineteen. He was going to Greece with Rufus Fletcher and Rufus Fletcher's girlfriend, who was an Honorable, the daughter of some titled person.

"You would think someone with her background would know better," said Lewis.

"Know better than what?" said Adam.

"Well, a single girl staying in places with a man like that." Adam laughed.

"How long will you be away?" said Beryl.

"I don't know." They never did know, or if they did, they weren't saying. Beryl might have saved her breath. "Term starts on October seventeenth."

"You're never going to be in Greece for four months!"

"I don't know. I might be. Greece is quite big."

"Staying in tents, I suppose. Sleeping on beaches." Lewis

had forgotten to be indifferent and aloof, he couldn't help it. "And what about that beautiful old house you've been unaccountably made responsible for? What about that? Is that to be allowed to go to rack and ruin?"

"It's not in ruins," said Adam, looking him in the eye. "I don't know what *rack* means. I've got someone from the village coming in every day to check up that no one tries making a nuisance of themselves. Squatters, I mean. There's a lot of squatting going on."

Lewis had known what he meant. He knew who Adam thought the squatters might be. It was a terrible way to speak to your own father.

Up in the short-term parking lot at Terminal Two, Lewis had to drive from floor to floor before he found a slot in which to put the car. He was back in the present now, having exhausted those resentful memories. Adam had gone to Greece the next day and not reappeared until September. Lewis and Beryl, of course, had never gone near Wyvis Hall; they would not have laid themselves open to such humiliation, to the possibility of their way being barred by some yokel, paid by Adam to keep an eye on the place. Where had Adam got the money to pay someone to look in at Wyvis Hall daily?

Lewis asked himself this question as he went down in the lift and crossed the arrivals hall of Terminal Two to await the exodus from Customs. The flight from Tenerife was due in fifteen minutes and he saw that there was a screen on the wall that would show when it landed. People stood around, meeting planes, men who seemed to be the drivers of hired cars carrying placards with the names of people or companies printed on them, families waiting for a returning father, a strange old woman in a red cloak chewing gum. Lewis wondered what visitor from Rome or Amsterdam or the Canaries was going to have the misfortune to stay with her.

Perhaps he should have told the police that there had been someone going into Wyvis Hall every day during those months of summer. Certainly it would not have been a respectable person, such as Hilbert's gardener or cleaner, but most likely some unemployed derelict Adam had met in a pub. This person might easily be the perpetrator of the crime that led to that appalling interment. And by association Adam would be involved in it too.

There did not appear to be any police in the crowd. No policemen had been sent to intercept Adam, unless of course they were in plainclothes—those two that looked like businessmen, for instance. They were probably detectives. Who else would be waiting at the arrivals barrier at Heathrow at this hour?

Lewis began to feel excited. Suppose Adam were to be arrested before he even reached his father? He imagined himself driving a tearful Anne and Abigail back to Beryl, then finding Adam a good lawyer. Adam would have to admit he had been in the wrong, had been extremely negligent, criminally careless really, in allowing any Tom, Dick, and Harry access to Wyvis Hall. He might not wish to reveal names to the police but he would have to. Pressure would be put on him. Eventually, he would come to confess that if his father had inherited the Hall as he had rightfully expected to do, none of this would have happened.

The arrival of Flight IB 640 from Tenerife came up on the screen. By this time Lewis was off into a fantasy in which a girl Adam had gotten pregnant had been abandoned by him with their child at Wyvis Hall, where she had later been murdered by a sinister caretaker. The first arrivals were coming out of Customs now: two middle-aged couples, a crowd of kids who looked like students, a family with four children and Grandma, a man who looked as if he had been drinking on the plane, his collar undone and his tie hanging. The detectives who were not detectives after all stepped forward to meet him, one of them shaking hands, the other slapping him on the back. A woman came out wheeling a big tartan suitcase, and behind her was Adam, pushing valises in a cart, Anne beside him looking brown and tired, pushing the empty stroller, Abigail asleep on her shoulder.

Adam's face, when he saw his father, was a study in some unpleasant emotion, not so much anxiety as exasperation.

6

The wonderful thing about the human mind, Adam thought, is the way it copes when the worst happens. Beyond that worst happening you think there can be nothing, the unimaginable has taken place, and on the other side is death, destruction, the end. But the worst happens and you reel from it, you stagger, the shock is enormous, and then you begin to recover. You rally, you stand up and face it. *You get used to it.* An hour maybe and you are making contingency plans. For what had happened was not the worst, you realized that. The worst was yet to come, was perhaps always yet to come, never would actually come, because if it did, you would know it, that would be reality, and there would be nothing then but to kill yourself. Quickly.

Now that he was able to, he assembled what had happened and laid the facts before himself. They had dug up those bones at Wyvis Hall and had decided it was murder they were investigating. Bones, skeletons, bodies, do not bury themselves. Those were the facts, as far as he knew them up to this moment. He would know more, much more, in the days to come. What was certain was that he could no longer use the escape key. It was defunct. The passages it canceled had, in any case, as in certain programs, not been lost but stored on some limbo disc from whence they must now be retrieved.

Adam sat in his parents' house, drinking tea. There must be a total retrieval now, the one good thing about which was that it might banish his dreams. He was aware of a slight feeling of sickness and of cold, an absence of hunger, though he had been feeling quite hungry when he got off the plane.

Anne sat next to him on his mother's cretonne-covered settee and Abigail lay on a plaid rug on the floor, kicking with her legs and punching with her arms. His mother kept poking toys at her which she did not want. A passage from a novel by John O'Hara came back to Adam. He had memorized it years ago in the Ecalpemos epoch: *The safest way to live is first, inherit money, second be born without a taste for liquor, third, have a legitimate job that keeps you busy, fourth, marry a wife who will cooperate in your sexual peculiarities, fifth, join some big church, sixth, don't live too long.* Apart from the last one, which he hadn't gotten to yet, and the penultimate one, which seemed to apply in America more than here (here he had joined the golf club) he had complied with all the rest. Or his nature and luck had complied for him. Nemesis had still come down like a wolf on the fold.

He had not wanted to come back here. But there had been no spirit in him, the shock of what his father told him had been too great.

"Something that will interest you, Adam, something to make you sit up. They've dug up a lot of human bones at my old uncle's house. . . ."

By the time he had rallied and got himself together and was thinking of things to say to the police, it was too late and they were heading north. Anne was furious. When Lewis said to come back with him and eat there, Adam had got a kick on the ankle from Anne and another kick when he hadn't replied.

He had turned on her and said with cold savagery, "For fuck's sake, stop kicking me, will you?"

He expected his father to rise and say something about that being no way to speak to one's wife or not in front of the child; he was capable of that. But he had said nothing, only looked subdued, and Adam realized why. His own terrible fear and anger had communicated itself to his father and shown him what the better part of valor was: keeping silent. Having put the cat among the pigeons, made mischief in his special way, he was lying low now and waiting. The old bastard. Adam only wished Uncle

Hilbert *had* left him Wyvis Hall and then there would have been no Ecalpemos, no Zosie, and no deaths. And Adam couldn't see he would have been much worse off. He and Anne would be living in a house like this one rather than that neo-Georgian palace. Children, after all, he thought, looking at Abigail, were happy wherever they were, so long as they were loved. . . .

His parents had not asked him what sort of holiday he had had or how the flight had been. The conversation was exclusively on the subject of the discovery at Wyvis Hall. Adam did not know whether to be glad or sorry he had not obtained an English newspaper while away. If he had, the shock would have been less, but on the other hand, his holiday would have been spoiled. He would have liked very much to be alone. Of course he knew there was no possibility of this, now or when he returned home, for when you were married, you never could be alone. Presumably that was the point. What was he going to tell Anne? How much was he going to tell her? He didn't know. None of it, if he could help it.

They sat at the table in the dining area to eat an absurdly early high tea. Lewis asked him if he could remember the day when he heard he had inherited Wyvis Hall and had walked in here and astounded them with his news.

"He had a beard then, Anne." Lewis's subdued air had changed to one of high good humor. "You wouldn't have recognized him, he looked like John the Baptist."

Adam could remember very well but he wasn't going to say so.

"What a funny thing," said Lewis. "We had ham salad that day too. What a coincidence! Oh, yes, I've been meaning to ask you, who was it looked after Wyvis Hall while you were in Greece?"

Adam could eat nothing. That other time, he remembered, it was his father who hadn't been able to eat. He didn't know what Lewis meant about someone looking after the house, but no doubt he, Adam, at the time had concocted some tale to keep his father quiet, to keep him away even.

"Someone from the village, you said," Lewis persisted.

"How can I remember that far back?"

"The police will want to know. It may be of vital importance."

"Aren't you going to eat your meat, dear?" said Beryl.

Abigail, who had been put upstairs in one of the bedrooms to sleep, set up a wailing sound. Adam was on his feet at once.

"I think we should go."

They had to wait until his father was ready. Adam would have preferred to phone for a hire car but Lewis wouldn't hear of it. Anne sat in the front in the passenger seat while Adam was in the back with Abigail. If his father could have found out what flight they were coming on, the police certainly could. It was possible they might be waiting for him. They would wish to interview every former owner or occupant of Wyvis Hall. He looked again at the newspaper account of the adjourned inquest that his father had saved for him. It would be owners and occupants of Wyvis Hall between nine and twelve years before that they would wish to interview, and those were Great-Uncle Hilbert, who was dead, himself, and Ivan Langan, to whom he had sold the house. As for other occupants, how would they know who else had lived there?

It was ironical that ten days before he had seen Shiva at Heathrow. The encounter he now saw as an omen, a shadow cast by a coming event. What would that event be? Adam did not want at this point to speculate; it made him feel sick. He turned the newspaper over so that he could not see that headline and those paragraphs. In high spirits, his father was talking about the immense advances made in forensic science in recent years.

As soon as they got home Anne started getting Abigail to bed. Their bags humped upstairs and put into the bedroom, Adam looked Rufus Fletcher up in the phone book. He was in there twice, at a Wimpole Street number and again at an address in Mill Hill: Rufus H. Fletcher, M.B., MRCP. All these years then, or for some of them, Rufus had been living three or four miles from him. He couldn't look Shiva up because he could not remember his surname. Women marry and change their names, he thought, there was no point in pursuing that one. Of course he could look up Robin Tatian but where, really, would that get him? He was reaching for the blue directory when Anne came back with Abigail in her arms, so Adam took her and carried her back to bed himself and tucked her in and kissed her. She was almost asleep. He wondered if Rufus had children, and if so, did he worry about them coming to terrible harm the way he himself worried. Was his whole life affected by what had happened at Ecalpemos? Adam

might have escaped the file memories for years, suppressed them
and jerked violently away from them, but he had never been able
to pretend he was unscathed by those events. Sometimes he felt
that he was the person he was because of them and acted the way
he did because of their effects.

He sat by Abigail's crib, not wanting to remember but
knowing that now he must. There was nothing in his house to
remind him of Ecalpemos. Everything that was left, everything he
and Rufus hadn't sold, had gone to Ivan Langan with the house.
For a song, too, because he had not been able to bear the thought
of going back, meeting a valuer, walking around the house,
picking things off shelves and out of cupboards. Only once had he
returned after they all left and that had been bad enough, like a
dream—no, like stepping into the set and scenario of some
frightening film, a Hitchcock movie perhaps. He asked the taxi he
had taken to let him off at the top of the drift and he had walked to
the house. It was almost a year since he had been there and in that
time nothing had been done, nothing had been touched. From the
pinewood he simply averted his eyes—till later.

The drift was thickly overgrown, a dank tunnel out of whose
bushy sides the tendrils of brambles and briar roses caught at his
clothes. One of these whipped back at him, and as he caught at it a
thorn drove into the fleshy pad of his finger. That thorn had been
there, festering, for months. A dull cool summer it had been, as
different as could be from the year before. No golden light bathed
the red brick of the house. It no longer looked mellow. Beautiful,
yes, but severe somehow, and to Adam's heightened awareness,
reproachful. He found himself encouraging, fostering, the
scenario illusion. Only thus, only by pretending unreality, pretending this was a part he acted, could he go on, cross the wild
shaggy grass, go past the black-branched cedar tree, arrive at the
porch set in its four Doric columns and insert his key into the lock.

In the film there would have been something terrible awaiting
him. A dead thing hanging in a noose over the stairs. There was
nothing, of course, only a faint smell compounded of dust and dry
mold. Ecalpemos. He no longer called it that. It was Wyvis Hall
once more, his house but bringing him no pleasure, no deep,
excited, almost sick joy. He breathed deeply, walked through the
rooms, went upstairs, being the actor in the film. In a few

moments the other participant in the sequence they were shooting would come, the real estate agent from Sudbury.

While they had been there the previous year there had been hardly any visitors. It was as if the magic house in the wood had had an invisible fence set around it or—what did they call it?—a shutting spell. The clear air, Constable's unique Suffolk light, had in fact been impenetrable, a barrier that held off intruders as a sheet of glass might have. This was all fantasy, of course, for one or two people had come, Evans or Owens from Hadleigh, the exterminator they called the coypu man, a meter reader, the man who wanted to do the garden and whom he had turned away with a lie. But for the most part they had been undisturbed in their magic island, or resort, that was closed to others but which they could leave when they pleased. Coming and going—there had been too much of that. Things would have been very different if they had stayed put.

The doorbell rang. It made him jump—inevitably. But it was just a bell that rang, it did not buzz or chime. He let in the real estate agent and took him through the house, into the drawing room and the dining room, upstairs to the Pincushion Room, the Centaur Room, the Room of Astonishment, the Deathbed Room, the Room Without a Name, and then back down the back stairs to that jumble of kitchens and scullery and wash house and coal store, most of it a nineteenth-century addition. What a lot of this sort of thing the Victorians had needed!

It was all quite tidy and clean, as Vivien had left it. But he could not say Vivien's name then, he could not even think it, only look about him fearfully, clenching his hands.

He opened the door to the gun room and showed the real estate agent the interior. There was a table in there and a windsor chair. The floor was of black and red quarry tiles and there were racks on the walls for the guns but these, of course, had gone, Hilbert's two shotguns had gone, one buried in the Little Wood, the other in his bedroom at home in Edgware, zipped up in an old golf bag under the bed.

The real estate agent suggested an asking price and took some measurements and then a photograph, standing on the edge of the lawn that had become a meadow, where Rufus had stood and taken photographs a year before. It was windy, and the cedar which he had likened to a galleon and Zosie to a witch, danced witchlike, its branches arms and leaping legs and flying skirts.

The car went off up the drift as many times Goblander had gone. Adam had given his only key to the real estate agent. He closed the front door behind him and started to walk. He had forgotten all about arranging for a taxi to pick him up or looking up bus times or anything like that. Presumably, the real estate agent would have given him a lift somewhere. It was too late now. Cold water drops fell on his head from the leafy roof of the tunnel. In the deciduous wood a pheasant uttered its rattling call. He emptied his mind, he walked like an automaton up onto the green ride, seeing at the end of it the cameo of stacked meadows, segments of wood, a church tower. He was holding his breath.

His head he was keeping averted, looking in the direction of the drift, at the wall of cluster pines with their black needles and their green cones. He knew the distance from the ride, thirty paces. When he turned his head he kept his eyes closed, let out his breath, opened his eyes, looked and heard himself give a little whimpering sigh. It was the sound a man might make when in physical pain but trying not to show it, suppressing complaint.

There was nothing to see, nothing to show. The place was as it had always been, a downland in miniature, a terrain of small green hills on which little dolmens had been raised, pink granite, white marble, a slab or two of gray stone. Wooden crosses. "By what eternal streams, Pinto . . ." Each in their narrow cells forever laid were Alexander, Sal, Monty, Ranger, Blaze. And to the right of Blaze the green turf lay undisturbed, very slightly irregular as the whole area was, a reticulation of tiny-leaved plants, minuscule flowers, netted into the grass, a small pit here filled with pine needles, a shallow rut there with a sandy bottom. Rabbits had mown the lawn here more effectively than any piece of machinery. Their droppings lay scattered about like handfuls of raisins.

Adam found he was holding both hands clamped over his mouth. He turned and ran, along the ride, up the drift, not looking back.

Anne, waiting downstairs for him with coffee and sandwiches on a tray, wanted to talk about the find at Wyvis Hall. He found himself unexpectedly touched by her simple assumption, the way she absolutely took it for granted, that he was innocent. Adam didn't want anything to eat. He was thinking of Hilbert's shotgun that he still had but which he should perhaps not keep much longer.

"You've never told me any of this," Anne began. "When you got the solicitor's letter saying you'd inherited the place it must have come as a terrific shock. I mean, didn't you have a clue?"

"I thought my father would come in for it. Everyone did."

"Why do you think he left it to you like that?"

"Not because he liked me. He hardly took any notice of me. He didn't like children, and when I got older I stopped going. I hadn't been near the place for four years. My parents went."

"Then I just don't understand."

"Look, he was an unpleasant old man." Adam looked hard at her. "My father is an unpleasant old man, and I daresay I shall be. Verne-Smiths are." She didn't say anything. "I think it happened this way. He saw through the toadying, of course he did. My father was just a blatant sycophant. He thought to himself, right, you've called the boy Hilbert to please me, to make me like him, so I damn well will like him, I'll like him more than you and leave him the place over your head."

"Do people really behave like that?"

"Some do." Adam thought. "Frankly, if it were me, I would. I might."

"Do you want some more coffee? No? I suppose you whizzed straight down there and had a look at your property?"

"No, I didn't as a matter of fact. I hadn't time, I had to go back to the university. Anyway, I was going to sell it, I wasn't all starry-eyed about my lovely house, you know."

That was just what he had been. Once, that is, he had seen it again after a four-year absence. But he had not guessed he would be and had postponed his visit till the term ended in June. All that term his father had been planning ways and means, trying to overturn the will, looking for compromises, plotting for all Adam knew a frontal assault. What he did know he had gotten from his sister, his ally against their parents if in nothing else.

"You'd been there for your vacations as a little boy? Did you love it then?"

"I don't think so. I can't remember. I think I'd have preferred the seaside. Kids do."

"And did they show you the animal cemetery when you were a child?" Anne persisted.

"I suppose so. I can't remember. Do we have to talk about it?"

In fact, he couldn't remember ever having heard of it until the day Shiva came in and told them what he had found. Vivien thought it was *children* buried there. Adam shivered as he remembered that. Well, an Indian would think like that, he wouldn't be able to understand the way the English went on about animals. Adam had a sudden awful vision of the spade going through that green turf and coming up with a skull on it. Something like that; it must have been like that.

Was the shot still there, among the bones?

Later he lay in bed beside Anne, trying to think of a satisfactory yet thoroughly noncommittal story to tell the police. Like most middle-class English people who have never had anything to do with them, Adam thought the police were fools. Anne had fallen asleep almost immediately. She had a habit, when she slept on her back, of making soft sounds in her throat. This was not snoring but a kind of clicking, irregular and sporadic—that was what made it irritating—and liable to start when least expected. Adam had only heard one other make these sounds, and when he first heard Anne make them his memory escape failed and those two nights were startlingly evoked, so disturbingly, in fact, that he had the terrible delusion that Anne was doing it to mock him. Of course that was nonsense. She had never heard of Catherine Ryemark and never would if he had his way.

Several minutes might pass without a click and then one would come and another would come and another one fifteen seconds after that. It drove Adam mad. Once, in a fit of temper, he had told her she only started doing it after they were married. If he had heard her do that in their single days, he would never have married her. But now, the soft clicks coming with typical irregularity, he listened to them painfully and let his mind slide back ten years to what he must remember, to the truth he must recall if he were going to be able to tell lies. He lay still with his eyes open, staring into the darkness that was only half-darkness because this was London and not Suffolk, where on moonless nights the small hours were black as velvet. Click, pause, click, a long silence. At last it had been cold enough to need a blanket and a quilt, to hold Zosie in his arms without the sweat pouring off them both. For a long time that night, too, he had not slept, had lain thinking, wondering what to do, listening to the delicate sounds like tiny bubbles breaking—and then hearing them no more.

Adam closed his eyes and turned his head away from Anne. A down-stuffed duvet in a printed cotton cover lay over them. It had been a quilt at Ecalpemos, faded yellow satin, brought in by Vivien from the terrace when the rain began. Quilts were what you lay on to sunbathe that summer, not for warmth on beds, but slung for lounging comfort as it might be on some Damascene rooftop. Night after night they had lain out there in the soft, scented warmth, looking at the stars, or lighting candles stuck in Rufus's wine bottles, eating and drinking, talking, hoping, and happy. That summer—there had never been another like it, before or since.

It was the hottest, driest summer any of them had ever known. The previous one, 1975, had been very good, especially the latter part, but that one, the summer of Hilbert's death and of Ecalpemos, had been glorious from April till September. If it had been gray and raining and chilly, he might have taken one look at Wyvis Hall and turned tail and fled to Crete or Delos or somewhere. Certainly he would have gone down there alone to spy out the land and check on his property. Rufus wouldn't have wanted to go and he would have had to go down alone by train.

There were so many ifs and conditions, so many other eventualities that easily might have happened. In the first place, he had approached Rufus only because Rufus had a car. If his father hadn't been so bloody-minded and had let him use the family car, he would no doubt have gone down alone and come back the next day, having called on some real estate agent in Hadleigh or Sudbury and asked them to sell the house for him, the very one probably that he saw the following year.

But things had not gone that way. It had been a glorious sunny day and he had wakened up in the morning rather early for him in those days. About nine. His father was on holiday, though he and his mother were not going away anywhere, in spite of what the doctor had advised, but staying at home and "going out for days." Or that was what they said. They hadn't been out for any days since Adam had been at home.

June 18 it was, a Friday. The date was stamped indelibly on his memory calendar, more than just stamped, etched in. He thought he would get up and go to Suffolk and take a look at his house. His generation—perhaps all generations at that age—hated making plans, making arrangements ahead. Adam had viewed with near incredulity his mother's preparations in the past for going on holiday, the way everything in the house seemed to get washed, the way she and his father wore their worst clothes for days beforehand because the best ones were packed, the phone calls she made, the notes she left for tradesmen. He liked to do things spontaneously, be up and off on the spur of the moment.

His father wouldn't let him have the car. It might be needed if they went out for the day. Adam said all right, not to worry, he would manage without, but this didn't seem to please Lewis either. He would have liked, Adam knew, to have lived in a time when a father could forbid his son to do things and the son would obey. Or rather, to have the rules of that former period prevailing now. Adam didn't say where he planned to go, though he thought his father guessed, but got on his bicycle and cycled over to Rufus's.

He couldn't remember what he had done with his bike when he got to the Fletchers', left it there, and collected it the next day perhaps, but he could remember most of the rest of it. What he had worn, for instance. Jeans cut off thigh-high to make shorts and a T-shirt he had made out of an old man's vest he had bought for twenty p in a sale under the arches at Charing Cross Station and dyed green and yellow. His hair was tied back with a piece of tinsel string he had found in the Christmas decorations box. Those were the days before people dyed their hair bright colors, the days of henna. Adam had put henna on his hair and that and the sun had turned it reddish-gold. His beard, though, was black and rather curly. He must have looked a sight but he didn't think so then. His legs were bare and he was wearing Indian leather sandals, the kind you had to soak in water before you first put them on. It showed what the weather was and how they had started taking daily sunshine for granted in that he hadn't got any sort of jacket or sweater with him even though he expected to be away overnight.

The Fletchers had a swimming pool. It was supposed to be a teardrop shape or shaped like a comma. This summer was the first anyone had made much use of the pool. Rufus was sitting on the blue-tiled rim of it with his feet dangling in the water. He was three years older than Adam and though they had been at the same school, Highgate, they had not been friends then. It was Rufus's younger brother Julius who had been in the same form as Adam, a rather dull, pompous boy, a sort of phony intellectual, and they had never had much to do with each other. Adam and Rufus had met as members of the same squash club.

That was what they seemed to have in common, that and Rufus's brother and Adam knowing each other already, but after a while Adam got to see things he admired in Rufus, his toughness, the way he'd got himself organized and in hand, the way he knew where he was going and yet still could be amusing and casual. Of course he had got to know him a good deal better at Ecalpemos. . . .

Rufus was very laid back and Adam liked that. He also liked Rufus's occasional sensitivity which didn't seem to go with the other aspects of his personality. And Rufus was wild, too, the way medical students had a reputation for being. Adam thought of himself and Rufus as being wild and laid back at the same time, equally like that, young adventurers with all the world before them and all the time they wanted to do what they liked with.

Rufus said, Hi, and come for a swim, so Adam took off his shorts and went into the water in his black nylon underpants. They would have swum naked, only Rufus's father had discovered them doing this and made a fuss out of all proportion to the offense, if offense it was.

"I reckoned I might go and take a look at my inheritance," Adam said, checking that the key to Wyvis Hall was safe in the pocket of his shorts.

"Now, d'you mean?"

"Yes. I guess so. Why not?"

"Want me to drive you?"

Rufus had an old Morris Minor van that he had bought third or fourth hand, but it went all right. It got you from A to B in one piece, as Adam's father remarked sneeringly of it.

That had been well before the motorway, the M25, was built. You went to Suffolk by the A12 through Chelmsford or took the country route. This was what Lewis had always called the route that went by narrower winding roads through Ongar and Dunmow, Braintree and Halstead to Sudbury, and that was the way he had driven them when they all went out to visit old Hilbert. Adam did for Rufus what Lewis would have called "navigating." It

maddened Adam, his misuse of this word, which couldn't of
course be applied to guiding anyone on land, coming as it did
from the Latin *navigare* and thence from *navis,* feminine, a ship,
and *agere,* to drive or guide. Adam loved words, was fascinated
by them, their meanings, and what you could do with them, with
anagrams and palindromes and rhetorical terms and etymology.
One of the subjects in the mixed B.A. curriculum he was taking at
the university was linguistics. . . . "Directing" Rufus was what
he was doing, he told himself. They had talked about words
during that drive, well, place names really, with particular
reference to the villages that were called Roding after the river,
High Roding, Berners Roding, Margaret Roding, and Rufus told
him they were pronounced Roothing from the old Danish, which
Adam hadn't known before.

It was a beautiful drive and the countryside looked wonderful,
a kind of sparkling shimmering green in the heat and sunshine.
The sky was huge, a pale bright cloudless blue, and the white
surface of the road ahead rippled in the heat mirages that made it
look like little waves. The farmers were haymaking, cutting the
tall feathery grass and its dense admixture of wild flowers. The
windows of the van were wide open and they had the radio on, not
playing rock, which they both hated, but Mozart, one of the better
known of the piano concertos.

In spite of all the times he had been there, Adam missed the
turnoff that was the drift leading down to Wyvis Hall. It was
somewhere along the lane between Nunes and Hadleigh, but so
much vegetation had grown up that spring that everything looked
different. They drove about a mile farther, right up to the group of
buildings called the Mill in the Pytle, and Rufus, turning the van
around, asked what a pytle was. Adam said he would look it up.
He told Rufus to drive a bit more slowly and this time he spotted
the six-foot-wide gap in the hedge on the right-hand side, almost
hidden by cow parsley growing up and elderflowers hanging
down, the wooden box on legs with its hinged lid into which
Hilbert's mail and newspapers and milk had been delivered. As a
little boy, Adam had sometimes been sent up here in the morning
to fetch the letters and the paper, carrying with him a wicker bottle
basket for the milk. There was no other sign that this was Wyvis
Hall.

"Why's it called a drift?" said Rufus, lighting another

cigarette. He had chain-smoked all the way down and Adam had had one or two to keep him company, though he didn't really like putting something lighted into his mouth. That was the trouble for him with dope. He liked the effects of it but didn't like having to smoke it.

"I don't know," he said. "I don't know why it's called a drift."

"You can look it up when you look up 'pytle,'" said Rufus.

On either side the drift was thick with cow parsley, its powdery white heads coming to an end of their long blooming. It had a sweetish scent, like icing sugar, like childhood birthday cakes, that mingled with the winy perfume of the elders. All the trees were in full leaf but the oaks and beeches had not long so been, so that their foliage was still a fresh bright color and the lime trees were hung with pale yellow-green dangling flowers. The pinewood looked just the same as ever, it always did, it was always dark and dense with very narrow passages through it that would surely allow nothing bigger than a fox to weave its way through. Imperceptibly the trees must have grown, yet they seemed to Adam no different from when he was a child coming up to fetch the milk and when, on sunless mornings, he had felt a kind of menace from the wood. Even then he had not liked to look into it too much but had kept his eyes on the ground or straight ahead of him because the wood was the kind of place you saw in storybook illustrations or even in your dreams and out of which things were liable to come creeping.

At the foot of the slope, through the thinning trees, a field maple, alders with their feet in the stream, a late-blooming chestnut, that dramatic lawn adornment, the cedar, the house came into view. Things, buildings, stretches of land, are said to look smaller when we grow up. And this seems only natural, just what one would expect. After all, the top of the table that was once on a line with our chin now reaches only to our thighs. Wyvis Hall, logically, should have looked smaller to Adam but it did not, it looked much larger. This must have been because it was his now, he owned it. It was his and it seemed a palace.

On the stable block, in which nothing had been stabled in Adam's memory, was a little tower with a running fox weathervane on it and below the small pitched roof a blue clock with hands of gold. The hands had stopped at five to four. Between the

block and the house you could just see the walls of the walled
garden, flint-built, crossed and coped with brickwork. A mass of
flowers covered the house, a pink climbing rose and a creamy
clematis. Adam had not known these names but later on Mary
Gage had told him. Because the sun shone so brightly the slate
roof blazed like a slab of silver.

Rufus pulled up in front of the porch. The whole area out here
was paved and small stonecrops and sedums with white and
yellow starry flowers grew up between the stones. In a couple of
narrow-mouthed stone vessels grew a conifer and a bay tree. The
rose which mantled the house must have put out a thousand
flowers and these were at the peak of their blooming, not a petal
yet shed, each blossom the pink of a shell within and the pink of
coral on its outer side. Adam got out of the van and felt in the
pocket of his shorts for the key. He was aware of a profoundly
warm, placid, peaceful silence, as if the house were a happy
animal asleep in the sun.

"And this is all yours?" said Rufus.

"All mine." Adam was equally cool.

"I should be so lucky in my avuncular arrangements."

Adam unlocked the front door and they went inside. The
windows had been closed for nearly three months and the place
had a dusty smell that got into your throat and made your eyes
smart. It was also very hot, for the drawing room faced due south
and the hot sun beat on the glass. Adam went around opening
windows. The furniture was all his, too, those cabinets with
bulging fronts and curved legs, chairs with buttoned backs, a
velvet-covered love seat, a big oval table supported on a wooden
base shaped like a vase, mirrors framed in mahogany and mirrors
framed in gilt, pale mauve and green water colors and dark
portraits in oils. He could not remember noticing any of this
before. It had been there but he had not seen it. Nor noticed the
pillars of rosy marble that supported the window embrasure, nor
the alcoves, glass-fronted, that were filled with china. Only the
overall impression was familiar, not the individual pieces. He felt
a little sick, engorged with possessions and the pride of ownership. In each room a chandelier hung from the ceiling, of
tarnished brass in the dining room, a cascade of prisms in the
drawing room, in hall and study Italianate glass tubes twisted
snakelike amid false candles. And everywhere the sun streamed or

lay in golden pools or rainbow spots or squares made by windows patterned with the shadows of leaves.

Rufus was among the bookcases in Hilbert's study. Adam took down Edward Moor's *Suffolk Words and Phrases*, couldn't find "drift" but here was "pytle" or "pightle," *a small meadow*. He went back into the drawing room, where he unbolted, unlocked, and threw open the french windows.

The sun came to him in a warm gust or like a warm veil enveloping him. It whitened the terrace beyond with a clear unbroken glare. All along the terrace, on the low wall that bounded it, stood the statuary his father had once told him had been placed there by whoever inhabited the place before Hilbert and Lilian came. They represented, in some kind of fine-grained gray stone, the loves of Zeus. He remembered them all right. As a child he had studied them with fascination, inquiring what the bull was doing to the lady, and receiving from his parents no very satisfying answer. Hilbert he had been too much in awe of to ask. They had come from Italy. Some cousin of Lilian's two or three times removed had found them in Florence while there on her honeymoon and had had them shipped home. There was Zeus as Amphitryon with Alcmene; Zeus coming to Danae in a shower of gold (difficult in stone, this one); snatching Europa; swan-shaped, wooing Leda; standing before the hapless Semele in all his destructive glory, and in half a dozen other metamorphoses.

Someone had been looking after the garden, you could see that. Flower beds had been weeded, dead heads removed, the borders of the willow-fringed lake shorn and trimmed, the lawns recently mown. As they walked along one of the stone-flagged paths and came to the gate in the flint wall they saw a neat pile of mowings waiting apparently to be composted.

The walled garden, too, had been carefully maintained. Inside the netted fruit cage Adam saw the bright ripe vermilion gleam of strawberries nestling among their triform leaves, raspberries yet green on the canes. All along the facing wall espaliered trees, their trunks dark and shiny and twisted and knobbed, bore among a rough dull foliage fruit turning gold. Nectarines, Adam remembered, and peaches too. Weren't there greengages somewhere that scarcely ever fruited but when they did were splendid? Red and white currants here in rows, berries like glass beads, gooseberries with a ripeness the color of rust on their green cheeks.

They each took a handful of strawberries. They walked to the lake, where there were two pairs of ducks, mallards with feathers as if painted in iridescent green, and from which a heron rose on gaunt wings, its legs dangling. Adam looked back at the house, at the honeysuckle that curtained the back of it in yellow and pink, at the martins, sharp-pinioned, that wheeled in and out from the eaves. He was in a state of tremulous excitement. He seemed only to be able to breathe shallowly. It was curiously sexual, this feeling, exactly the way he had once or twice felt with a girl he was mad to make love to and who he thought would let him but was not quite sure, not absolutely sure. The slightest thing would turn his fortune, snatch it, send him home frustrated, bitter, in a sick rage. He felt like that now. If only he could breathe properly! And here was the finest country air, transparent, sparkling sun, the distant low hills and soft basking meadows half-hidden by the blue haze of noon.

"You're actually going to sell this place?"

Rufus lit a cigarette, offered him one. Adam shook his head.

"What else can I do?"

What choice did he have? He couldn't live there, he couldn't keep it up. Adam lay in bed beside Anne, his mind repeating what he had said to Rufus on that wonderful day in June.

"What else can I do?"

Of course he should have said I don't have a choice. Come on, I'm hungry, let's go get some lunch and then we'll find a real estate agent. But they had bought food on their way coming through Halstead, the 1976 version of take-out, a couple of meat pies, apples, Coke, and they had had lunch lying in the grass by the lake. The magical quality of the place crept on them there like a spell, the warmth and the sunshine and the scents of the garden and the tranquil silence. But it was more than that. There was an indefinable ingredient, a kind of excitement. It had something to do with history and the past, that excitement, and something to do with potential as well, with what Orwell or somebody had said, that every man really knew in his heart the finest place to be was the countryside on a summer's day. I was happy, Adam thought, that's what it was.

The Garden of Eden. Shiva had called it that but in his mouth it had not been the hackneyed expression it would have been if an English person had so referred to it. He was drawing an interesting image from the mythology of another culture and it had seemed to him fresh and new. Adam had merely shrugged. The Garden of Eden was the way certain people would describe any charming landscape. Yet the phrase had remained with him, particularly in its darker aspect, the way it appears to most of those who are bound by the puritan ethic, not as a haven to live in and enjoy but as a paradise to be expelled from. It was almost as if a necessary condition of being in this paradise were the commission of some frightful sin or crime that must result in expulsion from it. On the day they had gone, when the summer was over and the skies gray and a wind blowing, he had thought of that image. Their departure had something in it of the bowed and wretched mien of Adam and Eve in the many "expulsion" paintings he had later seen, and by then the Garden itself had a ruined look, paradise destroyed.

He got out of bed to pee. He and Anne had a bathroom opening out of their bedroom but Adam, when he got up in the night, usually went to the other one that was on the far side of the landing. This was because his reason for getting up at all was to see if Abigail was all right. But he had used their bathroom and was back in bed again before he realized that he had forgotten to look at his daughter. His anxiety for her had been displaced by a greater worry—was that possible?

Ever since her birth he had been ultra-anxious without expressing, even to himself alone, his reasons for this. Of course he knew what those reasons were but he had never faced them. Now he did and they did not seem absurd, they seemed like good reasons. He got up again and padded across to Abigail's room. Suppose, after all, that he had not gone to look and in the morning they had found her stiff and cold, her eyes glazed and unfocused, her lips blue? He shivered, gooseflesh standing on his face and arms. Abigail lay on her side, well tucked in, the teddy bear she was too young for sitting in the corner by her feet. Adam stood watching her, listening to her silent sleep.

7

With the specialist's contempt for the layman's ignorance, Rufus read accounts of the inquest in two newspapers. More prominence was given to the evidence of Alec Chipstead than to that of the Home Office pathologist, Dr. Aubrey Helier. The stuff Rufus wanted to know would be beyond the average reader's comprehension. He should really have gone to that inquest. That could be remedied; he could acquire a transcript of the proceedings or simply a copy of the pathologist's findings, but he did not dare, he was not prepared to show his hand to that extent.

Instead, he tried to guess what might have been said. He put himself into the pathologist's shoes and stood in the witness box. He spoke of how he had established the sex of the larger skeleton. A fragment of the uterus remaining perhaps? It was this soft part that often persisted longest.

"Having established that the larger skeleton was that of a female, I set about making an estimate of the subject's age at the time of her death. It should be explained that between the ages of twelve and thirty the union of the epiphyses of most of the long bones with the shafts takes place and by the age of twenty-four most of the epiphyses have united. In the case of the subject I shall henceforward designate as Subject A, I found that the medial end of the clavicle had not yet fused, though fusion had taken place at the acromion and vertical border scapula. The bones of the arm had for the most part fused but fusion had not yet taken place between the radius and ulna, which would be expected to have occurred by the age of twenty-one. The heads of the metatarsals were fused, which one would expect to be accomplished by nineteen years, but fusion had not taken place in the secondary pelvic centers. The sutures of the skull remained open on their inner aspects. . . ."

Something like that it must have been. He would not have been able to put a precise age on the skeleton. Between seventeen and twenty-one, say. And the cause of death? Rufus had another look at the paper. The pathologist had said it was at this stage impossible to give an opinion but the report also said the police were treating the case as murder. There was nothing about how the pathologist had reached the conclusion death had taken place some time between 1974 and 1977. Rufus guessed again.

"Certain highly technical factors, intelligible only to the expert and with which I will not take up the time of this inquest, have led me to conclude that Subject A had been dead for more than nine years and less than twelve. Suffice it to say that I reached this estimate on the basis of the preservation of a vestige of the uterus and as a result of obtaining a chemical reaction for blood from periosteum. I should not have expected to obtain such a reaction if more than twelve years had elapsed since death."

It was only conjecture about that bit of uterus. Rufus wondered if he might have invented that part because he had so much to do with wombs in the course of his own daily life. He knew very little about tests done on blood from bones, only that they could be carried out. Identification of "Subject A" would be a more difficult matter altogether. There was no mention of hair, though Rufus knew hair could persist intact for far more years than those bones had been in the grave, and there was nothing about clothing. Would ten years in the earth have destroyed that cotton shroud? He imagined a policeman with nothing more to go on than a tiny, once brightly embroidered label, a square inch of bloodstained, earth-stained, half-rotted cloth, hawking it around boutiques in Kilburn and West Hendon, narrowing the field, finally coming to an importers' warehouse down below the Westway. . . .

But no, she hadn't been wearing that dress, of course she hadn't. He asked himself how accurate his memory in fact was, how much time and a desire to repudiate the past had blocked off. He ought to try to remember; he must. There were ways of bringing memories to the surface and he must use them to protect himself. It was imperative, too, to keep cool and not allow things to get out of proportion. Most likely they would proceed no further than they had with the identification of "Subject A," especially since there was no one (apart from themselves) to miss her and she had never been missed. In the case of a person missing ten years before but who had never been reported missing, what hope was there now of establishing identity?

It might be somewhat different with regard to the other occupant of the grave. Rufus became the pathologist again.

"Now to the remains of the infant I shall call Subject B. Examination of the pelvis usually allows sex to be determined with great confidence in very young children and even in the fetus. I found in Subject B the greater sciatic notch to be wide and shallow and the ischial tuberosities to be everted, the ilia inclined to the vertical and the brim of the pelvis almost circular in outline. The subpubic angle was rounded and somewhat of the order of ninety degrees. I can therefore state with total confidence that Subject B was of the female sex.

"The age of Subject B I estimate to have been more than four weeks and less than twelve. The skeleton in toto measured twenty-two and a half inches. The anterior fontanelle was open. There was no appearance of ossification in the humeral head, though the cuboid was ossified. . . ."

Rufus was getting into unknown terrain here. He had very little idea of how the baby's age could have been estimated. By the fusion of joints, certainly, it need hardly matter to him which ones. How old had the baby been anyway? Very young, without teeth. "A primary deciduous dentition had not yet commenced" was no doubt how the pathologist would have put it. But what of Subject A's teeth?

That was primarily how dead bodies were identified, by their teeth. On the other hand, if the particular person had never been missed or reported missing, their existence scarcely recorded in the great reference log of National Insurance and medical cards, passports and driver's licenses, if the chance of their even being named seemed thin, what obscure dentist was going to rise up suddenly producing the relevant chart?

A certain assumption might of course be made.

"There is considerable danger here of drawing the conclusion that because the two sets of bones were found in conjunction and on the same date, they must have met their deaths at the same time. Although this is probably so, I am able to offer no evidence in proof of it. Nor have I come upon any factor to prove the truth of another assumption which may be made: to wit, that Subject A was the mother of Subject B. Experience and probability point to this being so but that is all.

"I am unable to state with any certainty the length of time which has elapsed since the death of Subject B or offer any suggestion as to the cause of death."

That was something which could never be established after this lapse of time. Unfortunate in a way, Rufus thought. It would be an ironical stroke if investigations into the affair resulted not in the discovery of those happenings in which they had been guilty but only of those where they had been blameless.

The inquest had been adjourned. No doubt they were still digging up the little graveyard. Rufus was not squeamish, he had not been one of those medical students who became nauseated at his first sight of surgery, but, curiously enough, he did not much like to think of all those odd little bones, so alien to him, so unidentifiable, being dug up and sorted out and sifted through in case there should be a human fibula among them or a vertebra. Rufus did not even know if animal bones shared the same names as those of humans. Did dogs have fibulas? He was surprised to find himself shuddering.

If there was no shot in or among the human remains, in the cavities of the skull for instance, would it be possible to find it in the soil, among the sand and gravel and pine needles? Bird shot it would have been or somewhat larger. Rufus had seen it only while eating partridge which had been winged instead of shot in the head, and had nearly broken one of his teeth on the tiny ball of lead. He imagined gravel being sifted, all the particles, the minute stones, being picked over by some policeman whose job it was to do that, the tiny flints laid in one tray, the wood fragments in another, and then, in a third, the shot.

He could remember so much, he had clear pictures of whole

days spent at Ecalpemos, whole conversations recorded that could be rerun in his head. Why was it then that he couldn't remember where she had been shot? In the heart or the head or the spine? His mind blanked over that, and there was a complete loss of recall. When he tried and saw the sky covered with rushing clouds, the lawn that had become a hayfield, the cedar's wheeling branches, the gun leveled, there would come an explosion in his memory like the firing of that shotgun, a redness in front of his eyes with splintered edges, then blackout.

The gun he could remember, both guns. And the gun room and the first time he went in there with Adam. They had eaten their lunch down by the lake. Two pork pies and a can of Coke each but not the apples which were imported Granny Smiths and bruised, and anyway they had strawberries. They must have each eaten about a pound of strawberries, for they kept going back to the fruit cage for more. Sometime during the afternoon they decided not to go back but to stay there overnight. That meant there was no hurry, they could have lain out there in the sun till the pubs opened. But Adam had this idea of phoning his mother to tell her he wouldn't be back that night. Rufus wouldn't have bothered, he came and went as he pleased, and anyway didn't believe parents should be pandered to in this way. Of course it wasn't quite pandering with Adam. He didn't want to get on worse terms with his mother, whom he hoped to get a loan from for his holiday in Greece, nor did he want the kind of thing that might have happened, his mother phoning hospitals or getting the police because they could have had an accident in Goblander.

As it turned out he didn't make the phone call until the evening and they found a phone booth outside a pub in one of the villages, for Great-Uncle Hilbert's phone had been disconnected. But once they were indoors again they resumed exploring, found a genuine butler's pantry with a lot of silver in it packed away in canteens and boxes and green baize, and opening the next door, came into the gun room.

Adam, as a child, had been strictly forbidden ever to go in there. Anyway, the door was usually kept locked. Presumably, in pre-Hilbert days, during Bereland squirearchy, it had contained an armory of weapons, for all four walls were hung with gun racks. However, only two types of firearms remained, both shotguns. There was a row of hooks for hanging up jackets and waterproofs.

A glass case on the windowsill contained a fat stuffed trout, another, on the circular table, a turtle—this certainly not of English provenance. The front half of a fox, paws and all, its rear end replaced by a shield-shaped slab of polished wood, appeared to be leaping out of the wall just below the picture rail, in the manner of a circus dog emerging from a paper hoop.

"Those aren't the sort of things you shoot, though, are they?" Rufus had asked.

"You most definitely don't shoot foxes."

Adam said this in such a snooty lord-of-the-manor way that Rufus yelled with laughter. He took one of the guns, the twelve-bore, from the wall and Adam had another go at him, this time for pointing it in his direction.

"It's not loaded, for God's sake."

"Never mind. You don't point guns at people." It appeared then that Adam had actually been out shooting the last time he was there. He had been only fifteen and had been given the four-ten, the so-called lady's gun.

Since then he had often recalled what Adam said next, had taken the gun from him and remarked that it was a pump action shotgun.

"What does that mean?"

"You don't have to keep re-loading. It's got a repeating action. You don't have to put a cartridge in each time before you fire."

And Rufus, who didn't mind appearing ingenuous in this area, said, "I thought all firearms worked like that."

One of the drawers in the pine cabinet was stacked with cartridges, red ones and blue ones which Adam said indicated the size of the shot they contained.

"That's amazing, me inheriting a couple of guns as well. We might even get some shooting."

"Not in June, squire. Even I know that."

Was that the first hint, no more than a joke really, that they might stay at Wyvis Hall, that they might *live* there? And Adam had said: "I didn't mean now."

"I thought you were going to sell the place."

Adam didn't say any more. They went back down the garden and after that out to a couple of pubs, where they drank a lot and Rufus had to drive back to Wyvis Hall with one eye closed on account of getting double vision. They slept it off, not getting up till around eleven next morning, Rufus in the principal guest room, Adam at the other end of the house in what he christened the Pincushion Room because it had a picture on the wall of St. Sebastian stuck full of arrows. Rufus looked out the window and saw a man trimming the grass around one of the rosebeds with a pair of long-handled shears.

He was elderly, bald, very thin, wearing a striped shirt of the kind that have detachable collars. It was the sound of his clipping that had woken Rufus up. The sun was blazing down and there wasn't a spot of shade anywhere till you came to the wood below the lake. Rufus, who hadn't much appreciation of nature usually, nevertheless found himself gazing in something like wonderment at all the roses, yellow and pink and apricot and dark red, a hedge of white ones, a cascade of peach-red that covered a pergola. The man with the shears laid them down on the grass, took a handkerchief from his pocket, made a knot in each of its four corners, and placed this improvised sun hat on his head.

Rufus had never seen anyone do that before, though he had seen it in pictures on seaside postcards. He was entranced. He put on his shorts and his sandals and went down. By the time he got outside, Adam was already there, telling the man in the handkerchief hat that he didn't want him to come anymore, he was going to sell the house.

"This old garden'll go to rack and ruin then. I been coming down here watering most nights."

"That's not my problem," said Adam. "The people who buy it will have to handle that."

"It do seem a wicked shame." The gardener opened his shears and wiped the grass clipping off the blades with his forefinger. "But it's not my place to argue. Mr. Verne-Smith paid me up till the end of April, so that's seven weeks you owe me—let's say six and a half to be fair."

Adam looked rather shattered. "I didn't actually ask you to come."

"True, but I come, didn't I? I done the work and I'll want paying. Fair's fair. Look at the place. You can't deny I done the work."

Adam couldn't. He didn't try. In the cagey, suspicious way he sometimes spoke he said: "How much in fact would it be?"

"I come twice a week at a pound a time, so that's thirteen, say, and then there's all the times I've come with me cans. Fifteen I reckon would cover it."

It was ludicrously less than Rufus had expected. For all that labor it was ridiculous. But this was the country, this was horticulture, and they ordered things differently there. He and Adam went into the house, where they managed to scrounge up fifteen quid between the two of them, leaving them with just enough to cover the petrol for Goblander to get home on.

Adam paid the man and he went off on a bicycle, still wearing the knotted handkerchief on his head. It was only after he had gone that they realized they had never asked his name or where he lived.

"You could have kept him on for two quid a week. It's nothing."

"I haven't got two quid a week. I'm skint."

And it was lack of money that stopped them going away. He, Rufus, could have gotten just about enough together for the gasoline en route and maybe his own food. If Adam had had an equal amount they would have managed. In another year, at almost any other time, Adam would have touched his father or more probably his mother for a loan, but in June 1976 his father was barely speaking to him, and his mother would have been scared to go against her husband. Of course if Adam had invited his parents to make themselves at home at Wyvis Hall, use it as a hotel while he was away, they would have lent him any amount, but that was the last thing Adam would have done. He did ask his sister for money. Bridget had been one of those teenagers who work all through their school vacations in restaurants or shops, or cleaning houses, and she always had cash. But she would not lend him any. She was saving up to go skiing the next January, and she knew there wasn't much chance of Adam repaying a loan by then.

It was ironical that Adam, who was the owner of that big house and all that land and the contents of the house, nevertheless went down to Nunes the second time with less than a fiver in his pocket. And that was everything he had. Instead of Greece they went to Wyvis Hall because Adam was broke and Mary was close to broke and because that first time it had been so beautiful and peaceful and *private* there that you could hardly see what advantages Greece would have had over it. They had intended to stay a week. Rufus had suggested to Adam that he sell something out of the house, a piece of china or some silver. There were almost more antique and second-hand shops in some of those villages than there were houses. He had counted six in the place where they had gone to the pub. They talked about it on the way down in Goblander.

It was funny how good Adam had been at naming things, the rooms in the house, the house itself even, or at naming the idea of it, the concept, Ecalpemos. Goblander was not just an anagram on "old banger," it really expressed the way that decrepit old van had of gobbling up petrol as it chugged through the countryside making awful noises because it needed a new silencer.

"You'll never even get near Greece in this," said Mary. "It'll just collapse and give up the ghost somewhere in France. I'm warning you."

Her father was a life peer who had held some sort of office under a Labour government. It must have been the boarding school she had been to that determined her voice—affected, sharp, shrill. She found fault a lot. The car was wrong, his clothes were wrong or funny or somehow unsuitable, he smoked too much, he was too fond of wine, and his whole lifestyle left much to be desired. She started on Rufus for making that shameful suggestion about selling what she called the family silver. How dreadful! What a desecration! He ought to have a feeling of reverence for the beautiful things his great-uncle had entrusted to him.

"He's not coming back," said Adam, "to see how I've discharged my duties."

"He'll turn in his grave."

"No, there'll just be a small upheaval in his ashes."

He told her Great-Uncle Hilbert's ashes were the contents of an urn-shaped Crown Derby sweets jar that stood on the drawing room mantelpiece. Maybe she believed him, for Rufus had once caught her lifting the lid and looking into the jar at the wood ash Adam had scraped up from the site of the handkerchief man's last bonfire. Mary was rather difficult but she was also just about the most beautiful girl Rufus had ever come across. It gratified him to be seen in her company. He had always been a bit that way had Rufus, manifestly to be seen to be doing all right for himself, successful, forging ahead, accompanied by the best looking girl possible. Mary was spectacular to look at and her own knowledge that she was made her capricious and difficult and expecting the best of everything. All that was her due because she looked like the young Elizabeth Taylor, had dark brown curly hair nearly to her waist, large dark blue eyes, creamy velvet skin, and a wonderful figure.

It was June 20 when they went back, all Goblander's windows open, the weather being perfect the way you expected it to be that summer as if it were southern Europe where you woke up each morning to sunshine and unclouded skies. By that time, as Adam said, you would actually have been shocked if the temperature had dropped or a shower of rain fallen.

"It makes you think there mightn't be an awful lot of point in going to Greece," he said. "I mean this could be the best summer ever and we'd miss it. It's always like this in Greece."

They bought food in Sudbury, quite a lot of food. Adam said the first thing would be to get old Hilbert's fridge going. Of course, it was his own fridge, but he was still in the habit of speaking as if, as Mary had implied, his great-uncle might return.

It must have been a strange experience for him, Rufus had thought, knowing he owned all sorts of things but not knowing quite what or where they were. They were the sort of things, too, which the parent generation owned, those old people that Adam, until Rufus laughed at him, had inadvertently called the grown-ups: sheets and blankets and knives and forks and pots and pans and more complicated appurtenances of living that if one ever thought about at all one supposed one would have to get together for oneself eventually. Someone else had got it together for Adam, and there it all was. They found some sheets in a walk-in cupboard, linen ones with "LVS" embroidered on them. The sheets felt a bit damp, so Mary spread them out on the terrace in the sun to dry. They ate out there, too, and drank one of the bottles of wine they had brought.

It was an amazing amount of wine they got through down at Wyvis Hall, and not only wine. But that first day they had been able to afford only two bottles of Anjou rosé. Later on they went all over the house, assessing what they might be able to sell, finding out just what Adam's inheritance amounted to. Rufus had been astonished by the quantities of junk in that house, the ornaments and knick-knacks and stuff like vases and candlesticks and ashtrays and glass and brass Hilbert Verne-Smith and his wife had accumulated over the years. Mary got stroppy about it and

said it was wrong what they were doing, it was a desecration. But
Adam had retorted quite reasonably that it was *his* now, didn't she
understand that? It was as much his to do as he liked with as the
sandals on his feet and the change from that fiver he had in his
pocket after buying the rosé. And then Mary said she felt as if
Hilbert were there with them as they riffled through chests and
drawers and cupboards; she could feel his presence standing
behind them, looking over her shoulder.

By then it was dark, it was nighttime. And at Wyvis Hall,
below the woods and above the river, with the nearest road half a
mile away and the nearest house twice as far as that, total silence
prevailed. The sky was clear, the color of a very dark blue jewel,
and on the surface of the lake the stars were mirrored. The house
was full of moths because they had left the doors and windows
open after they put the lights on. Mary screamed when a bat flew
close to her, she said bats got in your hair, a bat had got into the
hair of some relative of hers and bitten her scalp. Mary's scream
sounded particularly loud in that dark silence. There was a loud
echo in the grounds of Wyvis Hall, Mary's scream ringing back
from off the wood and walls and starry waters, and Rufus, a town
dweller who had never spent much time in the countryside,
expected alarmed or annoyed people to arrive or the disconnected
phone to start shrilling with complaints. Of course nothing
happened. They could all have screamed the place down, Mary
could have been bitten to death by bats, and no one would have
come.

That was part of the trouble, that was how it was that events
were set in motion. If Wyvis Hall had been less isolated, less
silent . . .

Rufus had come a long way since the Goblander days, and the
car he got into to drive himself to the hospital he attended two
mornings a week was a BMW not yet a year old. At the garage
where he bought petrol they offered him a complementary sherry
glass because he had bought more than thirty liters. Rufus refused.
He already had two of the things clinking about on the backseat.
But the sight of the glass took him back into the past again, the
past which he believed he had exorcised but was now fetched back
in fragments and longer scenarios by every possible association.
He had sat in that locked room talking, therapist and patient both,

had talked it out over and over. To the site of his trauma he had returned and relived it. He might just as well not have bothered, for it was there still, it would be there forever, unless one day they found how to cut memory out of the brain with a scalpel.

On the backseat the two sherry glasses clinked as Rufus took a left turn rather too sharply. What they had eventually decided to sell before they went to bed that night (or the following morning really) were Great-Uncle Hilbert's dozen Waterford sherry glasses. As Adam said, none of them drank sherry and he didn't know anyone under fifty who did. Having wandered all over the house, they had ended up in the dining room, where the cabinet full of glass was. In another cupboard they found half a bottle of whiskey and a dribble of brandy in the bottom of a Courvoisier bottle. There had been something extraordinarily delightful and exhilarating about sitting at that big oval mahogany table drinking whiskey at two o'clock in the morning. The moon had come up and laid a greenish iridescence on the surface of the lake. It was so bright it made the stars disappear. They had to close the window because of the insects. Then they turned out the lights, the great brass chandelier with its false candles, and the moon's lemony radiance lay as still as cloths draped over the shining wood. Adam set the twelve sherry glasses that were cut in a Greek key pattern around their rims in the middle of the moonlight and said he would put them in a box tomorrow and try to sell them in Sudbury to the man who had the antique shop in Gainsborough Street that they had passed.

There had been a kind of innocence about them at that stage, Rufus thought. On one level they were just marking time, spending a few days in the country at a friend's house. On another they felt (as Mary put it) like burglars, prowling around the house, discovering treasures, half-expecting the true owner to return and surprise them.

"Suppose old Hilbert's face were to appear at the window now," Adam had said as they went up the back stairs to bed.

There was a window at the top, on the landing, but outside there was only the blue jewel night. They had all slept heavily, the sleep if not of the just, of the innocent and artless. None of them doubted that they would eventually get to Greece. In those early days, that last week of June, it was merely a matter of raising enough money. Not that this had been easy. The Sudbury man was not forthcoming, he had been suspicious, wanting all sorts of information about them and the glasses.

"He thinks you've nicked them, doesn't he?" said Mary, who hadn't come in but stayed outside in Goblander. "And of course he *would*. I mean, just look at you!"

Adam's cut-off jeans with the fringed hems, she meant, and his yellow and red headband that Adam insisted on calling a fillet, as if it were a bit of fish. And their long hair and bare feet.

"You reckon I should put on one of Hilbert's suits, do you?" Adam said.

He never did that. Instead, they drove into Hadleigh and found an antique-shop man who offered to drive to Wyvis Hall and give Adam a valuation for some of the furniture, the chandeliers, and the ornaments. Two days later he actually came, an oldish man, at least sixty, and valued two of the cabinets as worth five hundred pounds apiece. When Adam heard that, he didn't want to sell, he was sure they must therefore be worth far more. The man bought a brass lantern and two little tables with the surfaces carved with flowers and fruit, and the sherry glasses, giving Adam one hundred and fifty pounds for the lot.

Rufus could not remember the man's name, only that he had been the second visitor to Wyvis Hall, the gardener being the first. Would he remember? If still alive, he would be in his seventies by now. He had a confused impression of coming into the dining room while the man was there and hearing him rather grudgingly assess the value of the glass cabinet. The man had said good morning and Rufus had said hello and had returned to the task he and Mary were embarked on, covering the flagstones of the terrace with quilts from the bedrooms. The terrace faced south and got the full sun, so it was too hot to be out there by day but in the evenings and at night it was wonderful. They fetched a lightly padded patchwork quilt from the Centaur Room, a pink candlewick from the Room Without a Name, two of white cotton from the Room of Astonishment, and a bedspread of heavy yellow satin they found in a cupboard in the Pincushion Room. Mary arranged some pillows out there and cushions from the drawing room and by the time they were finished the antiques man had gone.

Leaving them with a hundred and fifty pounds.

So that evening they went out to spend some of it. Had they been noticed and noted as they drove through the village of

Nunes? Rufus had always heard that nothing can go on in a village without the gossips knowing. Perhaps this would apply if they had walked along that village street or sat on the green or drunk in the local pub, but they had not. For some reason they had not much liked the look of this pub called the Fir Tree, and though he had slowed a bit as they came to it, but had not stopped. Adam had seldom been to the village, and only once on foot, but he could remember the layout of it with surprising clarity.

A church that stood upon a grassy hill and to which you mounted by a flight of steep stone stairs. An avenue of yew trees. Behind it one of those screens of elms, all dead even by then of Dutch elm disease. A village street of houses and cottages, a garage, a grocer, but not a single antique shop. The green an isosceles triangle without a tree on it, but trees around the pub, the same kind as in Adam's pinewood, Rufus supposed, or very like, which the licensee or the brewery had probably thought its name required.

There was the inevitable council estate, the houses painted pale green, blue, pink, as in some child's drawing, and then, around a bend in the lane where you might have expected open fields, half a dozen houses of nineteen fifties or sixties provenance, lavishly appointed, glamorously gardened, with big garages and big cars outside them.

"Hampstead Garden Suburb comes to Suffolk," Adam had said.

Later on they had seen the coypu man's van parked on the front driveway of one of those houses. And they had had a discussion about it, speculating as to whether he actually lived there or was there to kill something, rats, moles, any sort of infestation. Snobbish Rufus had not thought it possible for someone like that to live there, but why not, after all? There was money to be made out of the destruction of pests in a country place.

Rufus had an outpatients' clinic and then a ward round, in the afternoon a very frightened woman to see in Wimpole Street, a woman who needed his kind reassurance, his urbane ways, the proffered cigarette, the support. His first cigarette of the day he smoked while he waited, extinguishing it two minutes before she was shown in, and he had to tell her that her cervical smear had shown precancerous signs.

Who would reassure *him*? Comfort *him*? No one, he thought, and despised himself for what was to him an unnatural need. The police would not necessarily assume that the bones in the graveyard were of people who had lived at Wyvis Hall, nor that those who had brought about their deaths had lived there. But it was *likely*. It was most probable. The existence of the cemetery was not generally known, and on the lane side of the pinewood the trees were separated from the grass verge by a close-boarded fence.

They would ask a lot of questions in the village. They would make inquiries at Pytle Farm and the house called the Mill on the Pytle. By some means they would discover all the people who were likely to have called at Wyvis Hall in the capacity of tradesmen or service operatives: dustmen, meter readers, gardeners, antiques dealers perhaps—why not?—the coypu man. Adam would be questioned, was possibly being questioned at this moment. Unless he had changed a lot he would not make a good impression.

Had the time come to forget the promise they had made each other, the guarantee they had given never to meet or speak? Rufus reached for the blue phone directory and turned to the Vs, to Verne-Smith-Duchini, and had actually begun to dial when his patient was announced.

He put the receiver back and created, forcing his lips to perform, a wide smile.

8

The lake water was clear and cool, not cold. Weeks of sunshine had taken off the chill. Soon after they got up—which was always late, which was lunchtime—he and Rufus went in swimming, keeping their feet off the gravelly or slimy bottom and their arms clear of the blanket weed which was like green hair. The lily leaves lay flat on the surface, their flowers waxen crimson and palest yellow, their stems tough, glutinous, slippery, a tangle of entrails.

"Reminds me of the duodenum," said Rufus, yanking out a long slimy stem and lassoing Adam with it, catching his neck in a noose of living rope.

They grappled together, the way schoolboys do, but they weren't schoolboys and Adam was suddenly aware of Rufus's body under the water, his hard muscles and smooth skin, legs briefly intertwined with his. And when Rufus's arms grabbed him from behind, ostensibly, of course, just to duck him under the surface, he found himself resisting in a way that Rufus recognized as real resistance and let him go. And Rufus knew why, grinning a little as their eyes met. He swam away and Adam swam away and very soon after that they came out of the lake and went back to Mary on the terrace.

A disturbing experience it had been, exciting and confusing.

Adam had not known he carried within his mind a directory of the forbidden. Selling what he still thought of—in spite of what he said to Mary—as Hilbert's things appeared only on the perimeter of it, in an area of doubt. Money they had to have. For the rest of the time they were there, money did not exactly overshadow them but the pressing need for it was always there, it was always in their minds. And Mary's condemnation was not enough to keep him from succumbing. He had let the dealer from Hadleigh come, a man called Evans or Owens, one of those Welsh names, and sold him a brass lantern and two little carved tables and the sherry glasses. The money he gave them they had meant to use for the Greek trip, but it was more than they expected and they had gone on a shopping then a drinking spree with it. Also Goblander had needed a new exhaust system and they had had that done immediately, not in the local Nunes garage though but at a big impersonal place in Colchester. Rufus had thought Goblander needed a thorough overhaul and the mechanic confirmed this, adding that it would cost him. The bill would be around seventy-five pounds but, as Mary had said, the van wouldn't get as far as Calais in its present state. Next day they had collected the rejuvenated Goblander, catching one of the rare buses to Colchester and taking all day about it. The cost of the service was nearer eighty-five pounds than seventy-five and they spent a further fifty on food and drink. Drink mostly.

Adam drank very little these days. It nauseated him and wakened him in the night with a palpitating heart. He had been better able to tolerate it ten years ago but then he had drunk alcohol to be like other people and to impress, not because he liked it. Rufus was different. Rufus had a great capacity and could metabolize (as he put it) large quantities of spirits and larger amounts of wine. It was not unusual for him, unaided, to drink two bottles of wine in as many hours. But he was wrong when he said it had no effect on him. The effects were very apparent, though they were not the common ones of slurred speech and unsteadiness and loss of memory.

Rufus used to say that if left to themselves most men would live on meat and cake. They might eat fruit and vegetables and dairy products but that was for their health, not because they liked them. It was versions of meat and cake that the three of them bought to store in Hilbert's—no, his—fridge, and they bought crisps and chocolate bars and a crate full of wines and liquor. He was a sybarite or an Epicurean, Adam thought, relishing words, but Epicurean sounded better, less pejorative.

No one drank the spirits but Rufus, and Adam suspected that he drank more than he let on about, probably keeping a private bottle somewhere.

"I don't see any point in self-denial," he used to say.

"My father says being denied things refines the character," Adam said.

Rufus grinned, for of course Adam had told him all about Hilbert's will. "He should know," he said.

Adam suspected that these days Rufus might be quite fastidious about wine, a wine snob even, the kind that savors bouquets and talks about nice little domestic burgundies and so forth, but in those days it was rotgut he wanted. So they bought the cheapest obtainable in order to get more of it, Nicolas, and stuff called Hirondelle.

"I shall have to sell the Gainsborough next," Adam said.

Of course it turned out not to be a Gainsborough, in spite of what Evans or Owens had said. Having secured the tables and the glasses, he had peered at the dark discolored oil of an elderly cleric in a shovel hat and opined that this was the work of "our local genius." Asked to explain, he said he meant Gainsborough who had been born in Sudbury. Hadn't they seen the statue of him in the market place where he stood with his palette, apparently painting the pub and King's the grocer's?

They took the painting to Sudbury to get an expert opinion and there the signature at the bottom of the canvas was pointed out to them, that of one C. Prebble. So they took it back to Wyvis Hall and hung it up again and then they lay out on the terrace in the sun, eating rump steak and potato crisps and drinking Hirondelle rosé. They used Hilbert's wineglasses because none of them could tolerate drinking from plastic or paper cups, but they ate off paper plates of which they had bought a hundred. It must have been that day or the next, Adam thought, that he or one of them, surely he, had first suggested the commune idea. But not then, not yet. He had brought with him reading that was expected of him during this vacation, works on sociology and on linguistics and some on where these two studies converged, but these were not the sort of books one much wanted to read under the hot sun and the influence of wine. Instead, he read Hilbert's books, notably selections from a shelf of classic pornography, not in any way hidden, the books not concealed under plain covers, but there on display for anyone to find. Adam rather admired his great-uncle for this. There was Guillaume Apollinaire and Henry Miller, Pisanus Fraxi and *My Secret Life*, Frank Harris's *My Life and Loves,* and a dozen others. That afternoon Adam, knowing it was not the wisest thing to be doing in his celibate situation, lay on the terrace reading *Fanny Hill.*

Rufus and Mary lay quite near him on a candlewick bedspread Rufus had found in one of the spare bedrooms. They had been for some ten minutes locked in a close embrace, the length of their bodies pressed together. Sweat was running down Rufus's back, between his rather sharp shoulder blades. In spite of being so fair, his skin had taken on quite a deep tan in the few days they had been there. Adam had tried not to look but now he could not help looking. What he had feared would happen was happening now, though the feeling he had was not of being in any way rejected, nor was it embarrassment. It was simply a breathless, increasing, pulse-hammering sexual longing.

The two of them slid a little apart, Rufus rolling onto his back so that his pronounced erection showed, like a great clenched fist under his black trunks. He kept his head turned toward Mary, though, as between parted lips they licked the tips of each other's tongues. Adam found Rufus's great endowment as disturbing as Mary's naked breasts, which lay round and creamy, soft and passive yet with hard, pointed nipples, between the open sides of her blouse. He turned his head away, pressed forehead and eyes hard down into the covers of *Fanny Hill.* After a while he heard the others move, heard Rufus take a great slurp of wine before they padded barefoot into the house and up the stairs to the Centaur Room.

When Adam was about eight his father had told him masturbating gave you scurvy. Saying scurvy was caused by a lack of vitamin C was just a blind, spread around by doctors and nutritionists, who ought to know better. Most of the people you saw with false teeth had masturbated when young, it was a well-known fact, only there was a conspiracy between dentists and what Lewis called the "vitamin C lobby" to keep it secret. It was in their interests to make work for the dental profession and sell vitamin C, not to let it get about that simply by keeping their hands where they ought to be young people could have healthy teeth and gums for life. Later on Adam wondered if his father had made all this up or if he really believed it himself. It was not a theory to be come across elsewhere. But the curious thing was that the idea had somehow and much against his will taken root in his consciousness. He did not believe it, he ridiculed it—to his sister, for instance—but it partially attained the effect Lewis aimed at. If Adam ever got as far as masturbating, and naturally he sometimes did, he always had the feeling afterward that his teeth were loose. His jaw would ache and once, when he cleaned his teeth that night, he found blood on his toothbrush.

So he had no recourse to masturbation that afternoon but went back into the lake instead, where it was cold enough to supply one of the well-known Victorian antidotes to sexual desire.

Wading out of the lake, his legs muddy up to the knees, Adam sat on the bank among the bulrushes and the great pale leathery hosta leaves and looked at the house with its canopy of roses and honeysuckle, the martins' nests under the eaves, the long terrace with Zeus in his various avatars and his loves disporting themselves along the flint wall. Some brightly colored butterflies, orange and yellow and black and white—his father would have known their names—sunned themselves on the mellow rosy brickwork, spreading their wings flat in the heat. The sky above the glittering slate roof was as blue as the curious lilies that had just begun to come out under the dining room window, trumpet flowers set like the seed head of a dandelion but as blue as—the sky.

There would be things just as beautiful in Greece, and it would be as hot or hotter. But it would not be *his*. He would not be proprietor of all he surveyed there. It was a revelation to him how important this was, how much it meant. He had never previously thought of himself as acquisitive or even as particularly materialistic. The truth was though that until now he had never possessed anything much, so how could he know? It gave him a good feeling, it was satisfying just to think, as he walked up the stairs, these floors are mine, this carved wood, these moulded ceilings. And when he came into the Pincushion Room and rested his elbows on the window ledge, he would look out the window at the garden bright with midsummer sun or bathed in moonlight and think, all this is mine, that garden, that fruit cage within the flint walls, that lake, the Little Wood, as far as I can see on either side of me and in front of the house and behind, all that is mine. . . .

He was beginning to think he could not bear to sell it.

It was a long time since Adam had had a dream about Zosie. Rufus, yes, and Shiva sometimes, and Shiva with Vivien, but it was a year since Zosie had come into his sleep and materialized before him.

Things happened as they must have happened, only in fact it was Rufus who had picked her up and brought her back to Wyvis Hall. Stopping on the way to exact his pound of flesh, of course. No, that was unfair. He would have done the same—in those days. In his dream it was he who was driving home to Nunes from Colchester, not Goblander though, but the car he had now, the Granada. She was waiting where in life she had waited, outside the station, near where the road forked, going in one direction to Bures, in the other to Sudbury. There had been a great Victorian pile of a hospital there then, maybe still was unless they had demolished it, its chimney concealed inside a mock campanile.

Small and delicate, fine boned, pale brown skin, beige really—pale brown wispy very short hair, fey-faced with a small tip-tilted nose and golden eyes like a cat. Someone had said she was like an Abyssinian cat and so she was. Very young, a child, only she was not that. Jeans and a T-shirt but you never noticed what Zosie wore. What was it they called that term in rhetoric? Zeugma or syllepsis? She stood there wearing a backpack and a face of woe.

He drew up ahead of her. She came running up to the van and climbed in beside him. It was a hot night but she was shivering. He asked her where she wanted to go.

"Anywhere," she said.

"Anywhere?"

"I don't know where I am, so how can I say where I want to go?"

"You came here on the train, didn't you?"

She started laughing and through her laughter her teeth chattered.

"I came out of there." She turned around and pointed back at the Victorian building with the campanile chimney.

"What is it?" he said.

"Don't you know? It's a bin. A funny farm. It's what my gran calls a lunatic asylum."

Adam woke up. He lay thinking of Zosie. Had she been a bit mad? Perhaps but temporarily and for a well-attested reason. And of course there was no question of her having escaped from a mental hospital or of ever having been in one. He shook the dream off him. Rufus had called her a waif and Adam had immediately ridiculed this word, said it was a romantic novelist's word, so they had looked it up in Hilbert's Shorter Oxford Dictionary and found illuminating things. "Something waving or flapping." "Something borne or driven by the wind." "A person who is without home or friends; one who lives uncared-for; an outcast; an unowned or neglected child."

"That's the one I meant," said Rufus.

And then Adam had read aloud the first definition: "A piece of property which is found ownerless and which, if unclaimed within a fixed period after due notice given, falls to the lord of the manor."

Well, eventually, it was true that Zosie had fallen to him. The waif who was ownerless and unclaimed had fallen to the lord of the manor. A father himself now, he thought of those parents of hers, her mother and stepfather, who had lost her and apparently had never searched, had never even declared their loss, been glad to be rid of her.

Adam wondered if Abigail sometimes woke up and looked for him in the dark, in the empty room, and fretted for a while before she began to cry. He could not bear the idea of it. It was deep night, three or four o'clock. Mark Twain had written somewhere: We are all mad at night. He got out of bed silently, in the dark. So many times he had padded across this bedroom to go to Abigail that he knew it perfectly in the dark, only requiring to hold his hands out before him, and like a blind man feel the beveled corner of the wardrobe, the lacquered wicker of a chair back, the top of the radiator, cold at this hour, the glass sphere of the doorknob.

Outside on the landing he put a light on. Abigail's door was ajar and he went into the room, bringing a segment of light with him, a triangle that fell short a yard from where she slept. Instead of bending over her, he knelt down and looked at her face through the bars. She opened her eyes, but, like Lady Macbeth's, their sense was shut. Awake, she never looked at him without smiling. She did not smile now, but her eyelids with those amazing lashes slowly closed and Abigail gave a sigh, wriggled her body, moved her head, and subsided back into deep sleep. Adam knelt beside her, thinking of Zosie and Zosie's mother and stepfather, who had not bothered to go to the police when their daughter unaccountably vanished. They had felt apparently as if a burden had been lifted from them and why tempt fate by attempting to get her back? But Zosie had been only seventeen. Or so she said, Adam thought. But perhaps she was a year or two older than that or even more. She was such a liar.

You might be able to tell a person's age after they were dead but often not while they were still alive. For instance, the newspaper had said the skeleton in the cemetery at Wyvis Hall was of a young woman between eighteen and twenty-one years old. Not that that was specially relevant. . . .

He got up and went to the window, looking out into his garden. A narrow plot of mean suburban proportions compared to the place he had once possessed. Streetlamps were on in the distance, greenish or blobs of orange light. There was no moon, only the perpetual chemical twilight that subsists in suburbs by night. Autumn had laid a misty chill over everything that grew. Plants had become sticks, leaves were rags of wet black plastic, tree branches were bones with arthritic joints. We are all mad at three in the morning.

There had never been another summer like that one. Nineteen eighty-four had been good but not as good as that. The night had been warm, too, not just the daytime, and even after sunset the temperature had not seemed to drop much. They had driven home arguing about which night was Midsummer Night. Mary said it was June 20 because that was the night before the solstice, the longest day, and Rufus said it was the twenty-fourth and he, Adam, said it was the twenty-third because that was the eve of the twenty-fourth, which was Midsummer Day. They were all rather drunk and, by analogy from the argument, Rufus had sung at the top of his voice:

Where the bee fucks
There fuck I. . . .

There was a rugby player side to Rufus. Mary, often so censorious, was sweetened by drink. Everything Rufus said made her giggle and clutch at him. They shared a cigarette, passing it from mouth to mouth. Lying on the backseat, Adam recited *Grantchester*, which in those days he knew by heart:

> And green and deep
> The stream mysterious glides beneath,
> Green as a dream and deep as death. . . .

Back at home they lay out on the terrace on the spread quilts and Rufus said he would sleep there. Gnats came in swarms from the lake to torment them, so they lit incense sticks to keep them away, peppermint and aniseed and sandalwood. Mary had found some oil of citronella in an old-fashioned medicine chest in the Deathbed Room, and they rubbed it on themselves for good measure. Or rubbed it on each other, rather. That was what started it.

All was silent. Sometimes you heard a soft splash as a fish jumped for one of the swarming insects. Or the whispering rattle of a bat's wing. And occasionally, from the depths of the wood, came less agreeable sounds.

"The noise made by something being murdered by something else," Rufus had told an acquaintance in one of the pubs.

Rabbit victims of foxes or weasels, Adam supposed it was. The thin pitiful cries were somehow unearthly when they wakened him in the dark small hours. But no cries came to them there on the terrace, the darkness lit by the moon, the bright stars spread like a net across a sky that never lost its blueness, the scented tapers burning between the statuary of the amorous god. Rufus had a bottle of red wine but he was drinking the wine out of one of Hilbert's brandy glasses.

"We're not going to Greece, are we?" Adam said.

"I shouldn't think so for a moment," said Rufus, whose speech grew more precise when he was drunk. "Why would we do that?"

"If you remember, it was our intention."

"I want to go to Greece," said Mary, but smilingly and rather sleepily.

"No, you don't, my sweetheart. You want to stay here and rub some of that disgusting stuff all over Adam."

Rufus was setting it up. Adam didn't immediately realize this but after a little while he did. Rufus was always a sensation seeker, wanting new experiences, new indulgences. He would have made a good bad Roman emperor. Adam had put out his hand for the citronella but Rufus stopped him.

"No, let her do it."

Adam had a shirt on, the kind that buttons up, not a T-shirt, but now he began to take it off, having an idea of what might be about to happen. The mixture of gin and wine he had drunk hammered in his head, distorting reality, opening limitless possibilities, showing him a fantasy world that rocked and shimmered. But all he could say was, "We'll save Greece for another year. We won't go to Greece this time. . . ."

Mary's fingers moved lightly across his back. Rufus had propped himself up on one elbow, watching. He leaned across Adam to light a cigarette from one of the incense sticks and he smiled, letting the smoke trickle out between his teeth. Mary told Adam to turn around and face her, she would do his chest. It was a bit like having someone rub you with suntan lotion, yet it wasn't like that at all—how could it be in the dark? What it was like was being anointed by some slave girl. Rufus threw his cigarette away and from behind her laid his hand lightly on Mary's bare shoulder. She was wearing a halter top thing that tied around the back of her neck.

All the time, right up till then and a little beyond, Mary hadn't known what was going on. Rufus, of course, had always known; Rufus had instigated the whole thing, and then, at this point, Adam realized it. The realization resulted in a leap of desire that was brought about as much by Rufus, by the recollection of their slippery buoyant contact beneath the water, as by the sight of Mary as Rufus untied the knot on her neck and slid the halter top down with his hands.

This movement, as Rufus had no doubt intended, sent Mary toppling forward into Adam's arms, her breasts lightly slapping into his chest in a way that would have been blissful if it had been allowed to continue, but Mary, drunk as she was, had sprung aside, actually sprung to her feet, and rather late in the day hugged her arms across her chest.

"Now what's the bloody matter?" drawled Rufus.

"I'm not doing tribadism, that's what's the matter."

"Troilism," sighed Adam, "not tribadism." He might be drunk and bursting with frustration, but words came first with him. An etymologist he was to the bitter end. "The confusion arises from that 'tri' which isn't Latin though but part of the derivation from the Greek verb 'to rub.' A tribade is a Lesbian, whereas a troilist . . ."

"Jesus," said Rufus, "I don't believe it."

He rolled about on the quilts, roaring with laughter.

"Pray continue," he said, "with your most interesting lecture on rubbing. If we can't do it, at least we can hear about it."

"You bastard," said Mary. "You perverted sod."

"Please, it was only a game. A midsummer night's game."

"It's not bloody Midsummer Night," she roared at him. "How many times do I have to tell you?"

She stalked off into the house. Rufus went on laughing, hiccuping with laughter. He lay on his back, pouring red wine down his throat.

"You're crazy, Verne-Smith, did you know that? I set you up a mini-orgy, a nice little threesome, and the minute it rocks a bit, nothing a mite of persuasion wouldn't put right, you start giving an address on the Greek verb 'to rub.' You slay me, you really do. I shall remember that to my dying day, I shall remember it all my life."

"You won't," said Adam. "I bet you don't."

"Do you reckon she's really a closet tribade?"

After that he often called Mary the closet tribade. She was right when she said he could be a bastard, he really could.

"How about going for another swim?" said Rufus, and he turned, his mouth all dabbled with wine, to look into Adam's eyes. And Adam had looked into his, the wind singing in his head, the incense tapers smoldering, scenting the warm dark air.

"Why not?"

But Rufus had lain there, not touching Adam, just smiling. He had languidly stretched one arm out and in doing so knocked over the wine bottle. It had fallen too slowly to break, but the wine had flowed out and made a dark stain like blood on the white bedspread. The tips of his outflung fingers just touched Adam's bare shoulder and Adam had lain still, aware of that warm faintly tingling pressure, but happily, even serenely aware, trying for some unknown reason to count the stars. The last thing he remembered Rufus say was uttered on a murmuring chuckle.

"The Greek verb 'to rub'!"

And then Rufus was asleep, his head turned onto the muscle of his upper arm, the fingers that had been on Adam's shoulder retracting as they relaxed. Adam slept, too, very soon afterward, and awoke shivering with cold at dawn as one does after sleeping uncovered in the open air. He had, and was going to have, the worst hangover of his life, but even in the throes of it he was aware of a sense of relief that they were staying there, they were not going to Greece. The sky was a clear pale dome, covered in the east by a flock of tiny clouds that were already turned to pink by the sun that was still concealed, that had not yet risen. The garden was no longer silent but noisy with birdsong, with twittering, cheeping, cooing sounds, and with the true clear notes of the blackbird and thrush. Adam got to his feet, and throwing one of the quilts over Rufus, went into the house.

Two things happened the next day. Or one of those things happened. He wasn't sure of remembering the date of the other thing. It might have been on the Saturday. The coypu control man must have come on a weekday, though, and it was with that hangover that Adam associated his coming.

Now when he and Anne had people to stay they ran around after their guests making sure they were comfortable. One or both of them got up early to make breakfast in good time. They made inquiries as to whether the beds were all right and the water hot. It was what their parents had done when they had guests. But a different system had prevailed at Wyvis Hall, or rather no system had prevailed at all. Everyone fended for themselves. That was the way Adam wanted it and had in fact been vociferous on the subject, vowing that neither now nor in the future would he ever give in to those bourgeois values and customs.

So he did nothing for Mary or Rufus that morning, did not even seek them out, scarcely knew whether Rufus was still asleep on the terrace or back in bed with Mary, and when he found further sleep impossible because of his shivering body and pounding head, he sat in the kitchen making instant coffee for himself but took none up to them. He had already taken two aspirin about half an hour before and now he took four more. The table he sat at was circular and made of pine or what Hilbert and Adam's father had called deal. Adam was thinking about this interesting word that used to be simply another term for pine but which originally meant a certain size of plank, from the Low German *dele*, when there came a loud knocking on the back door. It gave him a shock in his fragile state. He crept to the door and opened it, blinking at the bright light. Outside stood a man, middle-aged, with thinning dark hair and a black moustache, wearing jeans and a lightweight jacket in pale blue plastic. He said his name was Pearson, he was from control and would it be all right for him to take a look around the lake?

"What control?" said Adam.

"New here, are you? I used to see a Mr. Smith."

Adam said he was dead. Was "coypu" an acronym? The man looked at him as if he were mad.

Adam gave up. "Look all you want," he said.

"Right, and I'll take a shuftee around the wood while I'm about it. That field next to you's down to sugar beet this year. Your coypu is crazy for sugar beet."

They aren't mine, Adam wanted to say but desisted. In Hilbert's dictionary he found coypu defined as a South American aquatic rodent, *Myo coypus*, somewhat smaller than a beaver. He liked the Latin name so much that he made up a sort of rhyme about it and chanted this as he went back upstairs:

> *Flittermus, ottermus,*
> *Myopotamus* . . .

From the window of the Pincushion Room he watched the man pottering about the edge of the lake. In one hand he held a sack, in the other what might have been metal traps, or not that at all but some kind of implement. How could coypu have gotten into a Suffolk pond? Must be an escape from a zoo, he thought, just as mink could be from fur farms. Going down again in search of more coffee, he met Mary coming up the stairs wearing Rufus's jeans and a dirty shirt with Louisiana State University printed on it. Mary looked the nearest to ugly he had ever seen her. She gave him a sullen glare and said in a very distant way did he know there was some awful peasant trespassing around the lake?

"He isn't trespassing." Adam started singing "Flittermus, ottermus" to the tune of the Austrian hymn.

"You mean hippopotamus."

Adam said he didn't, he meant myopotamus, which in turn meant coypu, that were presumably now in the process of being exterminated, whereupon Mary burst into shouts of anger and distress, calling him a cruel beast and an enemy of ecology.

"There can't be anything ecological about preserving South American rodents in Suffolk," Adam protested, but by then Mary was tearing off downstairs, bent on tackling the coypu controller herself.

Adam took a look out of the window of the bedroom that had been Hilbert's. The van, which had "Vermstroy Pest Control Ltd., Ipswich and Nunes," painted on its side, was turning around on the open area in front of the garage. As Mary came running out of the front door it moved off up the drift toward the wood. It made him laugh to see her standing there, shaking her fist at the departing van. He had begun to feel better, the aspirin and coffee were doing their work.

Rufus was still lying asleep on the terrace, though at some point he must have awakened, for he was shaded from the sun by Hilbert's old black umbrella which he had opened and propped there to shelter his head and face. Adam sat down beside him, wondering if he would have to pay the coypu man.

"I could sell those guns," he said when Rufus woke up.

"Or more directly, dismiss the coypu man, keep the guns, and shoot the coypu yourself."

That was all very well but there were going to be a lot of things to pay. Rates, for instance. Adam found himself not at all sure what rates were for, but he knew that people who owned houses did pay them. And there would be bills for electricity and water. The guns could be sold and more of the furniture. Unless . . . unless he could rent rooms out to people, or better still, gather a group of people here who all paid their way, start a commune, in fact.

This was the first thought he had ever had of the commune; it was at that moment it first came to him, out on the terrace sitting beside Rufus under Hilbert's umbrella, while the Vermstroy man hunted his quarry along the woodland streams and Mary pursued him with cries of protest.

Adam, among his computers, reflected on the coypu man, whose bill he had later paid, but whom he had never seen again. Would the coypu man remember? And if he did, would he be able to declare categorically to the police that Adam and Rufus and Mary had actually been living there? It must have been on or about June 25, before the others had come. From the lake the coypu man would have seen Rufus sleeping under the umbrella on the terrace and no doubt also seen Mary and probably spoken to her—have practically been assaulted by her.

He was about fifty or rather more. Very likely he was still alive. Vermstroy operated from Ipswich but it also operated from Nunes. The coypu man lived in Nunes. Later on, on a rare trip through the village in Goblander, Adam had seen that van parked in the driveway of one of those big Hampstead Garden Suburb houses.

Of course it was possible the van was parked there only because the man was inside destroying coypu or moles or rats or woodworm, but somehow Adam didn't think so. He recalled the way it had been parked, its nose halfway inside the open garage.

The man had been in the wood and had perhaps seen the animal cemetery. Adam could not know if he had but it was quite possible. He would know that there were people living at Wyvis Hall. If nothing else, the appearance of the terrace, arranged like a huge bed, would have told him that. Evans or Owens, the furniture man, who had come twice to the house, had been at least sixty then. He was hardly a danger. The gardener who had worn a knotted handkerchief on his head, whoever he might have been, had had no means of knowing then or later that Adam intended to live there. The visitor whose footsteps he had heard circling the house that last dawn they had ever spent there, if indeed he had heard them and not, in his state of panic, imagined them—that man or woman would have had no evidence for thinking anyone lived there but for the presence of Goblander on the drive.

But the coypu man was different. The coypu man could not be dismissed or the danger of him glossed over. Hope lay only in the possibility, the fairly strong possibility, that he was one of those who do not push themselves forward into police investigations unless directly called upon.

The next day or the day after perhaps, when they had talked a lot about the commune project, Mary had come up with Bella's name. It had been more roundabout than that but that was basically it. She and Rufus and Adam himself had all been putting forward the names of people they knew who might want to be part of a commune, likely people of the right sort of age and the right sort of temperament. Mary herself was quite keen, stipulating though that she would stay only if Rufus did not. Since his sly suggestions of Thursday midnight, she had been unremittingly at war with him, though they still ostensibly shared a bed. In fact, Rufus had taken mostly to sleeping outdoors. He had no intention, he said, of being part of a permanent commune, he had his medical degree to get, but he might think of coming there for his holidays. He upset Mary further by saying he thought Adam's sister Bridget very attractive and it would be an inducement to him if she became one of the members.

Adam didn't want his sister, they didn't get on all that well. He could think of two of his fellow students who might be suitable but they, too, had degree courses to finish and Adam was beginning to think very seriously of not returning to college. The peculiar mixed course he was doing he had always had doubts about. The linguistics part he knew already, the English he could pick up on his own, and the sociology bored him. What was the good of a B.A. from that tinpot redbrick place anyway? He might as well be at a polytechnic. If he wanted a degree, he could just as well get one at the technical college in Ipswich. . . .

Rufus put up two or three names, one being of someone they had both been at school with. You wanted at least one person who had been in a commune before, Mary said, and perhaps you ought to advertise along those lines. In *Time Out*, say.

"Or *Gay News*," said Rufus. " 'Tribade seeks fellow travelers' help out of the closet.' "

"I do just wonder," Mary said, "why you go on and on and on about it. Could it just be you've got a closet of your own, d'you think?"

Rufus started laughing at that and said all the doors in his life were strictly never kept closed. "Open house and bring your friends."

"It's a mystery to me you've got any."

Adam hadn't liked the idea of advertising. Besides, money was short. Before they got onto the subject of the commune they had been discussing which item of Hilbert's former property they should sell next. One of the big cabinets, Rufus said, and no nonsense about it, get Evans or Owens back, but Adam could see his house being stripped bare. If people came and put money into the commune . . .

"There's a girl I know of called Bella something," said Mary. "I don't know her. It's my friend Linda that knows her. She used to be one of that Rajneesh lot, she always lives in communes, and Linda told me she was looking for somewhere. I mean I could find out more about this Bella."

It was through Bella, of course, that Vivien found them and with her the Indian, Shiva, whose other name Adam could not remember.

Mary was the only one of them, as far as he knew, who had ever walked to the village and walked around in the village when she got there. It would not matter what any inhabitant of Nunes told the police about Mary, for she had departed soon after that. And if people remembered her, they would not have known where she came from. She had gone to the village—as Vivien had later gone—to use the public phone booth outside the Fir Tree. Probably she went into the Fir Tree or the village shop to get change for those calls. She had been phoning people who might go to Greece with her or drive her there or, failing that, pay her air fare, and eventually she succeeded in getting a loan from an aunt and an offer of a place in a minibus from an old schoolfellow and her boyfriend.

The day before she left he thought of a new name for his house. For some days he had been mulling this over, trying to come up with something more interesting than Wyvis Hall. Myopotamus Manor, which had occurred to him, was just a joke. He began anagraming, twisting letters around, keeping in mind where they *had* been going, where Mary was still going. . . .

Ecalpemos.

He asked the others what they thought Ecalpemos was.

"A Greek island," said Mary.

"Not an island," said Rufus. "More like a mountain. A volcano."

"Or a resort on the Costa Brava."

"You just made it up," said Rufus lazily. "It does sound rather like a community. Oneida, Walden, Ecalpemos."

"It doesn't sound in the least like Oneida or Walden. I know what it is, it's like Erewhon that's 'nowhere' backward."

Adam was surprised at Mary's perspicacity but annoyed that she was leaving. He didn't like her much but he wanted her to stay. He was finding he resented people who did not care for Wyvis Hall as much as he did.

"You don't know the difference between an anagram and an inversion, do you?" he said. "Bloody illiteracy always puts my back up. Why talk about it if you don't know?"

"Hey-hey," said Rufus. "I'm the one that quarrels with her, remember?"

"Erewhon is an anagram of 'nowhere.' Ecalpemos is 'someplace' inverted."

"Well, well, very clever. Don't you find 'someplace' has too much of an American flavor?"

"I don't give a sod about that," said Adam. "It's not being called 'someplace' anyway, it's going to be Ecalpemos."

Which thereafter it always was.

The next day was the 30th of June, a Wednesday. Mary wanted Rufus to drive her all the way back to London, but he said Colchester was his limit and she could get a train from there. There was a certain rapprochement though as Mary came down with her things in the backpack Rufus had lent her and wearing jeans and a pair of sandals for the first time for days.

"I actually adored it," she said to Adam, "only I'd promised myself I'd go to Greece these holidays and I absolutely can't not go now."

"That's okay. Ecalpemos will still be here next year."

"I did wonder if you'd like me to send cards to your parents and Rufus's from Athens. I mean ones you'd write here and I'd take them with me."

"By a quite exceptional oversight," said Rufus, "I don't just happen to have any picture postcards of the Acropolis about me at present."

"It was just a thought," Mary said sulkily. "It didn't have to be cards, it could have been a letter."

"If mine got a letter from me," said Rufus, "they'd think I was dying or in jail."

It amounted to the same thing for him. And why bother to write anyway? What was there to say? Mary had some vague idea that Adam's parents might suspect he was down here and come to see him. But Adam couldn't see why they should. If only he had acceded to that suggestion of hers! The ironical thing was that all the time, in a stack in Hilbert's desk, secured by a rubber band, were fifty or so old postcards collected by Hilbert and Lilian presumably on early travels and among them were two of Greece, one of Mount Lycabettos and the other the very view Rufus had spoken of so scathingly.

But they hadn't known that then, and if they had could not have known how much one day such postcards would have supported the story Adam was beginning to think he would tell. Always supposing their parents had kept the postcards, which, considering their rarity value, they might well have done. Mary's offer had been rejected without their thinking twice about it, and she and Adam had said good-bye in a cool, offhand sort of way and Rufus had driven her off to the station in Goblander.

From that day to this Adam had never set eyes on Mary Gage and had hardly ever thought of her. If she had come into his mind, he had operated his canceling switch as he did when any of the denizens of Ecalpemos strayed into his thoughts. Once, not long ago, an old film called *National Velvet* had been on television and when the young Elizabeth Taylor appeared on the screen, he had at once been sharply reminded of Mary—and had exited, not with the escape key but the switch on the set.

He and Rufus had talked about money later that day. What could they sell next? Even to Adam's ignorant eye the Victorian water colors of moorland or mountain streams, mounted on gold paper and framed in gilt, were valueless. There was a strange picture in one of the bedrooms of a centaurlike creature, a horse with the torso and head of a man, presenting itself at a forge to be shod, where it was eyed with fearful fascination by the smith and a crowd of onlookers. When they cut away the paper at the back of the frame, it proved to be a Boecklin but a print cut from a magazine, the original being in Budapest. They called the room where it hung the Centaur Room. Another strange picture hung in Hilbert's room, one that Adam had never allowed himself to think about. Since the birth of Abigail it would have been torture. And, besides, the picture no longer existed, having been burned by Adam himself, destroyed on that pyre with certain other things.

A large gloomy bedroom had been the setting of it, hung with draperies, not the kind of thing you would expect a child to sleep in, but it was a little child that lay on the bed, white and still, the elderly man, evidently a doctor, who had seemingly just lifted a mirror from the parted lips, turning to the young father and imparting the news of death, while the mother in a transport of grief clung to her husband, her head buried in his shoulder. Adam confronted this remembered picture now with a kind of stoicism. He forced himself to see it and recall those things that were connected with it. How extraordinary it seemed that he and Rufus had stood in front of that picture and *laughed* at it! To remember this now brought him an actual physical pain in the deeps of his body, in his intestines. He and Rufus had stood there drinking wine. Rufus had the last bottle of wine in his left hand and a glassful in his right. They were walking around the house speculating as to what they should sell and had paused here in this far from gloomy room, this warm, sunny, charming room, and laughed at that gloomy picture, at its sentimental naiveté. In fact, he had even made some appropriately sophisticated comment.

"Dead and never called me Mother," it had probably been.

That was the reason they named it the Deathbed Room.

On into the Room Without a Name they had passed and through to the room it communicated with, the Room of Astonishment, so called because it had a cupboard in it with a little staircase inside that wound its way up into the loft. They considered the salability of a washstand, a swinging mirror, a flowered pottery basin and jug, and then as they descended by the back stairs, the plates in dull red and dark blue and gold glaze that hung on the wall there and might, from the hieroglyphs on their backs, possibly be Chinese and perhaps valuable.

Next day they had taken the mirror and the pottery and the porcelain to Long Melford because there were more antique shops in Long Melford than anywhere else they had seen, but twenty pounds was all they got for the lot. When people came to join the commune, Adam thought, they would have to pay, they would have to contribute. And how were any suitable people going to know about it when he had no phone, or no phone that worked, and Mary Gage had probably forgotten all about this Bella?

There, of course, he had been wrong. All the time he and Rufus were living it up, driving about the countryside in Goblander, driving to London once to buy marijuana from the dealer Rufus knew in Notting Hill, drinking and smoking (as he had put it) Hilbert's furniture away, all that time Vivien and her boyfriend Shiva were making arrangements to join Ecalpemos. And they were expecting, of course, a well-run settlement, a sort of East Anglian kibbutz, where the members had appointed duties, where vegetarianism prevailed and brown rice had an almost holy significance, and discussions on mystical or occult or philosophic subjects went on long into the night.

But first Zosie had come.

Rufus, driving back from London with the hashish his dealer swore was genuine Indian *charas* and a package of best Colombian, picked her off the street—"a piece of property that is found ownerless." And she had slept with Rufus in the Centaur Room, it being taken for granted she would share his bed, though Adam did not think her wishes had been consulted. Rufus was a bit of a centaur himself, a big roan stallion, and she was a little cat-eyed waif.

It must have been a day or two afterward that she had seen the picture. Exploring the house on the following day or the day after that, she had ventured into the Deathbed Room. She had gone in and looked at that picture and come running down the stairs crying, with her hands up to her face and the tears pouring.

"Why did you let me go in there? Why didn't you tell me what was in there?"

Just for a moment, standing by the window, dropping the edge of the curtain he had lifted and turning back toward the crib, Adam saw the picture again, saw it with an awful clarity on the darkness before his eyes.

The painting was destroyed. He had burned it himself on the fire he had made against the fruit garden wall and it might be that no copies of it existed, yet in his mind's eye it recreated itself, the child forever stilled, its face a waxen mask, the old doctor haggard with sorrow and lack of sleep, the mirror no breath had misted held in his hand, the parents in each other's arms.

9

Because he was without a qualification Shiva was not permitted to dispense. Kishan, with his pharmacology degree, did that, and Mira, Kisan's wife, helped out at particularly busy times. Shiva served in the shop and arranged the displays and kept a check on the stock and sometimes recommended remedies for coughs and spots. Kishan really needed a second assistant, but he couldn't afford one if he was going to continue paying Shiva a decent wage with small annual increases. Although Shiva didn't want to lose him, Kishan was an altruistic man and was always trying to persuade Shiva to go back to college and finish his courses so that he could set up as a pharmacist himself, not just work for one. Shiva knew he would never go back now; it would all be too fraught with memories and bitterness. Besides, he did not dislike the shop, the warmth of it and the delicious scents, the feeling of doing positive good when he was able to persuade someone of the virtues of vitamin C, the brief pleasure he took in selling a pretty girl a pretty shade of lipstick. He accepted. He did not expect to be fulfilled or enjoy job satisfaction or be happy.

Once he had been all those things. At school in the far west of London he had got three good A Levels and gone on to study pharmacology. This brought his father an almost delirious joy. Shiva's father was an uneducated though not an illiterate man, who had brought his wife and his widowed mother to this country some twenty years before. For some time he had worked for a tailor and his wife as a machinist but having a business sense and some foresight had observed the beginnings of the trend toward Indian-made clothes. Even he could not have imagined how immensely popular dresses and skirts and tops of embroidered Indian cotton would become or how the humble import business he started would make him if not a rich, at least a very comfortably-off man. It was in this comparative affluence that Shiva and his brother and sisters grew up, their home a big semi-detached house in Southall. Shiva's elder brother, though he had won a scholarship to the City of London School, had not lived up to his early promise and had embarked on a career in a High Street bank. It was on Shiva therefore that his father pinned his hopes and ambitions. Shiva had just completed his first year at a college of technology, where he had done very well, so well in fact that two of the lecturers there had privately told him—well, not exactly that he was wasting his time, but that he was mentally equipped for higher things. Both believed that he would be better suited to study medicine.

Of course he told his father. What should he do? Should he apply to medical schools? Probably that meant he would have to wait a year, always supposing he were accepted. His father, overwhelmed at the prospect of having a doctor for a son, was certain he would be accepted. And why not have a year off if that were necessary? There was money enough to keep him. It was all very pleasant to contemplate and think of at his leisure. Not entirely at his leisure either, for it would not have occurred to Shiva to live at home and do nothing. The business could always do with the temporary help of an extra pair of hands.

Another source of Shiva's happiness was his relationship with Vivien Goldman. Of her he said nothing at home, his parents were progressive and though his grandmother might wring her hands, predicting curses and disaster, they would not have considered arranging marriages for their children. Just the same, they took it for granted they would marry among their own people. They probably took it for granted, Shiva thought, that their children would not even get to know members of the opposite sex who were English.

Vivien was Jewish. To Shiva's way of thinking she was only

half Jewish because her father had been gentile, but Vivien said it was having a Jewish mother that made you a Jew. Not that she had seen her mother for many years, having been brought up in children's homes until she was eighteen. Shiva had met her at a party given by a fellow student who lived in a squat near the river at Hammersmith where Vivien was also living. He had not at first been specially attracted by her, indeed he had been somewhat daunted, but she had singled him out and talked to him. She had talked to him about Indian philosophy and Indian mysticism, subjects on which Shiva was not well informed, and confided in him how she intended to go to India to learn from a certain guru and sit at his feet. After the party Shiva had gone home with Vivien, not to make love but to talk and sleep and talk again.

Vivien was the only person Shiva had ever met whose aim in life was to find out what she was doing in this world, what the meaning of life was and to learn how to be good. To this end she had lived for a while on a kibbutz and in a commune in California and been a disciple of Bhagwan and attended hundreds of lectures and read hundreds of books. Shiva (whose mother described him as "education mad") asked her why she didn't go to college and study philosophy but Vivien despised formal education. After she left school and at the same time the children's home, she lived for a while on the dole, but coming to believe that this was wrong, went out cleaning apartments and in between the kibbutz and Bhagwan had been a children's nanny.

She was a small, dark girl with long hair she wore in braids or wound tightly around her head. Shiva had never known her to wear trousers or any garments of a masculine cast. Vivien wore robes rather than dresses, and sometimes she hung around her neck the Star of David and sometimes the Christian cross. Alone in the world and without ties, she seemed to have a hundred friends but no close ones and Shiva, when at last they made love, was only her second lover.

He parted from her with no thought of seeing her again until he returned to college in September. If he returned there. They would write to each other. The Hammersmith squat had no phone and Shiva would not have liked Vivien to phone him at home. He could imagine the scenes his grandmother would make if she found out he had an English girlfriend, and what praying there would be, what threats of retribution, and not made in vain either, for his mother was not so progressive as to fail in her deference to her mother-in-law and the old lady's opinions carried great weight in the house in Southall. So Shiva wrote to Vivien and received her letters which he told his parents were from a friend of his at college, a boy whose family was from Benares.

Then the letter came with the suggestion that Shiva might like to join Vivien in a community at Ecalpemos, wherever that might be, just for a trial period to see what it was like. She understood he would have to go back to college in September. But she might remain. It all depended on whether a center for meditation might be established there.

Would he have to go back to college, though? Shiva asked himself. Perhaps not, not if he changed his mind about the pharmacology course and decided to try for medical school instead. In that case he would not be able to start until a year from October and in the interim might have to take his A Level in math. But he could study just as easily at Ecalpemos as in Southall and perhaps more easily. A house with gardens and land in the country, in Suffolk, Vivien had written.

Shiva, though far more deferential to his parents than any European contemporary would be, holding them in far greater esteem, nevertheless had no compunction about lying to them. He reasoned this way. If he told them he was going to spend two months in a center for meditation with an English girl who had no parents to speak of and was partly Jewish, they would be very unhappy indeed and would worry, whereas if he said what in fact he did say, that he would be attending a summer school designed as a preparatory course for those contemplating a medical career they would be happy and gratified. Really there was no choice about it. That such a summer school did not and could not exist need be no obstacle since his father was ignorant about these things and trusted Shiva's word and opinions. He even gave them the address: Ecalpemos, Nunes, Suffolk, for he knew that nothing short of the death of one of them would induce the others to get in touch with him.

Shiva's father told him to help himself to a selection from the best of the Indian cotton shirts so that he might look smart during his stay. Shiva knew he would have no need of new shirts, so he took a dress instead. No Indian woman had ever worn dresses like these—with low square necks and big sleeves and high waists and floor-length skirts—or ever would, but this bright turquoise blue one embroidered on the bodice in scarlet and gold might have been made for small, pretty Vivien. It would be the first present he had ever given her.

The squat was in a row of condemned houses in a street very close to the river off Fulham Palace Road. It was all gone now, Shiva had heard, the derelict cottages replaced by hygienic local authority housing and a day center for the handicapped. When Vivien had been living there the row had been awaiting demolition and scheduled unfit for human occupation, but squatters had come just the same and knocked out openings in the communicating walls so that entering at number one, you could walk all the way through to number nine without going out into the street. Shiva walked through, stepping over people asleep on mattresses on the floor. No one in that squat except Vivien ever got up before midday. It was shabby rather than dirty and it smelled of the river.

He found Vivien in her room, sitting cross-legged and meditating. She turned on him her bright-eyed gaze but gave no other sign of greeting and he did not interrupt her. He sat down among the mats and cushions that furnished the place in a vaguely oriental way that was quite unlike the solid three-piece suites and carved wood and etched brass of his own home. There was a rack of essential oils in tiny vials on the windowsill and the case in which Vivien kept her Bach flower remedies. A reflexology chart hung on one wall and the chart of Vivien's own horoscope underneath it. Her book collection he found daunting, the Bible, the Koran, the Gita, the *Imitation of Christ*, the Tibetan *Book of the Dead*. The *I Ching* lay open on a cushion, what looked like slips of straw beside it, as if before he came she had cast to know what her fate would be at Ecalpemos. . . .

Since then he had sometimes wondered what the *I Ching* had told her. Not, surely, anything like an accurate forecast or she would hardly have gone. It was impossibly cryptic, anyway; it could be made to mean anything. He sat and waited, not minding, not impatient, but beginning to feel soothed and at peace as one did in Vivien's presence. Twenty minutes went by and then she got up. Her bag was packed but she opened it again and put the flower remedies in and a big dark red shawl in case it got cold in the evenings. The bag was a carryall made of carpet with padded cloth handles, for Vivien wore no leather or any animal material, not even wool.

"What time is the train?" Shiva asked.

"I don't know. If we go to the station, a train will come. They always do."

He thought it quite amusing that Vivien should have to teach *him* this serene fatalism. "Are you in a great hurry, Shiva?" she said. "Have you got some pressing business at Ecalpemos that will vanish or be lost if you aren't there by nightfall?"

It was just a tradition, an accepted way of life, that you made haste, you rushed busily, irrespective of what you had to do when the end was reached. His parents were as much afflicted by it as English people.

"We have time," Vivien often said. "We're young. It's when we're eighty and we haven't much time left, then we'll have to rush."

He gave her the turquoise blue dress and immediately she put it on, for she had no understanding of the concept of keeping something for best. What would "best" be? All days were alike to her and all places for her to look at, not where others would look at her.

It was a gray and cream striped Moroccan cotton robe she had been wearing. She folded it carefully and laid it beside the *I Ching*.

"I won't need that now. I've got another dress with me."

Shiva found her amazing. What other woman would go off for perhaps months with only two dresses?

"You can always collect it," he said, "if you have to come back to London for an interview."

She had applied for a job as a children's nanny before Bella told her about Ecalpemos. But Shiva could tell that though calm and unhurried, she was excited by the prospect before her. The job might be disregarded if Ecalpemos turned out to be what she was always seeking, a real community of dedicated people, all with ideas similar to hers, people that she might teach and who might teach her something. He watched her write a note to someone else in the squat, ending it: "Love and peace, Vivien."

Traveling with her was a placid, restful experience. They missed the fast Inter-city train because Vivien refused to run for it and got into a slow train instead that took fifteen minutes longer to get there, stopping at half a dozen stations on the way. The blue dress was very conspicuous, the embroidery on the bodice and low-cut neckline glistening like real jewelry. Vivien looked beautiful and exotic but a little bizarre too. Outside Colchester station, off the grass verge, she had picked a yellow flower of a very common sort, though Shiva did not know what sort, and stuck it in her hair. Perhaps because of the way she looked—and the way he looked, too, come to that, a lithe, small-boned, dark-skinned Oriental—it was a while before a motorist stopped to give them a lift. Vivien had given no thought to the proximity or otherwise of Nunes to Colchester but they learned at the station that it was twelve miles away. There were buses but these were infrequent and the last one had gone. The car driver who picked them up said he would go into the village of Nunes but no farther.

Shiva had seldom been out into the English countryside and it was with wonder and a certain amount of curiosity that he looked at the wide fields of yellowing wheat and barley across which exaggeratedly long shadows lay. It was the driver who told him they were wheat and barley; they might have been sesame and sainfoin, for all he knew. There was no wind. There were no animals in the meadows, which surprised him, for he had expected herds of fat black and white cattle. They passed not a single walker or cyclist and met few other cars. The houses which he thought would be the dwellings of the poor, ramshackle and mean, were for the most part large and prosperous-looking, set in gardens full of flowers.

It had been mid-July. The sun was on the point of setting but the sky was still a dense blue and quite cloudless. Vivien had found out from Bella precisely where Ecalpemos was and when she saw the first of the landmarks she had been told about, Nunes church, flint-walled with a square tower and narrow pointed spire, set on a grassy mound, she said they would get out and continue on foot. They walked along quite slowly, watching the sun go down and as it vanished below the dark wooded horizon, saw the sky warm at once to gold and gradually flush rosy-pink.

It was after about half a mile that they found the path. Both of them, Shiva knew, were disconcerted because there was no sign saying Ecalpemos. He suspected Vivien had anticipated a hand-crafted wooden sign with the name lettered on it and perhaps a carved flower or pair of acorns. But it must be the place. There were no other houses to be seen in any direction, only huge prairielike fields. A farmhouse called the Mill on the Pytle they

had passed ten minutes before. To the left of them was a dense
pinewood that looked quite black at that hour with the sky above it
reddening as if from a distant fire.

They turned down the path, wondering and hoping. It was like
entering a tunnel after a while, for the trees met overhead, though
through the black network of branches you could still see the
brilliant sky. This tunnel descended gradually, winding a little,
then running straight down. It was the quietest place Shiva had
ever been in, silent in a velvety, tactile way so that you felt you
might have been stricken with deafness. And there were insects,
flies and slow-wheeling transparent winged things with dangling
legs, and moths. A dustiness in the air and a dustiness underfoot
and a scent of something sweet and something rotten. Not like
England, he had thought, not what he had expected a bit. Vivien
had not spoken for some minutes and their footsteps on the sandy
surface of the path, the dry turf, were soundless.

The trees parted. Briefly and absurdly, Shiva had the notion
that the trees had stepped aside to reveal the house to him. It lay
bathed in the afterglow of sunset, its windows turned to flat sheets
of gold, a mansion it seemed to him, old and dignified and
belonging in an unknown world. The breeze of dusk, the little
wind that Shiva had come to learn always raised itself at about this
time, fluttered through the bushes, the treetops, a clustering of
feather-headed flowers, as if a living thing had passed and ruffled
the leaves with its invisible paw.

It was a gentle nemesis Shiva felt was in pursuit of him, its
approach slow and lightfooted, but as sure as that breeze. Whether
it was Vivien who had taught him to wait and accept, or if this
were an inheritance from fatalistic forebears, he did not know. But
he did not specially want an awareness of the true state of things,
of the progress the police were making. He would have liked
Adam or Rufus to get in touch with him. Their indifference, their
treating him as of no account, caused him a pain he thought he had
long gotten over. In one respect only he felt glad, he felt relieved,
and this was in that he had kept nothing from Lili. To his parents
and his grandmother he might have lied when the expediency of
lying appealed to him, but to his wife he had told only the truth.
His father had died four years before, but his grandmother lived
on, she and his mother sharing the Southall house, two widows,

though his mother had never adopted the white sari. Abandoning that ambition to read medicine had caused Dilip Manjusri an enduring bitterness and sorrow, so much so that he hardly seemed to notice when his son gave up the pharmacology course as well. Of course by then Shiva had been very ill, had suffered a true mental breakdown that included physical collapse. It was curious, he sometimes thought, how in stories and books someone who had brought about another person's death recovered from it immediately, was just the same afterward as before, was affected if at all only by the fear of discovery. The reality was very different. Lili understood that and it was this as much as anything that bound him to her. This was what he called his love for her.

The pharmacy closed early on Wednesdays. Shiva's bus took him to the top of Fifth Avenue, and he walked home along the sidewalk, beside the parked cars that were like a string of colored beads, past the pub that was called The Boxer and past the grocery, both of which had their windows boarded up. There had been trouble down here the previous Saturday night, starting in The Boxer, when the barman refused to serve a man who was already drunk. The man happened to be Jamaican and the resultant mini-riot ensued, Shiva had heard, when he and his friends accused the barman of racial discrimination. A lot of windows had got broken and by the time the police arrived, someone had got as far as overturning a car. From inside their own house snug in front of the television Lili and Shiva had heard that car go over and Lili had been afraid. But the sound of the police sirens seemed to put an end to all of it, which was far from always being the case.

How horrified his father would have been if he could have seen this! He had loved England with the innocent worship of the immigrant who *has* made good, who has found the mother country indeed to be the land of milk and honey so many of his compatriots had warned him it was not. In many ways it was fortunate he died when he did. There had been rioting before that but he was too ill to realize. London had been a cleaner place then, too, Shiva fancied, not all this litter lying around the streets, cans in the gutter waiting to be kicked to make that characteristic night sound of a city street, a hollow empty meaningless clatter.

Was there more packaging than there had been ten years ago? Or more eating in the streets? More children around who were never told not to throw wrappers on the ground? Suddenly a memory came very sharply to him. He could almost hear that drawling upper middle-class voice, Rufus Fletcher's: "These days breaking into most people's houses is easier than opening a packet of biscuits."

In the kitchen at Ecalpemos, Vivien in her peacock blue dress with a large bowl of strawberries in her arms, Rufus naked but for ragged shorts, stabbing at the cellophane covering on a custard creams pack with a pair of scissors. The tough transparent stuff split open with quite a loud crack, with an explosion almost, and the biscuits tumbled out onto the table and the tiled floor, breaking and scattering crumbs.

And Zosie sitting on the edge of the table, picking one up and putting it whole into her mouth and someone saying—Adam? Rufus? He couldn't remember—but saying: "Zosie is the same color as those biscuits, matte, smooth, and lightly baked."

Dark Shiva was more conscious of the color of his skin when he was at Ecalpemos than perhaps he had ever been before. Though not more than he had been since. He should have said, "And I suppose I'm the color of a gingernut."

Lili worked all day on Wednesdays and she had just an hour off at lunchtime but she made a point of coming home specially to get his lunch for him and be a proper Indian wife. She wore the kamiz and salwar, her neck and shoulders covered by a dupatta in very much the same shade as the blue dress he had given Vivien. It dismayed him to see her dress like this; it embarrassed him. Her ancestors were not from the Punjab—why did she wear the costume of Punjabi women? To be not *an* Indian but all India, he knew that. Their notions about this were diametrically opposed. Assimilation was the only answer, in his view. Would all those European Jews have died if they had assimilated, if the Diaspora had not set itself apart and exclusive? If Shiva had a dream it would be that the world might become like the ideal in a popular song he remembered from his childhood in which it was advocated that all races be blended in a melting pot. Shiva did not care about what was lost thereby, the kamizes and saris, the festivals and phylacteries, the tongues and the traditions. They could all go if the gas chambers and the burning cars went with them.

"I'll be going straight to my Bengali lesson after work," Lili said.

"I know. I'll walk over and meet you."

"Oh, why? You needn't."

"I'll walk up and meet you," Shiva said.

Two stressful sounds met Adam as he let himself into his own house, as he pushed open the front door: Abigail's crying and the phone ringing. The crying came from the living room, the door to which, on the left, stood ajar, the ringing from the phone that was on a table at the foot of the staircase straight ahead of him. Adam, seemingly without thought, instinctively perhaps, went to the phone and picked up the receiver. Immediately, before he even said hello, he thought with a pang that caught him in the chest: I went to the phone first, I put her second, I went to the phone first.

It was the police.

Anne came running downstairs and into the living room. A voice was saying to Adam that he was Detective Inspector Someone-or-other and could he come to see him to "clear a few matters up." Abigail's crying stopped quite abruptly.

"What matters?" Adam asked because he knew an innocent person would ask that.

"I'll explain all that when we meet, Mr. Verne-Smith."

Adam asked when he wanted to come.

"I'm sure you'll agree there's no time like the present, so shall we say half an hour?"

"All right."

Anne came out with Abigail in her arms and Adam kissed his child and took her from Anne. In the way babies can, Abigail looked as if she had never cried in her life, would not have known how to cry. She had a glorious angelic smile and her cheek against Adam's own felt cool and fat and satiny like a new-picked plum.

"My God," Adam said, "I came into the house and heard the phone ringing and her crying and I went to the phone first. What sort of a father does that make me?"

Had Anne only known it, he was confiding in her, was opening his heart to his wife, and this might have been the beginning of a greater confidence, an abandonment of his self into her keeping, but she did not know it, she saw his outburst simply as another symptom of neurotic self-absorption. It exasperated her.

"But there was nothing wrong with her. She was only frustrated because she had thrown her teddy out and couldn't reach it."

Adam shrugged. He held Abigail pressed against him. Suppose they were to take him away and he were not to see her again for years, for ten years, say? Of course that was nonsense, it must be nonsense, he was getting hysterical with worry. The fact was that he was terribly tired. To break into an area of memory that has been deliberately buried and turfed over for a decade was an exhausting process. It was his own thoughts that had worn him out, this once-buried thing that now obsessed him. He wished he could drink, he wished drinking could do something for him.

"Would you get me a small whiskey with water in it?"

Anne looked at him in surprise.

"A lot of water." He apologized. "I can't get it without putting her down."

He sat in a chair with Abigail in his lap. Taking off his watch, he held it to her ear and then he remembered—for her face registered nothing—that it was his new watch, the one with the battery, and which therefore did not tick. Instead, he gave her an ornament from the mantelpiece, a small china cat. Abigail put its head into her mouth. Adam felt sick with love for her, he felt as if his love for her were being pulled out of him with tongs, and he knew beyond a doubt, it was laughable even to consider a doubt, that he had never loved anyone before. Not even Zosie.

His drink was brought. Anne took the china cat away from Abigail and gave her a rattle which had just been washed and which smelled of the stuff with which her bottle and other utensils were disinfected. Adam said: "The police want to come and see me. Something about that house my great-uncle left me."

"When?"

"What do you mean when?"

"When do they want to come and see you?"

"Now." He looked at the watch which did not tick. "Well, in twenty minutes or so."

"I see. What's it all about, Adam? I mean, you're not going to get into some sort of trouble, are you?"

Sometimes he felt tremendously distanced from her. She was less than the intermediary that produced Abigail from his seed. Worse than that, he felt he didn't know her at all, she was just a woman who had come over for something. Collecting for a charity perhaps. Canvassing for a political party or a religious sect. He did not know her, she was a stranger, even her face was unfamiliar, not an attractive face or a loved one, not a face he could ever have kissed.

"I can't tell them very much," he said. "It isn't as if I ever lived there. Well, I stayed there for a couple of weeks, and then I went off to Greece."

"But you had someone come in to look after it, didn't you?"

"Actually no. I told my father that at the time to stop him from saying I was letting the place go to ruin. How could I have afforded to pay anyone to go in there? I was broke. I had to sell some of Hilbert's furniture in order to get to Greece."

"It was the bones of a girl they found and a baby."

"I know what they found," said Adam, and holding Abigail's round strong plump body, he closed his eyes.

Those two girls, the barmaid and her friend, that he and Rufus had picked up and brought to Ecalpemos for the night, would they go to the police? Hardly. One of them had been married, her husband away on a selling trip. A discreditable drunken spree ending in messy sex was scarcely a memory she would want to revive. That must have been very late in June, the twenty-ninth or thirtieth, a Wednesday anyway. And a few days later, the beginning of the following week Zosie had come and then Vivien and the Indian. Adam thought he would tell the police he had left Wyvis Hall for Greece the first weekend in July and then if by any remote chance those two girls had talked to them, it would still appear all right.

The Indian wouldn't go to the police. Perhaps he wasn't even in this country any longer. Maybe when Adam saw him he had been going abroad somewhere, possibly even to take a job and live there. Adam could still remember the slight feeling of dismay he had had when the Indian had come that night, had walked around the side of the house with Vivien a little way behind him, stood on the grass below the terrace wall (between Zeus with Danae and Zeus with Europa) and looked up at him and Rufus and Zosie and the inevitable wine bottles on the terrace.

Adam had never before spoken to an Indian. Well, that wasn't quite right, for of course he had spoken to Indian post office clerks and supermarket assistants and ticket collectors but he had never been on social terms with one. He had never had a conversation with an Indian, for the Indian students at his college, of whom there were in any case not many, kept to themselves. This one looked as if he might be—well, there was no word for it these days, but what old Hilbert might have called a killjoy or a wet blanket. Adam sensed at once a disapproval at the mess on the terrace, the air of indolence, the atmosphere perhaps of debauch. The girl on the other hand who announced herself as Vivien seemed only smiling and friendly. She climbed up the steps at once and accepted the glass of wine Rufus offered her.

Had they spoken much to the Indian that night? Already Adam had been drunk, tired, and feeble the way drink always made him even then. And Rufus had been as he always was, alive and alert, unaffected one might think until one knew him well. His eyes had gone speculatively to Vivien, summing her up, the level of attractiveness she might have on the scale he kept in his mind, the precise relationship she might be having with Shiva. To Adam that relationship was obvious from the first and he had never even asked them if they would prefer to sleep apart but took them up to Hilbert's room as a matter of course, to the room where the painting of the dead child and its parents and the doctor hung on the wall facing the bed.

Next day Shiva had asked if he called it the Deathbed Room because his great-uncle had died there. He was the sort of person who is very bound up with family and relatives. Adam knew Hilbert had not died there but outside the door at the top of the back stairs, though perhaps his body had lain in the room to await the arrival of undertakers. Anyway, they all came to believe it, to accept that it was Hilbert's death chamber, along with the other absurdities of Ecalpemos.

Zosie used sometimes to say she saw Hilbert's ghost up there and a ghostly little dog at his heels. The extraordinary thing was that she described Hilbert very much as he had been, a small, spare man with a round face and thin gray hair and gold-rimmed bifocals. She must have looked into one of the photograph albums in the study. And Adam did not think she had ever mentioned the little dog until after Shiva had been up in the pinewood and found the animal cemetery and Blaze's grave. . . .

The smell of the whiskey made him shiver a little. He took a sip of it and as he set the glass down heard a car draw up outside. The police had come. He shook his head at Anne and went himself to let them in, carrying Abigail in his arms, as if their hard hearts might be softened by the sight of a father with his child.

10

One of Rufus's patients had a drug-addicted daughter. Mrs. Harding came for her check-up and her smear and then she would tell him the latest on Marilyn. Last time it had been the Methadone overdose Marilyn had taken, believing thus to get herself off heroin the sooner. Now Marilyn, though experiencing a precarious cure, was afraid she might have become a carrier of AIDS through using infected needles. Rufus, smoking a companionable cigarette with Mrs. Harding, urged her to make Marilyn have a test done.

While commiserating with her he found himself wondering what she would think if she knew of his own less than innocent past in this connection. It was of course long over. Rufus had not smoked cannabis or eaten hashish or swallowed "acid"—with heroin he had never experimented—since the expulsion from Ecalpemos. An addictive personality he might have, did have, but he knew where to stop. Rufus stopped at the rationed cigarettes and the half glass of vodka behind the curtain. He got up and opened the door for Mrs. Harding and she said, thank you *so* much, you don't know how marvelous it is just to *talk*. . . .

The stuff he used, he thought, had all come from the same dealer, an American who had originally come to England to escape the Vietnam draft and who lived in Notting Hill. Rufus wanted supplies before all the money ran out, the money Adam got from selling plates and a mirror and then, at his instigation, a set of silver fruit knives and forks. Whoever ate fruit with a knife and fork? The shopkeeper seemed to feel the same, which was why they hadn't got all that much for them. But what they did get Rufus took with him to Notting Hill, going up from Nunes in Goblander around lunchtime on—when would it have been—July the first or second?

He had got to Notting Hill late in the afternoon, waited for Chuck for what seemed like hours in a pub called the Sun in Splendour, and eventually gone to Chuck's flat which was the basement of a house in Arundel Gardens. Chuck was displeased to see him, had forgotten their arrangement, and kept saying it looked bad to have a stream of people arriving at his door at all hours. Rufus, naturally, couldn't have cared less. He got his Colombian and his *charas,* fifty sodium amytal capsules for good measure, paid for them, and set off back to Nunes.

If he had had any money left, any real money instead of just enough to buy petrol and ten cigarettes, Rufus would have stayed in London much later and found something interesting to do with his evening. He had occasionally thought of that since, how everything would have been changed, whole lives would have been changed, including his own, if he had had twenty pounds in his pocket instead of two pounds fifty. For if he had left London at eleven, say, instead of seven-thirty, Zosie would not have been waiting outside the station at Colchester to hitch a lift to Nunes.

"Some great brute of a truck driver would have picked you up," he had said to her a couple of days later, "and maybe raped and murdered you and left your body in a ditch."

"Well, you raped me," said Zosie.

"I *what*?"

"I only did it to get my lift and a bed for the night. I only did it for *sanctuary,* and that's rape really."

It was never policy with Rufus to recall ego-defacing rejoinders of that sort. He allowed himself to remember instead how from the first she had known it was Nunes she wanted to go to. She had never been there but she knew it was where she was heading. Home is where you go to, someone had written, and they have to take you in.

She looked about twelve until you got up close to her. Then, even in the dark, in the greenish lamplight, you could see she was more than that. Her hair was like a little cap of fawn satin. He hadn't said that, Adam had, Adam the wordsmith. She had a face like all the drawings there had ever been of fairy girls on birthday cards and illustrated children's books. Adam had said that too. Rufus saw only a small, slender, finely made girl in jeans and a T-shirt with a backpack that looked as if it hadn't much in it. And a face of despair or desperation that expressed itself in a big-eyed stare.

He drew up a few yards ahead of her and she ran up to the van.

"Where do you want to go to?"

"Anywhere!"

"Come on, give me a better idea than that."

She hesitated fractionally. "Nunes."

"Surprise, surprise. By an amazing coincidence I'm going there myself."

Frankly, and he had been quite frank about it to himself at the time, he had picked her up because he thought there might be a chance of sex and he had had no sex since Mary went (the encounter with the barmaid's friend not having amounted to much, he being too drunk at the time). At first she had not seemed particularly attractive. Zosie was like that. Her attractions made themselves felt slowly and then they grabbed you by the throat. She looked impossibly young.

"Could I have a cigarette?"

"I've only got six."

"You could buy some in that pub."

"I could if I had any money. I just bought a gallon of petrol. It was either that or a long night's smoke on the side of the road. Have you any money?"

"Of course I haven't."

She couldn't have sounded more astonished, more *sullenly* astonished, if he had asked her if she had a mink coat in her backpack.

"What's your name?"

"Zosie."

"Zoe?"

"Not Zoe and not Sophie. *Zosie.* What's yours?"

"Rufus."

"Woof-woof," said Zosie.

He gave her a cigarette and he had one. He pulled Goblander off the road onto a car track down one of the lanes leading to Boxted and they smoked their cigarettes and he remembered the packet of marijuana in the pocket of the door. So he took one of his four remaining cigarettes to pieces and rolled a joint and they smoked it, moving gradually closer and closer together, touching each other's faces and lips with fingertips and each other's bodies with hands, until it was time to climb into the back of the van. . . .

It was the quickest sexual encounter of Rufus's life, with the least preamble, the least working up to. Almost as easy as when you are married, Rufus thought now. He did not ask himself if she had liked it, had wanted to do it. She had moved in the right way and made the right noises and the expression he saw briefly on her face, blank yet wild, was probably indicative of pleasure.

Back in the front, driving on, his left hand on her knee, moving in a vaguely affectionate way, he asked her where in Nunes she wanted to go to.

"Where are *you* going?"

"To my friend's place. Maybe you know it? Wyvis Hall, a rather handsome Georgian house with a lot of land."

"I've never been to Nunes. This friend of yours—is it his parents' place?"

"No, it's his. He owns it. Just he and I live there."

"Rufus," she said, and her voice was very small, very young, "can I go there with you? Just for a little while? Just for the night?"

"Why not?" said Rufus, and then he said, "Where had you been meaning to go?"

She said nothing for a moment or two.

"Okay, you don't have to tell me. That's your business."

"I was just hoping something would turn up," she said.

"Haven't you really got any money?"

She said fiercely, "What d'you want me to do? Pay you for it?"

"Okay, sorry. I just wondered how you expected to get very far without money."

"I've got fifty p." She fished in her backpack for some coins to show him. The pack was half empty. There was a gray knitted sweater in it, a black leather belt with studs, a copy of *Honey* magazine, and a half-eaten chocolate bar. Zosie pulled the shawl around her shoulders and sat hugging herself. "I'd have gone home," she said.

He could tell she didn't like being questioned, so he hadn't asked where home was. By then they were going along the road from which the lane led up to Nunes and the church and the village green. She stared out of the window, into the white moonlight, the dark spaces. He noticed she was shaking, though it was warm.

"Are you feeling all right?"

"I'm tired," she said. "Christ, I'm tired."

She sat back and closed her eyes. He drove past the Mill on the Pytle, not a light showing in the house, not a light anywhere, and turned down Adam's drift. When Goblander stopped she woke up, whimpering like a child.

"Here we are," said Rufus.

She got out, stretching herself, pushing her fists into her eyes.

"I'll carry that," said Rufus, taking the backpack from her.

Yawning hugely, she looked up at Wyvis Hall, at the pillared porch, at the lemony glow of the dining room window through which the chandelier could be seen above the pool of light it made on the surface of the oval mahogany table.

"This friend of yours, it all belongs to him? I mean, just him?"

"That's right."

"How old is he then?"

"Nineteen."

"That's amazing," said Zosie.

She wanted to know if she could go straight to bed. By then they were in the house and Adam had come in from the terrace. Rufus couldn't be sure how Adam felt about Zosie's arrival. He was looking at her speculatively, seemed indeed unable to keep his eyes off her. It was different somehow, this picking up of Zosie, from when they had brought the two girls, the barmaid and her married friend, home with them from Sudbury. Adam said: "I'll show you where you'll sleep."

Rufus didn't object. He had decided to open a bottle of wine. Their footsteps could be heard overhead, which meant Adam must be showing her into his, Rufus's, room, the Centaur Room, and that was all he cared about. He stood on the terrace with the wineglass in his hand, looking at the waters of the lake in which the white reflection of the moon lay like a disc of marble. He and Zosie had smoked all the cigarettes and Rufus had never liked getting through the night without a cigarette in the house. . . .

He screwed his eyes tightly shut, opened them again to look at the Players packet on his desk. It was slipped into the top drawer as the receptionist announced his next patient.

When Adam approached home after they had expelled themselves from Ecalpemos he felt, for the first time in his life, the wish to die. Alternatively he had the feeling man attributes to sick animals, that of needing to find a hole far away from the herd to creep into and hide. And he had hoped, after Rufus had left him and he had uttered with ridiculous drama Cassius's farewell to Brutus, that he would at least be able to get into the house unobserved and go up to his bedroom and be alone. But this was not allowed him.

His father stood in the front garden with a pair of clippers in his hand. When he saw Adam he did not greet him but spoke in what Adam thought was a very strange way for someone who has not seen his only son for nearly three months.

"An afternoon is all it takes me to get this place shipshape, the whole lot weeded and tidied up. It's not as if I had a decent-sized garden, a few acres, something you could call a garden."

Adam said nothing but stood there feeling hopeless and helpless.

Lewis Verne-Smith said, "That's my old uncle's golf bag you've got there." He seemed to recollect that the bag must now, however unfairly, however productive of resentment, belong to Adam. "You can imagine how my uncle treasured that. He used to take care of his things. I don't suppose you can understand that. I expect it's just an old golf bag to you, something to be thrown about any old how."

"I'm not going to throw it anywhere," Adam said.

He went around the side of the house to the kitchen door, aware that his father was following him. He was beginning to think his father was going a bit mad. The loss of Wyvis Hall and brooding on that loss had unhinged him.

"So you've been to Greece," he said.

"Mmm-hmm."

"Is that all you can say?"

"What do you want me to say?"

"If I had had the incredible good fortune at your age to be permitted to have ten weeks holiday in Greece, I should have had a good deal more than 'mmm-hmm' to say about it, I can tell you."

By then they were in the kitchen. His mother and Bridget were nowhere around.

"I don't imagine you've been near your inheritance all these weeks. It might have been broken into, set fire to, razed to the ground for all you know." His father had worked himself into one of his rages. "You're totally irresponsible, do you know that? No one knew where you were, nobody could have gotten in touch with you. We might all have died, that glorious house you don't give a damn for might have been razed to the ground—and where were you? Swanning around the Aegean."

Adam went upstairs, carrying his stuff with him, and entered his bedroom and locked the door. He was glad now that he had let his father believe he had on that day returned from Greece. Later on, he remembered, his father had commented on his tan with ancillary remarks about dolce far niente and lotus eaters. But all he had been able to think of at the time was that phrase of his father's, "swanning around the Aegean," and before his eyes as he climbed the stairs, as he entered his room and sat down on the bed, he had had a sort of vision of a dark blue sea dotted with little green islands, the sun shining and the sky blue, and a team of white swans with golden collars around their necks and golden harness pulling a magic boat, a boat that was shaped rather like a gondola, in which he sat like some hero of antiquity, robed in white and trailing one graceful hand in the water.

The vision was so beautiful and reality so awful that he had lain on the bed and to his horror and shame burst out crying. He stuffed bedclothes into his mouth to muffle the sounds in case his father were standing outside the door. He had not cried for long. After a while he had got up and made himself undo the golf bag and remove the shotgun, the twelve-bore. He wrapped a dirty T-shirt around his left hand and held the gun with it and then he wiped the gun with a dirty sock. The golf bag with the gun in it he put under his bed.

Hadn't he been afraid his father might come poking around and find it? Adam made it a rule to keep his bedroom door locked always, but that is not the kind of rule which one keeps and he often forgot. Still, if his father had found the gun, he had never said and Adam had never moved it. He left it there when he went back to university a month later and it remained there until a year later when he moved out and into a house of his own that he bought with the money he got from the sale of Ecalpemos.

The gun was no longer in the golf bag but in a cupboard in the smaller spare bedroom upstairs. Adam did not have a license for it. But although made nervous by the arrival of the policemen, he was not in a panic, he was not in a state to believe that on this initial visit they would search his house. Their attitude to him was impersonal—that and incredulous. No, not quite incredulous, this was the wrong word, signifying as it did an astonished overt disbelief. They were not like that. They behaved rather as if as a matter of course they never believed protestations of innocence but would all too readily accept admissions of guilt. And yet none of it was as explicit as this. He also had the impression that what they were doing was mere routine, boring to them even, something to be gotten over. But instead of comforting him, this served rather to increase his anxiety because he felt that important questions were being saved up, were postponed until the time when certain evidence and certain remarks of his had been sifted and studied. Then the policemen would come back and the subsequent interview would be very different in kind.

The inspector's name was Winder, the Detective Constable's name was Stretton, the former a bit older than himself, the latter a bit younger. They looked like his neighbors or the people he worked with. He offered them a drink but this they refused. What Adam found a bit upsetting was the way neither of them, though politely acknowledging Anne, took the slightest notice of Abigail. Of course Anne took Abigail away to bed almost immediately after Winder and Stretton arrived, but even so Adam thought it strange that neither of them said good night to her as she was carried from the room or commented upon her after she had gone.

Winder started by asking him if he had ever lived at Wyvis Hall and Adam replied, well, not *lived,* stayed there for a few days just to check on the place. He had been short of money and while there he was afraid he had sold some of the contents of the house, ornaments rather than pieces of furniture.

"It was yours, wasn't it?" said Winder in his dull neutral voice.

"Yes, it was mine. I had a right to sell it."

"How long did you live there, Mr. Verne-Smith?"

"Stay there? A week or two. I don't remember exactly." Adam waited to be asked if he had stayed there alone but he was not asked. Neither man was writing any of this down and this gave Adam a small amount of confidence. He did not like the impersonal, breezy, almost automatonlike tone of Winder's voice, but it might be natural to him; it might be that he always talked like this, even to his wife and children.

"And after you left at the end of the week or two, did you ever go back?"

"Not to live there," said Adam.

"You never lived there in the first place, did you? Did you ever stay there again?"

"No."

"You put Wyvis Hall on the market, is that correct? Your father has told us you put it on the market in the autumn of 1976 and then withdrew it from sale in the spring, when you had had no acceptable offers. You offered it again in the autumn of 1977, finally selling it to Mr. Langan."

None of this was being written down, but this time Adam told the strict truth.

"I didn't offer it for sale at all until the late summer of 1977."

"So your father is mistaken?"

"He must be." Anticipating a fairly obvious question, Adam said, "I was in my last year at university. I had my finals coming up. I didn't want the bother of selling property. Besides, I was told that if I hung on to it, it would go up in value and it did."

This seemed to satisfy them. Stretton asked him what he had been dreading but knew must come, the first of a series of questions that would lead up to the matter of the animal cemetery and the contents of the grave.

"Did you know there was an area on your property where family pets had been buried?"

"I used to go there when I was a child, you know. I think I must have been shown it then."

"You think, Mr. Verne-Smith?"

"I don't remember," Adam said. "I knew there was an animal

cemetery there somewhere but I don't remember when I first saw it."

"You didn't, for instance, go up to look at it while you stayed at Wyvis Hall in June 1976 or again before you offered the property for sale in August 1977?"

"I don't think so. Not that I recall."

"You are aware, of course, of what was found buried in the animal cemetery a couple of weeks ago?"

"I think so."

"The skeletons of a young woman and a baby. Death occurred between nine and twelve years ago—which really means most probably ten or eleven years ago? Would you agree?"

Adam wasn't at all sure if he would. That is, he would not in general agree to an assumption of that sort and he was quite sure a court would not. On the other hand, he knew very well when death had occurred—ten years and two months ago.

"The young woman met a violent death. The child, too, possibly. Suicide is a possibility in the woman's case but she didn't kill herself and dig her own grave. She didn't bury herself."

Adam nodded. A rueful smile would have been in order but he could not smile. Winder had said "kill" and not "shoot," which meant they did not know a gun had been used, they didn't know about the pump action twelve-bore. Nor, perhaps, had they found the lady's gun, buried in the Little Wood. He had thought that if you shot something—for up till then he had shot only birds and few of them—the victim staggered, fell, and died. Like on the screen, like on television. He had not anticipated the flying blood, the fountains of blood, as the ball bearings struck arteries, great and small blood vessels. So it had been. So it must have been for Sebastian up in the Pincushion Room, the arrows summoning forth spouts of blood instead of the flesh receiving them passively as it might so many acupuncture needles. . . .

He had to exert himself not to drop his head into his hands.

"While you were down there in the summer of 1976—when would that have been exactly?"

"From the eighteenth of June for about a week," said Adam.

"You didn't happen to see a young woman about, I suppose? Pushing a baby in a pram, for example? A girl might have taken a child for a walk down the entrance drive."

"It's a private road."

"Well, yes, Mr. Verne-Smith, but the village people do use it occasionally. That sort of rule is more honored in the breach than the observance, don't you find?"

Adam shook his head. The idea of people having walked up and down the drift without his knowledge made him feel almost faint.

"You never saw a girl in the vicinity while you were there?" He waited for Adam's denial. "You won't mind my asking, I'm sure. It was a long time ago. You never had a girl staying with you there?"

"Absolutely not." Adam was astonished at the vehemence with which he could lie.

Vivien came into his mind—inevitably. He saw her in her bright blue dress, the bodice embroidered with crude birds and flowers in red and gold. She had been a squatter. London was full of squatters in the mid-seventies.

"I believe people might have used the house in my absence. When I went back in 1977 there were—well, signs that people had been in, sort of camped there."

They were keen on that. They wanted to know more. Yet even as he invented, describing a broken window in the washhouse, the paper wrappings nibbled by mice, a few missing ornaments, he sensed their disbelief. He sensed that they were simply interested in hearing what he would come up with next, that they were patiently paying out the rope, yards and yards of it, with which he would ultimately hang himself.

But it was over. They were going. They had not asked him where else he had been that summer and he had not had to invent a Greek holiday or involve others in an alibi. As he slowly eased himself from his chair, getting up ponderously as if he were prematurely arthritic, as he was poised there, supporting himself by his forearms pressing the arms of the chair, Winder said: "Is there anything else you would like to tell us?"

It was uttered with the utmost casualness, lightly thrown away. But Adam found the question deeply disconcerting. It sounded sinister and deliberate.

He said again, "I don't think so," reflecting what an absurd rejoinder this is, this squeamish, cautious substitute for "no."

He opened the front door for Winder and Stretton, and Winder thanked him for his help, adding as if this were an afterthought, a

tiny minor matter, something so unimportant that it had nearly
gone out of his head, that perhaps in the next few days Adam
would not mind going into his local police station and there make
a statement to the effect of what he had just told them. They were
Suffolk police, but "liaising" of course with the crime squad, and
if Adam were to ask for CID or better still for Sergeant
Fuller . . .

Anne had come out into the hall and was listening to what they
said. She looked disdainful but at the same time quite upset.

"Sergeant Fuller would take the statement from you," Winder
said. "Anytime will do, at your convenience, but let's say before
the weekend, shall we?"

"It's a funny thing," said Stretton, prolonging their departure.
"It's a funny thing how people—the public, that is—how they
think that just because a crime was committed a long time ago, I
mean, say, ten years ago, it's less important than if it had been
committed, well, yesterday. But that's not so at all. I mean, that's
not the way the police look at it."

"No," said Winder in a preoccupied way. "No, you're right,
it's not. We'll say good night, then. Good night, Mrs. Verne-
Smith."

After he closed the door Adam felt a little like he had that day
when he came home with the gun in the golf bag and found his
father in the front garden. He longed to be alone but he should not
have married if he felt like that. One of the objectives of marriage
was to have an ally.

"Just what is all this?" Anne said.

"It's nothing to do with me. They think squatters got into
Wyvis Hall and lived there without my knowing."

"Why did that man want a statement from you then?"

Adam did not answer her. He looked up Rufus's phone number
once more. If she comes up behind me and touches me, he
thought, if she says any more, I'll kill her. And then he thought
how that phrase, which was the general routine threat of the
harassed person, was banned to him forever, because to those
others it was fantasy while to him it was real.

Anne was sitting in the armchair reading, but she was
watching him with half an eye. Adam learned Rufus's number and
repeated it over and over to himself. He put the phone book back
and thought how much he longed to talk to someone who *knew,* to

one of them. It seemed to him that he had soldiered on, bearing this alone through eons of time. Ten years in fact, but most intensely for five days.

"I thought I heard Abigail," he said.

"Did you? I didn't."

"I'll just go up and look."

Anne's face wore that peevish exasperated expression that always signified he was being too concerned a parent. In the hall Adam looked at his watch and the digits told him nine fifty-six. A bit late to make a phone call but perhaps not too late. Five to ten at Ecalpemos had been the start of the evening, the infancy of the young night. And he and Rufus, like sultans, had reclined on quilts and smoked hashish, the pungent trails of smoke rising into the dark air and mingling with the scents of the summer night. For ever and forever farewell, Rufus. And whether we shall meet again I know not, let us therefore our everlasting farewells take. . . .

In his bedroom he lifted the receiver and put his forefinger to the nine button on the phone. Rufus's exchange was nine five nine. Adam knew he was being hysterical, a bit mad, those policemen had sent him over the edge, but he did not just want to talk to Rufus, he *longed* for Rufus. He wanted, at that moment, to hold Rufus in his arms and possess Rufus's body with his body, and be lost in him as he had once wanted to lose himself in Zosie.

He was trembling. He dialed the number very quickly before his nerve could fail. If a woman answered he would put the phone down. He was holding his breath. The phone was answered and Rufus gave the number. It was the same languid drawl, very cool, very Rufus.

"This is Adam Verne-Smith."

"Ah," said Rufus.

Now that he had done it he did not know what to say.

"I rather expected to hear from you," Rufus said. "Sometime or other."

"I have to talk to you."

"Not now." The voice was stony, remote.

"No, all right. Not now. Tomorrow? Thursday? We could meet." Adam would know the minute Anne picked up the receiver downstairs; he would hear the click and have the sense of a door opening somewhere along the line, yet knowing this perfectly well he was nevertheless afraid he might already have missed hearing and sensing it and all the time Anne had been listening, was even now attending to this rather sinister exchange between him and Rufus. "Hold on," he said, and he went to the head of the stairs, looked down, of course could see nothing, and had to come right up to the living room door and look in to make sure she was still reading. She looked up and stared back at him, unsmiling. Adam returned to the phone and Rufus. "Some policemen have been here."

"Christ."

"I didn't mention you—or anyone. I said I'd never lived there."

"Where do you work?" said Rufus. "I mean, where's your office or whatever?"

"Sort of Victoria, Pimlico."

"Call me tomorrow in Wimpole Street. We might have a drink."

"All right."

Rufus replaced his receiver first. But Adam found he did not much mind, it wasn't a rejection and it didn't hurt. It was strange how Rufus's tone had changed while he, Adam, was downstairs checking up on Anne. In those thirty seconds he had become the old Rufus again, his best friend, once very nearly his lover, his partner in crime, his Cassius. Suppose this were to pass away, all of it, suppose by a miracle they were to escape, would it be possible to be friends with Rufus again?

He found he was trembling at the thought of it and he got up from where he had been sitting on the bed and went into Abigail's room. Standing by her side, looking down, he thought how unlikely it was he would sleep that night, how he must anticipate lying wakeful for hour upon hour.

And then he really looked at the crib, looked into it in the light that came in here from the landing, and saw his daughter lying face downward, utterly still, her face buried in the small flat pillow. His breath caught and held, he stared. He lowered the side of the crib. There was no movement at all; she wasn't breathing, there was no delicate rise and fall of the frail shape. The sheet and blanket and down quilt lay motionless on her small, rigid body.

The room was silent, warm, expectant of the most appalling disaster. Adam cried out, a yell of terror, and snatched up Abigail in his arms. Very much alive, she burst into screams of fright. Anne came running upstairs. The light was put on, was painfully bright, making Abigail sob and cry the more, poking fists into her eyes.

"What the hell are you doing to her?"

Adam gasped. "I thought she was dead."

"You're mad. You're insane, you ought to see someone. Give her to me."

Without a word he handed her over. Instead of his wife and child, he seemed for a moment to see Zosie standing there with the baby in her arms. He could have married Zosie, he thought. She had wanted to marry a rich man and in her eyes then he had been rich, the lord of Ecalpemos. Avoiding such thoughts, he had never considered it till now, but was it he she had had in mind when she talked of her career? And had he thrown her away through simply failing to recognize this?

Exiled from Abigail's room, he went downstairs again, aware of his aloneness, appreciating this rare solitude. Anne he had deeply offended, but he was indifferent to this. It meant, anyway, that she would not pursue him with questions. He indulged in fantasizing briefly, in a dream of her leaving him, walking out on him and Abigail. He would have to get a nanny, of course, but he could afford that. Someone like Vivien perhaps . . .

All roads led back to Ecalpemos. Whatever he thought of brought him back into the Ecalpemos file which Undo and Quit keys only briefly expelled from his mind's screen. Or he had lost the knack of escape.

He was dozing in the armchair but he was awake, he wasn't dreaming. Zosie was coming across the garden and his hands were red, but with raspberry juice, not blood.

11

The garden was beginning to get a dried-up look, the grass not growing much but the sun bleaching the green out of it. And in the full heat of the day the flowers hung down their heads. Even the leaves on the bushes and small trees drooped when the sun was at its hottest. But inside the walled garden the fruit swelled and ripened, maturing to un-English reds and golds. The strawberries were over but the raspberries were at their peak, the height of their season, fat juicy crimson fruit the size of rosebuds and safe from birds on their canes inside the cage, currants growing alongside them, black, red, and the ones they called white which were really golden, and gooseberries with purple-flushed hairy cheeks that had overripened and split open. All along the old weathered wall of agate-colored flints the nectarines had turned from green to yellow to orange and on some a rosy blush was appearing. Distantly, beyond the screen of walnut trees and hazels—for Adam had left open the arched green door in the wall—could be seen a yellow field of barley, almost ready to cut.

He was inside the cage eating raspberries. It was around noon and very hot, the sky cloudless and the sun high. Adam looked up and saw Zosie appear in the doorway, look around her until she saw him, then pull the door to behind her. This was her second day at Ecalpemos. She wore her jeans, which she had cut off a good six inches above the knees and frayed the hems, a white cotton vest he thought might have been Hilbert's, and a pair of pink espadrilles through which her toes had made holes. Her exposed skin, of which there was a good deal, was a uniform pale biscuit color and her hair was this color, too, and her eyebrows and her lips. Her eyes themselves were a little darker, the color, he thought, as she approached the cage, of milkless tea. A good tea, Earl Grey perhaps. She looked at him gravely and then she smiled, showing small, very white teeth. Adam thought he had never seen such a small girl with such long legs. There was a slight but attractive disproportion here, so that for a moment Zosie seemed less like a real girl than some artist's impression of an ideal, the legs longer, the neck more fragile and attenuated, the waist extravagantly narrower than could have been in nature.

She came into the cage, carefully attending to the various hookings and pinnings necessary for closing the wire door.

"Have some raspberries," Adam said.

She nodded. "Thanks," but she didn't pick any fruit. "Adam," she said, "would it be all right for me to stay on for a while?"

He thought, well, you're Rufus's girlfriend, aren't you? If he says so, I suppose you can stay. He didn't say this aloud, though; he didn't know why. There was something mysterious about her, something odd. Last night, when they all went out to the pubs in Stoke-by-Nayland, she had insisted on crouching on the floor of the van until they were beyond Nunes village. He was disturbingly attracted by her and very confused by this, partly because she was Rufus's and partly because he had an uneasy feeling she might be very young indeed, she might only be about fourteen. On the other hand, there were times like now, when she remained quite still— she had sat down cross-legged on the ground—and she had fixed on him unblinking eyes that her face became hard and she looked in her early twenties.

"I really meant," he said, "for people to sort of pay their way. I want to get a commune going with people contributing."

"Well, I haven't got any money," Zosie said.

"No."

"I expect I could sign on."

The expression was not familiar to Adam, who had never worked for his living or really known anyone who had lost his job and drew unemployment benefits. He looked at Zosie and put his eyebrows up.

"I could sign on and get the dole and give you some."

"Could you?" Perhaps he could do that too. If he didn't go back to college. It would be a way of living. If she stayed, he thought, she might still be here after Rufus went. . . .

"There are other ways of getting money. I can always get money."

He could see the outline of her small round breasts through the white cotton, and the nipples, soft and meek, not erect, but evident enough.

"I wouldn't want you doing that."

She wrinkled up her nose, a gesture of puzzlement with her where another girl might have cocked her head on to one side.

"Doing what? Oh, I see." She laughed in the funny breathy way she had without smiling. "I didn't mean *that*. I suppose I would do that though, it wouldn't bother me. I expect you'd call it that when I let Woof-woof fuck me to get a bed for the night."

Adam came as near to being shocked as was possible with him. At the same time he was pleased, exhilarated almost.

"What did you mean then?"

"About getting money?" She looked away. She picked a raspberry and then another, put the fruit into her mouth, tasting it as if she had never tried such a thing before. And she said, "I've never actually picked fruit and eaten it like this. It's sort of always been bought in shops."

"What did you mean about getting money?"

"I don't think I want to say. You'll see."

"Zosie," he said, "where did you come from when Rufus picked you up? I mean, did you come on the train from somewhere?" He disliked asking questions of this sort; it made him like his parents. They always wanted to know where one had been and where one was going and what time one would be home. But something impelled him to ask these things of Zosie. He wanted to know about her, he had to know. "Had you just got off the London train?"

She shook her head. "Suppose I said I came out of the booby hatch."

"The *what*?"

"The laughing house, the bin."

"*Did* you?"

"Suppose I said I escaped and they're out looking for me? Psychiatric nurses in white coats that drive around in white vans? Why d'you think I don't want anyone seeing me when we go out of here? Why d'you think I get down on the floor when we're in Woof-woof's van?"

"Okay, you don't have to tell me."

So they had picked a couple of pounds of raspberries and filled the bowl Adam had brought out with him and eaten them for lunch on the terrace with a bottle of wine. Zosie had also eaten an incredible amount of bread and cheese and chocolate cake and drunk about a pint of milk. Sometimes she would eat like that, enormously, ravenously, and at others she seemed indifferent to food. Wine did not seem to affect her, she could drink it as she drank milk.

Everything changed with the coming of Zosie. Simultaneously with her arrival, or perhaps because of her arrival, Ecalpemos itself underwent a change for Adam. Whereas before he had simply liked it very much and been proud to own it but nevertheless looked upon it as a source of plunder, a kind of lucrative treasure chest, he began now to *love* it, to learn the house and grounds, to value it and to want desperately at whatever cost to keep it for himself. An instance of this change took place the very next day when, to Rufus's mirth, he set about watering the garden, using cans filled from the lake and humped a hundred yards across the lawn that seemed to sizzle in the sun. Zosie helped him. But they must have done something wrong, watered while the sun was still hot probably, for all the plants in the flower beds had scarred and blistered leaves next day.

Out in the yellow meadow the farmer had begun cutting the barley with a combine. The great lumbering machine wheeled quite close by where the Ecalpemos land ended at the grove of walnuts. The terrace was visible from there and the heaped quilts on it and the people who lay there sunbathing. Had the farmer noticed? Would he remember? Ten years was a long time if you had no special reasons to remember. Adam had too many special reasons for forgetting to be possible.

It must have been the next week or the week after that Shiva and Vivien had come. No, it was St. Swithin's Day, July 15. St. Swithin's Day, if thou dost rain, for forty days it shall remain.

. . . Rufus said it always rained on July fifteenth, but in fact it
didn't that day; there was nothing for the rain to come out of, not
even a tiny cloud, not even those pale high strips of cirrus that had
lain on the horizon for two or three days past. St. Swithin's Day, if
thou be fair, for forty days shall rain no more. And it had not. For
six more weeks the fair weather had continued, the Mediterranean
come to England, tropical Suffolk, perpetual sunshine, and on the
forty-first day a storm and rain and winds blowing and the summer
gone forever. . . .

She dressed herself in a pillowcase. All she had with her was
what she stood up in and a gray sweater and a leather belt with
studs on it, so when she washed her shorts and her T-shirt she had
to find something else to put on. It was a white linen pillowcase
with Aunt Lilian's monogram LVS in a circle of embroidered
leaves. Zosie unpicked the stitches in the middle and a little way
down each side and made herself a sort of tunic. Wearing the belt
made it more like a dress. Zosie looked beautiful in it; she made it
into a new fashion.

It was what she wore when they drove into Sudbury to sell the
silver, fish knives, and forks this time and a filigree candy basket
and two sauceboats. Rufus said no one would want to use those
things, they were quite useless, they would just lie in the bottom
of a drawer or stand in a cupboard and no one would look at them
for a lifetime or if he put them out, they would go black with
tarnish. As it was, all the silver and brass that lay around was
badly discolored from lack of attention. Adam did not at all want
to sell the silver but neither could he think of anything with which
to refute Rufus's argument. That they were his and a part of
Ecalpemos, and the whole that it was, the perfect whole, must be
made up of its parts, he did not feel able to say to Rufus. They
needed money; they had very nearly nothing.

"If we can't have booze and a few fags and go out on the
razzle when we want," said Rufus, "there's no point in being
here."

Adam did not see it that way, though he admitted he liked
those things, they were a kind of prerequisite to enjoyment.

Zosie had said no more about drawing the dole. She still slept
in the Centaur Room but mostly Rufus did not. He had taken to
sleeping out on the terrace all night and usually, around midnight

or later, Zosie would creep away alone. As Goblander came up out of the drift into the lane and turned toward the Mill in the Pytle, Zosie got down on the floor and crouched there in the yoga praying position. It was only when they were out on the Sudbury Road that she emerged.

She came with them to sell the silver. The place they chose was an antique shop on Friar Street where the man had been forthcoming twice before and had asked no questions, though Adam suspected that the prices he paid were absurdly low. The shopkeeper stared at Zosie's pillowcase, which left about eight or nine inches of thigh showing. The mini-skirt had been out of fashion four or five years by then and people had got out of the habit of seeing it. She walked around the shop examining everything. Adam and Rufus went into the back to carry out their transaction, got sixty-five pounds for the silver which made Adam feel sick because he thought just one of the sauceboats must have been worth that alone. Zosie was sitting on a bentwood chair, her hands folded in her lap, waiting for them.

Rufus bought wine, the cheapest stuff, bin ends and from places one would never have thought of as producing wine, like Romania. Zosie had gone off somewhere, saying she would meet them back at the van which was parked in the marketplace under the shadow of Gainsborough. The girl in the wineshop gave them a box to put the bottles in and Rufus's pack of two hundred Rothman King size. Adam pulled the bundle of notes out of his pocket and paid the girl, controlling his face, not showing to Rufus his misgivings, his dismay, until they were outside.

"He gave me sixty-five for the silver, didn't he?"

"Sure. Why?"

"I only had fifty-five when I paid for that lot."

"Come on. You must have miscounted."

So they set down the box full of bottles and Adam counted again, subtracting thirty-four seventy-two for wine and cigarettes.

"Twenty twenty-eight," said Adam, "and there ought to be thirty twenty-eight."

"You dropped a tenner somewhere."

"I didn't."

At this point, as Adam was unnecessarily counting the money again, as they stood in the middle of the sidewalk outside the Town Hall, the missing ten-pound note appeared in front of them in the shape of a new pair of jeans on Zosie, who came rather diffidently toward them from behind the Gainsborough statue. They did not have to say this to each other. They knew. But neither of them felt they could put an accusation into words. They looked at Zosie, at the jeans, which were of the cheapest kind, the poorest quality, and better to be described perhaps as cotton loons, the red T-shirt of the less-than-a-pound reject shop kind, at this new ensemble which was nevertheless infinitely more respectable than Aunt Lilian's pillowcase.

It brought Adam a good deal of humiliation to understand that Zosie had picked his pocket without his having the least idea of it.

"I had to have some clothes. I felt funny in that pillow thing."

With that manner of hers that was at once meek and apprehensive she held out to Adam her closed fist. She opened it above his hand and dropped into his palm three screwed-up notes, a twenty-pound note and two tens.

"Where did all this come from?"

She shook her head. "Never mind. It's for us. You said everyone had to contribute." Turning her head this way and that, she darted alert glances across the marketplace. She reminded Adam of a hare he had seen sitting up on the edge of the barley field. "Let's go home now, can we?"

As they passed through Nunes she got down on the floor and stayed there until they were outside the front door of Ecalpemos. He kept the money she gave him, he asked no questions, he had a pretty good idea anyway what had happened, what she had done, and he made a mental resolve not to go near the shop in Friar Street again.

That also was the day Zosie saw the picture in the Deathbed Room. Rufus had opened a bottle of thick dark red wine, bull's blood stuff that Adam knew would give him a headache. But he took a glass and so did Zosie and they were drinking it at the kitchen table when Zosie said it was all right now, wasn't it, she could stay on now? Adam said yes but he said it rather unwillingly because the afternoon's happenings had shaken him and he had a feeling Zosie might bring trouble down on them all. On the other hand, he was beginning to realize, to his own discomfort, that more than anything in the world he wanted her to stay. It was almost that if she left, Ecalpemos would lose its point and he would no longer want to be there. The curious yearning, the breathless hungry feeling that was never to be fully satisfied even when he had made limitless love to her, that had begun. When she asked him if she could stay, the request pierced him with real pain, it made him wince.

"Can I go and explore the house? Can I go and look at everything?"

He would have offered to go with her but he was afraid to trespass on Rufus's territory. He looked at Rufus after Zosie had gone upstairs and Rufus grinned, smoke curling out from between his teeth.

"It's all yours if you want it," Rufus said.

"I rather thought . . ."

"A brief aberration. A two-night stand." Rufus refilled his glass. He always drank twice as much as anyone else twice as fast. "Zosie is a woman of mystery. You'll have noticed I've been sleeping on the terrace this past couple of nights. Why don't you take her into Pincushion and let me have Centaur back again?"

Before he could answer—what could he have answered though? That she was not his slave, his creature?—Zosie came back saying she had seen an old man at the top of the stairs, a little thin old man with gold-rimmed glasses and a bald head. Rufus had laughed and Adam hadn't taken any of it very seriously, for she had been in the study looking at photographs. It was different when, half an hour later, she rushed in with the tears fountaining from her eyes.

"Why did you let me go in there? Why did you let me see it?"

It took a while to elicit from her what she meant. Rufus pushed a glass of wine across the table to her.

"It's only a picture," Adam said. "It's not a photograph, it's just a sentimental Victorian painting."

But Rufus only looked at her and looked away, nodding a little, as if he had received confirmation of something he suspected or almost knew for sure. Zosie dried her eyes and felt better after a while and Adam said she need never go in there again, there was no reason for her to go in there, and soon perhaps other people would come and use the room. He had not of course known how soon this was to happen.

Some of those who steal, steal love, the psychiatrists say. Those who have inside their lives an empty space need to fill it with love if they can, and if they cannot, with things. And they need to please others in order that others may give them love. Those who need love with the hunger the rest of mankind keeps for food, for the necessaries of life, give their bodies simply and without reflection for a return of love, would give their soul if they knew how, are reduced to thievery of the basest kind and of the basest things because this is the easiest way. Adam knew none of that then but he did think Zosie might be a little mad. "Disturbed" was the word he used to himself. He thought she might be "schizoid" (the fashionable expression) for she seemed to have no idea at all of reality.

"Flittermus, ottermus/Myopotamus," Adam said to Zosie, expecting her to correct the last word to "hippopotamus" as Mary Gage had. But she only nodded and pushed at the poor corpse with the toe of her sandal.

"It's a coypu."

He was surprised she knew but he did not want to tell her how the creature had probably died, he didn't want hysterics. Let her think it had met a natural death.

"Some of those things," she said, "they give them pellets with cyanide in and then you mustn't let the carrion crows get them. They give moles worms with cyanide. Isn't that hateful?"

Adam was pretty sure the coypu man hadn't had poison with him, only traps, yet how then had this large, coarse-pelted animal died? "We ought to bury it."

They had been in the fruit cage, gathering more raspberries, had walked back along the farther shore of the lake eating raspberries, the red juice staining their fingers. Rufus saw their red hands and said, "You didn't touch the thing, did you? You could get leptospirosis." A rat was a rat as far as he was concerned, irrespective of size or variety. They put on gardening gloves they found in the stable block and took down a spade from the wall where a primitive tool rack had been made by knocking long nails into the boards. There were two spades, Adam remembered, this one and a bigger one with a slightly rounded blade; it was this bigger one which they had used later on when they dug the grave. . . .

But on the evening of the fifteenth of July, a Thursday evening, Adam had used the smaller lightweight spade and dug a shallow pit in the Little Wood. He lifted the body of the coypu in and they put back the earth and trod it down hard. The grass and weeds would soon grow and cover it, he said to Zosie, but they had not. It was too dry and hot for that.

Side by side at the kitchen sink they washed their hands, hygiene-conscious Rufus standing over them. He wouldn't give them any wine until he was satisfied their hands were clean and pure once more. It was the bin-end hock and the Romanian chianti they drank that night. Adam had made little hashish cakes with flour and sugar and an egg and the *charas*. Somehow he had expected Zosie to refuse to have anything to do with them but she had eaten two of them greedily, as if starving for a change of consciousness.

They were all on the terrace, stupid with hashish and wine, silent, lying on the quilts and watching the sky change from blue to gold and gold to rose as the sun set, when Shiva and Vivien came. A breeze ruffled the garden as always at this time, as if it were an invisible creature that passed over the grass and between the rose trees, swayed the leafy ropes that hung from the willows, blew the reeds, and set them shivering. Adam lay on the white quilt and Zosie only a yard away from him on the yellow and they looked into each other's dazed faces, eye to eye, and Adam's hand moved to the edge of the white spread and Zosie's to the ruffled border of the yellow satin, but their fingers did not quite meet. Rufus lay sprawled on his back, an outflung hand grasping the almost empty fourth bottle of wine. And it was thus that they were found by Shiva and Vivien walking around the house in search of signs of life.

On the lawn below the Loves of Zeus they stood and Adam thought he saw disapproval in their faces. It was Chinese people who were called inscrutable, but Adam wondered if perhaps this did not apply even more to Indians. The Indian's expression was curious and watchful. There were murmurs of Mary Gage's name and of Bella's, and the girl said she would have phoned first to ask if they could come, she had looked him up in the phone book, but all she got was a strange beeping.

The Indian said his name was Shiva and gave his surname, which Adam had since forgotten, if indeed it had ever registered with him.

"And this is Vivien Goldman."

The real trouble, at the time, was that he was in no fit condition to speak at all, still less talk about terms and conditions. Stupefied with wine and hashish, poisoned with these things really, he could hardly stand, hardly cope with the banging in his head. Rufus, of course, was indifferent. Having elevated himself onto his elbows and said hi, he had lain down again and lit a fresh cigarette, Zosie crouched on the yellow quilt, her hare look back again.

Adam took them into the house. He was unsure now what he could in fact recall of that night and what came later. Small, dark Vivien, with her long hair braided and coiled around her head—had he observed and absorbed that on this evening? She had been wearing the blue dress that one thought of as inseparable from her, as if she were an exotic bird, as if it were her natural plumage. From the first, from that evening, he had been aware of her disappointment. As they walked through the house and up the back stairs, she looked about her warily, ruefully, at the furniture, the pictures, the carpets, because she had expected rush matting and earthenware pots and earnest folk meditating or pounding up herbs.

Why hadn't he summoned up the strength to tell them this place was more a hotel than a commune? He wanted to be paid. They could camp out for tonight in one of the outbuildings, but tomorrow they must go unless they could pay their way. In fact, he was sure he had never mentioned money. Poisoned by drink, born without a taste or capacity for liquor, he staggered up the stairs ahead of them, showed them into the Deathbed Room, muttered in a thick, slurred voice he was ashamed of even at the time that they would find a kettle and tea and coffee in the kitchen, wine if they wanted it. After that his memory blanked. The last thing of that night he could recall was Vivien opening the big cylindrical carpet bag she carried and his seeing for the first time all those Bach flower remedies and little bottles of homeopathic pills and herbal stuff. Or was he manufacturing a memory out of what he knew had come later?

The Indian was so neat and clean. "Dapper" was the word, thought word-loving Adam. Someone, a downtrodden mother or sister probably, had ironed creases down the fronts of his jeans. His crisp starched shirt was the color of the blue lilies that grew outside the dining room window.

"What a beautiful house this is," he said very politely. "It is quite a privilege to be here."

Had that been next day or the day after? It was on the morning, Adam thought, when the postwoman appeared with the letter for him. He had just gotten up, for it was hardly morning, it was past noon, and was sitting in the kitchen, much hung over, feeling as if he were recovering from some long, debilitating illness, when something red and shiny flashed past the window. It was the postwoman's bicycle but he had not known this immediately. The letterbox on the front door made a double rap sound, something he had heard every now and again years before, when Hilbert was alive, but not since.

What she had brought was a demand for the half year's rates. And at that hour it must have been the second post. Rufus had seen her, Rufus was outside and had seen her and she had seen him. No doubt she had also seen Goblander.

"Some young rustic beauty," Rufus had said. "A milkmaid on a bike."

The box at the top of the lane was supposed to be for the post. Perhaps she hadn't known that, or perhaps she was sticking dutifully to the rules. Shiva had said in his sententious way: "They are obliged by the law of the land to bring your mail up to the door."

Eventually he had paid those rates. Deeply humiliated but with no other course before him, he had borrowed the money from his father, who had required its return plus all the accumulated interest as soon as Adam had sold Wyvis Hall. That year Adam couldn't bear to think of, from the time when he had returned home with the gun in the golf bag to the return to Ecalpemos and his meeting there with the real estate agent. For months the hue and cry over Catherine Ryemark had gone on. Back at college, at any rate, he had not been obliged to see newspapers. But in the Christmas and Easter breaks, at home, each time the phone rang, each time the front doorbell rang, his stomach clenched and turned. . . .

As it was clenching and turning now. Alone in his office in Pimlico, he dialed Rufus's Wimpole Street number. He didn't need to look it up, he knew it by heart. Rufus, when he came to the phone, sounded distant and preoccupied. How he, Adam, had longed and longed to phone Rufus during that year, but had never dared, had never been prepared to risk the receiver being put down without a word spoken! Besides, he had always had that irrational fear that the Verne-Smith and Fletcher phones were bugged, that the police were waiting patiently for this very thing to happen, for them to get in touch.

Adam had no such notions now. Patient they might be, but they would never have waited ten years. He and Rufus arranged, without discussion, to meet at six. Adam went down the passage to the lavatory and threw up with violent painful spasms, leaning against the wall afterward and gasping for breath.

12

On her skin was a fine tracery of bluish marks, like the downy feathers of a little bird a cat has plucked. They were all over the tops of her thighs and the iliac crest and faintly on the flat stomach. More than feathers, they looked like silk where, through stretching, the weft has been compressed to expose the warp. One day they would fade and bleach white, but that had not yet happened and they would never go away entirely.

Rufus had twice made love to Zosie before he saw the marks, once in the back of the van and once in the bed in the Centaur Room (erstwhile scene of placid slumbrous nights enjoyed by Lewis and Beryl Verne-Smith), but it was not until the third night that he actually looked at her naked body. She lay waiting for him like a sacrificial victim, and though she was silent her whole attitude, supine, receptive, patient, uttered to him: I will do anything you want, I am yours—or not, I know I must pay for my board and lodging and for sanctuary and this is one way I know how to do that.

It was scarcely provocative. Rufus, however, did not much care about this, but about what the marks signified he did, and as he stood there he thought about what involvement might mean and about his future career and the risks he was taking—had indeed already taken—and instead of getting into bed with Zosie he took a pillow from the bed and one of the blankets he had long discarded and dumped on the floor, and departed for the terrace.

That was before she stole the silver bracelet, for that was what she had done a few days before Shiva and Vivien came. While they were in the back of the shop in Friar Street selling the fish knives and the sauceboats Zosie had helped herself to the bracelet from a display table of jewelry. Because she looked somewhat disreputable in the pillowcase, she had bought jeans and a T-shirt with the tenner she nicked out of Adam's pocket, taken the bracelet to a dealer in Gainsborough Street, and sold it for forty pounds.

Of course it was all of a piece, all understandable. Rufus had watched it, wondering what Zosie would do next. It had been a case history for him and he had even thought of writing it up. The pattern of the stealing had been so interesting, not meaningless kleptomania any of it, but calculated thieving of salable goods or edible items. The food had been produced so proudly to be stowed in the back of Goblander as any henchman of Robin Hood might have robbed for the poor.

Until the incident of the little boy, of course. And that, or something very like it, might have been predicted. Well, something very like it had happened.

A woman of mystery, he had called her. Zosie as woman was an almost laughable concept. She was a child. And yet of course she was not; she was in some ways older than any of them. She had done and known more. Adam would have said—and did say—that she had suffered. They had tried to ask her about her life, who she was, where she came from, where she was going.

"Are you a student?" Vivien had wanted to know.

The other three were, so why not Zosie?

And she replied with absurd naïveté, with what sounded like disingenuousness but was not, was simply Zosie's way: "I'm just a person."

Vivien had persisted: "Do you have a job?" She was wearing, as Adam put it, her "social worker's hat."

"I don't have a job and I'm not a student." Zosie added after a pause for thought, "I was at school."

"We were all at school," said Shiva. "In this modern world you have to go to school. It's compulsory." He smiled with pleasure because he had amused the others.

"What do you want to do then, Zosie?"

"Well," she said, and she sighed a little. "Well, I don't *want* to do anything. I'd quite like to live here forever, in this house, and just never do anything ever. But what I will do is marry a rich man and maybe he'll buy this house, Adam. Maybe he'll buy it off you for me. Would you like that?"

They wanted to know why she was called Zosie, what did it mean, what was it short for? It was for someone named Zosima in a Russian book, she said.

"Do you mean Dostoevski?" said Adam. "Father Zosima's a man."

"My mother's very ignorant, she wouldn't know. She'd just have liked the sound."

So Adam wanted to know where Zosie's mother and father lived but she wouldn't say, only that she hadn't a father. Her father had died and her mother remarried. And Zosie sat on the terrace with her knees drawn up to her chin and her arms clasping her knees and darted her eyes this way and that like a nervous animal and Rufus, who admitted to himself he was not usually sensitive or caring, suddenly felt they were all persecuting her and changed the subject to talk about where they should go that night.

A pub presumably it had been or perhaps that drinking club they found in Colchester. A place very different at any rate from where he was now heading to meet Adam, who in other circumstances would have changed from the Victoria onto the Northern Line at Warren Street but had agreed to get off at Oxford Circus and meet him in a pub not far from Langham Place.

Rufus would not have recognized him. But there was simply no one else there that it could have been. The beard had gone—had long gone, Rufus suspected—but this depilation usually makes a man look younger and Adam looked older than he was. He looked careworn and irritable, sitting there with a drink in front of him that might have been gin and tonic but was probably Perrier. Rufus did not remember Adam having such a high-domed forehead, and then he understood, almost grinning at the realization, that it had not been so high ten years before but that in the meantime Adam's hair had receded.

He walked up to the table and stood there and they looked at each other. To Rufus's surprise Adam was blushing, his face darkened to a mottled purplish color. Neither of them said hello. Rufus finally said: "Well, well, after all this time," and then he said, "I'm going to get myself a drink."

Gin and tonic but not much tonic. This sort of thing inevitably shook one up. Rufus sat down. It was the only vacant chair in the place, which was smoky and hot and full of laughing, chattering people, semi-hysterical at being released from work for another fourteen hours.

"I'd like to dispense with all that how-are-you and what-have-you-been-doing-all-this-time stuff," said Adam, "if you don't mind, that is. It's a mere matter of form, we can't really want to know."

Time hadn't improved him, Rufus thought. The basic rudeness was more than basic now. He shrugged but didn't say anything, tasting his gin and thinking how the whole of life and its pain and its irritations and its stress were worth that first taste that came just once a day.

"The others haven't contacted me. I rather expected they would." Adam moved his glass around, making wet rings on the wood, and then more rings to link up the first ones. "I thought they might be anxious about what I would tell the police. About them, I mean, mentioning their names."

"And have you mentioned names to the police?"

"No," said Adam, "no, I haven't."

"But they've been to you? They've questioned you?"

"Yes, but I haven't mentioned you or anyone."

"I see." Rufus did not really see. He felt, though, an overwhelming surge of relief, the kind of surprising relief we feel when we have not known how horribly anxious we have previously been. He found himself really looking at Adam for the first time since he came into the pub, at his tired, reddish, rough skin, and receding hairline and the dark marks under his eyes and the little pulse that jumped at the corner of his mouth. And he had a strange, incongruous feeling of loss, of a ruined past and friendship destroyed and wasted, and rage welled up in him so that he would have liked to sweep the glasses from the table and overturn it and sweep the glasses from the next table and overturn that and make general mayhem. He controlled it as he usually did. "Why not?" he said.

"I've told them I wasn't there. I mean, they asked me if I had ever lived there and I said no, only stayed there for a week or two." Adam looked up at Rufus and away. "At the beginning of the time we were actually there. They didn't ask if I was alone, so I didn't have to say. They asked if I had a girl with me and I just said no, certainly not."

Rufus could not stop the start of a grin.

"It's not funny. Christ, it's not *funny*."

"Everything is funny in a sort of way," said Rufus.

"Do you want another drink?"

"Of course I want another drink. I haven't changed that much. It's gin with something in it. I don't care what they put in it, it doesn't matter."

Adam came back with just one glass, Rufus's. He must be an uncomfortable sort of man to live with, Rufus thought.

"I suppose you're married?"

"Yes. And you?"

"Yes." They weren't going to talk about this sort of thing, all this was among the private life history to be avoided, and Rufus was a little surprised when Adam said: "I've got a daughter."

"Have you? I can't imagine you with kids."

"Thanks very much," said Adam, looking displeased. Two frown lines appeared between his eyes and then his whole forehead corrugated. He seemed to be holding his breath. Exhaling, he said in a rush, "I've more or less undertaken to go into my local police station sometime before the weekend and make a statement and sign it. Well, not more or less. I've said I would."

"If you've already answered their questions, that's not such an ordeal, is it?"

Like a peevish schoolboy Adam said, "It's all very well for you. You haven't got to perjure yourself, because that's what it amounts to. It's one thing talking to a couple of blokes in your own living room and another thing signing sworn statements. I've managed to keep you out of it—so far."

Rufus didn't believe in altruism. "It wouldn't help you to mention us, come on. If you stick to what you've already said, they'll accept it. Why wouldn't they? They've come to you only because you're one of the past owners of the place. Whoever you sold the place to is coming in for the same."

"I hope you're bloody right," said Adam, but he looked a

little less wretched. "Do you think I ought to get in touch with Shiva Whatshisname?"

"What *was* his name? I've been trying to remember. You're afraid he might go to the police and make a voluntary statement? I don't think he would do that."

An unasked question lay between them. Rufus was not fanciful, he liked to boast that he had no imagination, but he was aware, just for a moment, of something very strange happening. It was as if a third had come and sat down at the table, an invisible being on an invisible chair, bringing with her the scent of herself, dry and salty and young, and laying on his arm a finger like a moth alighting. He actually brushed at his sleeve. There was no one there, of course, there was no room for anything to be there. He looked at Adam.

"Women get married and change their names. That's the difficulty."

"She isn't in the phone book," said Adam, and it was as if the words were being wrenched out of him on hooks. Someone laughed nearby and Rufus missed whatever else it was he said.

"Why don't you just go ahead and make that statement. You'll probably feel a good deal of relief once you've done that."

"You reckon it will be cathartic, do you?"

"Why not?"

"I don't know if you've ever thought about this, but there were a lot of people who knew we were living there or must have guessed we were."

"Not a *lot*."

"There was the gardener and there was the antiques man from Hadleigh."

"Yes, what was his name?"

"Evans, Owens, one of those Welsh names. He was quite old, though, and he may be dead by now. There was the pest control that we called the coypu man and there was the post girl that came with the rates that time, and came"—Adam hesitated—"on that last day too."

"And the farmer, come to that. Presumably he lived or lives at Pytle Farm."

"In detective stories," said Adam, "people in our sort of situation go around murdering possible witnesses."

"I don't think I've ever read a detective story."

"And there are Mary Gage and Bella. And didn't you come back in a taxi one day? There's the taxi driver. He was young. He won't be dead. The post girl looked about eighteen."

"Mary Gage married someone and went to Brazil." Rufus had meant to say something about their collective guilt, and now he thought he would. "I expect, in the eyes of the law, we'd all be guilty, you know. I mean we were all there. Not to be guilty one of us would have had to go rushing off to the police."

"Like Vivien," said Adam very quietly.

"Well, Vivien wasn't guilty of anything, that's for sure. When you've made that statement, give me a ring and tell me, at Wimpole Street, would you, Adam?"

It was the first use of a Christian name. Adam's face had a rigid look. He compounded the détente.

"Your wife knows nothing of all this, Rufus?"

Rufus shook his head. "And yours?"

"No."

Silence locked them within itself. Rufus experienced a great quiet, while aware that the hubbub around them was still there, was if anything more intense. Adam was looking at him. The memory came, quite unsought, of that evening at Ecalpemos, while Mary Gage was still there, after she had left the terrace to go to bed, and Rufus had meant to make love to Adam. He would have laughed in derision if anyone had suggested he might have homosexual or even bisexual feelings, but that night he had wanted Adam. Because he loved him. It had been as simple as that. An intensity of love for Adam had come to him like a release of heat breaking over the body, and the only natural thing to do with it seemed to be to make love to its object, to turn to Adam and take him in his arms. Rufus had never done that with any man and he had not done it with Adam that night because he was drunk, and with his mind full of muzzy love and amused tenderness, he had fallen asleep.

He got up and pushed his chair back.

"Soldier on," said Rufus with a faint smile.

It was likely enough he would never hear another word about it. Rufus realized as he went to find his car that he had said nothing about the shotgun, the twelve-bore. Adam would speak to him again once he had made that statement and there would be time enough to ask about it then. Who was it that had suggested

those guns be sold? Shiva, he thought, or perhaps Vivien. No, not
Vivien, she had reacted to the very existence of the guns as anyone
else might to an instrument of torture in the house, a genuine
medieval rack or wheel. Mary Gage's dismay at the presence of
the coypu man had been nothing to Vivien's distress at the guns
and the purpose for which they had been used. You might have
expected therefore that she would be glad to see them sold, but not
a bit of it, as she would not have dreamed of profiting from such a
sale. Shiva it was who had taken the lady's gun down from the
wall and said to Adam: "I expect this is quite valuable. You could
sell this and the other one instead of your beautiful family silver."

"I don't want to sell them. I'm going to use them."

"What, shoot birds?"

"Birds, hares—why not? Meat's expensive."

"Please give me advance warning of when you're going to do
that and I'll go out somewhere for the day," said Vivien.

She was the kind of person Rufus found ridiculous, had done
then and did now. With her to Ecalpemos she had brought a
medicine chest full of remedies, mysterious and very nearly
occult, for every known disease. Some of the plants and flowers
that formed their ingredients had to be picked at certain stages of
the moon for perfect efficacy. Rufus adjudged all that with
incredulous contempt, with the disgust of the orthodox medical
practitioner. Vivien also had among her baggage something called
a "rescue remedy" of which she urged people to accept a few
drops if they ever received anything in the nature of a shock, if
they got an insect bite, for instance, or a minor burn. She was a
devotee, too, of many alternative therapies—charlatanism, Rufus
called them—iridology and reflexology and aromatherapy. She
meditated, she was a sort of Hindu of the kind, Rufus thought,
that takes the shortcut to enlightenment. On the whole she did not
talk of it much, she did not inflict all this on the rest of them too
overtly, he had to admit that, but it was so much a part of her, it
was her, that she carried with her an ambience of it wherever she
went and all the time.

If it had been left to him, he would not have let her stay. She
and Shiva would have been asked to go if not the moment they
arrived, certainly on the following day. Rufus liked people to be
amusing and wild and rather "way out," or he had done then, and
Vivien was none of these things. Shiva was quite abysmally none

of these things. But before Adam could have been brought around to this way of thinking, Vivien had consolidated her position, had done this the very next morning, by taking over the management of Ecalpemos. Rufus had not thought they needed a cook or a cleaner, an herb grower and homemaker. When the sun shone and there was wine and marijuana, who needed all that? Adam, apparently, thought very differently. Subtly Adam was becoming a householder who wanted a clean, polished house and his money saved by the food being cooked at home. And then—although Rufus had not realized this before, had not dreamed of it, and viewed this revelation with wonder and an amount of distaste— Adam and Zosie both, it seemed, wanted a mother and found their mother in Vivien. Like brother and sister, albeit by then an incestuous pair, they came to Vivien's apron strings for comfort or giggled together in rebellion against her, while Shiva, an awkward elder brother, watched with anxious wistful smiles, rubbing his hands, longing himself to be accepted and not knowing how to go about attaining this.

I am not in this world to live up to your expectations and you are not in this world to live up to mine. I am I and you are you. And if we find each other that's beautiful, if not, it can't be helped. Something like that, he might not have got it entirely right, there might have been more of it. It was called the Gestalt prayer and Vivien pinned it up on the kitchen wall. Rufus had laughed and said how did anyone know, that might be why one was in this world, why not? But Zosie had liked it and said she longed for people to live that way and Shiva nodded sagely.

"Love is about allowing," said Vivien. "Love is about letting people be free. You leave the cage door open and if you're really loved, the bird flies back to be with you. That's the only kind of love worth having."

Rufus had seen something like that printed on a T-shirt, so he did not receive it with the awed gravity of the others—well, not Adam. He winked at Adam behind Vivien's back and Adam half-grinned back.

"You weren't very allowing about me shooting birds," he said.

"That's different," Vivien said, frowning. She was quite without a sense of humor. Her small, earnest face was often puckered with worry about moral questions. She pondered on such matters as Jesuitical responses, half-truths, on doing good by stealth so that the mind may avoid a consciousness of virtue. "I said I'd go out, anyway. I didn't say I'd stop you."

She had wanted to organize them, to give them all appointed household tasks, like a big family or a kibbutz. There would be a rota pinned up on the wall beside the Gestalt prayer. And the day was to begin with meditation; she would teach them to meditate, an appropriate mantra provided for each. Of course no one had agreed to any of this; even Shiva, usually meek and obliging, had rebelled. Picking all the fruit and selling it at the top of the drift, coppicing the wood to get timber for winter fires, learning to weave, keeping a goat, growing potatoes, all these ideas of Vivien's were met with incredulity, then with firm refusals. It was too hot, it would be too boring, it was much easier to sell Hilbert's silver.

No one changed their ways. They went on drinking and smoking and lying in the sun, swimming in the lake, and going on pub sprees and then on selling and buying trips. It might have been expected that Vivien, finding that nobody was interested in truly communal living, in working to be self-supporting, which was the idea, might herself have yielded and joined in. But she never had. Without support and without much in the way of thanks, she cooked for them and baked bread, cleaned the rooms and took the bedlinen to the launderette in Sudbury. She did not explain why until pressed.

"It's to earn my keep. I can't contribute any cash."

No one else thought of it in those terms.

And yet Vivien had no intention of staying at Ecalpemos. Perhaps she might have if the set-up had been different, if it had been more like her idea of a commune. But that would have meant foregoing the job she had already applied for. Shiva would not stay either, for whether he continued with his pharmacology course or gave it up for medicine, he would have to return eventually and present himself submissively to his father. For his part, Rufus intended to be back by the first week of October, if not sooner, to enter his fourth year at University College Hospital. Only Adam would remain—and Zosie. Adam and Zosie, orphans of the storm, the babes in the wood.

One afternoon, looking for his secret drink which he had hidden on some sill or shelf, behind a curtain or a row of ornaments, Rufus came upon them embraced. They were on the sofa, lying close, lost in each other, their faces joined at searching, sucking mouths. He looked at them for a moment or two, feeling ever so slightly a pang of envy, of the rejection such a sight induces in all but the continuously satiated. And then it was gone and he was grinning at them. But they were oblivious of him, they did not see him, fused together as they were, striving to make their separate bodies one. For a long while that day they disappeared together, returning to the company quite late at night, vague-faced and with smiling, glazed eyes. There were candles burning on the terrace, candles that were set in saucers between the statuary. Vivien sat cross-legged, Shiva had his own candle to read his math book by, Rufus had just opened a fresh bottle of wine. Such pleasure, the withdrawing of the cork, the first pouring! The air was full of moths, soft-winged, dusky, feathery, floating on the candlelight as if made languid by the warmth. The moon was rising, a huge red orb, ascending with mysterious aplomb out of the dark low hills crested with black woodland. Adam came out of the house and sat beside him, and then he saw Zosie standing in the shimmer of the candlelight, her arms wound around one of the heads of Zeus, his curls of stone, his flowing beard, her head lifted to gaze at the red moon. In that shiny, slippery light she looked herself like a statue, only one made of bronze, fey-faced, nymphlike, unreal.

"Oh, she doth teach the torches to burn bright!"

Rufus looked at him. "Bloody hell," he said.

He didn't sleep on the terrace that night. He knew he would find the Centaur Room empty. And when he went to bed at last, the remains of the last bottle of wine with him, he found that Zosie's things had gone. He opened all the windows to get rid of the smell of her that was salty and flowery like the smell of a child.

At home, his dinner eaten, Rufus went to the cabinet and fetched himself a second drink, identical to the first which he had left in the room called Marigold's studio, where the television was. She was watching *Bookmark* on television because there was a segment on it about a now quite famous poet that her mother had once lived next door to. This double measure, slightly diluted in a squat spirit glass, would be his evening's "secret drink" to be tasted immediately and then concealed behind the hem of a curtain or among Marigold's proliferating houseplant pots and swigged from at intervals until bedtime. At times of stress Rufus indulged in this neurotic behavior even when he was alone. Of course he knew it was neurotic but he did not particularly on this account wish to change it. At some point, when the level in the secret glass fell below the halfway mark, he would secretly recharge it, putting in another single measure of vodka. The legitimate or above-board drink was to be sipped from in front of Marigold and made to last the whole evening. The thing about all this that did cause Rufus some anxiety was the disproportionate excitement and actual happiness, a kind of exultant glee, having this hidden drink brought him.

He sat down on the settee next to Marigold. Poets did not interest him much because they were not, in his view, commercially successful or entertaining or possessed of obvious intellectual superiority. This one, small and bearded, stood at a lectern reading from his own works. Adam, as far as Rufus knew, had never written poetry but he used to recite it sometimes and Vivien had wanted them to devote an evening to each of them reading aloud their favorite poetry. Rufus had soon squashed that. They had lain out there in the garden long into the small hours, everyone unwilling to go to bed, until a lightening appeared in the sky, a pale glow that gradually suffused it and Adam with his arm around Zosie, who had fallen asleep with her head on his chest, said in a vague remote voice: "I suffer from eosophobia."

"From *what*?"

"An irrational fear of the dawn."

Rufus wondered what had made him remember that. Something the poet on the screen had said perhaps. That was the day, the next day rather, when Vivien had her interview with Robin Tatian. Of course they had all wanted to sleep on and on and Rufus would have stayed in bed until the afternoon but Vivien came in and woke him, had shaken him awake, then presented him with coffee and breakfast on a tray, reminding him he had promised to drive her to London.

Wasn't it rather strange that it had been he and Vivien and Zosie who had gone, leaving Adam and Shiva behind? Not that there had ever been any question of Shiva's going. Off on one of his exploratory walks, he had on that afternoon discovered the

animal cemetery. Adam, Rufus seemed to remember, had balked
at going to London, anyway to North London, on the grounds that
he might encounter one or both of his parents, who believed him
to be in Greece.

Vivien, before she came to Ecalpemos, had applied for a job
as nanny to the child of a man who lived in Highgate called Robin
Tatian. Tatian was an architect and presumably a successful one
and rich, to judge by the address on View Road. Rufus and Adam
both knew the neighborhood well, having been to Highgate
School. It seemed strange to Rufus now that he had never seen
Tatian, but knew what he looked like only from Vivien's
description when she came back from the interview.

"He's tall and suntanned and he's got brown curly hair. About
thirty-five."

"Sounds yummy," said Zosie.

"I didn't actually see him," Vivien said. "The woman showed
me a photograph of him with the baby. She's his sister. She said
she 'handled all the staff for him.'"

"A snooty bitch by the sound."

Tatian had probably been at his office or studio or wherever
architects worked. It was a Thursday, the third or fourth week of
July, Rufus thought. And the hot weather went on and on. They
had all Goblander's windows open and it wasn't too much, even
when he was driving quite fast up the A12. The girls sat in the
back because they hadn't been able to decide which one should sit
in the front with him.

"I'm saving up to go to India," Vivien said. "If I save up all
my salary for six months I'll get enough to go to India. If I don't
spend anything and I needn't, I'll be living in."

"What do you want to go to India *for*?"

"There's this mystic—well, a *saddhu*. I've read about him.
People go to him and learn, lots of people." Vivien became
reticent and embarrassed but she went on explaining, her voice
getting low. "I would go and live there and it would be a *start* for
me. I might stay there or I might come back here, I don't know,
but if I never go I shall feel I've missed my chance, I'd regret it all
my life."

"Is there some sort of ashram there for you to stay in?" Rufus
asked. "I mean, will you wear yellow robes and ring a little brass
bell?"

When he mocked her she reacted by treating his remarks as if they had been perfectly serious. It wasn't a bad technique either, he had to admit it. If it was a technique. If it wasn't, which was what he suspected, a simple lack of even a rudimentary sense of humor.

"I shall take a room in the village," she said.

"You will make yourself ill," said the doctor in Rufus, "on unwholesome food and infected water and very likely get amoebic dysentery."

"I don't think so. I shall be careful."

"Well, at least you don't say what does the welfare of the body matter compared to the soul."

"I'm not stupid," said Vivien, and Zosie said, "I wish I could go with you!"

Rufus couldn't see Vivien because she was in the back and he was driving but he imagined she must be holding out her arms in hieratic fashion and smiling with uplifted eyes as she uttered the single word: "Come!"

The interview was to be at Tatian's house at three o'clock. Vivien was wearing the bright blue dress with the embroidered bodice and her hair was plaited and wound tightly around her head. She looked like a minor character in a Rosetti painting, one of the maidens holding up the canopy in *Dante's Dream* perhaps, not at all the prospective nanny. This picture was one of the few Rufus could actually recognize. A reproduction of it hung in his parents' house and, curiously enough, now in his. Marigold, the first time he took her home, expressed enthusiasm, fervor, for this painting. Afterward she told him she was just being polite. But the result was that his mother gave it to Marigold as part of her wedding present and it now hung in a corner of the hall. As the poet faded from the screen, Rufus got up and went out into the hall, pausing on the way for a nip from the secret drink.

Rufus could no longer see any resemblance. The girls in the painting were both redheaded, one wore a dress of a pale lettuce green, the other's was a darker, bluer shade. And the pale, delicate faces with their wistful expressions were more like Zosie's than Vivien's. Rufus closed his eyes. Vivien had just the two dresses, one of cream cheesecloth and that blue one, both with long skirts, square necks, full sleeves which, in those hot days, she wore rolled up to the upper arms, to the shoulders. He couldn't remember that he had ever seen her legs. But her feet he remembered and her thin, bony ankles. As often as not she went barefoot. That day, though, she was wearing blue cotton espadrilles.

"Have you got any references?" Zosie said, a display of worldly knowledge that had rather surprised Rufus.

"I've looked after someone's baby before. She'd give me a reference, I think. I'm going to give her address if I'm asked."

He hadn't been able to see Zosie any more than he had Vivien, and it was hindsight that made him recall a stricken face, a faltering note as she asked: "Do you like babies?"

"Yes, of course. I'm a woman."

Rufus burst out laughing.

"It isn't funny. Women naturally like babies."

Zosie always spoke with great simplicity. She was like a child, yet more straightforward, more naïve. "Why doesn't his wife look after her baby?"

"I suppose she's too rich," said Vivien. "The baby's got a nanny now but she's leaving soon. There's another child, a bit older."

Returning to Marigold, Rufus took a longer pull at the vodka behind the curtain, then decided it was in need of recharging. He took the glass to the bottle, not the bottle to the glass. This is the way of all secret drinkers who will thus not, or less probably, be caught with a bottle in their hands. The glass he restored to its niche behind the curtain hem.

It was then, as they came into the far eastern suburbs of London, Romford and Ilford and Newbury Park, that he had thought of drawing Zosie out, of eliciting from her the answers to a few questions. The time seemed ripe, the conversation tending in appropriate directions. And he had started in with: "That wouldn't do for you, Zosie. You wouldn't have anything to do with babies, would you?"

The silence was long. The traffic was getting thick, three lanes of it, brakes groaning and squeaking as it pulled up at lights. As if she had been drowning, coming up with a gasp to clutch at a lifeline, in the voice of someone whose head has been underwater, Zosie said: "I would. I'd like six, I'd like twelve."

That made him laugh. They were stopped at a red light. He turned around and looked at the two girls, at Vivien, who had taken Zosie in her arms and was holding her. It was so hot he could see a wet patch on Zosie's back where the sweat had come through her T-shirt. Vivien's strong, capable hands, large for someone so small, held her shoulders with maternal sureness, not patting in an embarrassed way, which is what most people do when called to take part in a spontaneous hug.

They delivered her to View Road. The house was called Cranmer Lodge, white, with a green-tiled roof and green iron balconies. Topiaried trees cut in tiers, cones of thick dark plates, stood on either side of the front door. The front gates were of wrought iron and there were stone pineapples on the gate pillars.

Zosie, who had been silent in the back except for an occasional muffled sound that might have been crying, said, "I love that house. Isn't it lovely?"

It was big, Rufus had thought, you could say that for it, imposing and rather pretentious. He had been back there just once and that was to pick Vivien up an hour and a half later. But never again, never nearer than North Hill out of which View Road turned and on that occasion he had been taking one of the routes out of London up to the North Circular Road. The district had an unpleasant feel as if—and this was more a typical Adam reaction—it were full of eyes and memories. The school years were lost, the later days remembered. He wouldn't dream of considering moving to Highgate, which Marigold had suggested.

Sitting down next to her, he tried to think where they had gone, Zosie and he. They had gone somewhere to kill time while Vivien was in that house—some big store it had been, or group of big stores, some shopping center. It might have been Brent Cross, or John Barnes which, at that time, had still been at Swiss Cottage.

"When did Brent Cross open?" he asked Marigold.

She turned to him, astonished. "What made you ask that?"

"I don't know. When did it?"

"I was still at school," she said. "I was only about eleven, I think."

So it might have been Brent Cross. He had a distinct memory of somewhere that was air-conditioned. You hardly ever needed air conditioning in an English summer, but you did that year. The van he had parked nearby, in a car park he thought, which argued for its being Brent Cross, and now he recalled a central hall and escalators, and a feeling of excited anticipation, the stomach muscles tautening. Zosie would steal something and he wanted to see her do it. He found himself observing her as one might watch the behavior of a laboratory animal in a drug trial. All desire he had ever had for her was dead. He would not even have cared to touch her.

In and out of shops they had wandered—or simply through the departments of stores? A food department he could remember and all those clothes and the crowds and the heat. So perhaps there had been no air conditioning or only part air conditioning. If Zosie took anything from a shelf or out of one of those bins filled with stockings, with panty hose, with underclothes, he didn't see her. He lit a cigarette and a man in a suit with a lapel badge came and asked him to put it out. Then the message came over the public address system. The exact words he had forgotten but the gist of it he remembered.

"Will the parent or person in charge of a small boy aged about three dressed in a white shirt, blue shorts, and blue sandals, please come to . . ."

And there had followed directions to some manager's office where the child could be claimed. Rufus could remember perfectly where he had been when he heard the message, by some trick of memory—so arbitrarily selective, so lacking in respect for the recall one most needed—photographed forever and printed on some wall of the mind. On one side of a bank of shelves packed with cosmetics he had been and the black and silver Mary Quant packaging he could see now. Zosie was on the other side of it, hidden from him but no more than six feet away. He heard the message about the lost boy and immediately turned to find Zosie, but she was gone; she, too, was lost.

He looked for her. The place was very crowded. The curious thing was that though Zosie was beautiful she was not very memorable, she was not unusual to look at. Thousands of young girls looked like her—or superficially like her, they looked like her from a distance. They all wore jeans and T-shirts and sandals and no makeup and had hair that was very long or very short.

She knew where the van was as well as he did. She knew the time—or did she? Of course she didn't possess a watch. But he didn't care, he wasn't going to wait for her past ten past four. They were due to pick Vivien up at four-thirty. If Zosie got left behind in

London, she would find her way back. Home is where you go to when you have nowhere else to go. Home is the only port in a storm.

Rufus sat in the van, smoking. He saw Zosie coming toward him along the aisle between parked cars, the metal glittering, the tarmac surface quivering with heat distortion, her shadow and that of the little boy black, short, dancing. He was fair-haired, blue-eyed, bewildered. He had a white shirt on and blue shorts and blue sandals, and he was holding Zosie's hand.

"Open the door, Rufus, quick. He can come in the back with me. Let's get away quickly."

Rufus wasn't often frightened. He prided himself on being easy, laid-back, cucumber-cool. But he was frightened then, fear hit him in the pit of the stomach, it was as physical as that. He jumped out, he slammed the van door.

"Are you mad?"

He knew she was. It wasn't a real question.

"Take him back. How did you get hold of him? No, never mind. I don't care. Just take him back. Put him inside the doors and leave him, anything."

"I want him, Rufus. He's called Andrew. He said he was called Andrew. He was saying Andrew wants Mummy so I walked in and I said here's Mummy, Andrew, whatever happened to you? I said, and come on, let's go. They didn't stop me, they didn't ask anything, and he just came. Look, he likes me. We can take him back to Ecalpemos and he can live with us."

From the first Rufus had been always aware of his future career, that he must keep his hands clean. That, at any rate, he must appear to have clean hands. It ruled him, that principle, it kept him from the worst excesses. Shiva had it, too, but Shiva was a loser; Shiva, through not being ruthless enough, would go down. Rufus had nightmares about doing something or something happening to wreck his qualifying and prevent forever what might come after qualifying. They were nightmares, but he had them in the daytime when fully conscious.

"Take him back!"

The child, up till then stunned perhaps by events, began to cry. Rufus picked him up and held him up on his shoulders. His heart was in his mouth, he literally had that feeling of choking, of imminent nausea and throwing up. But he ran across the tarmac with the child in his arms, the child who by then was screaming, ran under some sort of covered way and in through glass double doors and into the first shop he came to, a shoe shop, where he thrust the little boy into the arms of an assistant and shouted: "He's the lost boy, he's called Andrew. There was a message . . ."

Between them they nearly dropped the boy. His screams shattered the air. Rufus turned and fled. He jumped into the van, aware that he was swearing aloud, muttering every obscenity he could think of, spitting out at Zosie that he would kill her, that she was criminally insane. She was crying, lying back on the seat with her head hanging back and weeping. He brought the van out as fast as he could, his heart knocking, his hands shaking. To think of it now even started his heart going. He brought the illicit drink, the one on the table by him, up to his mouth. The vodka had warmed and sweetened. But then, nothing compared to the first taste of it.

They had driven a long way in silence—silence but for the sound of Zosie's sobbing. He should have known then, he should have been warned. The marks on her body he had seen, the blue and therefore recent stretch marks. He had seen her look at the picture and now she had tried to steal a child. What had happened to her own baby? He did not ask, he did not speak at all. They were late collecting Vivien and, incredibly now, he was more concerned about the delay than about Zosie and what she had done or what she might do. Indeed, he had not thought at all about what she might do.

The traffic was building up because it was close to rush hour. He drove along Aylmer Road, down Archway Road and into North Hill, with a whole lot of stopping at lights that gave him the chance to turn around and tell Zosie to shut up, to control herself. There was no one following them. Of course there wasn't. What had he expected? Police cars? Posses of policemen brandishing truncheons? The conclusion reached had probably been that he, Rufus, had found the child wandering after his second abandonment and carried him in to safety.

Zosie turned her face into Goblander's threadbare upholstery and drew her legs up into the fetal position. She had stopped crying. Rufus turned into View Road, seeing ahead of him Vivien waiting, seated on a garden wall, her bright blue dress incongruous among all the greens and grays, the hard whiteness of the light and faded lawns.

She got in beside him, gave Zosie a glance, and looked discreetly away.

"How did you make out?"

"It was his sister I saw, not his wife. His wife's dead. She died when the child was born, she had an embolism or something."

"Unusual," said Rufus, "but it still does happen." He started driving back toward North Circular Road.

Zosie put her head up. "What's an embolism?"

"A bubble of air in a vein, and if it touches the heart or the brain you die. Is that right, Rufus?"

"More or less," he said. Already, even at that time, he disliked discussing these esoteric matters with lay people. "Did you get the job or don't you know?"

"They're going to let me know. The sister was interviewing some more people before she goes back to America. She lives in America. They've got a nanny now for Nicola—that's the baby— and the other little girl, Naomi, but she's leaving, she's getting married."

Zosie said, "How old is the little baby?"

"She's nine months old."

"What is she like? Is she lovely?"

"Yes, of course. Beautiful." Vivien hesitated. She lightly touched Rufus's arm. "Do you know, I think I've done something silly. She said she'd write to me and I told her my address was Ecalpemos, Nunes, Suffolk. It isn't really called that, is it?"

"It's Wyvis Hall," said Rufus, laughing. "You'll have to phone them and set them right."

"Or just wait and phone in a couple of weeks time. She said she'd let me know in about two weeks."

Recalling this, Rufus thought that at least the presence of a Miss Vivien Goldman at Wyvis Hall in July 1976 could not be traced through the post office. No officious clerk with a superlative memory would be around to remember an envelope. Nor had that pretty postwoman ever brought a letter from Robin Tatian to the front door and left it in the box at the top of the drift. Such a letter had been written, addressed to Ecalpemos, and perhaps eventually returned to its sender, marked "unknown."

Only Adam had received letters while there: that demand to

pay the rates, and on the last day an electric bill. Sometimes, though, Rufus had lifted the lid off the big wooden mailbox that was up near the road on the pinewood side and looked inside. He had done so that day on their return from London and found lying there, a dead leaf on top of it, a copy of the Nunes parish magazine.

Halfway down the drift they met Adam and Shiva coming up, off to view the animal cemetery which Shiva must have just discovered. He parked Goblander and it was then that Zosie showed him what else she had stolen—a small, mass-produced camera. They all got out and followed the others up to the pinewood, Vivien scolding Zosie in a mild motherly way, reproaching her for being "a little thief." Rufus could remember Zosie's sulky face and the way she took dancing steps and fluttered her hands. He could remember the slanting rays of the sun penetrating the wood, and the muted tuneless twitter of birds going to roost.

"Do you want another drink?" said Marigold.

He shook his head. She turned off the television, picked up his empty glass, touched his shoulder in a vaguely caressing way as she went from the room. Rufus retrieved his secret drink, wondering if she knew about it, if she had known all the time, but tactfully did not say. Once or twice he had forgotten to remove and wash the secret drink glass, but it had been gone next day.

The phone began to ring.

Rufus picked up the receiver, said hello. A voice he would not have known, just a young woman's ordinary voice, said, "Rufus, this is Mary Passant, Mary Gage that was."

13

The Gestalt prayer on the kitchen wall was a daily reminder to Shiva that Rufus and Adam were not in this world to live up to his expectations. They did nothing, they seldom got up before noon. They used drugs and Rufus drank excessively. Shiva had looked forward to discussions on the nature of existence, the future of the world, varieties of religious experience and other aspects of moral philosophy, but Rufus and Adam, though obviously mentally equipped to hold views on these subjects, talked only of trivia, of food and drink, of places they had been to and films they had seen, of people they knew, and they engaged in incomprehensible, presumably witty, repartee.

Shiva had difficulty in finding ways to pass the time. He worked at his math. He helped Vivien in the kitchen, though feeling rather resentful that the other men never did though they came from a less patriarchal culture than his own. He tried to engage Rufus in conversations about medicine and the medical profession, the various medical schools and his chances of getting into one of them, but Rufus was not very forthcoming. Though perfectly kind and pleasant, he seemed curiously indifferent to the subject, acting on the amazing assumption that anyone could get into medical school if he or she wanted to.

One of the ways in which he filled up his time was by

exploring the place, though he seldom went out on the roads. He could have roads at home. He walked the fields, where strictly he should not have been, but he did not know this. In these days of mechanized agriculture there was no one to warn him off. Sometimes he walked through the high yellowing barley and wheat but he was too lithe and lightfooted to harm the growing crops. The names of plants and trees were quite unknown to him, he literally could not tell a dandelion from a dogrose, but perhaps they were all the more wonderful to him for this reason, for their mysteriousness. He followed the course of the little river, looking at the weed like green hair that streamed beneath the surface, and sometimes seeing dragonflies skim the water. Once he saw a kingfisher that was the color of Vivien's dress but more jewellike, more glowing, as if a light burned inside the bird's bright blue feathers. Overhead the sky was always blue, occasionally covered by a reticulation of thin, fuzzy cirrus, but more often cloudless, and every day the sun renewed itself, hot, powerful, seemingly permanent.

It was after he and Vivien had been at Ecalpemos for about two weeks that he found the cemetery in the pinewood. Vivien and Zosie had gone to London with Rufus for Vivien to have her interview at the architect's house in Highgate. Adam was lying on the terrace reading a nineteenth-century dirty book which had been his great-uncle's. It was late afternoon or early evening, though the sun seemed as hot as at noon, and Shiva remembered he had promised Vivien to fetch in some kindling so that she could light the kitchen stove and bake some bread.

Really it was too hot to consider heating up a stove that would make the place even hotter, but Shiva fetched from the stable block the shallow flat basket Vivien said was called a trug and set off. He walked up the long almost totally enclosed tunnel that the drift had become, remembering a fallen tree that lay on the northern border of the wood.

At first all the trees were of the deciduous kind, oaks and ashes and beeches and limes. All the coniferous ones were at the top near the road. The scent which grew stronger as he got to the top of the slope reminded him of a certain kind of bath essence. Putting two and two together but still with a sense of serendipity, Shiva concluded that the pine which was the bath essence perfume was the same as, or similar to, these trees, and he looked at them with new eyes. They were of a very dark green, nearly black, their needles borne in dense, round clusters. Among the clusters grew long, pointed cones of a pale fresh green, but the cones that lay on the ground, on a brown blanket of millions and millions of fallen needles, were also brown and with a shiny look as if each one of them had been hewn from a block of wood, carved in a pineapple design and polished. The pines grew thickly, close together and in symmetrical rows, so that the wood, to Shiva's fanciful imagination, looked like some ancient pillared hall, overtopped by a roof of somewhat forbidding darkness.

It occurred to him that the cones might make better kindling than fallen wood and he began picking them up and putting them into his basket. But as he gathered them it seemed to him that there were always finer cones lying deeper in the wood, and he gradually made his way farther and farther in, soon finding that he had to squeeze between the pine branches, so closely had the trees been planted. It was dry, silent, and rather stuffy in there. It was very still. The wood was not very large—he knew this from having seen the whole of it spread out when returning one afternoon from Hadleigh in Rufus's van—so there was no possibility of his getting lost. What he had also seen from this hilltop if not quite aerial view was that a sandy ride bisected the wood, running from north to south, a provision supposedly for getting logs out. Very soon, Shiva thought, he must reach this ride, and after struggling on for another fifty yards or so, gathering cones as he went, he saw light gleaming ahead and a thinning of the trees. Above his head a bird's nest hung from a branch, a nest shaped like a little basket, but Shiva did not see the goldcrests, a pair of tiny, twittering yellow birds, until he had reached the ride and come out into the open.

As soon as he emerged from the densely ranked pine trees he saw that the ride going southward must lead uninterruptedly to the open area of grass that divided the pines from the deciduous wood. He would go out that way and avoid the awkwardness of groping through a maze of wooden columns and stiff sharp branches. He looked around him. On the opposite side of the ride, a little way to the right, the straight line of pines was broken, or, rather, indented, the trees there forming three sides of an open square. This square space was turfed as the verges of the ride were, but instead of smooth as were those verges, raised into a dozen or perhaps fifteen shallow tumuli. The effect was of a range of little green hills, a midget country viewed from a midget aircraft, or of molehills the grass had grown over. The whole place, however, was scattered with what seemed to be monuments. Carrying his basket of cones, Shiva came closer.

It was a graveyard that he was looking at. The monuments were mostly of wood, gray as stone or greened over with a patina of lichen, and some had fallen over and lay on their sides. Here and there was a headstone of marble, pink, mottled gray, white, and on this last Shiva read engraved the single name Alexander and the dates 1901–1909. On another monument was a verse he found incomprehensible but the simpler tributes touched him. He was moved by *Gone from us after three short years* and *By what eternal streams, Pinto*. . . . The dead who lay here had known such short lives, the oldest being a certain Blaze, who had died in 1957 at the age of fifteen. Shiva had little doubt he had come upon a children's graveyard. These were the dead offspring of the Verne-Smith family lying in their ancestral burying place. The earliest date was 1867, the latest excepting that of Blaze's death, 1912. Infant mortality during those years in England he knew to have been quite high and he felt his heart wrenched by the thought of these losses, by that of the little three-year-old, by Alexander, who had died at the age of eight. But as he walked away along the ride it cheered him up to realize he now had something to tell the others, for the first time he would be able to impart to them a piece of interesting information. Adam, he was sure, knew nothing about it. Adam had told him he had never been into the pinewood.

Enjoying in anticipation, however, the element of surprise, Shiva told Adam only that he had something interesting to show him. He said the same to the others whom he and Adam met in Goblander as they were returning up the drift. Later he was greatly relieved that he had not announced his discovery of children's graves. It would have been hard to live that down.

Vivien didn't know either. He and she came from very different backgrounds but they were closer to each other than either was to Rufus or Adam. As for Zosie, she merely stood staring, holding one fist up against her mouth. The two Englishmen had behind them a long tradition, a mythology rather, which Shiva knew he would never understand, which his father would not have understood for all his vaunted love of England and admiration of English ways.

Adam laughed when Vivien reacted as Shiva had—well, not as Shiva had, far more impulsively than that, with a cry of pain for bereaved parents and bygone suffering.

"They are dogs and cats," Adam said. "I suppose there may be a goat or a parrot there as well, but it's mostly dogs and cats."

"How can you know?"

"I just know," Adam said, and Rufus nodded. He just knew too. "People like the Berelands—they were my great-aunt's family—they were the sort to have animal cemeteries."

Vivien said, "And I was thinking what short lives those poor little dead ones had."

"They were quite long-lived really, weren't they? Old Blaze lived to be one hundred and five in dog years."

Zosie's eyes were swollen as if she had been crying, Shiva had already noticed, and she looked as if she might begin crying again. She spoke in the childlike, ingenuous voice she reverted to when distressed.

"Do you think anyone else will ever be buried there?"

"If by 'anyone' you mean any more animals, I shouldn't think so. I can't imagine I'd ever keep a pet."

"Oh, Adam, wouldn't you? You don't mean you wouldn't let anyone else? Couldn't I have a dog if I wanted one or a kitten?"

Adam put his arm around her but he didn't give her any answer. Zosie was quite possibly mentally retarded, Shiva thought as they all walked back to the house. He had never known anyone to behave the way she did. Her conduct in coming to Ecalpemos as Rufus's girlfriend—he had gradually gathered all this—and then removing herself to Adam's bed profoundly shocked him. A kind of precociously vicious child-whore was how he thought of her. He had never really spoken to her and had they ever found themselves alone together he would not have known what to say.

"She had had a baby," he said to Lili. "This child had had a baby. It was born before she had her seventeenth birthday."

"That was very sad, Shiva." Lili was faintly reproving.

"Well, it was not sad for the baby. The baby was adopted. My goodness, it must be ten now. More than ten. She was a tremendous liar, you know. One day she told Vivien her stepfather was the baby's father and another time it was a boy at her school or a teacher at her school. Who knows what the truth was? She opened her heart to Vivien. Vivien was like a mother to her and Adam.''

"Do people open their hearts to their mothers? I never do to mine.''

"That was a manner of speaking, Lili. Anyway, she didn't really open her heart if half of what she said was lies, did she? But it was clear she left school because she was going to have a baby and after it was born she went to live in this place where young girls who were not married lived with their babies until they were adopted. She didn't go back to live with her mother, though of course she meant to later. She thought she *had* to later because there was no one else till Rufus found her by the roadside.''

"She was sick in her mind," said Lili. "You always said she was sick in her mind.''

"Some women get sick that way after they've had a baby, don't they?''

Lili looked away. "There's something called post-partum depression.''

"It wasn't depression. Zosie wasn't depressed. She was unhappy, mad with unhappiness. She was broken-hearted. Rufus knew. He was halfway to being a doctor. He should have done something, got her to a doctor. But they encouraged her, Rufus and Adam, they encouraged her to steal. It amused them. It was love she was stealing, a psychiatrist would say.''

With a shrug Lili said, "She had her parents—well, she had her mother. Didn't she love her?''

"Zosie told Vivien her mother was embarrassed when she got pregnant. Not angry or upset, mark you, but embarrassed. She was afraid of what the people she knew would say.''

"Why didn't Zosie have an abortion?''

"Vivien said she wouldn't face up to things. She pretended it wasn't happening. By the time she told her mother it was too late to do anything. The only thing her mother could think of was having the baby adopted. It was a piece of luck for her—the mother, I mean—that she and her husband were moving just about the time Zosie was due to give birth, so that with luck the old neighbors wouldn't know and the new ones would never find out. That was why Zosie was supposed to go to this hostel place for single parents after the baby was born.''

"They used to call girls like that unmarried mothers. Did you know? I read it in a novel."

"Some of them must have been too young to *be* married. Zosie almost was. She had the baby in a hospital in London and she was only there five days and then she came out and went to this place. A week after that she gave up the baby to the adoption people and it went to its new parents."

"Was it a boy or a girl?"

"I don't know," said Shiva. "I didn't ask and Vivien didn't say."

"It seems important."

"Zosie couldn't stay on there without the baby. She couldn't go back to her school. Her mother and stepfather had moved but of course she had their new address. Her mother wasn't as bad as that. She probably expected Zosie to come home—that is, to the new place. And Zosie went because there was nothing else to do. She had nowhere else to go and no money."

Shiva stopped and picked up the paper once more. It was a paragraph on an inside page that had started this conversation. This said that new evidence was leading police to believe a positive identification might soon be made of the remains of a young woman and a baby found in the animal cemetery at Wyvis Hall. That was all. Shiva reread it carefully.

"You weren't to blame," said Lili. "It was nothing to do with you. It was only that you happened to be there."

"No, it was more than that. I should have left anyway. When I saw the way things were going, I should have left. Instead, I actually persuaded Vivien to stay on. When she heard she had got the job with Robin Tatian she thought of going back to London, back to the squat. Things hadn't worked out at Ecalpemos the way she had expected them to. Nobody did anything but her, you see. They didn't pull their weight and they took what she did for granted—like you take what Mother does for granted. You can stay on, Shiva, she said. It doesn't mean you have to go because I do. I knew then that whatever there had been between us was over. Do you mind me talking like this, Lili?"

She shook her head, looking at him with a fleeting smile.

"I didn't think you minded. You've no cause. It was never much of a love affair we had, more a friendship. We slept in the same bed at Ecalpemos, but we never touched. I believe Vivien was coming to believe there wasn't room in her life for the distractions of sex, and in a funny sort of way there wasn't time. I used to wake up sometimes in the night and see her sitting in a corner of the room with a lamp on but shaded, reading the Gita. That made me feel strange, her doing that when I was the Indian and I hadn't even read it.

"I persuaded her to stay on. The others—well, the others were very distant from me. I'll be frank. I was in awe of them, I was even a bit afraid of them. Not Zosie, I don't mean Zosie, I mean the men. I've said Vivien was like a mother to Zosie and Adam but she was like my mother, too, I'll confess it. I felt she was a protection, a sort of shield between me and them. I said to her please to stay just till she went to her job, not to desert me, and she said all right, she wouldn't. I don't think she wanted to but she was practicing what she preached, you see, she was being good.

"After she said that she thanked me for being Indian. We'd never even talked about Hinduism, I don't know anything about it anyway, but she said that for her purposes it was enough my just being Indian, it pointed the way for her. I've never really known what she meant."

He fell silent. Lili waited, looking at him, and then she picked up the book she had been reading. She turned a page and stared at the text but he did not think she was really reading it. Shiva went out into the hall and looked up Adam's name in the blue phone directory and then Rufus's in the pink one. It was not so much that he was afraid to phone either or both of them as that he did not know what he would say. What was there to say? Don't mention my name, don't say I was ever there. They would either say or not say and nothing he begged of them would make a difference.

Closing the pink directory, he switched off the light. They were economical with electricity on Fifth Avenue. He looked out of the little window and across the half-lit street. The people opposite were moving out. They had been one of the last white families left in this particular section of Fifth Avenue, a young couple with two children. The For Sale sign had stood there for months and months but at last the house had sold. For five thousand less than was asked, Lili had told him, and five thousand was a big percentage of the kind of prices they could ask down here. All day the moving van had stood outside, but it was gone now. No one had moved in and the windows were without curtains. If the new occupants didn't move in fast, thought Shiva, squatters would come or else all those windows would be broken.

The two lines of parked cars were strung up over the hill, colorless in the sodium light, their roofs glittering, the pub lights orange, as if fires burned behind the leaded stained glass, but not a soul to be seen. There was something sinister and menacing about urban emptiness. A street of houses should have people in it but it was a measure of the kind of society they lived in, Shiva thought, that he was glad when the street was empty of people, he was relieved, he was thankful for the safety that came with the absence of his fellow men.

Living beings are without number: I vow to row them to the other shore.

Defilements are without number: I vow to remove them from myself.

The teachings are immeasurable: I vow to study and practice them.

The way is very long. I vow to arrive at the end.

He did not know where it came from, some Hindu or Buddhist writings presumably. They were all like that, all posing for the devotee impossible goals. That passage Vivien had copied out and the sheet of paper it was written on lay on the table in their room underneath the painting of the dead child, its parents, and the doctor. It was there all the time they were, the paper weighted down with Vivien's bottle of sandalwood oil. He remembered it now because for six weeks, the duration of their stay, he had seen and read it every day.

Vivien had been alone in the world, brought up in a children's home. Shiva could remember her saying that her mother had had so many children, there had not been time or room for her. She was taken into care because her mother had been ill and could not cope with her large family. When she recovered and indeed settled down somewhat, marrying the man she had been living with, somehow Vivien and one of her brothers also in care were forgotten. Neither of them ever went home again, and one day Vivien found out that she had been truly abandoned, for a whole year before her mother and the rest of the family had moved away to quite a distant part of the country.

This account Vivien had given in a not at all self-pitying way but speculating as to how many siblings she might actually by then have. Zosie had been there and had listened with a kind of staring intensity, her elbows on the table and her little pale face held in the cup of her hands.

"My mother's abandoned me too," she said.

That was before she had told Vivien about the baby. She was still the mystery girl, come out of nowhere.

"My mother doesn't know where I am," she said. "She doesn't care, does she? She hasn't tried to find me, she hasn't looked for me, she hasn't told the police. I'm missing but she doesn't care."

"How do you know?" Rufus said. "It was you ran away from her not she from you. Or so one gathers. How do you know she's not going mad with worry?"

"We've had the radio on every day and there's been nothing. I bought a paper while we were in London. I've looked at papers every time we've been in Sudbury and there's never been a word. She doesn't care, she's glad I've gone."

"So what?" said reasonable Rufus. "Isn't that what you want? I thought you said the last thing you wanted was to go home. You don't want your mother fussing around you, do you?"

Shiva thought he had understood. Vivien certainly had. Vivien said it was one thing a young girl running away from home and being glad to leave her parents but quite another for her to find out the parents were relieved she'd gone. And Zosie said: "Don't you see how terrible it is? I'm missing from home and my mother isn't worried. I might have been murdered. For Christ's sake, I'm only seventeen."

She began to cry, tearing sobs. Vivien sat down beside her and put an arm around her, then she turned her around and held her in her arms. It was later that day that Zosie had told Vivien everything—or almost everything. At any rate she had told her about the baby. And things about Adam. Adam had told her he was in love with her, he was mad for her, and by the way he looked at her, devouring her with his eyes, Shiva had no difficulty in believing this. How Zosie felt about this, whether or not she reciprocated, she had not told Vivien, or if she had, Vivien had not repeated what she was told. One thing she had said to Vivien was perhaps significant.

"If I'd known before, I could have kept my baby."

Vivien had asked her what she meant.

"He wants me to stay here with him. He wants me to live here with him forever. That's what he says. He's not going back to London, he's not going back to university. This is going to be my home for always, he says. I keep thinking, if only I'd known, if only I'd known before I gave up my baby. I could have had my baby here and we could have lived here, all three of us, like a family. And I can't bear to think of that, how it might have been if only I'd known."

The few lines about the prospective identification of the bones at Wyvis Hall Adam happened to read while he was waiting to make his statement to the police. He was actually sitting in the police station waiting to be attended to and he took a look at the evening paper which he had just bought. Immediately he imagined that all eyes were on him, that the policemen who stood behind a kind of counter, the two or three other members of the public who were also waiting, all knew exactly the position of that paragraph on the page, knew to what it referred and were measuring the degree of his guilty involvement. He folded up the paper, trying to do this nonchalantly. But his heart had begun to beat painfully as he registered the import of what he had read.

Five minutes afterward he was in a small, bleak office with the man called Sergeant Fuller. Adam, though nervous enough about this interview, had told himself over and over that after all, he had already said everything he intended to say to Stretton and Winder. It was they who were au fait with the case. This Fuller would know nothing about it, he was a mere official whose rank or simply his availability placed him here as the recipient of this statement. He was therefore very taken aback when, having repeated what he had said to Winder and seen it taken down on a typewriter by a policewoman, Fuller said in an idle, conversational sort of way: "In point of fact, just for the record, where were you for the rest of the summer holidays? At home with your people, were you, or did you go off somewhere?"

"I went to Greece," Adam said.

"On your own, were you?"

"I don't see what this has got to do with Wyvis Hall. I wasn't there and I should have thought that was all that mattered."

"All that mattered?" said Sergeant Fuller. "That would be a

very tall order, don't you think? All that mattered—whatever that might be."

Adam was afraid to say he had gone to Greece on his own in case his father had already told the police he had gone with Rufus. Why hadn't he checked with his father as to exactly what he had told them? He said: "If you've finished with me, I do happen to be rather busy. . . ."

"You have to sign it, Mr. Verne-Smith."

Adam signed.

"You were going to tell me who you went to Greece with," said Fuller.

"I went with a friend of mine called Rufus Fletcher. He's Dr. Fletcher now."

"Perhaps you'd give me Dr. Fletcher's address, Mr. Verne-Smith."

Adam regretted it as soon as he had said it. "He's in the phone book."

Fuller said nothing but he looked hard at Adam and Adam knew what he must be thinking. If this man is a friend of yours, how do you know his name is in the phone book? You would surely either remember his phone number or have it written down in a personal directory. Or did you mean he *used to be* a friend of yours but is this no longer and you know he is in the phone book because you had to look up his number in order to phone him and warn him, or discuss this case with him or concoct an alibi? And if this is so, Mr. Verne-Smith, it gives rise to all kinds of interesting possibilities. . . .

He would have to warn Rufus. They would certainly want to confirm this with Rufus. Adam felt weary of it, he felt slightly stunned, as if he had been struck but not hard enough to knock him out. Usually at this time, returning home, he began to feel an anticipatory joy at the prospect of seeing Abigail, but thinking of the child now only filled him with despair. As for Anne, he understood now, all humbug and self-deception past, that he remained with her solely because of Abigail. He had loved just two people in his life, Zosie and Abigail, and the Zosie he remembered came back to him as nearly as young and small and vulnerable as his daughter.

The bluish-white marks on her body he had at first taken for some peculiarity of her own, what Rufus would have called ideopathic. Zosie's skin was pastel brown, matte like biscuits, and the little white feather marks were not like scars but in themselves rather beautiful, piquant. Idly, one afternoon he asked her what they were. She was lying on her side, resting on one elbow and cupping her chin in her hand, a characteristic gesture of hers. She was looking at the painting of St. Sebastian facing an archery squad of Roman soldiers.

"I was shot full of arrows," she said.

"Come on, Zosie, tell me."

"My skin was stretched and stretched and when the stretching stopped it could never go back to what it used to be. Imagine doing it to a piece of silk, go on." She jumped off the bed and got hold of the hem of one of the old faded pink silk curtains. She held it in her fists and pulled. There was a splitting sound. "Oh, dear, it's too old, it's rotten. I'm young you see, so I didn't split."

He said to her Zosie, Zosie, what do you mean?

"Shall I tell you? Shall I tell you now?"

He held out his arms to her and she came into them, nestling close and confidingly, whispering into his shoulder. The curious thing was that it had not meant much to him. To hear now of a girl of just seventeen having a baby and giving it up for adoption, running away from a hostel and sleeping first with one man, then another, while she was still post-parturitive, without any proper medical examination and using no contraceptives would shock him and rouse his indignation. But then he had not seen it like that. About the contraception or lack of it he had not thought at all; it had not crossed his mind. He had not even known in those days that a woman should not be sexually active after childbirth until six weeks have elapsed and she had been given medical clearance. Apart from all that, he had not even given much consideration to the baby or what Zosie's feelings for it might have been. And he was ashamed now to recall his gross insensitivity. The truth was that at nineteen he had thought of a baby as an encumbrance any single girl would wish to be rid of, either at birth or preferably earlier by abortion. So when she told him that those blue-white feathers were the stretch marks of pregnancy, he had given her the only sort of sympathy he thought she wanted.

"They don't spoil you, darling Zosie, they're not ugly. They're sweet, I think they're lovely."

A shiver ran down the length of her. Her nipples were erect

from the shiver, not from desire. He longed and longed for her to desire him as he desired her, for he suspected that she never did at all, but why this should be he could not understand, and thought it must only be necessary for him to be more expert and more inventive, to achieve a longer performance. It never occurred to him that she might be suffering from a post-childbirth frigidity, he did not know of such things. It had been a case of hopeless misunderstanding, Adam now thought. Not once, that July and August, had he ever attributed Zosie's unhappiness to her separation from her baby or supposed that her sometimes strange behavior might be a form of postnatal psychosis. Because she slept with him and let him make love to her whenever he wanted to—which was at least once a day and often two or three times— he assumed that she wanted it. And she was not passive, she was not limp and dry, but she moved and moaned and writhed her limbs, and those hot nights the sweat lay on her in drops like glass beads and rolled off her pear-shaped breasts and down her thighs over the feather scars. How was he to have known anyway? How was any man ever to know? It was a dark wood, that place of woman's response. How was any man to know what was real and what they pretended to for their own ends, though God knew what those ends might be.

Has any woman ever come with me? Adam thought. I don't know. I am married but even so I don't know. I know only what they have said. And Zosie did not even say. She wept sometimes and sometimes she laughed in a mad sort of way and sometimes she squeezed me in-out, in-out, and drew up her legs and bounced her buttocks—and I never knew it was all payment, it was all to make me let her stay. As if I could have sent her away! But I didn't know anything, I didn't understand anything. She said to me, "If only I'd known you lived here and you'd want me to live here with you, I needn't have given up my baby, I could have kept my baby. Why don't things happen in the right order, Adam?"

"What would we do with a baby here, Zosie?" he had said. "It would be a terrible nuisance and we wouldn't be able to go out."

When Abigail was born he had been present at the birth and he had felt as much her mother as Anne was. Abigail had come out in a rush and the midwife had lifted her up in triumph to gasping, smiling Anne, and Adam who was weeping, down whose face the tears were coursing. Later on Anne had reproached him for that, saying she thought the Verne-Smiths (you bloody Verne-Smiths) didn't know the meaning of emotion, yet here he was crying because he'd seen a baby born. It was impossible to explain that he had wept for joy and for the delight of loving once again and for becoming a parent, which to him was a miracle. Later, too, when he saw the child clean and dressed and in Anne's arms, nuzzling at the breast, he remembered Zosie and for the first time he bled for her.

Having a baby when you were very young and then having that baby taken away from you might drive you over the edge, might make you mad for a little while, a kleptomaniac and a visionary, might make you see ghosts. He had never been afraid *for* Zosie, he thought, only afraid *of* her, of what she might do. His fear that she might steal something in one of those shops had made him leave her in Goblander and thus left the way open for her to commit something far worse than simple theft. . . .

It was nearly a month before that when she and Rufus and Vivien went to London and she had stolen a camera. In the evening they had all gone up to the animal cemetery for the first time, Vivien admonishing her for being a thief, telling her the camera should go back and Zosie sulky and giggling by turns. She must have stolen a film too or Rufus had bought a film, for he took pictures of the cemetery and then one of the house. He stood on the grass in front of the cedar tree as the breeze of dusk blew and swayed its branches and took a picture of the house. Then Zosie posed on the terrace like Juliet and he posed on the lawn below like Romeo and Rufus took more pictures. What had happened to those photographs? Rufus might have them still, but if there was danger Rufus would destroy them.

Was that the night the temperature dropped so low? Adam thought he could recall that happening on the last or nearly the last night of July. It was getting dark and Zosie was at the end of the passage, having come up by the back stairs, when she saw Hilbert ahead of her and the little dog Blaze with him, running around his legs and jumping up at him. Only it was an old man she saw and a puppy, which did not quite fit the facts. It was all made less believable by her mentioning the dog only after they had all seen its grave in the animal cemetery.

The night was cold and they were glad of the heat from the

kitchen range. This was the end of the fine weather, they all thought that, but it came back next day, it came back for nearly all the month of August, as hot as ever. That cold night, enveloped in her gray sweater, Zosie asked him if she could have a kitten of her own and he had said yes, but later, when the others had gone and they were alone, a cat and a dog and a lamb and a pony, too, for all he cared.

"I wasn't allowed to have them at home. Anyway, I wouldn't have, I wouldn't have dared. Cliff kills animals."

"Who's Cliff?" he said.

"My stepfather." She sat close to him, hugging him as a child might. Her face was buried in his neck, her lips touching his skin. "He kills little things, he has no mercy."

"You mean he hunts and shoots?"

"He hunts them down, yes. He hasn't hunted me, though, has he? Perhaps he doesn't know where to begin, he doesn't have a scent." And she laughed, nuzzling his neck, nuzzling like a child at the breast.

One of the few nights that had been when he could hold her close without the heat stifling them, without the sweat rolling off their locked bodies. . . .

Entering the house rather later than usual, Adam went straight upstairs. He could hear the sounds of Abigail being bathed, the splashing and the shrieks. The bathroom door was ajar. He called out to Anne but did not put his head into the doorway lest the enchanting sight of Abigail with her floating dolphins and her duck and her inflatable fish seduce him from his task. He went into the spare bedroom where he kept the shotgun, Hilbert's twelve-bore. It seemed to him imprudent in the extreme to keep that gun in the house a moment longer. The arrival of the police with a search warrant would not in the least have surprised him.

The shotgun was still in the golf bag in which he had fetched it away from Ecalpemos. Would it still work? Or would it have to be cleaned and oiled first? Carrying it downstairs past that bathroom from which issued those sounds of innocent hilarity, he thought for the first time of using the gun on himself, of the peace that would ensue and an end to the torments of anxiety. Tired with all these, from these would I be gone / Save that to die I leave my love alone. There was Abigail to think of. . . .

Several times these past few days there had come to him a

thought that was deeply distressing. Zosie *could* have had her baby back, she could have fetched it and lived there with him, all of them could have lived on at Ecalpemos the happy paradise that was someplace spelled backward, for it was by no means too late for her to have said no to the making of an adoption order, only she had not known it and he had not known it then.

Adam lifted up the lid of his car trunk and put the gun inside, concealing it under the plastic sheet he kept there for covering the windshield in icy weather.

14

M ary Gage was into her second marriage, she told Rufus, and although she did not quite say so, he gathered it was no more successful than the first. She had read the papers on her return to London on a flying visit. Five days more and she would be gone again, back to Rio, but she had felt somehow, what with one thing and another, that she ought to phone him. Of course she did not really suppose that the discovery in the grave in the animal cemetery had any connection with Adam and him. . . .

"I don't remember any animal cemetery," she said.

Marigold came through the room on her way to have her bath. She looked at her husband, her eyebrows up. Rufus covered the mouthpiece with his hand.

"Mary Passant," he said.

Of course Marigold didn't know who that was but that he had spoken the name so openly would allay any possible suspicions on her part. And later he would explain. He would be the frank, honest husband who trusted and expected trust in his turn and who therefore could tell his wife this was a former girlfriend, calling him up because she happened to be home on holiday for ten days.

"Who were you talking to?" Mary Gage said.

"My wife."

Marigold must have heard that reply, too, before she closed the door.

Mary gave a little sigh. "So you don't know anything about it? Well, how could you?"

"How indeed? Adam and I didn't stay long after you left."

"So that girl Bella never found anyone to make up a commune with you?"

"What a memory you have, Mary," Rufus said in his light, bantering way, though he had felt a brief sensation of coldness, almost a shiver. After ten years she had remembered Bella's name. It was a tremendous relief to hear her say: "Oh, I only remember because someone told me yesterday that she had died. She died of some awful thing and she was only thirty."

Rufus felt quite buoyant and euphoric suddenly. Bella was dead so Bella could never be found by the police, could never tell them how she had sent Shiva and Vivien to Ecalpemos on July 15, 1976.

"When exactly do you go back?" he said.

"In five days time—well, four really. I mean Tuesday, and I'll be making an early start."

The earlier the better, he thought. There was no reason to think she would speak to the police unless they sought her out, and how could they?

"Do you know, we haven't actually spoken since that day you drove me into Colchester and I got the train to London."

"That's right," said Rufus. He resigned himself to a chat. From upstairs he could hear Marigold's bath water beginning to run out down the plug hole. He reached for the secret drink and sipped it. It tasted stale, warm, and sickly.

"Are you drinking?" she said. "My God, it doesn't sound as if you've changed much."

One minute more and they had run out of things to say. He wished her a good trip quite cordially and said good-bye. Really he should be happy she had phoned. It was good news she had brought—the best. Vivien's origins now remained lost in obscurity. Rufus lit a cigarette, his last of the day, and drew a deep lungful of smoke. If Adam could not remember Shiva's surname, all the better. What he could not remember he could not tell the police. He would not mention Zosie at all if he had any sense, poor little doomed, mouselike Zosie. It was strange how when one thought of her it was often to compare her to some small, pretty animal whose vulnerability is great and life expectancy short. As a hare one thought of her in her alert listening aspect, a mouse when her eyes grew round and large, or a little cat that sleeps yet never really relaxes. She had been so frightened and so desperate. . . .

Rufus went up to bed, Mary Gage almost forgotten, his thoughts at Ecalpemos.

Because of Zosie's theft and subsequent sale of the silver bracelet, they had felt unable to carry out any more of their dealings in silver and ornaments in any of the Sudbury shops. Adam believed, and perhaps accurately, that the two relevant shopkeepers had risen up in their wrath and alerted all the others so that now the whole antiques and secondhand dealers' fraternity of the town was lying in wait to trap them when next they appeared with goods to dispose of. And if this were so, would their description and reputation for dishonesty not also have spread to Long Melford, to Lavenham, to Colchester even?

In the back of a long, deep drawer in the kitchen cabinet Vivien had found two large, heavy spoons. They had been in a section of the drawer at the back, the front divisions containing carving knives, a fork, and a sharpening stone. Rufus had once seen a pair like them on the table at the regimental reunion dinner to which his father had taken him.

"They're stuffing spoons," he said. "For hoiking the stuffing out of chickens and whatever."

Adam said they looked old, they looked valuable. "Isn't that a Georgian bead pattern?"

The trouble was that they were afraid to hawk them around any of the local towns, just as they were afraid to hawk the dozen liqueur glasses, the two hexagonal salvers, and the mask jug, all scheduled to be disposed of next. Money was getting very short. Zosie said she would steal food for them, she would steal bottles of wine, but Adam stopped her. He was afraid she would be caught and he would lose her.

"I could sell my ring," she said.

She wore it on the little finger of her left hand. Zosie's fingers were very small and delicate and Rufus frankly doubted if the ring would fit anyone but a child. It was of gold, of several strands of gold, fine as wire, and plaited together in an intricate braid. Zosie had only recently taken to wearing it. For the first weeks from her arrival it had lain in her backpack along with the sweater and the boots and the studded belt. It used to turn her skin black, she said, there was something about her skin that when she wore gold made a black streaky deposit. She kept studying her hand to see if this was happening again, but so far it did not seem to be.

"I don't want you to sell your ring," Adam said, putting his arm around her.

Shiva had a look at it. "Besides, who would it fit? An Indian girl perhaps. The English mostly have thick fingers. And I don't think you would get much money for it, gold or no gold."

That made Adam cross. "I should think it would fetch at least fifty pounds, but I don't want her to sell it. I hate the idea of her selling it. There are other ways of getting money. It may be that we'll have to take some stuff to London. Somewhere like Archway Road is full of places offering good prices for silver."

They were a commune in only one way but that perhaps not an insignificant one. What they had they shared. Of course this mostly meant that what Adam had they shared, but at this point Rufus contributed something. He pawned his gold neck chain. Strictly speaking, it was not his but his mother's. Rufus rather fancied himself in a shirt open to the waist with the gold chain and pendant hanging against his deeply tanned chest. His mother never wore it so he helped himself. He said nothing to the others about pawning the chain. Indeed, he did not know if you could still pawn things, or if the practice had become obsolete. He went to Colchester to the pawnshop on Priory Street, doubting the validity or significance of the three brass balls, but it was all right, there was no difficulty, pawning still flourished apparently, and the pawnbroker gave him a hundred pounds for the chain.

Thinking about those last weeks, the weeks of August, Rufus recalled for the first time that he had never redeemed that neck chain. Probably it was still there. It might by now be worth five hundred pounds. His parents were both dead, had died within a year of each other four and five years ago. They had not been young, approaching forty, when he and his brother were born. If his mother had missed the neck chain, she had never said.

The money he handed over to Adam and Vivien with the proviso that some of it be spent on wine. Meanwhile, Zosie kept her ring. After a day or two the black streaking reappeared and she was always taking the ring off to wash her hands. The ring was often to be found on the edge of the kitchen sink or in the bathroom or lying anywhere around the kitchen, jumbled up with utensils.

Rufus tried to remember when it was that Adam, and Zosie with him, had gone to London to sell the stuffing spoons, the liqueur glasses, and the mask jug. Not then, not until nearly the end of August, for Adam had been reluctant to go to London at all on account of his neurotic fear that he would encounter one or other of his parents. Rufus told him he was like those antipodeans who, when one of their neighbors is off on holiday to London, tell him to say hello to their cousin or friend, should they meet these people in the street. But the fact that there were about nine million people in London, that he was going to Highgate and his parents lived in Edgware, had little effect on Adam's fear. He wanted to go, he needed the money, but he kept putting it off. Rufus did not allow himself to indulge in what his father had used to call "jobbing backward." It was useless to regret and say, if only he had never gone.

Much later in August, nearly at the end of the month, the London trip with all its consequences had taken place.

He was jumpy and nervous, he didn't trust Adam. Adam was one of those people who go to pieces under stress. In an emergency they are useless. Look at what happened on that last morning when the post girl came. Adam had already been in a panic over footsteps he imagined he had heard circling the house in the early hours and had actually stalked that invisible nonexistent intruder with a shotgun cocked. And the gun had come readily to his hands again when they saw the red flash of the bicycle, heard the letterbox make its double rap sound. He panicked. Hysteria bubbled up in him and erupted.

Rufus told himself to keep calm; he at least was not one of those people, he wasn't the sort to jump when the phone rang. But he did, this morning he did. His receptionist was very selective about which calls to put through to him while he was with a patient, but if Adam were to plead urgency . . .

Adam couldn't stand on his own feet, he couldn't hold out alone, never had been able to. He needed constant support and then kicked you in the teeth. He had no patience either. What must he be like with this daughter of his? Rufus could not imagine, could only see Adam as he had been at nineteen, humping the portable crib up the stairs at Ecalpemos and never bestowing a glance inside it, Adam who had loved Zosie, who said he wanted to live there forever with her in their Garden of Eden, but who when she began crying had shouted at her: "Shut up or I'll kill you!"

Rufus held himself still, told himself to be cool and calm, to be optimistic, but he was not totally under control. He got hold of the wrong notes for Mrs. Hitchens and was about to tell her that her symptoms were menopausal, when he looked up and saw he was addressing a girl of no more than twenty-eight.

It was just before one when Adam phoned, and by then Rufus had given him up for the day.

"I'm sorry, but I had to tell them I went to Greece with you. If I wasn't at Wyvis Hall, they wanted to know where I was and who with. I had to say; I couldn't just invent someone."

"Thanks very much," said Rufus.

"The ironical part is that after I'd made the statement I rang up my father and asked him exactly what he had said about me to the police and he'd never mentioned me being in Greece."

"Ironical is what you call it, is it?" Rufus's nurse was going off to lunch. He waited till she closed the door behind her. "You've involved me in this quite unnecessarily. Why the fuck didn't you phone your father first?"

"I didn't think of it, that's why. And why shouldn't you be involved anyway? I don't see why I should carry the whole burden of this alone."

"You shot her, that's why. You fired the bloody gun."

Rufus crashed down the receiver. The blood was pounding in his head. He sat down and made himself breathe deeply, regularly. He began telling himself that the worst that could happen would be for the police to ask him to confirm that he was with Adam Verne-Smith in Greece during July and August 1976. As far as he could see, they couldn't prove he hadn't been. The passport he had had then had expired and been renewed, but even if they asked to see the old one and he showed it to them, as often as not passport control officers did not bother to stamp the passports of other Europeans.

"A little place called Ecalpemos," he could say if they asked him precisely where he had been. "It's very small and obscure. You won't find it on your map."

Of course he wouldn't say anything so risky. The really worrying thing was that Adam was unreliable, Adam would crack. If he had blurted out Rufus's name the minute they had asked him to name a traveling companion, what might he not say if they became actually suspicious? Suppose, for instance, they told him the antiques dealer with the Welsh name or the coypu man or the farmer from Pytle Farm were all prepared to swear that Adam and a group of friends had been living at Wyvis Hall with two girls among them? Suppose the refuse collectors had seen them? True, they had always taken their rubbish—wine bottles mostly—up to the top of the drift on whenever it was, Tuesdays or Wednesdays, because Hilbert had done so, Adam said, but one of those men might remember collecting it week after week. What would Adam say if the police confronted him with that? As likely as not he would break down and confess everything. The best thing would have been to have refused to answer when asked where he had been. He had a right to refuse, everyone had. Rufus, who would have liked to do that, realized that now he couldn't, for this would incriminate Adam and therefore, by association, all of them.

Since he had started permitting himself to think about her, he thought about her all the time. She came into his dreams, entering in strange guises, once in a nurse's uniform of blue dress and white cap to tell him Abigail was dead. She, Zosie, had taken the greatest care of Abigail, had watched over her and sat by her bed and loved her, but nevertheless she had died. She had turned her face into the pillow and died. Out of that dream he awoke fighting, flailing at the air. Anne said: "You're ill, you're sick. For God's sake go to the doctor."

He got up and at two in the morning was driving down Highgate West Hill. He took the turn into Merton Lane and left the car halfway down, carrying with him Hilbert's shotgun which, after taking careful thought about this, he had wrapped up first in strips of rag, then in part of an old brown curtain that in the past had been used for covering up furniture while he painted a wall. Secured with string, this made an innocuous-looking package. At least it no longer looked like a gun. The rags, he reasoned, would disguise the identity of the gun but not protect it.

There was no one around. It was dark but there were streetlamps on all night. He walked down to the ponds, where he lost his nerve. If he merely put the gun into the shallow water it would soon be found and he did not dare throw it so that it fell in the center. He could imagine the splash. There were too many houses and apartments around there. He went back home again. Anne was sitting up in bed with the light on.

"Where have you been?"

"Not to the doctor," said Adam.

Next morning, which was Saturday, he drove around until he found, north of the North Circular Road, a huge used car dump, a mountain range of broken, torn, rusted, disintegrating metal. It looked abandoned, was quite unattended. All the piled, dumped vehicles were far beyond rescue, rejuvenation. All that could happen to them would be either that they were simply left there, an eyesore, an awful detritus, forever, or that individually they were picked up and crushed flat or by means of some marvelous machine that could do such things, compressed into a small cuboid block of metal.

Adam walked in among the metal mountains, where there was no vegetation and the ground was hard and dusty. On either side of the central walkway rose hills in which the strata were blue and red and cream with here and there outcroppings of black rubber and slivers of glass and spars of chrome. There was an all-pervading smell of motor oil, which contains a high proportion of metal filings, a bitter, unnatural odor.

He poked the gun through the broken rear window of what had once been a Lancia Beta saloon. It was unlikely that it would be found there and if it were, the finder was most unlikely to take it to the police. But probably, when the time came, it would be crushed up in the compressor along with the metal shell that now housed it.

Walking back to the car, he found it impossible to remember why he had ever brought the gun away from Ecalpemos in the first place. Why had they not buried it in the Little Wood along with the lady's gun, the four-ten? Had he actually thought the time might come when he would *use* it again?

He had not known anything about cleaning or oiling guns, but on the twelfth of August he had gone into the gun room and taken this one down from the wall, "broken" it, and begun his cleaning operations. After all, cleaning was cleaning. There was presumably only one way you could do it. Zosie came in and watched him.

"Today is the glorious twelfth," he said.

"I don't know what that means."

"It's what they call the day grouse shooting begins. It's the twelfth of August, which is today, and it's called the glorious twelfth."

"I wouldn't know a grouse if I saw one," Zosie said.

"There aren't any here. I don't think there are any south of Yorkshire. I'm not planning to shoot grouse anyway. I might shoot pheasants or pigeons or something. Or a hare. I expect Vivien could cook jugged hare."

Rufus said you couldn't shoot pheasants before October the first.

"You mean there are secret gamekeepers hiding in the wood to stop me?"

"You're right. No one would know," said Rufus, and he laughed.

But Vivien had been appalled at the prospect of his attempting to shoot a hare. She made more fuss about it than Mary Gage had about the coypu man. So Adam promised to confine himself to birds and did actually succeed in shooting a couple of pigeons, which they ate, though the purple-brown flesh was tough. But it taught him to like the feel of the twelve-bore in his hands, and after that he took it out every day, aiming at squirrels or pigeons or sometimes at a hole in a tree trunk. He could imagine himself becoming an English country gentleman, a landed squire, living here with Zosie. In a couple of weeks time Vivien would be gone and Shiva with her. A further week would see Rufus's departure. Adam could hardly wait. All that worried him was money. What were he and Zosie going to live on? They had nothing.

"We shall have to get jobs," he told her as they lay at dusk on the bed in the Pincushion Room. The windows were open and the sky, just after sunset, was a soft rich violet-pink, not clear but covered with innumerable tiny flecks of cloud as if overspread with flamingo feathers. "We shall both have to work."

"I can't do anything," said Zosie. "What could I do?"

"Can you type?"

She shook her head. He felt her hair rub silkily against the sensitive skin in the hollow of his elbow.

"You could work in a shop."

"I'm bad at counting up," she said. "I'd get it wrong. I'm best at stealing really. I can't do honest things. I told you I should have to marry a rich man. Do you know what my mother calls me? Well, *called* me. She called me Lady Muck because I'm idle but I like nice things. Why doesn't my mother come and look for me, Adam?"

"She doesn't know where you are."

"No, but she hasn't tried to find out, has she? I'm so young, Adam, you'd think she'd be *concerned,* wouldn't you? Why doesn't she love me?"

"I love you," said Adam.

"You love screwing me."

"Yes, I do, yes. But I do love you, Zosie. I adore you. I love you—with all my heart. Don't you believe me? Say you believe me."

"I don't know. It's too soon. If you're still saying it in a year."

"I'll still be saying it in fifty years."

She turned to him with trembling lips, in tears that seemed to him shed from no understandable cause. He made love to her in the pink light that muted to purple, to dark. It was warm and humid and he tasted on her skin the salt of sweat and the salt of tears. Afterward she sat up and said, "I won't hide myself on the floor when next we go out in Goblander."

He smiled and held her, pleased by this sign of rational behavior.

"We must think about working next. We must think about money."

"Do you know at school they were always reading out that bit from the Bible at prayers about the birds of the air not sowing or reaping but your heavenly father feeding them just the same. Only he doesn't, does he? Birds die and so do people and he doesn't do anything. I don't understand that."

"Nobody understands that, my sweetheart," said Adam.

One evening, in a pub in Colchester, Rufus picked up a girl who was the wife of a serving soldier. The soldier was away somewhere in training. Someone had told Rufus that Colchester was unique among English towns in having at the same time a port, a garrison, and a university, and it was perhaps in consequence of this that it had the highest rate of venereal disease in the country. He repeated this to the girl because it amused him. Later on they went back to the girl's house in married quarters. Now he was uncertain of what her name had been, Janet or perhaps Janice.

There was no uncertainty in his mind, though, as to whether he had ever taken her back to Ecalpemos. He hadn't. They had met on half a dozen more occasions but he had always spent the night at her place. Rufus had not been averse to the others knowing where he had been and what he had been up to. His amour propre, his machismo, had suffered through his being seen to lack a woman while the other men (less attractive to or successful with women than he was, he thought) had girlfriends. Adam had seemed relieved, was even congratulatory. Rufus guessed he felt guilty about Zosie, as if he had stolen her from Rufus instead of, as was truly the case, Rufus himself voluntarily relinquishing her. But Shiva had been shocked. One good thing about that, Rufus remembered, was the effect it had of stopping Shiva constantly asking him about his chances of getting into medical school. Instead, Shiva settled down at last and applied to every teaching hospital they could jointly think of, consulting the public library in Sudbury for the required addresses. From time to time he eyed Rufus as one might eye the Antichrist if one were so unfortunate as to see him.

That August, on the seventeenth, Rufus had had his twenty-third birthday. Ten years ago and two months. But that twenty-third birthday had been the first he had not looked forward to with pleasure at being a year older. He had thought how much better pleased he would have been to be twenty-two.

"Another year older and deeper in debt," Adam said, quoting something no doubt, on the birthday morning. And that was true too. There was scarcely a tenner left out of the pawnbroker's money.

It was hotter than ever the night they went out to celebrate his birthday, first in the Chinese restaurant in Sudbury, then in the pubs, where Rufus remembered he had given up wine for that night and drunk brandy. The tipple for heroes, Adam had said, quoting someone else. He had sold to the man called Evans or Owens a Flora Danica wall plate to raise money for this spree and Rufus was grateful. Together they had gone to Hadleigh, to the shop, and now Rufus, with a sense of chill, remembered the old man saying: "Settled in at Wyvis Hall then, have you?"

And Adam had replied with some enthusiasm that he was happy there, that he intended to go on living there. Had Adam forgotten that? Had he forgotten the old man going on to say—and he had not been so old, he had been a spry and vigorous sixty-odd—that he must come down again in the next week or two: "Try and twist your arm around that cabinet I've got my eye on."

The cabinet in the dining room with the curve pattern in the veneer that he called "flame-fronted." Adam hadn't wanted to sell and didn't want to sell now.

"I'd make it three hundred, you know, and don't tell me that's not a tempting offer."

It hadn't tempted Adam. Why hadn't it? What was there about possessing all that old furniture that meant so much to him? The lord of the manor syndrome, thought Rufus, it probably wasn't all that uncommon. Rather than sell Owens or Evans an old cupboard he never looked at from one week to the next, he preferred to do that stupid, terrible thing that brought retribution down on all of them, and out of which in any case he never made a penny.

He hadn't done it for money, of course, he had done it for Zosie because he was in thrall to Zosie. The idea of the money had come from Shiva. Ten thousand pounds. It didn't seem so much today, but things had changed a lot and he had changed and his circumstances. It was fairy gold anyway, at the end of an impossible rainbow, while Evans's or Owens's three hundred pounds would have been notes pressed into the hand.

A lively little man with an undercurrent of Welsh in his voice that a lifetime of living in Suffolk hadn't got rid of. He had walked around the house as if he had some sort of right to buy, as if their poverty and his comparative affluence and expertise gave him the right to what he wanted. And in the shop he held the Royal Copenhagen plate in his hands and looked at it and then at them as if he wanted to possess it yet despised them for selling it.

It may be crazy but I'm going to go there, Rufus thought, I'm going to go down there. There are things I have to know. Thank God it's Saturday.

And thank God, too, for a woman who did not probe, who was not apparently sensitive to his moods or any more aware of apprehensiveness in him than she was of his inner sighs of relief. He could have an affair or a nervous breakdown and she would be none the wiser. That he would himself have to pay for this by a lifetime of being misunderstood, he judged a fair bargain.

It took him a little while, though, to think up a convincing lie. He had a private patient rushed in as an emergency to a hospital in Colchester, he told Marigold. Of course he did not especially want to go down there and visit her, but he thought he should. He would have been surprised if Marigold had asked any questions, yet at the same time it seemed to him faintly odd that she didn't. It would have been natural for a wife only three years married to demur at being left alone all day on a Saturday.

Nor did she say how she would herself spend it. She was wearing her new Edina Ronay sweater and Rufus noticed how long she had let her hair grow. It tumbled down over her shoulders, beautiful thick shiny blond hair, and she had washed it when first she got up. She appeared neither glad nor sorry he was going to Colchester. Certainly she was not relieved. But still Rufus thought, suppose if I had been here she had said to me that she was going to her mother's, or to someone's coffee morning, or made any excuse for going out, I would have thought nothing of it, I would have accepted. She won't have to say that now. It may even be a source of satisfaction to her that because I shan't be here she won't have to go out.

With all these minutiae of reactions he felt he could not concern himself now. The abyss between them that they bridged with "darlings" widened a little more, that was all. By ten he was on the motorway whose approach road was only a quarter of a mile from where he lived.

The yellow-brick pile by Colchester station that might have been a hospital or a children's home or some sort of institution for the mentally handicapped was gone and a high fence put up around the site. It was there, on this spot, just beyond the bridge, that he had picked up Zosie. For the first time Rufus was really aware of the difference between himself now and the Rufus of those days, a lifetime seeming to separate them, not a mere ten years. That clapped-out van, the drugs under the backseat, his hair long and shaggy, a stubble growth on his chin, naked to the waist, nicotine-stained hands, a predatory way with women. He felt a hundred years older, he usually did feel old for his age. The Mercedes glided smoothly, purring as it did its automatic gearshift. He put up his hand to his face involuntarily, felt the smoothness of the skin, and felt, too, the deep indentation that now ran from nostril to jaw.

Nunes might have changed but he didn't know, he couldn't be sure. He had no eye for things like that. That house might be new, that one extended. What altered it most was the season, the grayness of October, the leaves falling and the leaves that had already fallen, a sodden mat of them everywhere. A sign on a pole had been planted outside the church, asking for donations for repairs to the roof. He drove past the Fir Tree and the phone booth to which he had taken Vivien to make her call to Robin Tatian. There had been a police car parked by the phone booth, the particolored green and white kind they called a panda car, and if not exactly alarmed, they had both been made wary by the sight of it. Of course its presence there had nothing to do with any of them, but they had both thought of Zosie, who must be classified as a missing person, and of the things she had stolen.

But he had parked Goblander behind the police car, which was in any case without driver or passenger, and Vivien had gone into the phone booth, this very phone booth, to say the phone was damaged and not working. So he had driven on and found another booth outside a cottage converted for use as doctors' offices and waiting rooms. There had been a plaque on the gatepost, Rufus remembered, and here it was, still the same, though doubtless some of the GPs in the group had gone and others come. There, on the grass verge, now glistening with water and scattered with shed leaves but then dry springy turf, he had sat and waited for Vivien because it was too hot to stay inside the van. And people had come by and looked at him, two women and a bunch of children and a dog. Rufus was glad now that he had never succumbed to the prevailing fashion of the time and painted Goblander with moons and stars and flowers and hieroglyphs.

He slowed, pulled in, and consulted his road map, though he had no need to. He wanted to appear to passers-by as a man consulting a road map. But there were no passers-by. It was desolate October and here in the country everyone ate lunch at noon, everyone was indoors. He lifted his eyes to the red phone booth, the length of brick wall hung with ivy.

Vivien had come out and given him back what remained of his change, down to the two pence pieces. She was always meticulous about money, overconscientious. And she had told him that Robin Tatian had himself been at home, had answered the phone. Yes, of course she could have the job, he had written to her. Hadn't she had his letter? Vivien wouldn't tell lies, even of the whitest kind, and confessed she had inadvertently given him the wrong address. Rufus had not asked if at this point she had given him the correct one. There had been no reason to ask, no need then for prudence or caution, any more than Adam thought he had needed those things when Evans or Owens asked him if he was settling in at Wyvis Hall. But Robin Tatian might even now, he thought, be reading in his newspaper about the prospective identification and seeing the name Wyvis Hall and the name Nunes, remember that his children's former nanny . . .

"I'll stay for a year," she had said. "By then I'll have enough to get me to India and once I'm there—well, if I starve in India, I won't be alone, will I? The thing I dread is that I may get too fond of the children."

"The children?"

"The Tatian children, Michele and Nicola. I may get to love them, in a way I hope I will, but then it will be such a wrench to part."

"It's just a job surely?" Rufus had no special feeling for children, had not had then or now. "You'll look on it simply as work, won't you?"

She gave him a strange look.

"You think it's that easy?"

He misunderstood her. "I didn't say it was easy. It's badly paid bloody hard work but it's your choice presumably."

"That's not what I meant, Rufus. I'm afraid I shall naturally come to love those little girls because I'm a woman with a woman's feelings and I'm afraid, too, that they may come to love me and be even more upset than I when we have to be separated. I'm afraid that if that happens I may not have the strength to go. Have you ever thought what a nanny's life must be? A succession of bereavements, joy succeeded by loss."

"You exaggerate," he said.

He had never liked her. She was a tiresome woman, uncomfortable to be with. He could not remember her ever laughing, and her smiles were not occasioned by wit or amusement but by wonder at some remarkable sight, a bird or a flower or a sunset. Well, those ambitions of hers had come to nothing, broken, lost, destroyed. The trouble was that he could easily have imagined her sitting at the feet of some dirty emaciated fakir or with a begging bowl or robed as a nun. Things do not work out as we expect them to, though they had for him.

If he was going to Hadleigh, he had better get on with it. Hadleigh, as he remembered it, more or less closed down after lunch on Saturdays. No one went shopping, and half the shops closed. He drove past the post office and the Hampstead Garden Suburb houses, postponing inquiries there till later. What he hoped for was that the shop kept by Evans or Owens, a shop whose position on High Street he could perfectly remember, would be gone and replaced by a hair-dresser's perhaps or a florist. And the florist would tell him the old man had died and left no children to take over the business.

They seemed to stretch before his mind's eye in a procession, those people who might remember the company at Wyvis Hall, and as soon as one was discounted—as in the case of Bella— another rose up to take her place, just as threatening, just as dangerous. He had seen something like that in a play, a line of dangerous people, kings perhaps, whose numbers were endless, but he couldn't remember what the play was. Adam, no doubt, would know. Bella was gone but now he remembered the men from the council's refuse department who emptied each week the dustbins they took up to the top of the drift. Someone must have come down to read meters, too, even if they had never been admitted to the house. . . .

Hadleigh was changed, seemed more cared for, made more consciously ancient, preserved, precious. There were traffic lights at the approach to the town that he couldn't remember from before. He drove in, over the river bridge. Down there on the right it had been, past the wineshop but before you reached the butcher, a low shop you went down a couple of steps to reach. . . .

And still was.

He parked the car on the opposite side, outside the vet's, crossed the street, and walked a little way along. Outside the shop he paused and looked in through clouded windowpanes at polished furniture within, elegant, sparse, a porcelain leopard, brown spotted golden glaze, lazing in the center of a circular mahogany table, and behind it, standing there and talking to a customer, a brisk-looking very young man, a mere boy.

Rufus went down the steps and into the shop. The woman was leaving, hastened her leave-taking when she saw him. Rufus said: "I see you've changed hands. There used to be someone called Evans or Owens . . ."

"Mr. Evan, that's right, not Evans. That's my father. What made you think we'd changed hands? I mean, it doesn't matter, but I'd be curious to know."

Before Rufus could reply, Evan himself had come into the shop from a door at the back and was standing there spry and slightly smiling, looking not a day older than he had ten years before.

15

The riots of the night before dominated the morning paper. Two of the eastern suburbs. It had begun when police went into a house in Whiteman Road to arrest a man suspected of robbery with violence and in the scuffle a woman had been knocked unconscious. The inhabitants of the house were black and one of the policemen was Indian and this had contributed to the outbreak of violence. A photograph showed the name of the street which was itself an irony. Down the road in Walthamstow they had overturned cars in Forest Road. Nearly every window for half a mile had been broken and a fire started down one of the side streets.

Anne, who liked to go shopping near there on a Saturday morning, was afraid to go near the place, so Adam went alone. But in places the damage was so bad that whole areas of street had been closed and the traffic diverted and Adam found himself in Hornsey, passing Hornsey Old Church, a route he had always consciously avoided, for this was the way he had come into London with Zosie.

This time, of course, he was driving in thick traffic in the opposite direction and it was the church itself that alerted him to where he was, the church that looked as if it might be Victorian Gothic but was in fact a single medieval tower. It was a key in his memory that immediately gave access to the file of those last days. Here, with the church ahead of him on his left, he had nearly turned left and headed down to Holloway, Islington, the outskirts of the City. Zosie had the street atlas on her lap and he had said, "I don't know why I'm going so far west. It might be better to go down to Holloway."

And she had said, "Go on then. *You* know. I've never been here before."

But, "If I was going to, I should have turned down the Seven Sisters Road."

So he had driven on and changed his whole future. If he had turned left, Zosie and he would have married and been living together at Ecalpemos still. Why not? And the turf in the cemetery would have lain undisturbed and the guns still been hanging in the gun room, Abigail unborn but other children born to him, and he would not have been a murderer in daily expectation of arrest.

Adam reached the shopping precinct and managed at last to park the car. He thought he had put Anne's shopping list into his pocket but he couldn't find it. He would have to do his best from memory, but it seemed that all his memory could *do* for him at the moment was dig into the documents of the past. Later Anne's parents were coming to them for supper. It would be the first time since the previous Christmas, so they could hardly get out of it. Then there had been a family gathering with his own parents among the company and his sister and Anne's sister. They had been summoned to arrive in time for a present-giving ceremony before lunch. Anne's father had given her mother a mask jug. She collected Victorian porcelain. Anne's father knew nothing about antiques and boasted of this, saying that the woman in the shop had vouched for its authenticity and value—well, he could vouch for that by what he had had to pay. The jug was of pale cream and yellow china, its spout a face in profile with hair depicted in gold as flowing back around its rim.

"That's called a mask jug," Adam's father had said. "You can see why. It's on account of the spout being in the form of a mask."

Everyone already knew this. They could see. But his father went on instructing them, taking the jug from Anne's mother's hands and holding it up to the light, swinging it around and tipping it upside down until Adam was in a sweat that he would drop it. It was only the second mask jug he had ever seen in his life.

"My old uncle, the one that had this rather splendid house in Suffolk, a mansion really, he had one of these jugs. White it was, white picked out in gold." He remembered then that Adam must have inherited the jug along with the other contents of Wyvis Hall. "What became of it, I wonder? Got it over at your place, have you? Or did you sell it along with all that other priceless stuff?"

"I don't know," Adam muttered. "I don't remember."

But he did, only too well. Back at that time he was in the habit of escaping from or canceling Ecalpemos thoughts. So good was he at this that on that Christmas Day, even if he had tried, he would have had difficulty in recalling the shape or coloring of the jug. Now there was no such difficulty. He could see it: about twelve inches high, a high white glaze, the spout or lip a smiling Silenus face with flowing locks lightly gilded, and on the almost spherical body of the jug a fernleaf pattern in gold. Zosie had wrapped it in tissue they found lining a drawer and then in newspaper. Whenever they went anywhere she bought a newspaper to see if her mother had told the police yet and there was a hunt on for her. There was quite a pile of newspapers mounting up. They used more sheets to wrap the stuffing spoons and the thimble-sized glasses etched with a Greek key design.

Vivien found a cardboard box to put the things in. It was one of Rufus's from the wineshop. Rufus had considered coming with them, Adam remembered. What had stopped him? He had a date with that girl, the married one, that was it. It would be his last chance to see her before her husband came back.

"He is doing a wicked thing, I think," Adam overheard Shiva say to Vivien. "Like your King David."

"Rufus didn't send her old man into the forefront of the battle," Adam said. "He's only gone on a gunnery course."

"How would Rufus feel if he got killed?"

"Bloody awful, I should imagine, only the chance is a bit remote, don't you think?"

So Rufus had stayed behind, though his date wasn't till eight-thirty. Things would have worked out differently if he had come. If he had stayed at home past eight o'clock they might well have worked out differently. There had never been any idea of Vivien or Shiva accompanying them. Shiva meant to go on one of his nature walks and Vivien always baked bread on Mondays. She was setting out her things just as they were leaving—scales, a big earthenware bowl, a measuring jug, a large bag of wholemeal flour, a lump of yeast. She poured flour into the bowl, started cutting up the yeast to drop it into warm water and just in time saw Zosie's ring stuck on the underside of the lump. That little ring of plaited gold strands was always lying around getting caught up on dough, scooped into vegetable peelings, threatened with being washed down the sink.

It was odd what Zosie did then, though not perhaps so odd when you knew Zosie. She put the ring on her little finger and put her arms around Vivien's neck, hugging her. Vivien held her, having little regard for her floury hands which made mealy marks on the back of Zosie's pale blue T-shirt.

"What's the matter, lovely?"

"I don't know, I feel so funny sometimes, as if I'm not anyone, as if I'm a shadow or a dead petal that's dropped off and someone will sweep me away. When I put my ring on I feel a bit more real, I get to be the person who wears the ring."

Adam hated her to talk like that. He felt bereft because she had gone into Vivien's arms and not his. "The usual tradition about rings," he said, "is that they make the wearer invisible, they don't *reveal* them."

She seemed to shrivel. She edged away from Vivien, drawing her arms back, pulling in her fingers like an animal retracting its claws.

"I'm not invisible, am I?" She looked from Adam to Vivien and back at Adam, her eyes vague and strange. "You can see me, can't you? Say you can see me."

"Don't be a fool," Adam said roughly. "Of course we can see you."

Vivien spoke his name warningly.

"Zosie, love . . . ," he said.

"Am I your love?"

It embarrassed him being spoken to like that in front of Vivien. It was almost as if they were in the presence of his mother. "You know you are."

"If I went away, would you tell the police? Would you look for me?"

She harped on that always.

"If you'd only tell me where your bloody mother lives, we could go there and find her and find out the truth of it."

"I will one day, I really will."

"In the meantime," he said, "we're supposed to be going to London. It's past one now and if we don't get on with it, it'll be too late."

"I'm coming," she said. "I'm coming."

He could see that tiny ring on her tiny finger now, the plaited gold. "It must be a child's ring," he said to her, "it must have been made for a child."

"It was. It was made for me when I was little. I wore it on one of my big fingers then."

The idea of her having big fingers made him laugh. She took off the ring and showed him a Z engraved inside.

"So you really are called that. I did wonder."

She sat beside him with both arms around his neck and her head on his shoulder and it was beautiful (If we find each other that's beautiful, if not it can't be helped) only he wasn't a good enough driver to contend with distractions like that. Her right arm she left along the back of his seat, her hand resting against his neck, the other with the ring on in her lap. It really was a lap because she had a skirt on, the first time he had ever seen her in one. It was a wraparound thing, white with pale blue checks. Perhaps it wasn't a skirt at all but a curtain she had found somewhere. She looked older dressed like that and less like a pretty boy. He had made love to her only two hours before, but seeing her like that, her brown polished thighs showing where the hems of the curtain parted, feeling her fingers in his hair, made him want to drive into one of those fields and carry her to a hedge bank where the wild clematis was in bloom and the tall weed flowers gone to seed.

It was hot, oppressively hot, but not as it had been. This heat was humid, making you sweat as soon as you went out into it, causing breathlessness. There was air all around you but you wanted air, you gasped for it. The horizon was lost in a foggy blueness. It did not need a meteorologist to forecast that the long-enduring fine dry weather was drawing to its end. They had all the windows of Goblander open but the heat was still thick and enveloping. Adam knew she had fallen asleep when he felt her hand drop. How she must trust him, he thought. There was no one he could think of he would let drive and go to sleep beside them.

He drove on down the A12 and still she slept, breathing with a gentle childlike rhythm. For a while he thought about words, about two words no one could spell, desiccated and iridescent, even the good spellers could not spell them, and then his mind had drifted back to Zosie and he wondered as he often did if she loved him, if she really loved him, and if his lovemaking gave her pleasure. Did she enjoy it or was her response an act put on for some secret purpose? How could one know? Adam wondered if it was possible she played this game *because she wanted him to go on loving her* even though she might feel no love for him.

He had driven into London along Forest Road, through Walthamstow and Tottenham. There was a smell of oil and soot and stagnant water. By this time Zosie was awake, staring out of the window, saying she had never been here before in these ugly northeastern suburbs. Riots had been unheard of in those days, apart from the old troubles in Notting Hill and the occasional fracas at a soccer match. Zosie had the street atlas open on her lap and she wanted to know where all the reservoirs were (she called them lakes) and the parks and open spaces she could see on the area plans when everything outside was just buildings in a gray heat haze.

At Hornsey Old Church he had gone straight on and up Muswell Hill toward Highgate Wood. If on that journey he had passed within sight of Archduke Avenue where he now lived, he did not think he would have considered buying the house. But he had not and there was nothing about his house or the street in which it was situated to remind him of that drive. Only the gray stone tower had reminded him of it and reading of the riots along the route they had taken.

Adam took a shopping cart and began walking dazedly around the store.

It had not been their Evan but his younger brother. Their Evan was dead. It seemed to Rufus that his adversaries were being bowled over and swept away in rapid succession, first Bella, now the old antiques dealer.

"I was always around," he said to Rufus blandly. "We were partners. Pure chance we never met, it must have been, though the fact is my brother tended to be the one that went around buying while I minded the shop."

He drove back to Nunes, absurdly relieved, dying for a drink.

Of course there was no question of having a drink when he had
seventy or eighty miles to drive home. He lit a cigarette. In those
people's place, he thought, in the shoes of the coypu man or the
meter reader or the farmer or the post girl, he would have gone to
the police and volunteered what information he had. He would
have thought it his duty, would even have *enjoyed* it. For the first
time he saw himself and Adam and Shiva and Vivien and Zosie as
the local people must have seen them, wild, feckless, curiously
dressed or half-naked, driving around too fast in a dirty,
dilapidated van, hippies, drug addicts, the kind it was a pleasure
to tell the police about. If they remembered. If they made the
connection.

On the Hadleigh side of the village stood the four Hampstead
Garden Suburb houses. They seemed far smaller than he remembered. Ten years ago he had not noticed the name of the little
curve of road: Fir Close. It was separated from the main road by a
half moon of grass on which were planted four or five saplings,
sticks without branches that had shed their few leaves. He drew
the car in along Fir Close, but found he could not remember on
which garage drive he had seen the Vermstroy van, on one of the
two center ones, he supposed, but he had no idea which. Nor
could he remember what the coypu man looked like. He had only
glimpsed him once and that had been when he, Rufus, was lying
on the terrace and the coypu man had appeared on the farther
shore of the lake, a distance of some two hundred yards.

"Like a brigand," Adam had said. "Fierce-looking with a big
black moustache."

But Adam had a too-vivid imagination. A woman came out of
one of the houses and Rufus wound down the window of the car
and asked her if she could tell him where it was the pest control
people operated from. He could see at once she didn't know what
he meant.

"We've only been here two years," she said. "The people at
the end have got something to do with a hardware firm in Sudbury.
It wouldn't be them? The man next door to us committed suicide
but that was years before we came and the widow moved anyway.
Did you say a white van? The people at the end had a white van
but it was more a mobile caravan."

They had no real reason to believe the coypu man had lived
there. It was an assumption that had been made on very thin

evidence and somehow become part of Ecalpemos mythology. Rufus got to the post office ten minutes before it was due to close until Monday morning.

Ten years before it had not been there. The post office had been a prefabricated hut which none of them had ever gone into. After all, they had bought no stamps, sent no letters. This was a shop that took up part of the ground floor of a cottage almost opposite the Fir Tree. Rufus had already noted that the present landlord of the Fir Tree was not the same man who had kept it ten years before when he had met Janet or Janice there for the last time. The landlord's name was printed above the door to the public bar and Rufus knew it was not the same, though he could not remember what the other one was.

He went into the post office with no story prepared, trusting to inspiration. There was a kind of cubicle with a wire grille behind which a middle-aged man in glasses was intently performing those mysterious tasks with forms and slips of paper and rubber bands postmasters everywhere seem to spend their time at. A youngish woman, stout and smiling, tired-looking, was behind a sweet and newspaper and postcard counter. Rufus picked up a copy of the *Daily Mirror*. There were no other papers remaining, perhaps there had been no others.

"Where would you recommend me to get some lunch?"

She hesitated, looked at the postmaster.

"I don't think the Fir Tree, do you, Tom?" The Suffolk accent was strong, a coarse intonation with glottal stops and what Adam had once called a "concavity of vowel sounds." "No, I wouldn't recommend that. That's the best place, the Bear at Sindon."

"He doesn't know where that is," said Tom in the voice of a retired army officer.

"It's a long time since I was around here," Rufus said quickly. "A good many years. Did you know a Mr. Hilbert Verne-Smith at a place called Wyvis Hall?"

"Everyone knew him," she said. "A friend of yours, was he? My uncle helped him out in the garden, used to go down there to see to the garden twice a week year in, year out. But the young fellow who came in for it, the nephew, he didn't want him, turned him off with just what was owing."

Rufus had an immediate picture of an old man with a knotted handkerchief on his head. "Is he dead?"

"Mr. Verne-Smith? He died a good ten or eleven years back, didn't he? I said the nephew came in for it."

"I meant your uncle."

"Dead? No, he's over to Walnut Tree on account of needing a bit of care but he's as fit as a fiddle really."

Seeing Rufus's puzzlement, Tom said, "Geriatric ward in Sudbury."

"Oh, I see. Yes."

"He never went back," the woman said. "Never set foot on the land again. It as good as broke his heart. Except for just the once, once he went back, to pick up the tools that was his own, his old spade and his dibber, and he went down there five one morning so as not to disturb folks and took a look at that garden—his garden, like he called it—and it was gone to rack and ruin, all burned up and the weeds gone mad and grass like a meadow. Mind you, it was that hot summer we had, whenever it was, 1976."

"So as not to disturb folks," Rufus repeated in his own mind. He understood now whose the footsteps were that Adam had heard very early on that last morning. And Goblander had been outside and Vivien's wash on the line. He was in a geriatric ward, the old gardener, but fit as a fiddle really.

"The Bear at Sindon you said?"

She began giving him elaborate confused instructions for finding his way there. Rufus looked at her face while she bent over the counter, drawing maps with her forefinger on the cover of the *Radio Times*. There was something familiar there, something that recalled a red bicycle to him, a waving hand, solid legs pumping pedals up the steep drift. . . . He could think of no way to ask her if she was that post girl who had brought the demand for rates to their door and then the electricity bill and without asking he could never be certain.

There was no question of going to Sindon to find some lunch. He had no appetite. And he felt that he had accomplished nothing. He had complicated matters. Driving past Pytle Farm he thought, the farmer may already have been to the police. They would certainly have been to him when the inquiry began. "So as not to disturb folks"—the phrase ran through his head. It made him appear in his own eyes naïve, as if he could reasonably have supposed for a moment that they could have lived down there for two and a half months and no one know.

Down here.

He stopped at the top of the drift. A sign on a post, lettering on a piece of oak, bore the name Wyvis Hall and under this: *Private Road*. It came to Rufus quite suddenly that not the Evans, father and son, nor the woman at Fir Close, nor the postmaster or the woman who might or might not have been that post girl, had mentioned the animal cemetery to him or what had been found in it or said a word about police. He wondered why this should have been but came up with no answer.

Simple fear prevented him from turning down the drift and driving to the house. Not normally imaginative, he pictured curiously a reception committee down there, the owners of the house—Chipstead, were they called?—police of course, the real post girl, eighteen still, the meter reader, the farmer, the coypu man. . . .

After a little while he began the drive home. Rain had started to fall as on that last day, the day of the expulsion from paradise. It was the same sort of rain, the kind that comes in spurts, wind-driven. And dismal rain had continued to fall in the ensuing days after he was back home, keeping him indoors, lying low and staying silent with his parents and his brother, waiting always for something to happen.

Just as now, he read the papers carefully every day, read everything about the baby, his tension mounting when the papers said the police had a clue, a shaming relief flooding him when it seemed they were further than ever from finding the truth. He used to wake in the night and wonder if he would ever go back to medical school, if he would be free to go back. He had done nothing really, he had only been there, but he never tried to deceive himself into believing he had no share in the collective guilt, the collective responsibility. It never crossed his mind, though, to break the undertaking they had all given and attempt to see the others. He didn't want to see them; he wanted to be rid of them for good.

There had been some sort of old school reunion around that time but he hadn't gone. He avoided Highgate from then on, sometimes making quite elaborate detours to keep clear of

Archway Road and North Hill and the Highgate police station on
the corner of Church Road.

Adam and Zosie had driven along the Muswell Hill Road
where it winds and dips up and down between Queens Wood and
Highgate Wood and up to the lights at the crossroads where
Archway Road runs northward and becomes the A1. There he
turned right and started looking for somewhere to park Goblander.
This would not have been possible in Archway Road itself. Adam
had not been there since he left school some thirteen months
before but the little antique and secondhand and junk shops were
here as he remembered them and he even saw in a window a sign
inviting customers to bring their silver to sell.

He had turned left into Church Road. Any of those side roads
would have done, he had thought since, but he had had to choose
Church Road and that in spite of what Zosie said.

"That's a police station on the corner. You're not going to
leave it outside a police station!"

"Why not? We're not doing anything illegal."

God help him. . . .

"Drive a bit farther up," she said.

So he had taken Goblander to the other side of the junction
with Talbot Road. He didn't want Zosie coming with him. Ideally,
he would have liked her to sit in the van and wait for him. At that
time he had the beginnings of an awareness that what he would
really like would be to keep her utterly to himself, shut her away
for his exclusive society, an Albertine to his Marcel.

She looked up at him, large clear golden eyes, childlike and
innocent.

"Do you know what? That's View Road over there. On the
other side of what's-it-called, North Hill." She had been studying
Rufus's street atlas. "That's where Vivien's going to be a nanny.
We took her there, Woof-woof and me."

"Oh, yes?" he said, not interested.

That was it, he hadn't been interested. He was glad Vivien was
going, he would be glad to see the back of her and Shiva, but
where she was going he didn't care about.

"I'll be about half an hour," he said. "Maybe a bit more. Say
three-quarters of an hour."

She nodded, back at her map reading. He got out of

Goblander, carrying the wineshop box with the liqueur glasses in it and the mask jug and the stuffing spoons. That was when he heard the first of the thunder, a long way off, like muffled drums.

"You never told me," Lili said to Shiva, "how they came to take the baby. But I suppose that's something you don't really know."

It was not she who had started on the subject but he. Traffic was diverted down Fifth Avenue away from Forest Road and he stood watching the streams of it, comforted because his street was a safe place and off the beaten, broken, dangerous track. All the glass down here was intact and last night it had been peaceful and even the exodus from The Boxer orderly. And then, abruptly, not knowing why really, he had turned away and come to Lili in her pink sari and Marks and Spencer cardigan, and said he wanted to talk about that time, about Ecalpemos.

He shook his head. "I know all right. My goodness, *I know*. But I didn't at first, not on the first day.

"You see, when they came home we thought the baby was Zosie's baby. It sounds a bit crazy, you'll say, but we knew Zosie had had a baby and we knew she wished she'd kept it and when they came back with a baby, we just took it for granted it was hers. That is, Vivien and I did. Rufus wasn't there. He was with that woman who was deceiving her soldier husband. A fine thing that, wasn't it? Rufus was a bad person, through and through, I don't think he had a redeeming feature."

"Never mind Rufus, Shiva. You mean they just walked in with this baby and you accepted it? Just like that?"

"You have to understand that Zosie was always mysterious. There were all sorts of things we didn't know about her and new things were always coming out. When they came home, Vivien and I had finished our evening meal and I was out on the terrace reading and she was doing something to her herb garden. She'd cleared a patch and planted this herb garden and she had to water it every night or it would have died. We heard the van come, or I did, and then a bit later I heard a baby crying. Vivien came around the house with her watering can and said what was that. I said it sounded like a baby. Then Zosie appeared. Was there any milk? She wanted it for the baby. She had a feeding bottle in her hand and she was—well, she was absolutely *alight* with happiness and excitement. That's why we thought, I'm sure we both thought, that it was her baby.''

"Did she go to London deliberately to kidnap it?''

"It wasn't like that,'' Shiva said. "It was more an accident, a chance happening. It was like this—or that's what they told me. It was about three-thirty when they got up there and Adam parked the van down a turn off the top of Archway Road. The road where he parked was a sort of continuation of the road where Vivien was going to work, but I think that was just coincidence. I went there once, months afterward, it had a sort of fascination for me; dreadful though it all was, I wanted to see for myself. And when I got there I could see it wasn't all that much of a coincidence. If you wanted to go shopping in Archway Road, that's where you would park, down one of those side streets up there, that would really be the only place.''

"So Adam left her in the van. Why didn't she go with him?''

"He didn't want her going in those shops. You can understand why not. He thought she'd take things. 'Unconsidered trifles' he called them. He thought she wouldn't be able to resist 'nicking' things—his word. That business in Sudbury was in his mind, you see. Anyway, he took his box of stuff and went off to look for the shop that had the notice in its window about high prices paid for silver. He left Zosie sitting in the van. She said she might walk around a bit. It was too hot to stay in there.

"She was mad, you know. She had a sort of postnatal insanity. Her thought processes didn't work like other people's, she wasn't rational.''

"You mean you think most people are rational, Shiva?''

He paused, remembering the night before, the noise of it, the shattering of glass that seemed to go on for hours, the shrieks and animal roars that punctuated the continuous cacophony of the sounds of destruction. The loud but dull and meaningless crunch, a reverberating noise of dissolution, that was a car being overturned. Brakes screaming, the pounding of running feet, far off a dull explosion. No, men were not rational.

"They have some idea of reality,'' he said, though doubtfully. "Some notion. Zosie thought of a baby as a doll she could have to comfort her. But no, that's not quite it. It was more as though she thought that what she had done was no worse—no different really—from, say, a kid stealing a doll from another kid. And yet it wasn't as if she didn't look after the baby. She loved the baby."

"Little girls love dolls but they get bored and then they stick them on a shelf."

"She didn't do that. She didn't neglect the baby. Of course she didn't really get the chance."

"But how did she come to take it in the first place?"

"Her," said Shiva. "It was a girl. She went for a walk, you see. She got out to stretch her legs and walked over to the house where Vivien was going to work. She had been there before. I don't think she had any idea then of stealing Mr. Tatian's baby, but she knew there was a baby there. The house looked as if there was no one at home. Remember, it was so extremely hot, but all the windows were closed nevertheless. She walked around to the edge of Highgate golf course and then she came back. She hadn't a watch, you know, but she calculated it was more than half an hour since Adam had gone.

"This time there were windows open upstairs in Mr. Tatian's house and she saw a woman come out with one of those things you transport babies in, what do you call them?"

"A portable crib?"

"That's right, a portable crib. Zosie said she didn't look at her, she didn't see her, and she can't have. She put the portable crib on the backseat of the car and she left the car door open, because it was so hot presumably. Anyway, she went back into the house, in by the front door, which she didn't close behind her. It was as if she'd forgotten something, Zosie said, or gone back to check on something.

"Zosie said she couldn't help herself. She didn't think of what she was doing, not of the dangers anyway. She had to have that baby and she took her. It was the little boy in the department store all over again, only this time Rufus wasn't there to stop her. There was no one to stop her. She put her hand into the car and pulled out the portable crib and walked off down the street with it. The baby was asleep and she went on sleeping. She was a remarkably quiet, sleepy sort of baby, I suppose, but I don't know anything about babies." Shiva looked up at Lili and quickly away again. "The traffic was at a standstill at the lights at North Hill, she said. She went over and down Church Road. She didn't meet anyone. I suppose the drivers of the cars that were stopped must have seen her, but if anyone saw a girl in a blue checked skirt holding a portable crib they didn't come forward. She put the crib on the backseat of the van and sat in the passenger seat in the front and in a matter of seconds Adam came back.

"He got into the driver's seat. He said to her, 'That was a bloody waste of effort' and he started up the car, turned into North Hill and headed for Finchley and the North Circular Road. Zosie looked to her left and down View Road. The car was still outside with its rear door open and she saw the woman coming back down the path."

"You mean Adam didn't know? He didn't know the baby was there?"

"He didn't know until they were right out Enfield way. They were parked at some lights and the baby woke up and started to cry."

16

The road sign pointing to the garrison recalled to Rufus that girlfriend he had had for a few days or a couple of weeks or whatever it was and whose name was tantalizingly present to him in two alternative forms. Had she been Janet or Janice? It was rather like the way Adam couldn't remember whether the antiques man had been Evans or Owens. He had turned out to be Evan, so perhaps Rufus's girlfriend had been Janine or Jeannette even.

He would never remember. She had had dyed red hair and been rather thinner than he liked a woman to be. He was sure he had never given her his address at Nunes and he had had no phone number for her to wheedle out of him. Certainly he had never brought her back to Ecalpemos. In any case, she would be the least likely person to go to the police with her story of ten years in the past, especially if she were still married to the soldier, perhaps had children by him.

He associated her somehow with the taking of a taxi home. And with the only time he had ever gone on foot into the village of Nunes, there to meet her in the Fir Tree and for some reason or other read the name over the public bar doorway of the landlord, now certainly changed. But why should he have walked when he had Goblander?

Janet or Janice (Janine or Jeannette) had come in her own car, or her husband's, to that last rendezvous they were ever to have, and he had walked there, not greatly enjoying this very nonmacho activity but even then, he remembered, being unwilling to let her know precisely where he lived. Very likely he had been apprehensive of her confessing to her husband in a moment of frankness or guilt and the soldier hunting him down.

And, of course, yes, that was it—he had not gone to this date in Goblander because Adam and Zosie had gone to London in Goblander. That was the evening they had brought the baby home. He had not been there, he had not seen the homecoming, for he had been with Janet or Janice first of all in the Fir Tree and later in some other pub or restaurant, where they had quarreled nastily over the meal because Rufus had nothing but the tenner which remained of the pawnbroker's money and he had made it plain he expected her to fork out for the rest of the evening's drink.

But they patched things up and made all well again in her double bed with the photograph of the soldier turned face downward on the bedside cabinet. And said good-bye next morning with no regrets, Rufus only hoping there was more relief on his part than on hers. She hadn't offered to drive him back to Nunes though. In fact she had gone so far as to say she couldn't afford the petrol, it being something like a twenty-four-mile trip there and back. That was why he took a taxi, of course it was, and when he got back to Ecalpemos he had had to keep the driver waiting with his meter running while he went inside and got the money for the fare off Adam.

Only he hadn't gone inside or only just, for Adam had either been in the hall or on the porch. He had started moaning about how badly he had done trying to sell that stuff down on Archway Road. He had gotten less than a hundred quid for the stuffing spoons and the mask jug put together. No one wanted spoons like that, he had been told. What use were they nowadays? The liqueur glasses he hadn't even been able to sell. Rufus got the four pounds for the taxi out of him with difficulty, but he got it.

Would the taxi man remember? He had been young, no older than Rufus himself. It had been a mistake to let him drive down the drift, for some reason he had felt that at the time, but there had been no help for it. He would hardly have consented to wait at the top for his money.

Of course he would have had dozens of fares that week, many

of them in rural places too. There would be nothing specially memorable about driving down the winding lane through the wood to Ecalpemos. Unless he had heard the child cry . . .

No, that was impossible. Rufus himself had not heard it until the departing taxi was almost lost to sight. And young he might have been and even observant, but he would not be able to identify Rufus after ten years or Adam, come to that, who had stood there holding out the money and looking in the expression current at the time "spaced out." Rufus had even thought he might have been smoking dope, only he couldn't have been because they hadn't been able to afford any more.

"Are you okay?" he had said as the taxi went off up through the hedge tunnel. "Or is it merely a king-size hangover?" (How we judge others by ourselves.)

Adam didn't answer. They walked down to the front door which stood open. It was then, for the first time, he heard the baby's crying. It greeted them plaintively, as unlikely a sound in that house at that time as a lion's roar. Or perhaps not, perhaps not . . .

"Christ," said Adam.

"I take it that this means Zosie has brought her child here."

"You said that in a glacial voice," said Adam. "That's what novelists would call it, 'glacial.'"

"Only very bad novelists." The crying stopped. "I suppose one will have children of one's own one day and be obliged to put up with that sort of thing, but I do rather draw the line at now. However, it's your house."

Adam didn't say anything and then he said, "Later on I'd like to explain about that. Well, I wouldn't like to but I'll have to."

Stiff and haughty Rufus had been. "Not on my account."

"How did you know Zosie had had a baby, anyway?"

"How do you think?" said Rufus. "It's my business to know things like that or it soon will be."

It must have been the middle of the afternoon before he saw the baby. Adam, very nervous and jumpy, had been telling him about his attempts at selling the spoons, when Zosie came out onto the terrace with a swathed bundle in her arms. Zosie had been at Ecalpemos nearly two months and the baby had presumably been born about a month before she came. That was how he had reasoned that afternoon. Not much of its face showed between the folds of Vivien's dark red shawl in which it was wrapped but enough to tell him it was very young, very tiny, three months old or so. Vivien followed Zosie, carrying a feeding bottle and one of Lilian Verne-Smith's embroidered towels, with Shiva bringing up the rear, looking mystified, out of his depth. Quite a retinue.

Of course they all (except Adam) thought the baby was Zosie's. What else could they have supposed? And what amnesia, or even aphasia, was Adam subject to that he did not realize what Vivien's innocent approval implied? But perhaps that did not especially matter, for a kidnapped child is a kidnapped child.

For the time being, Adam thought he was done with the police. Or the police were done with him. He had answered their questions and made that statement. Of course he could imagine they might come to his house again, this time to arrest him, that idea was with him always, constantly haunting him, but never imagined he might receive a phone call from them.

He was at home and the evening paper which he had bought but not read lay on the arm of the chair beside him. He did not feel himself equal to looking through it, to searching for the small item of news which might, in plain print, reveal the identity of the adult bones found in the grave. Some extra sense of *fingerspitzengefühl* told him it would be there and while he knew that if it were not there, that he had another twelve or even twenty-four hours to wait for it, he would feel relief, he still could not bring himself to look. His parents-in-law were coming, he could not remember for what reason Anne had invited them, but he resisted the notion of having more to conceal, more company from whom to conceal it, a greater load to bear and still to present a casual, relaxed appearance.

When the phone rang he was alone in the room, for Anne was preparing Abigail for bed and had not yet brought her down to him. He thought it was Rufus phoning, he was convinced it must be. Rufus was phoning to tell him he had spoken to the police and confirmed the details of the Greek trip and they had seemed completely satisfied, had perhaps even told him it was unlikely he would hear any more from them . . . ?

He picked up the receiver. It was the policeman called Winder. Adam went cold, his throat contracting.

"Oh, Mr. Verne-Smith, just a few small further inquiries. I won't keep you."

His voice sounded as if he had a bad cold. "That's all right," he said while thinking what a stupid and meaningless rejoinder this was.

"I wonder if you can remember. It's a long time ago."

"What?" said Adam.

"While you were living at Wyvis Hall in the summer of 1976 . . ."

"I told you I never lived there," Adam said. "I stayed there. I stayed there for a week."

"Well, live, stay, it's all a manner of speaking. What I wanted to ask you was: Can you recall ever being called on by some pest control people called Vermstroy?"

This was it then. The coypu man had remembered. He had remembered the encounter at the back door and the sight of Rufus on the terrace and Mary Gage's pursuit of his van and her shouted remonstrances.

"No," he said, "no, I don't remember."

Holding his breath, he waited for Winder to tell him they now had proof he had not been there alone, that another man had been there and a girl, when he had assured them no girl was ever there. What could he do but deny it? He would always deny it, he would never admit.

And Winder persisted, though not yet taking the tack Adam expected.

"A biggish dark man with a moustache? You've no recollection? We understand he used to destroy vermin for your— grandfather, was it? Uncle?"

"My great-uncle."

"Oh, yes. Your great-uncle. Rats and moles, too, I believe. Oh, and those peculiar things—what are they called?"

Adam knew he wanted him to tell him but he wouldn't be caught like that.

"Never mind. It doesn't matter. Well, Mr. Verne-Smith, if you can't help us, you can't, and that's all it amounts to. You'll be glad to hear that in any case our inquiries are almost complete. Sorry to have held you up. Good night."

Adam sat holding the receiver in his hand, listening to the dial tone that droned from it. After a moment or two he put it back.

They must be thinking the girl the coypu man had seen was Vivien. He imagined the coypu man voluntarily going to them with his information.

"He asked me if it was an acro-something and I said, no, it's a rat, isn't it? And there was this fellow lying asleep out on a sort of terrace along the back and a girl that came chasing after the van. End of June, July, somewhere around then . . ."

Perhaps he had come at other times, later times. Who knew? And there had been the bill, paid to an Ipswich address. Up into the wood he had gone and there, no doubt, had come upon the animal cemetery which he could testify had at that time been untouched, undisturbed. Possibly, too, he had returned in September and seen the newly dug grave, the squares of turf replaced. Flittermus, ottermus, myopotamus . . . How young I was, thought Adam, how carefree, how *frivolous*, to invent these artless rhymes. Was I the same person?

Adam knew he should phone Rufus and tell him what had happened but he lacked the will and the vigor to do this. It had been a shock, that phone call from Winder, and it had debilitated him, a shock almost as great as what he had felt when his father came to meet him at Heathrow or as on that evening when he and Zosie were driving back to Suffolk from Highgate.

He allowed the memory of it to flow back into his mind. The heat of the evening first, the unbreathable thick air, his hands slippery on the wheel, the droplets of sweat gleaming on Zosie's forehead and upper lip, sweat gumming his body and his clothes to the car seat. He thought of it, feeling everything that had happened before, remembering, avoiding for a moment the recollection of that shocking sound that had broken into tranquility and disrupted a world.

It nearly made him bang into the back of the car in front of them. The cry was a sudden wail with no murmur or whisper to herald it. The van was in low gear, the clutch half out, and the shock made him let the clutch in and jam his foot on the accelerator. It was lucky for them the amber light had come on with the red and the man in the car in front was one of those quick ones at a getaway.

Goblander shot forward. He stamped on the brake and she bounced out of her seat, nearly hitting her head on the windshield.

"For Christ's sake," he said.

"Please don't be angry. You mustn't be angry."

He looked into the back and saw the crib, no head or face, but a tiny hand upraised. He could see it now, that starfish hand. The truth didn't occur to him then, what she had done didn't occur to him. As all the others were later on to believe, he believed it must be Zosie's own child. In his case, of course, the delusion was brief. But momentarily, as he pulled in to the side of the road and stopped the van, he had some sort of idea that during the bare forty minutes he was away Zosie had somehow repossessed herself of her own baby.

She gave him her fearful look, her mouse look, eyes bright and round and desperate, darting to him and darting away. Her lips were pursed into a little mouse mouth. She got down from the van as if she were running away from him, as if she were going to run and scream for help. But all she did was open the doors at the back and pull the portable crib out. She came back with the baby in her arms. It looked very small, too small to be crying so loudly.

Zosie spoke confident words but spoke them nervously. "What a bit of luck that this was in the crib with her." She was holding a feeding bottle half full of milk. "Otherwise we might have had to go into a shop and buy one. I expect I can manage all the rest of the stuff we'll have to have."

Adam, closing his eyes, thought this must be what people mean when they said they felt faint.

"What do you mean luck?" he said. "What do you mean, in the cot with her?"

"I took the cot as well. When I took her, I took her cot too. She was in it. In the back of Mr. Tatian's car."

That told him everything. Or he thought it did. "Zosie, we have to take it back. We have to turn around and take it back where you found it."

" 'Her.' She's a girl. Her name's Nicola. Vivien said she was called Nicola."

"Okay, now we turn around and take her back where you found her."

Zosie started crying. She and the baby sat in the front seat and cried noisily, Zosie's tears falling on to the baby's face. Adam couldn't bear to see her cry. It killed him. Oh, God, and he had left her behind in the van because he was afraid of her stealing things in shops. How much better would that have been than the theft she had actually indulged in!

"We must take it—her—back. Her parents'll be doing their nuts. You can imagine. Zosie, please don't cry. Please don't, I can't bear it. Zosie, you can have a baby of your own. You and I, we'll have a baby."

It embarrassed him now to remember it, his pleadings, his promises. He had come close to tears himself. They were children themselves, their combined ages no more than thirty-six, and life in its most awful aspects had attacked them and they could not fight it off. He had felt as if it tore him apart. He loved her, he longed for her happiness, yet he was almost hysterical with fear.

"I won't give her up," Zosie screamed at him. "If you turn around, I'll throw myself out of the van. I'll jump out and throw myself under a truck."

"Zosie . . ."

"I want her, I love her. I took her and I won't give her up." She was nearly ugly in the ferocity of her expression, her snarling mother-tiger face. "I want her to love me, don't you see? If I look after her, she'll have to love me, I'll be first with her. Don't you know what it means to want to be first with someone?"

"I love you," he said, levels in his mind falling away, down, down to a bottomless pit. "You're first with me." His voice strangled, he croaked the words out. "I'll love you forever, I'll never change, I promise, Zosie, but please, please, for God's sake . . ."

How had it happened that he had given in, had fallen in with what she wanted, and had driven on? He no longer knew, he was not the boy he had been then. Since then a hardness, a tired indifference, had encrusted his character. Perhaps it was not her pleadings that had won him but fear of returning, of the reception awaiting anyone who came back with their story—with what story? So he had started the van and gone on, driving slowly on the inside lane because his hands were shaking. Zosie lay back, spent, and the baby lay in her lap, on the skirt that was a blue checked curtain, sucking at the bottle nipple, later relinquishing it and falling asleep. Zosie's face was beautiful and curiously matured in its maternal placidity, her tears dried on her cheeks in little drifts of salt.

The heavy sultry day drew into a stuffy evening. Great clouds rose in mountain shapes and the moon sailed among them like a white galleon moving through the straits that divide volcanic islands. The clouds were blown by a warm wind that came in sporadic gusts. In front of the house the cedar flapped its rough black arms like a living creature, like a witch in black skirts, Zosie said. It was the last night of his life on which he had been happy, he thought, the last time he had known joy.

Of course that couldn't be so. It was an exaggeration. He must have been happy since then, oblivious, euphoric, he must have been, but he couldn't remember any specific occasion. That particular night he could remember, though, in all its strange details, their homecoming down the drift and the wind blowing the branches that met overhead, Zosie running into the house with the baby in her arms and himself following with the cot. Like young parents, first-time parents bringing their child home from the maternity hospital, and with as little idea of what to do and what life would bring. Only when this had happened in his own life, when Abigail was brought home, he had been at work and Anne's mother had gone to fetch her.

The baby gave one single sharp cry which Vivien must have heard. Vivien was watering her herb garden, nursing along sad little sprigs of parsley and coriander, but she came into the house and helped Zosie prepare the feeding bottle. Zosie took the baby straight upstairs to their room and pulled a drawer out of the walnut tallboy to make a cot for her. She put a big oblong cushion from the drawing room into it for a mattress and she covered the baby with her own bedclothes and Vivien's red shawl. She tore up one of the towels to make napkins. Adam could hardly believe it when she said she was going to bathe the baby but she did bathe her in the bathroom washbasin and pinned a clean strip of a towel around her and then put her back into the pink outfit she had been wearing, lamenting that she had nothing fresh to dress her in. The baby cried but not distressfully. Zosie held her in her arms and fed her milk.

Adam went downstairs and fetched glasses of milk for both of them and some of Vivien's fresh bread with cheese and their own early apples, Beauty of Bath, striped red on wrinkled yellow skins. They sat on the bed and ate the food while the baby slept in her drawer and Adam managed somehow to forget for the time being the awfulness of what they had done, not to think about the misery that must come about through this theft, the anguish and panic. The wind shivered away, blew itself out, and left a purple sky, clear as some dark streaked petal, the clouds in distant ranges. He opened the window onto the ruined, dried-out garden. Shiva was standing by the lake, holding a book in his hand, though it was too dark to read, looking up at the stars. It was early still, no more than ten. They had never been to bed so early. They were parents now, Zosie said, and parents had to go to bed early because their baby would wake them at dawn. She was mad and he knew she was mad but he did not care.

He took her in his arms and made love to her and for the first time—the first and the last, the only—she made love to him, she responded. She was passionate and lascivious, wet and soft, and the warm, crumpled bed smelled of salt flats and fresh-caught fish. Her tongue was a small slippery darting fish but inside her was a warm pool of space that grew and enclosed him in warm weeds and as he drowned caught him up and threw him on the shore. She caught him with a shock that was almost pain, that made him cry out as she did, made him close his eyes and arch his back and sink on her with a sigh and a rattling gasp. She was looking at him when he looked at her, smiling, she was, and surely satisfied.

Or was she? Had she been? How did he know? How does any man ever know? Besides, he knew now that it was the baby, the possession of the baby, that had brought her to this, not he. Already the baby, *her* baby for only the past four or five hours, was more to her than he was. But he made love to her again, he stirred her and himself into excitement again, then and later in the night, in the early hours. He was young, he had thought it was always like that and always would be at all ages. And he had believed, too, that love lasted and he would love her forever.

Adam sat with Anne and Anne's parents, who were drinking whiskey and coffee. A sickly mixture, he thought, but he hated both anyway. Winder's questions and sly taunting comments rotated in his head. In the conversation he took no part, keeping silent, bolstering his reputation as "not very talkative." On these occasions he often wished Abigail would wake up so that he could go upstairs and comfort her, cuddle her. But it was a long time now since she had wakened of her own volition in the evenings but slept undisturbed, in a beautiful noiseless serenity. It had been different with that other baby, who in her sleep made faint whistling sounds and occasionally soft irregular clicks. Was that why Anne's clicking in her sleep had so enraged him?

The clickings had grown more frequent and there had been a grunting and whimpering before she awakened. And then cries. That crying had been disconcerting, bringing him a feeling of incipient panic, very like what he felt now. At first he had wondered what it was, where he was. And it had been the same the next morning, the sky he saw when he opened his eyes, red as if somewhere a great fire were burning, and it had taken him a moment to realize that this was the dawn.

"I suffer from eosophobia," he had once said, "an irrational fear of the dawn."

Zosie went down and got milk for the feeding. She changed the baby's napkin, she knew how to do that, they had made her do that in the hospital where her own baby was born, even though they knew she was giving it up for adoption. They slept again, all three of them. And outside the world was going mad looking for that baby; outside the charmed circle that enclosed Ecalpemos, outside the invisible walls the shutting spell had erected.

By the time they got up there were four wet napkins in the bucket Zosie had brought up from the kitchen. Vivien washed them because she had to wash her own blue dress. She looked at the baby and talked to it and held out one finger which the baby got hold of in its own tiny pale fingers, but she asked no questions, desisting as a very caring, kind mother might. And even then he had not thought what this meant, what Vivien's acceptance meant.

They had no newspapers and if they had the radio on, no one ever listened to the news. If Vivien, going about her work, had heard talk of a missing baby, would she have made the connection? She and Rufus accepted that the baby was Zosie's, concluded presumably that she had had the adoption order set aside now that she had a home of her own and a man of her own.

He was only a little bit afraid, that day. When the car with the lamp on its roof came down the drift—albeit a yellow lamp and not a blue one—he thought for a moment it was the police. It was only Rufus returning and without enough money to pay the cab fare. And he was strangely intimidated too by the weather. It seemed crazy to say the weather frightened him but it did because it was different. Overnight it had grown cold, the temperature falling from over ninety degrees—they still thought in Fahrenheit then—to less than sixty. And he could not help seeing it as an omen of a change in their fortunes, as an end of the good times and the beginning of an encroachment of disaster.

What else had they done that day? Nothing much. When he looked back on it he remembered Zosie as inseparable from the baby, cuddling the baby and feeding it and changing it, and himself as restless and nervous, glad of the night coming, of being able to go to bed early. The baby woke up and cried and he thought, Oh, God, what a drag, is this what my life's going to be?

The new cold made him bad-tempered. The morning was dull and stormy and Zosie cuddled the baby and talked to the baby and suddenly he knew the baby would have to go back. Of course she would. How had he ever believed they could keep a kidnapped baby and not be found out?

He considered reasoning with Zosie, a pointless task at the best of times. He couldn't just grab the baby and take her to London on his own. The help of the others might be enlisted, except that the others didn't know.

They were soon to find out. Once Shiva gave him the lead, handed him the opportunity, he wasn't going to stay silent. Not even for Zosie's sake. Besides, it wouldn't be for Zosie's sake in the end, it would be better for Zosie to relinquish the baby—or he thought so, he couldn't see further than the moment, the cold, increasingly alarming present.

It was Shiva who asked.

"Whose baby is it, Zosie? Is it yours?"

Vivien smiled and nodded. Rufus wasn't there, he was lying hopefully out on the terrace where once the sun had shone. Shiva sat at the kitchen table, looking from one girl to the other. Now Adam had his chance and he took it.

"She isn't Zosie's," he said. "She's someone else's baby."

"She's mine," Zosie said.

"Only," said Adam, pedantic to the last, "in the sense that she's presently in your possession."

Shiva said, "I don't understand what you mean."

Zosie, who had been heating milk in a saucepan, stepped away from the stove, her shoulders hunched, her eyes the eyes of the mouse in the corner, its back to the wall. The baby was in Vivien's arms. She and Zosie had been, as it were, joint priestesses of some maternal mysteries, performing together the rites of an ancient cult, and Vivien had smilingly confirmed Zosie's motherhood in a way that excluded males. But in all this she had been deceived and at Adam's denial she sprang back, clutching the baby tightly to her, her face a mask of shock. Adam had a feeling that anyone else, at this revelation, might actually have dropped the baby but Vivien held onto it the more firmly as if by the mere utterance of certain words, it was placed in danger and required her special protection.

He spoke steadily, without emotion. "She's a baby Zosie took out of a car when we were in London. She kidnapped her, if you like."

"I don't believe it," Shiva said in a slow wondering voice.

"Of course you do. You know people take babies, women do when they've lost their own. It's a well-known fact."

"She just took a baby out of a car? Didn't anyone see her do this?"

"Obviously not. Look, we've been through all this. I'm sick of it. I know it was wrong and terrible and all that, I know that. I'm not feeble-minded. I know the baby's got to go back, and the sooner the better, as far as I'm concerned."

Vivien spoke. She still held the baby. She wouldn't relinquish the baby. "It was a wicked thing to do, an evil thing. I think you are feeble-minded, both of you, that's just what you are. This baby has to go back to her parents now, immediately. You have to drive back to London now with her and give her back."

"I quite agree," Adam said wearily.

"Do you know who her parents are? I suppose you don't. You took her out of someone's car, you say? You're mad completely, you're sick in your minds."

"Oh, shut up."

"Rufus will have to know about this. Rufus should be in on it."

It must have been the first time Vivien had ever made an overture of any kind to Rufus. Still carrying the baby, she put her head out of the window and called him.

"Rufus, would you come in here, please?"

Zosie had filled the bottle and was holding it under the cold tap to cool it. She dried the bottle on a cloth and came to Vivien, lifting up her arms. For a moment it seemed as if Vivien would hold onto the baby, for she briefly raised her left arm to shelter its face and head from Zosie.

"She's a human being you've stolen," she said in a wondering voice. "A *person,* not an animal or a toy. Do you realize that? Do you *think*?"

The baby broke into wails at the sight of food held tantalizingly a yard from her. Vivien said: "I thought she was yours, I thought this was your own child you'd somehow got back."

"Please give her to me, Vivien."

Cigarette in mouth, Rufus walked in just as the changeover was taking place, Vivien putting the baby into Zosie's arms while turning her head sharply away. Shiva had begun to laugh, not wildly, but softly, ruefully, while shaking his head. Rufus said: "What's going on?"

"Zosie's stolen this baby out of someone's car. She just took it yesterday afternoon. She's mad, of course. Presumably she thinks she can get away with kidnapping. I know you thought it was hers, we all thought it was hers, but it's not, it's someone else's. They don't even know whose baby it is, they don't even know who the parents are."

"Oh, yes, we do. It's Tatian's, it's that man's you're going to work for."

Vivien looked at Adam. She put her hands up to her face which had gone as pale as the cream cotton of her dress. The baby in Zosie's arms sucked away at the nipple, its miniature hands, pink as shells, holding on to the bottle. Vivien took a step toward Zosie, in a threatening way, it seemed to Adam, and he half-rose, but she was only looking at the baby, staring into the baby's face.

"Are you saying you think this baby is Nicola Tatian? Is that what you thought? Nicola's *nine months old,* she's big, she crawls around. I ought to know, I've seen her. God knows who this is, God only knows. What made you think you'd taken Robin Tatian's child?"

Zosie didn't speak. She doesn't care, Adam thought, she doesn't care whose it is, it's hers now, that's the way she thinks.

"It was in a car outside his house. Zosie naturally thought it was his."

Shiva's had been a nervous giggling and had ceased now, though the shaking of the head continued. But it was simple raucous laughter Rufus gave vent to, peals of laughter that shook him so that he had to sit down at the table and bury his face in his arms.

"Put the radio on," said Vivien. "Keep it on till we get some news. There's bound to be something on the news. You're useless, aren't you?" she said fiercely to Rufus. "You'd think anything was funny. You'd think murder was funny."

"Maybe I would," he said, throwing back his head. "Maybe I would."

But he did not when the time came.

Shiva put the radio on and rock music thrummed out. Almost at the same time, as if the radio had started it or the music had provoked it, thunder rolled out of the distance, a sound like a load of stones being rattled out into a pit of stones. And then the music stopped and a man's voice began announcing the news bulletin.

His father-in-law was talking about Wyvis Hall. Adam, lost in his reverie, his hearing shuttered, had missed whatever it was that triggered this off. He sensed, though, that it might be some news item his father-in-law had read or heard but which had escaped him, something fresh that the media had just got hold of, and while one part of him burned to know what it was, the rest cringed from it, would have given anything not to know it, covering eyes and blocking ears. Nor did he want to answer the questions that were now being put to him about his ownership of the place, what sort of a house it was, what was the extent of the grounds, what kind of people lived in the neighborhood.

He did answer, though, in an abstracted kind of way, thinking all the while that he had only to inquire what made him ask for Anne's father to revert to whatever had begun it. Those lines in the evening paper he was afraid to look at, perhaps, or even something on television. But he did not ask. Instead, he found himself saying abruptly that it was an unpleasant subject, it was something he didn't want to talk about. Anne was looking at him with those suspicious, narrowed eyes that seemed a habitual expression with her nowadays. And suddenly Adam thought, my marriage won't survive this, we shall split up over this. In a way it would be the least of evils. If the sole result of all this were to be the breakup of his marriage, he would have got out of it lightly. But it could not be the sole result, not now, not with the coypu man appearing on the scene and saying his piece.

* * *

Adam remembered lightning, a bright flash of it, flaring in the kitchen. It was only then that they realized how dark it had become. It had given them an illusion of nighttime but it wasn't night, it wasn't even evening but three in the afternoon. He had gone to the window and looked out on a gray and purple sky, where the clouds were mountain ranges capped with snow. Like the Himalayas, warm and close in the foothills, clear and icy on those distant peaks. A tree of lightning grew out of the blue horizon, branches forking through the cumulus, and the thunder cracked this time, a sound like gunfire.

He listened to the voice coming out of the radio, they all listened, even Rufus. "The missing Highgate baby" was the way the voice referred to the child in Zosie's arms, not by name. Zosie rubbed the baby's back, cuddling it against her shoulder. For a few seconds she held her head on one side, listening to the words which the announcer delivered in ominous tones, but not as if it had any application to her personally, and with no more interest than she might have given to news of an earthquake taking place on the other side of the world.

She had torn up another towel and was changing the baby's diaper. Shiva recoiled from this with wrinkled nose and downturned mouth.

"I'd like to go to Sudbury, please, and buy her some clothes. She ought to have another outfit and underclothes and things. She ought to have real napkins."

Adam wondered what it was this reminded him of. He closed his eyes. Of his sister, yes, of Bridget when she was a child of seven or eight, and had for a few days become obsessed by a birthday doll.

"You're not going to Sudbury," Vivien said. "You're going to London to take that baby back."

She was Mother, she was in charge, hers was the voice of authority. Only it no longer worked so effectively. And Rufus surely had been Father. Why do we need these roles, Adam had wondered then and wondered now, why do we cast ourselves in them?

"A small local difficulty," said Rufus, "is that we don't yet know who it belongs to."

"It'll have been in the papers. It'll have been in this morning's paper." Adam was beginning to see what he must do. "I'll take Zosie into Sudbury and buy a paper and find out whose it is."

"I don't see why," said Zosie, "seeing that I'm not taking her back."

Adam put his arms around her. He put his arms around her and the baby, the baby was between them, keeping them apart. For more reasons than one, he wanted to be rid of the baby.

Shiva, who had been silent, who had seemed to be listening intently only as might someone whose grasp of the English language was imperfect but who needed to understand every word, now said slowly: "Do you realize it's fortunate it wasn't Mr. Tatian's baby you took? You would have been found by now if you had, the police would have found you."

They all looked at him. It was the first mention of the police.

"Because they will want to know about everyone connected with the Tatian family. Mr. Tatian would have said he had this new nurse for his children coming on Thursday but he didn't know much about her, it was his sister-in-law who had interviewed her. He would have said there was something odd about her address, she had given him a false address. There was no such place as Ecalpemos but it might be true that she lived at Nunes in Suffolk. What do you think they would have done then? They would have been here by now, they would have found us, they would have called at every house here."

"Congratulations," said Rufus. "One of these days you will make a great detective, a credit to the force."

A flush came into Shiva's olive face. "It's true, though, isn't it?"

"My guardian angel was looking after me," Zosie said.

"How about this baby's mother's guardian angel? He was on leave, was he?"

"I thought you were on my side, Rufus."

The radio was playing music, rock, not very loud. Rufus turned it off. He lit a cigarette.

"Did you now?" he said. He was looking at Zosie in a speculative kind of way and yet as if he found her an astonishing creature. "I'll tell you whose side I'm on. Rufus's. And that goes for always."

Adam had an uneasy feeling that the grown-ups had come. He looked at Rufus, needing him, needing him for guidance, for

direction. And what Rufus said next struck him like a blow under
the ribs. He felt the blood run into his face and the skin grow hot.

"Frankly, this is no place for me. Not any longer. It's time for
me to quit." He smiled at Adam but not pleasantly, without
camaraderie. "So if you'll excuse me, I'll be on my bike in the
morning."

Adam had to maintain a cool manner. He had to put up his
eyebrows and shrug.

"As you like. It's your decision."

"Right. But I'm afraid I shall have to deprive you of the van."
He said "the van" and not "Goblander" and this twisted a knife
in Adam. "So if you want to buy newspapers and baby clothes, I
suggest you run into Sudbury now while the going is good."

Very laid back was Rufus, cool as a cucumber and with a
cutting edge to his voice. He didn't have to put it into words. It
was plain what he was thinking: I am a medical student at a great
teaching hospital with a future before me. And I am good, I am
going to be good, I am going to be a success. I have two years still
before I qualify. I have far to go up the ladder but up it I am going
and be damned to the lot of you. The last thing I mean to do is
jeopardize my career for a crazy girl with kleptomania—the kind
of kleptomania that has babies not things as its object.

From goodness knows where, Rufus produced a big square
bottle of gin Adam didn't know he had, poured himself a generous
measure, and drank it down neat. He didn't say any more but went
off through the house, carrying his bottle. As soon as he was gone
Zosie started telling them about the little boy she had tried to
abduct from some shopping center when she and Rufus and Vivien
were all in London together. It was the first Adam had heard of
this and it turned him cold. The baby would have to be returned.
Rufus could go, he would soon be going anyway, and all Adam
really wanted was to be alone with Zosie. Without the baby.

Sometime later on, if he could divert her, if she would go to
sleep, say, he might be able to take the baby back. And what
would that do to their relationship? What would keeping the baby
do to it?

The empty portable crib was on the backseat of Goblander.
Zosie sat holding the baby, wrapped in Vivien's shawl. Her
childlike hand on which the plaited ring gleamed stroked back the
cobweb-fine hair, touched the round satiny cheeks. Her face was

rapt and her guardian angel sheltered her with his wings. She no longer reminded him of his sister but of girls he had seen in paintings, Renaissance madonnas whose ardent faces and shining eyes had nothing to do with piety.

Like a small ill-treated animal begins to trust the first human being who is kind to it, the first who does not kick it or desert it, she trusted him. She wasn't afraid to leave the baby in his care. He supposed he should be flattered and in a way he was. It pleased him, it meant that later on he could do what he had to do. But first he left her with the baby, and bought the *Daily Telegraph*. The missing baby story was big on the front page and the name was there. The child who slept in the portable crib on the backseat of Goblander was called Catherine, her surname was Ryemark and her parents whose guardian angel had been on leave lived on the other side of Highgate, in the area called the Miltons.

Her arms full of packages, a shopping bag hooked on one arm, Zosie came back, came dancing back in spite of her burdens. The shopping she had done must have made a big hole in the mask jug and spoons money.

"Catherine," said Zosie when he told her. "I like Catherine better than Nicola."

The baby seemed to smile at her. It was very quiet, placid, staring. The large blue eyes were calm and mild, not wandering but fixed on Zosie's face. Adam read aloud a minute description of the portable crib, cream with a white and cream checked lining, the linen white with a pink blanket and a pastel-colored patchwork quilt. He wondered why all the people passing by did not look into the van and see the crib and rush off to denounce him.

A few drops of rain had fallen, widely separated, each the size of a large coin. They watched the sparse rain with surprise, almost with curiosity. It was so long since they had seen it, it came as a phenomenon.

"It says here she's fourteen weeks old," Adam said as they began the drive back.

"Doesn't that seem tiny? You can't imagine being fourteen weeks old." Zosie sat in the back with Catherine. She had taken her out of the crib and held her in her arms. "My baby was a little girl. I haven't told you that before, have I? The funny thing is I feel just the same about her as I did about my own little girl, just the same, no different. Do you know, Adam, it won't be long before we forget she's not our own baby."

Adam didn't say anything. He would have liked more information than the newspaper gave, but he did not like the sound of a "nationwide hunt" for Catherine Ryemark. There was nothing in the story about motorists stopping to let a young girl in a blue top and blue and white checked skirt holding a portable crib go across the pedestrian crossing at North Hill. Perhaps no one had seen her.

At Ecalpemos Vivien was waiting for them, standing under the front porch waiting. The rain had never really come, though the sky was still a rolling mass of cloud and the thunder growled distantly. A wind had risen, swaying and shivering the trees. She began telling them before they got in the door how the baby must go back, how they must not even bring her in but take her home at once.

Adam agreed really but he knew that if he was to accomplish the child's return he must seem not to agree. He pushed angrily past Vivien. Rufus was nowhere about, probably he was up in the Centaur Room. Because she had been awakened at dawn and after that had dozed only briefly, Zosie was sleepy and yawning, putting her fists into her eyes as children do. It was no more than five but it was as if dusk had come and the rooms had a gloomy, almost wintry look, though stuffy and close. They had closed all the windows on account of the threatening storm and Adam went around opening them again.

Upstairs in Pincushion he found Zosie lying fast asleep, stretched out on the bed, and close beside her, not in the portable crib but on the mattress, the baby Catherine Ryemark lay also sleeping in the crook of her arm. Adam bent over and kissed Zosie softly on the forehead. It was done almost as if he intended to wake her, as if he would in this way prevent himself from betraying her. But she did not wake. His kiss had an effect of assisting him in his purpose, for it disturbed her enough to make her whimper quietly, turn herself toward the wall and withdraw her arm from under the baby's head.

Adam picked up the baby, put her into the portable crib and carried the crib along the passage toward the Centaur Room. None of them had ever been into the others' rooms. How odd that was! It had almost been prudish of them, an old-fashioned and unexpected respect for privacy. Adam did not know whether he should knock or not, but he needed to speak to Rufus to ask if he could borrow Goblander to take the baby back to London. Preferably, would Rufus himself drive him and the baby to London? Holding the portable crib, he stood indecisively outside the door. Then he did knock but there was no reply. He opened the door and looked inside. The room was empty, the bedclothes tossed back on to the floor and the windows wide open.

Adam looked at the reproduction of the Boecklin painting, *The Centaur at the Forge,* and noticed for the first time that among the crowd of curious bystanders eyeing the man-horse who had come to be shod was a woman holding a baby in her arms. He turned away. He would have to find Rufus and quickly. It would be just like Rufus to have gone off to the pub.

He went back along the passage, thinking about where they would take the baby. The best way would be to leave it on the steps of a church or some public building. Provided the storm did not come, of course. Well, they would have to take care to leave it under cover.

The house was darker at this hour than he could ever remember having known it, though of course he had been here in the winter and it must have been darker then. A momentary uneasy feeling came to him that it was here, at the top of the back stairs, that Zosie had seen Hilbert's ghost, or said she had seen it. Of course there was nothing and no one, only Vivien throwing open the door of the Deathbed Room and starting on him again.

"Okay, the baby goes back tonight," he said. "But don't keep at me. I have to think of ways."

Where had she disappeared to? How was it he had gone into the kitchen alone and found Shiva there, sitting at the round deal table, reading with great concentration the story of the stealing of Catherine Ryemark? He could not remember, any more than now as he said perfunctory good-byes to his parents-in-law, preparing to explain to Anne his silence and his "rudeness," he could not remember where Rufus had been. Not out in Goblander, for from a side window of the kitchen he could see the van parked on the drive. In the drawing room perhaps with what he called his Happy Hour drink and the secret drink, too, that he thought (through the only naïve chink in his armor) no one knew about.

Shiva looked up and at the portable crib and then he quite

simply told Adam about this idea of his. He smiled as he spoke, looking roguish.

"We couldn't do that," Adam had said.

"Why not? You have the name, the address, everything. It will take a load off their minds, be a relief."

"I don't know," he had said. "I don't know."

But he did.

Abigail awoke crying just as he was getting into bed. He got up and comforted her, changed her diaper, fetched her orange juice in a bottle which Anne said was wrong, encouraging bad habits. It would be bad for her teeth, but she had only four. All the time he was thinking that the occasions on which he would perform these simple paternal tasks were numbered, could perhaps be counted on the fingers of one hand. As he laid her down again he seemed to see the baby Catherine's face instead of hers, a face that was more infantile, more feeble and vulnerable, the eyes glazed and not quite in focus. He twisted his head away, closed his eyes. When he opened them again it was his own child he saw who looked gravely at him and then favored him with a radiant smile.

In the suburban dark that is not dark he lay listening to Anne's steady breathing and the soft clicks that came irregularly. They no longer annoyed him. It was rather as if these sounds were visited upon him as a kind of retribution because he had agreed to Shiva's suggestion. All sorts of fanciful ideas came to one in the night. At this hour it was quite possible to believe the dead child's spirit made those soft delicate clicks through the medium of Anne's slightly parted lips. Or, more readily if one understood about guilt and fear, that Anne never made them at all, that there were no sounds, they did not exist, but that his fevered imagination recreated them from that night ten years ago when at last the rain came and the air grew cold. When he lay listening to the rain fall and abate and fall again and then to the baby's breathing, the occasional just audible click, the whimper which seemed a threat of crying that never came.

He remembered but he did not dream. He knew he would not sleep. It was raining now, the sluggish drizzle of winter. He could just hear the whispering patter of it. That night they had forgotten to shut the window and one of the things they found in the morning was water lying on the broad oak sill.

One of the things.

The Sunday paper came early and he got up and went down to fetch it, praying please, please, please, touching wooden surfaces all the way, banisters, the front door, the architrave of the front door. Abigail cried out but for once he left it to Anne to go to her.

The page where the news was. His hands trembled. When he saw the paragraph, homing on to the headline, he couldn't look. He closed his eyes. Opening them, he stared, not understanding what he read, thinking anxiety must have broken his mind. The bones from the grave at Wyvis Hall had been identified as those of a Nunes girl and her infant daughter, the identification having been made by a Mrs. Rita Pearson of Felixstowe.

That was all.

17

The police must have come for him, Shiva thought, when the two men came into the shop just before closing time on Monday and one of them held out his warrant card on the palm of his hand. He, too, had seen the paragraph in the paper, indeed had known of this piece of news since the previous morning, when Lili herself had pointed it out to him, tucked away inside the *Sunday Express*. It had not stopped him sleeping, for he was no longer anxious. He was resigned. Lili had withdrawn herself from him; it had been too much for her, as she had warned him it might be. If he said too much, it might destroy her feeling for him and he had said too much. There had been nothing else for them to talk about, they had talked about it all the time, and he had told her the ultimate which tipped him over the edge of her love.

But it was not for him that the police had come. They wanted the pharmacist. They wanted to talk to him about a tip-off (Shiva guessed) they had had that Kishan had been buying suspect-source drugs, repackaging them, and selling them at the current retail price. Shiva suspected he had been but he did not intervene, turning the sign inside the glass door to Closed, saying good night and going home.

Home where Lili would be—would she?—waiting for him with eyes no longer tender, with no more reassurance and practical comfort. He had received the last of that last night before he told her.

"You weren't to blame," she had said. "You just happened to be there. Unless you mean you should have told the police off your own bat."

"I don't mean that. It isn't that. I was to blame. If I hadn't put up this idea of mine to Adam, he would have taken the baby back then and there. As soon as he found Rufus he would have taken her back to London and if he had taken her back she might not have died."

"Would he have taken her back?"

"Oh, yes, he was ready to do that. He was going to get into the van and do that—but I stopped him."

Lili said nothing, but a change came over her face. Without actually moving she seemed to shrink from him. It was as if her spirit, her soul, her mind, or whatever you called it, receded more deeply inside her. She was wearing a dress of Indian cotton, embroidered and with bits of mirrorwork, not unlike the one he had given Vivien from his father's warehouse. Did Lili know Indian women never wore clothes like that? He found himself wondering about it with supreme irrelevance. She put her hand up to her face and rubbed her pale Austrian cheek.

"When you told me about this before you didn't tell me that."

"No."

"Did you really do that, Shiva?"

"It seemed a harmless thing. I swear I thought it couldn't do any harm. It wasn't hurting anyone, I thought, it wouldn't even make them more anxious. At least the parents would know the baby was alive. I didn't suggest it for myself, Lili, I was going to leave there almost immediately. When Vivien was due to go I was going too. I wanted to get home. I thought there might be some replies from the medical schools I'd applied to. I swear to you, it wasn't for myself. Adam needed money and I thought this was a way of getting money."

"You were always trying to get in with those two. You would have done anything to make them like you. But they despised you really."

"I don't know. Maybe. They are the sort of Englishmen who always think themselves superior to someone like me. They can't help it, it's ingrained."

Walking along to the bus stop, he found he was nodding to himself. Adam had seen him at Heathrow but had deliberately not seen him. Of course that could be explained away. They had made a pact not to recognize each other and that was before this business began in the newspapers. (Shiva thought of it as "this business in the newspapers," though he knew very well there was a reality, a series of physical happenings, behind the printed lines.) But he sensed that the pact not to communicate had since been broken and Adam and Rufus were following events together. He imagined one of them phoning the other, their meeting, their perhaps daily colloquies. But neither of them had been in touch with him. Manjusri was an uncommon name, he and his family were the only ones in the London phone book. They could easily have found him. But they thought him insignificant, of no account, an unnecessary third he would have been, at their conferences. Shiva felt very alone and an end to his isolation would not come when he reached home.

It was true what Lili had said. He had been making a bid for Adam's attention. In all the time he had been at Ecalpemos he had never felt more left out than in that hour or so before Adam came into the kitchen with the portable crib. The facts about the snatching of the baby he had had to get secondhand from Vivien or pick up himself from the conversation. No one had explained anything to him, still less consulted him. He had gotten hold of the paper Adam and Zosie brought back from Sudbury and sat at the table reading it, making himself conversant with the facts. And Adam had come in and asked where Rufus was. Or had he asked that? Had he spoken at all? Adam was always going around asking where Rufus was, so it might be that he was remembering wrongly and Adam had said nothing, had not even glanced at him as he passed through the kitchen on his way to the back door with the baby in the portable crib.

"It had started to rain," he had said to Lili, "and Vivien had gone out onto the terrace to bring the quilts in. The terrace had been like a great bed covered with quilts from end to end. She was out there and Rufus was in the study listening to the radio and drinking gin."

"What did Adam say?"

"When I suggested the ransom? First he said we couldn't do it and then he said he didn't know and then how would we do it. He put the crib on the floor and sat down at the table. I thought they'd trace a phone call and anyway we didn't have the number and we couldn't very well ask directory inquiries for it. So I said send a letter, cut words out of this newspaper and stick them on paper. Adam said we mustn't ask very much. I mean not some huge sum. He said we should ask ten thousand pounds because any ordinary middle-class people could raise ten thousand pounds if they had to."

"I don't suppose we're middle-class then, are we?" said Lili.

"Adam took the kiddy upstairs again. We cut the newspaper up, sitting in our bedroom, Vivien's and mine. The Deathbed Room, Adam called it, because of this picture on the wall of a dead child and its parents crying. When we'd done the ransom note, Adam took the picture down and said he was going to take it out of the frame and burn it. But he didn't. Not then, not till later on.

"We'd decided to post the note in London but we couldn't do that till the next day. Adam said he'd get Rufus to post it since Rufus was going back to London anyway, and he was sure Rufus would do it, it was the kind of thing that would tickle him. I'm only quoting, Lili, that was what he said. But he couldn't tell him then because Rufus had gone out, he'd gone off to the pub in Goblander on his own.

"Vivien was standing in front of the stove drying herself. Her dress was wet but the other one, the blue, that was wet too, still out on the line. Adam told her he was going to take the baby back that night.

"What happened after that was rather strange. Vivien didn't seem to know Rufus had gone out. She went up to have a bath and when she came down I was there alone—as usual—and Adam and Zosie were off together somewhere, in their room maybe. I didn't exactly tell Vivien that Adam and Rufus had gone out together to take the baby back, but I let her think it. She asked me if that's where they were, you see, and I said that's what I understood, though the ransom note was in my pocket all the time and the kiddy was upstairs. I don't know what I thought would happen when the baby cried, but I didn't think of it. You don't when you're not used to babies."

"I suppose not," said Lili.

"Vivien sat sorting out her flower remedies and she went to

bed early. We all did—except Rufus. You see, we'd lived outside in the sun and warmth all the time we'd been there and suddenly there was no sun and no warmth anymore. We didn't know what to do with ourselves. The baby didn't cry, or if it did we didn't hear it. Zosie came down to the kitchen for some milk just as I was thinking of going to bed. She was just like a young mother, she was changed, happy and practical and looking tired. I lay awake for a long time and so did Vivien. We talked and she kept saying how relieved she was they'd taken the kiddy back. She wanted to know where they had taken her, what plans they had made. They would be sure to have taken her somewhere safe, wouldn't they? Did I think they would have thought of phoning the parents to let them know? All that sort of thing. She went on and on and then, somewhere around midnight or later, we heard Goblander come back.

"Rufus used to go to pubs that didn't keep to licensing hours, they'd stay open till one or two sometimes, it was all a fiddle, you know, pretending they were the landlord's private guests. Rufus didn't care about it being illegal. Vivien thought Adam was with him, she thought they'd come back from London, and I didn't contradict her. I wanted to go to sleep and I thought it would all sort itself out in the morning."

"Well, it did," said Lili. "And now you blame yourself because if you hadn't suggested asking for a ransom, they really would have taken the baby to London and been coming back."

"Yes."

"I think you're right to blame yourself," said Lili.

He had thought she would adjust to it and hold him in her arms but she had not. And later on she had said she did not think she would come to bed but he should go, she wasn't tired, she would sit up for a while. It had been a very quiet night, humanity and the elements equally silent. Shiva lay in bed in that silence remembering noise, remembering the sounds of Rufus's return, his running feet slapping on the wet gravel, the front door slamming behind him as he came into the house. Vivien had turned over and sighed and murmured, "Good night, Shiva," and slept immediately, her breathing gentle and regular. All their nights except one cool one had been warm, moonlit or starry, blue velvet nights, the curtains flung back, the windows open. That night was cold and from time to time rain slapped against the glass. . . .

A rain so fine that it hung rather than fell, misted Fifth Avenue. Shiva walked along the deserted street. At the Forest Road end all the windows were boarded up after the riots of two nights before, giving the street a strange look as if it were scheduled for demolition. No one spoke to him, no one catcalled him as sometimes happened. But as he passed The Boxer and was crossing the street a stone no larger than a piece of gravel struck him on the cheek. It struck him with a sharp, painful sting and Shiva put up his hand to feel the place.

Another stone, uncannily describing the arc of the first, stung the back of his raised hand. Shiva wheeled around in the misty dark. A door slammed somewhere. The street was empty but he sensed, or imagined, many watching eyes. At least it had happened to him and not to Lili. He stopped outside his own house and stared at the fence.

The graffiti, done with aerosol paint, read: *Go Home to Pakistan*. Shiva stretched his mouth into a bitter smile. He was remembering forbears of his, his grandfather and his father's uncles, who had hated the name of Pakistan more than any Walthamstow Jamaican or Irishman could conceive of. Tomorrow he would try to clean that off or maybe spray over it; he would have to think about that. What he disliked was the knowledge it would be there overnight, it marked his house, it located him and Lili as enemy-victims or potential victims.

He went in, closing the door quietly behind him. A letter, waiting to be posted, addressed to his mother-in-law in Salzburg, lay on the shelf where the phone was, where Lili had laid down her gloves. He thought, when women leave their husbands, they go home to their mothers, they write and ask their mothers if they can come home to them. It was nonsense he was thinking, he told himself as he went through the little house to find her.

Adam had not told Rufus about the ransom note that night. This was because he had a half-formed idea that he might be able to get Rufus to post the letter without telling him what it was. Rufus had shown no interest in the parentage of Catherine, had not even glanced at the newspaper as far as Adam knew, and now the paper was not available for him to look at, for after Adam and Shiva had cut the words out they had stuffed the remains of it into the kitchen stove.

Rufus would wonder, though, why Adam had printed the name and address on the envelope and used a disguised, back-sloping printing at that. It was no good hoping Rufus would not bother to look at the envelope. He would be bound to because he was going to have to buy a stamp for it. Neither Shiva nor Adam had any stamps. Adam thought Rufus might not want to be involved, even remotely, in what would be, after all, a criminal act. When he thought of it like that, Adam himself felt quite sick and at the same time he felt it was all unreal and he could not truly be involved in it, not he. On the other hand, they were going to have to hand the baby back sometime, and however they did it, at some risk to themselves, so why not get paid for that risk?

For a long time that night Adam had lain sleepless, listening to the rain, the thunder that grumbled softly like a beast stirring in its sleep, the light breathing of the baby and the uneven clicking in her throat. It was cooler than it had been at any time since they came to Ecalpemos, so they had a couple of those quilts over them as well as the sheet, and for the first time Adam was able to hug Zosie in her sleep, to hold her in his arms and rest his head against her fragile shoulder. It was also the last time, and if he had known that, he would have luxuriated in it more, given himself totally to the joy of it, instead of worrying about Rufus and stamps and printing on an envelope.

Now, ten years afterward, he could not remember what the ransom note had said. It must surely have told those Ryemarks how to contact him or have said how he would contact them. Instructions must have been contained in it, a location proposed for where the money should be taken, a prohibition on calling the police, and so on. But all he could now recall of it was the sum named, the ten thousand pounds.

He and Zosie could have lived on that for two years, he had believed, and naïve as he was, green as he was, he had still somehow known that this would suffice him, that if he could have her at Ecalpemos for two years, it was the best he could hope for or ask, and then he would return to the real world, sell the house, go back to college. What he had felt was impossible would have been to return home when the others returned, give up the house, become a student again, for somehow he knew that his relationship with Zosie, his love for her, would not survive out there in the harsh light but only here in the dream country of Ecalpemos.

He held Zosie, her back curled against his chest, as if lying down she were seated in his lap, and he held her right hand in his right hand, feeling the gold ring on her little finger. They would be alone here together, everyone else gone and perhaps the baby gone too. They could have a baby of their own if Zosie wanted one— why not? Zosie might be pregnant with his baby already for all he knew. He had done nothing to stop it.

Downstairs the front door slammed. That was Rufus coming in. He heard Rufus mount the stairs and go to the Centaur Room and after a while he was aware that the rain had stopped. The only sound was a steady drip-drip-drip from the guttering on the corner of the house and that, too, slackened, the gaps between the drips growing longer, finally ceasing altogether. A profound silence spread over land and sky, the air washed clean and sharply fragrant, the wind fallen. It was black-dark but the open window showed up dimly as a gray, very faintly luminous rectangle. His legs felt stiff and his left arm ached, but if he turned over he would have to relinquish his hold on Zosie and he could by no means be sure that she, too, would turn and put her arms around him. Was that a test of love? If in your sleep you instinctively turn to embrace the lover, was that a test? He had not come up with an answer but had turned over just the same, though Zosie, he recalled, had not turned with him to hug him in her arms.

For all that, he had slept quite quickly once he was on his right side. The Romans—or was it the Greeks—made their slaves sleep on the right side so as to rest the heart. There was something soothing and reassuring about the black silence that was not broken by any sound from the baby sleeping in the drawer.

An old Morris Minor van stopped at the lights ahead of Rufus. He drew the Mercedes up behind it. The van was the same dark green as Goblander had been, the same age, too, judging by the license plate, so therefore very old by now. Holding up well though, Rufus thought; it had probably been carefully looked after while Goblander would long ago have perished. Things were always going wrong with it even in those days.

Because he expected it to be rickety and uncomfortable—and because, let's face it, he was very drunk—he hadn't noticed anything particularly amiss when he came home alone from the pub. It had seemed a bit bumpy coming down the drift but it was always pretty bumpy. He woke up next morning about ten with a dry mouth and banging head, though nothing like the hangover he would have had today after the amount he had drunk. He got dressed and carried out a bundle of his stuff to put in the back of Goblander, intending to leave around lunchtime. By then, he remembered, he'd been looking forward to getting back to London, a better place to be when the weather was gray and wet. The flat tire was a nuisance but no worse than that. By a piece of luck, when he had had that big repair job done back in June, he had replaced the spare tire with a new one. He was standing there, making up his mind to start changing that wheel, when Shiva appeared carrying an envelope.

He came out of the front door holding up an umbrella and he was very formally dressed for any inhabitant of Ecalpemos in gray flannel trousers and gray and white striped shirt and black leather jacket.

"The rain it raineth every day," Shiva said in a way that sounded a bit like Adam.

The umbrella had a gold band around the handle and was probably Hilbert's as was the gray Pringle sweater Rufus had found in a drawer and pulled on over his T-shirt. He took the envelope, read the printing.

"What's this?"

The rain had started to come down quite heavily and Shiva held the umbrella over Rufus. "Adam wants you to post it for him when you get to London."

"Does he now? What is it, some sort of ransom note?"

Now, that had been guesswork on Rufus's part and even as he said it he did not really believe the envelope could actually contain a demand for money. He could not believe this of Adam. His disbelief was founded not on moral grounds but on simple incredulity that anyone he knew as well as he knew Adam would do anything so foolhardy. He was not even sure that he believed the account he had been given of the stealing of the baby. There was more to it than he had been told, or less to it. A very strong instinct for self-preservation was sending him home that day to a safer environment, but at the same time he had never accepted that he or any of them were in very great danger. Games were being played, that was all, and games of which he was largely ignorant and wished to remain so. If he had been aware of the whole truth, he would not have slept the previous night, but he had in fact slept soundly. If he had known what had actually happened and what Adam and Shiva were up to, he would not have waited till the morning but have gone the night before. Or tried to.

"You've a flat tire," Shiva said.

"Yes, I know."

"I will give you a hand."

"Not dressed like that you won't," said Rufus. "Who are Mr. and Mrs. Ryemark and why has someone printed this address?"

So Shiva explained. He was careful to explain that the ransom idea had been his own, and he seemed proud of it. Rufus said: "Come back into the house."

They went into the drawing room because Vivien was in the kitchen. She had the radio on and a burst of music and then a man's voice were just audible.

"What's in this letter?"

"Adam is asking for ten thousand pounds. The mother is to bring it to Liverpool Street Station, one hundred yards along platform twelve. One hour later she'll find the baby in the station mothers' room."

"I don't believe it!"

"No one will be hurt, Rufus. Adam won't hurt the baby if they don't pay. And when they pay, why is it worse than ordinary stealing? I don't see why it's different from Zosie stealing that silver bracelet or that camera. Except there's more money involved."

"I'll have nothing to do with it," said Rufus. "And if you take my advice, you won't either. What are you thinking of? You want to do medicine as a profession, don't you, yet you'd get yourself into this shit?"

"I'm not going to take any of the money, Rufus."

"For Christ's sake, there won't be any money. There'll be a policewoman with a suitcase full of paper and another one to go and get the baby."

"If that's what you think, Rufus, you'd better tell Adam. But I can tell you he's sold on the idea."

"I shan't tell him anything," Rufus said. "I shall change the tire on my car and get myself out of it."

But he had got no farther than the front door when Adam came down, wild-eyed, his face working, white as a sheet, and from upstairs came a long, keening wail.

SIDS, Rufus very well knew, ranks after congenital abnormality as the most usual cause of death in very young babies. Generally it affects infants from two weeks to one year old, but its peak incidence is between two and four months. All classes are affected by it, though there is a statistical relationship to poor home conditions and a degree of neglect or mere inattention. About 1200 babies in Britain die of SIDS every year.

This much he had known then while he was still a student but he had never seen a case. Catherine Ryemark was the first and because of her, when he saw another as a house officer in a hospital in the East End of London two years afterward, he was able to diagnose at once. But his hand had trembled and his mouth gone dry.

That day, that first time, he had gone up the stairs two at a time and run into the Pincushion Room and snatched the child out of the cradle Zosie had made for her in a drawer. Zosie was sitting naked on the bed rocking from side to side, an unearthly unhuman sound issuing from her closed lips, a thin, catlike wail. The baby felt cool but not cold, her face waxen but not blue, her blue eyes clear and staring but empty of their vital force. Rufus tipped her upside down and began compressing her chest with his thumb. He gave her kisses of life, his mouth over her cold, pearly lips.

"She was lying with her face down," Adam kept saying. "She was lying with her face down."

Zosie's keening rose an octave.

"Make her shut up," Rufus said. "Take her away."

She wouldn't go, she clung to the bedpost. Rufus continued to work on the baby, but he knew she was dead, it was useless, hopeless, she had been dead before he began. He could feel what little warmth remained in the tiny fragile body receding under his hands.

"What is it? What happened to her?"

Rufus didn't stop even then. He didn't look at Adam.

"Sudden Infant Death Syndrome," he said. "Cot death to you."

18

They were not experienced parents. They didn't know about babies, how they don't let you sleep until ten or eleven in the morning. Adam had not even thought about it. He would have been surprised and even angry if the baby had disturbed him in the night or wakened him early, but he wasn't at all troubled by these things not taking place. Nine years afterward, when he was married and Abigail was newly born, he scarcely slept, he was too afraid, and when he grew hopelessly exhausted and fell into a doze he would wake and jump up in horror, certain Abigail had died while he slept. For nearly three months, until Abigail had passed the age of Catherine Ryemark, he had made Anne take turns with him in staying awake to watch over her. Or, rather, he had tried to make Anne take turns, and it was her unwilling half-hearted compliance and her ridiculing of his fears that had caused so much damage to their marriage. It made an abyss between them, only Adam knew that it was his own past experience and personal knowledge that had really caused this rift.

He had fallen asleep that night while it was still very dark, two or three hours before dawn probably. Just before he woke up he dreamed he was out with Hilbert's gun in the wood when a large animal appeared between the trees in the distance. Adam saw, though without surprise, that the animal was a lioness, a beautiful nervous beast of a pale straw color. He lifted the gun and took aim, but before he could fire, someone seized him. He woke up to find Zosie shaking him.

"You were making awful noises. You were snorting."

The room was full of clear gray light. It was broad daylight but for the first time for months there was no sun. He turned over and put his arms around Zosie and she cuddled up to him.

"Isn't Catherine good? She's slept for hours and hours. She must like it here, she must like us."

"I don't suppose it's very late. It's probably only about six. Go to sleep again."

"I've had enough sleep," said Zosie. "I do feel happy. Are you happy?"

"Of course I am."

"I wish I could show her to my mother. But I don't suppose I can."

"Don't even think of it." Worries of the day ahead had begun to crowd into his mind, pushing sleep away. Rufus was going and with him they would lose their transportation. He couldn't remember what he had done with the letter, brought it up here with him or left it with Shiva. He put out his hand to the table by the bed, feeling blindly for the envelope he might have left there, encountered instead his watch. "You were right," he said to Zosie. "It's ten past eleven."

She sat up. In seconds she was out of bed and across the room. "Poor Catherine will want her breakfast!"

What fools they had been, what children, not to know that when a healthy baby wants breakfast it yells for it. It doesn't lie meekly waiting like some elderly hospital patient. Zosie knelt down, she bent over the drawer, gave a shocked gasp, then a long high scream. He would never forget the sound of that scream or his own sight of the baby, her face deep into the pillow, her body utterly still, and the feel of her skin, cool and waxen.

They got Rufus, or he did. Zosie sat on the bed, hugging herself, swaying back and forth, making a noise like a cat howling. Adam meant to try to explain lucidly to Rufus but all he could say was, "She was lying face downward, she was lying face downward."

Rufus turned the baby upside down and massaged her chest and gave her the kiss of life. She had been dead long before he got to the Pincushion Room, before they even woke up, perhaps before dawn. If he had looked at her while he lay wakeful listening to the rain and the dripping gutter, could he have saved her then? He knew it was what they called cot death before Rufus told him.

Zosie pushed him away screaming when he tried to get her out of the room. She knelt at Rufus's feet and put her arms around his knees and said in a little thin mad voice that the baby had died because she had swallowed her ring.

"She did *what*?"

"Of course she didn't swallow your ring," said Adam. "You've got your ring on."

It was the only thing Zosie did have on. He pulled the sheet off the bed and wrapped it around her. She began keening again. In a singsong voice she said, "I put my ring on her but her little fingers were too small for it."

"It's nothing to do with your ring," said Rufus. "It's not known what causes cot death but it may have something to do with the respiratory center in the brain that controls breathing shutting off."

Adam was trying to control a desire to scream himself. "What makes that happen?" he said, stammering.

"It could be some sort of infection or have something to do with inhaling food—I mean milk in this case. Perhaps she had a cold. Did you hear her wheezing?"

Adam couldn't remember. He said helplessly: "What are we going to do?"

Rufus didn't answer him. He said something Adam would never forget, that would haunt him forever, whatever the outcome of all this. And he said it to be cruel.

"There is a theory that cot death could be due to fear. Things are not the way the child has been used to. The tranquility of routine has been disturbed. It isn't the mother's face that the child sees when first she wakes."

Adam shuddered. He felt himself shrink in pain. They both looked at the demented girl rocking herself this way and that, her head flung back, animal sounds trickling from her half-open mouth. Rufus's words had not touched her. She hadn't heard them.

"I've got something I can give her." Rufus meant a sedative drug. "And we ought to make her a hot drink."

It was then that Adam caught sight of the envelope with the Ryemarks' name and address printed on it sticking out of Rufus's pocket. He made a sound of pain and put his hands up over his mouth.

"Christ," he said, "that bloody letter."

"It doesn't matter now."

"Did you mean that? Is it true? I mean about the baby being afraid because it's the wrong face it sees?"

"It's what I've heard. It's a theory I read somewhere."

"Why should she die because she was afraid?"

"I'm not saying she did. It's only a theory. No one's proved it. You know how animals play dead? Pretend to be dead to deceive a predator? The theory is that it's something like that babies do and then they really do die."

Adam turned away his face.

"You're not making me feel any better."

"I'm not in the business of making you feel better," Rufus said roughly. "I'm telling you what I think, what the possibilities are. Right?"

"You won't go, will you, Rufus?" Adam said like a child, pleading like a small child. "For God's sake, don't go and leave me with this lot."

"I won't go," said Rufus.

Zosie had stuffed the end of the sheet into her mouth. Her head hung down over her knees. The sounds she was making were like the grunts of a gagged person.

"What are we going to do?" Adam said again.

"Stay here. I'll get her something."

Adam tried to put his arms around Zosie. He tried to pull away the sheet from her mouth. The muffled noises she made turned to a thin, choked scream emerging from the folds of sheet. He turned away, twisting his hands within each other, wringing them. He looked at the dead little baby with feelings of terror and pity and disbelief. She lay on her back, her eyes wide open, her skin bloodless, pale as ivory. Remembering something he had read of or perhaps seen in films, he pulled Vivien's red shawl up to cover her face.

Rufus came back with something hot in a mug. He had got

barbiturates from somewhere, "downers" that he had bought from Chuck, Adam thought. Zosie hit out at the mug and Rufus nearly dropped it, tea splashing everywhere. But after a while he did manage to calm her, easing the sheet from between her lips, talking softly to her, not comforting her but telling her screaming and crying wouldn't help, would make things worse. He held the two red and black capsules out on the palm of his hand and offered her the half-empty tea mug and, silent now, white and aghast, she took the capsules and drank, gagging on the tea with a sob, but drinking it down.

Watching Rufus's every movement, Adam realized he was relying on him utterly. Rufus would save them; Rufus would be their rock.

"Don't ask me what we're going to do, please," Rufus said. "Don't ask me that again. I don't know yet."

"Can we keep it from the others?"

"Shiva knows," said Rufus.

Zosie went to sleep very quickly. She had already slept for about twelve hours and a couple on the previous afternoon, but that didn't stop her sleeping again.

"If she's never had these things before," said Rufus in a tone of satisfaction, "she'll probably sleep all day and half the night."

They told him nothing. Shiva had minded more about that than about the baby's death. Well, then he had, at that particular time. Remorse came later. At the time his exclusion from the drama, the tragedy being enacted at Ecalpemos, mattered more to him than anything.

He and Rufus had been talking about the ransom note and Shiva had felt quite sufficiently put down and admonished. Rufus was going back to change the tire on the van and he, Shiva, was thinking he would offer to help and thereby—yes, he admitted it— get himself back into Rufus's good graces. Up till then, up till that moment, he still cherished dreams of Rufus saying, "Let me know when you get into medical school. Give me a ring. We might meet and have a drink." But then Adam had come running downstairs, saying he wanted Rufus, Rufus must come because he thought the baby was dead.

Shiva just stood there in the hall. Then he walked through the house to the kitchen and started to make tea. He made all the movements mechanically just to have something to do, to keep moving. Besides, he felt the need for strong hot tea. At that time he thought Adam—or Zosie—had somehow killed the baby. He decided he would tell Vivien—to be revenged upon them presumably.

In a little while Rufus came in and saw the teapot on the stove and said: "Pour me a cup of that, would you?"

Distant, doctorlike, indifferent.

"What's happened?" Shiva said.

"You heard Adam say, didn't you? The baby's dead."

Rufus took the note out of his pocket, opened the door of the stove and thrust the envelope inside, on top of the glowing coal. He went back the way he had come without another word, carrying the tea mug. Shiva went outside and into the garden, looking for Vivien.

He had told all this to Lili last night, before he made his confession, how he meant to find Vivien and tell her everything. The two of them together could go to the police and explain everything that had happened. The ransom note seemed unimportant, an irrelevancy. It was destroyed now anyway, burned, and it might never have existed.

And then, as he walked along the grass below the terrace, passing the stone figures he had always thought ugly and antierotic, he realized that Vivien would ask him why Adam had not taken the baby back on the previous night as he had undertaken to do and he, Shiva, would have to explain that it was he who had stopped him. A glimmering of that feeling of self-hatred began at that moment. He stood still, his hand to his forehead, looking around him, looking at the garden.

"If I had been asked," he said, "I would have said the garden was a blaze of color, a mass of flowers, but in fact by then there were no more flowers. They were all over, finished, or else dried up. I looked at the place that morning, I looked with new eyes, I suppose, and it was just a wilderness I saw, a desert. The rain had come too late. There were dead trees with the leaves shriveled on them and plants dried up like straw. The apples were being eaten up by wasps and the plums Vivien brought in from the fruit garden were full of worms.

"We sat in the kitchen cutting up the plums for stewing, cutting out the maggoty bits. It made you feel sort of sick, you didn't feel like eating them. I knew I wouldn't eat them when Vivien had cooked them anyway. I just went on doing it mechanically. What I wanted to do was run away. I wanted to run away and hide, cut myself off absolutely from that place and everyone in it. It was dreadful being in that kitchen with Vivien and hearing her talk so—well, innocently. Rufus had told her the baby had been taken back to its parents, that Adam and he had taken it back, and she was relieved in a grave sort of way. She said to me she didn't think she could go to Mr. Tatian now, though. She couldn't take the job after what she knew, the Ryemarks being people he knew, you see. It would be wrong, it would involve deceit.

"Vivien was so circumspect in every aspect of her life. She daily examined her motives and her actions, it was all-important to her. Although she wasn't prepared to tell lies, she thought she could go so far as to phone Mr. Tatian and tell him circumstances beyond her control prevented her taking the job. That was true, after all. It grieved her to let him down at the last moment, but as she saw it, she had no choice. The facts that she would have nowhere to live, nowhere to go, no income, didn't affect her decision at all. As soon as the van came back she would get Adam or Rufus to take her to the village and from there she would phone.

"I felt responsible for her and I didn't want to be. I just saw all this as adding to my troubles. If she didn't go the next day, what would Adam do? I was afraid all the time, too, of the police just turning up.

"In the middle of the afternoon I packed the two bags I'd brought with me, I didn't have much and they weren't very heavy. I'd made up my mind to walk to Colchester. It was ten miles, but I thought I could walk ten miles, as I'd been having a lot of exercise lately, I was quite fit. Some motorist might stop and give me a lift, I thought."

"What about your responsibility for Vivien?" said Lili.

"I'd tried to dissuade her from phoning Mr. Tatian. I'd tried telling her that sometimes she should put herself first. It was useless. And I was no good to her anymore. She took up with me in the first place because I was Indian and she had some sort of mystical feeling about Indians, that they had something special to offer her, that they were more civilized than other people. But she'd found out that I was just ordinary, just like anyone else only inside a brown skin. I wasn't a prophet or a poet or a saint.

"I told her I was going, I didn't just sneak off. Rufus I couldn't get hold of, he had shut himself up in the Centaur Room and locked the door. She didn't put up any objections, I think she was glad to see the back of me. I walked off up the drift carrying my bags and when I got halfway up I met Adam coming out of the wood.

"He begged me not to go, he implored me. It was flattering, that, to be wanted at last. He said he relied on me to take Vivien away. If she was allowed to do what she wanted and phone Mr. Tatian and give up the job, she would stay on at Ecalpemos, he would never get rid of her. So I went back to the house with him. I gave in."

"Did you try to get Vivien to go?"

"Where could I take her? That was the trouble with all of us. We had nowhere to go except back to our parents. We could either stay where we were or go back to our families. And Zosie, or so we thought, didn't even have that. In the end Rufus drove Vivien to the village to phone Mr. Tatian, but she couldn't get a reply. There was nothing to do but for her to try again the next day.

"You know what happened the next day. I've told you before."

"I know what happened," Lili said.

"And after that I went home and immediately I got ill. It was a sort of nervous breakdown, they said. I was ill for a year and by then I'd given up the idea of being a doctor. I gave up the pharmacology too. You see, I could never make myself see it as all inevitable, as something I couldn't have prevented. If I'd stuck by Vivien in the first place, Rufus would have supported us, he was nearly there. If I'd said the baby must go back, we'd have taken her back somehow."

"And Rufus—and Adam—might have had some respect for you."

Shiva shrugged. "Perhaps the baby wouldn't have died. Rufus thought she wouldn't have if she'd been at home or with people who knew how to look after her. Adam and Zosie neglected her, though that was the last thing they meant to do. They didn't know, they were ignorant.

"I could have taken Vivien to my auntie. It would have been a hassle, there would have been a lot of explaining, but I could have done it. It seemed easier to try to persuade her to go to Mr. Tatian as she had undertaken she would. I thought I could talk her into it. I didn't see what harm waiting another day would do. . . ."

It was a windy, cool evening of sporadic rain. Of all of them the only one who was innocent and tranquil was Vivien, who cooked a lentil dish and made a salad. The plums had been turned into a sort of mousse. While the food was cooking, Vivien stood in the kitchen ironing the blue dress. And upstairs, drugged by Rufus's barbiturates, Zosie slept on.

Adam could remember very clearly destroying the radio. He took it up into the wood in the afternoon, smashed it with a heavy stone, and buried the pieces under the thick soft leafmold. Coming back he had met Shiva sneaking off, running away really, but he had made him stay on. When she had finished her ironing, Vivien started looking for the radio. She wanted to hear what the Ryemarks' reaction had been to the return of their child, she wanted to rejoice with them, she said. Adam went upstairs to look at Zosie. Every five minutes he went in to look at her. She was still asleep and he didn't like it in spite of what Rufus had said, he didn't like her sleeping on and on like that, dead to the world.

Vivien thought she hadn't come down because she was too upset at parting from the baby. She said she would go up and talk to her and offer her some of her Bach rescue remedy and when Adam said no, not to do that, she was asleep, she said: "Will it be all right if I stay on a bit, Adam, just till I find myself a job?"

"You've got a job," Shiva said. "Why don't you just go ahead and take the one you've got?"

"I've told you why. It wouldn't be right. I should be deceiving him. Mrs. Ryemark might come to the house with her baby and I should be acting a lie even if I wasn't telling one."

"Life is too short to be so circumspect."

"How do you know it is, Adam? You're no older than me, you're not as old, so how do you know better? I think life's too long to do anything that we know is wrong before we begin."

She had been so earnest, yet so meek, too, never aggressive but talking in that soft low serious voice, humorless, utterly sincere. He saw her as one of those incubi that appear along life's route, clinging, insinuating, almost impossible to shake off.

"You can't stay here," he said, surly, short, looking down at the plate of food she had cooked.

She was terribly taken aback. This was not what she expected. "I mean for only a week or two."

"I am staying here alone with Zosie and that's final."

She looked at him, her hand going up to her mouth.

"Okay, so you think I'm ungrateful. I'm not. Thanks very much for all you've done. But it's over, right? The party's over, the summer's over. Shiva's going and Rufus is going and I'm afraid you'll have to too. Now excuse me, will you?"

He just made it to the bathroom. He held his head over the lavatory pan and was repeatedly sick. *Mal au coeur* was what the French called feeling sick and that was about right, that was how he felt, sick at heart. In the Pincushion Room Zosie slept, lying on her back, breathing regularly. He thought, suppose she isn't asleep, suppose she's in a coma? But he had to trust Rufus, he would trust him.

In the Deathbed Room where the newly ironed blue dress hung on a hanger from the wardrobe door handle, he unhooked the picture from the wall and with the dusty paper backing outward and the painted scene turned against his chest, he took it downstairs and outside into the garden. He was going to make a fire.

The site for it was just this side of the fruit garden wall. Adam had never before made a bonfire, but he thought paraffin might assist him and he found some in a can in the stables. The gale had blown dead branches and twigs down from the big trees. He went around gathering them up, looking with dismay at his wrecked garden. His lost Eden. The picture he threw into the flames without removing it from its frame. There was nothing subtle or ominous about its burning. A sheet of fire leaped from the shellac on the frame and engulfed glass and picture in seconds. The portable crib burned less easily. No doubt it was purposely made from some nonflammable material.

Later on, because he could not bear to think of sleeping—or even just remaining—in the same place with it, he took the drawer and its contents into the Room of Astonishment. He couldn't even remember why they had called it that, for there was nothing astonishing in there except a staircase that wound up into the loft from a closet The room was on the opposite side of the passage from the Deathbed Room but north facing and always rather dark. No one went in there.

He did not immediately get into bed beside the still heavily sleeping Zosie. His fire was still burning. He had lit it too close to the wall of the fruit garden and the smoke had blackened the bricks. That much could be seen from the window in the lasting glow from the fire. The night was dark, gusts of wind rising from time to time, moving black branches against a faintly paler sky. Earlier, before they separated for the night, he had said to Rufus that a kind of poetic justice would have been for the flames to spread to the house and set it on fire. At this point there would have been a rightness about the destruction of Ecalpemos.

A light moved on the lawn. It was someone with a torch. Adam saw that it was Shiva going up to look at the fire and obscurely he resented this, seeing it as interference. But he did nothing, only watched, saw Shiva take hold of a dead branch and poke at the fire, sending cascades of sparks into the air like fireworks.

Lili had left Shiva a note. It wasn't that sort of note, the sort he dreaded when first he saw the white square held firm on the table by a small vase with two chrysanthemums in it, but the customary line or two she sometimes wrote to remind him she had gone to her Bengali lesson.

He got himself some food from the fridge, tried to watch television. There was nothing about Wyvis Hall on television but there never had been since that first time. If he wanted an evening paper he would have to walk the length of the street to get it and he did not much care for the idea of that. He had not looked at his face in a mirror since he reached home but now he did and saw that his face was cut on his right cheekbone, a dried trickle of blood running down from the punctured skin.

Lili would be home by nine. He decided to meet her. The presence of the graffiti made him decide that, though he was by no means sure how he would be received, whether or not she had rejected him. The idea dismayed him, and if he had not clenched his hands and set his teeth, panic would have taken hold of him. He turned the television on again and made himself watch a quiz show. At about a quarter to nine he went out into the hall and picked up the letter to Sabine Schnitzler. There was no stamp on it. Shiva had a stamp in his wallet, he had several, eighteens and thirteens. Neither would be sufficient for a letter to Switzerland, but two thirteens would be enough. He stuck two thirteen-pence stamps on the envelope and thought, suppose she is writing to her mother to ask if she can come to her when she has left me, I should be carrying, so to speak, my own death warrant to the executioner. But he took the letter with him just the same and mailed it on the way to Lili's friend's house which was on Third Avenue.

He had timed it so that she was just coming down the steps from the front door. Salwar and kamiz she was again wearing this evening with her brown tweed winter coat over the pink silk trousers. In the dark the pallor of her skin did not show. If she took his arm, he thought, he would know all was well. She did take it, but lifelessly, and he knew nothing. They walked along in silence and there were no flying stones, no catcalls, no other people even.

The graffiti on his mind as they turned into Fifth Avenue, Shiva nevertheless decided not to point out the spray-paint letters to Lili. Approaching from this direction she might not see them. Of course she would see them tomorrow, but things were different in daylight. They came up to the gate and Lili wasn't looking to her left and didn't see them. In the distance Shiva heard someone make a whooping sound and then the noise of a tin can being kicked began. He hustled Lili quickly into the house and drew across both bolts on the front door.

As they were getting ready for bed he forced himself to ask her if she had forgiven him.

"I don't see that it's for me to forgive you things you didn't do to me," she said quite reasonably.

"All right then. Can you forget?"

"I don't know," she said. "I haven't forgotten," and that was all she would say.

Shiva lay in bed beside her—at least tonight she had not stayed up till goodness knows when, saying she wasn't tired—and thought what a fool he was to talk of forgetting when things had not really begun yet, when the gathering forces were only just starting the work of retribution. She would not be *allowed* to forget, he thought.

The sound of running feet awakened him. Feet came running down from the Forest Road end of Fifth Avenue, pounding on the sidewalk—two pairs of feet, he thought, but there were no vocal sounds. And that was odd, for those people never moderated their voices or restrained their words because it was the early hours and others were sleeping. The footsteps slackened, it seemed outside his own house, and it came to him that they might be writing more words on the fence. But then his letterbox, the box on the front door, gave a double metallic snap and he knew that they, whoever they were, had put something through it. Not something disgusting, he hoped. He heard feet stamping and the gate banged. Once before a parcel had come in this fashion and though he had never opened it, from the feel and the smell he guessed it was full of viscera, the insides of a chicken probably.

The feet that stamped kicked at a tin can. The clanging the can made, not merely kicked but kicked from one side of the street across to the other, woke Lili. She sat up and held him. Shiva put a bedlamp on. Even in his fear he was happy that it was to him she turned instinctively, holding onto his arm, looking up into his face.

"Something came through the door," he said. "I'll go down."

"Don't go down."

The sound of the rolling can went on and on, growing fainter but still audible. They had left the window open a little way at the top and the curtains quivered.

"I suppose the morning will do," he said. "It won't go away, will it?"

He put the light out. He felt the tenseness slowly go out of her, knowing that as soon as she relaxed she would sleep. Her back just touched his back and he was pleased because she did not flinch away. The deep silence that had succeeded the clatter came into the room and filled it with peace and filled Shiva's head, too, bringing the beginnings of sleep, the first hesitant waverings on the edge of unconsciousness.

It was the smell that brought him back from the brink and into total wakefulness. Because he was confused he thought for a moment that he was smelling the contents of the parcel. And in a way, of course, he was.

A crackling sound ripped through the house, a mindless chattering. Shiva got out of bed, smelling the burning which was strong enough to make him cough, to choke him, sucking the oxygen out of the air. He ran across the room and threw the door open and saw the whole hall on fire, a pit of fire down there, the flames strong and thrusting and greedy, as if fire were eating the house.

He gave a cry that was lost in the roaring of the fire. The flames came to climb the stairs and eat the banisters. Through it he could not see the door to the living room, which they had left open and through which the fire had burst and driven. A cascade of sparks broke over the burning staircase. Shiva retreated into the bedroom, slamming the door behind him, covering his mouth with clamped hands,

Whimpering, crying out, calling to Lili, he threw up the window sash and as he did so a great tongue of flame shot up from the burning bay below him. It seared his face and he backed, his hands up, as the long, curling, crackling flames licked into the room.

He turned blindly back to the bed and picked up the sobbing Lili in his arms.

19

The somber photograph of the blackened house, the account of the preceding fire and the search for arsonists, served only to remind Adam of that last night at Ecalpemos. He recalled how he had half-hoped, half-dreaded, his own house catching fire. It was an Indian man and his wife who had lived in that little terraced box on Walthamstow Street and they were both dead, the man dying in an attempt to save his wife, she surviving for an hour or two after the ambulance reached the hospital. A deliberate racist act, some policeman said on television. Adam did not catch the name of the couple or bother to read about them in the newspaper.

He fancied that during the previous night he had heard the sirens of fire engines. But would such vehicles be permitted to have sirens on at that hour? He didn't know. Perhaps he had imagined it, just as, ten years ago, he had imagined the sound of footfalls circling the house on that last night, or had dreamed of them.

Sometimes he thought that it was then he lost the ability to sleep soundly. His sleeping since had always been light, precarious. The footsteps passed beneath his window, went on, stopped, continued toward the corner of the house where the Centaur Room was and Rufus slept and went on to the stables. The sky was lightening, with dawn not sunrise. A bird cried, it could not have been called a song.

What had he feared? That they had tracked the kidnappers of the baby here? If so, what he did was foolhardy in the extreme. But he had not known what he was doing, he was overwhelmed and conquered by his instinct for self-preservation. He ran downstairs and into the gun room and took Hilbert's shotgun down off the wall. He loaded the gun and stepped into the dining room, approached the window, hiding behind the curtain.

There was no one there. He went into the hall and listened. The birds had begun their chorus, the twitterings of autumn, not spring birdsong. But there was no other sound. He opened the front door and went outside, the gun cocked. He must have been mad. Suppose it had been the police out there, for who else would have come searching for Catherine Ryemark?

Ecalpemos lay gray and barren in the gray morning. It was rather cold, the air having a chilly, humid feel, and he could smell stale woodsmoke. Still carrying the gun, he went to look at the site of his fire. It was dead, a sprawl of gray ash with the blackened metal frame of the portable crib balanced on a half-burned branch. He was aware of an awful silence, the deep silence of the countryside at dawn which the sound of birds does not seem to mitigate, as if the birdsong were something else, were on a different level of perception.

Had he dreamed those footsteps? It would seem so. He had no inclination to go back to bed but took himself into the gun room and huddled there in the windsor chair with the gun beside him. He must have dozed off, for he awoke freezing cold in spite of Hilbert's old shooting coat he had slipped his arms into. From the kitchen he could hear Vivien moving around and singing. Perhaps she always sang when she got up in the mornings. He had in the past been too far away to hear. It was "We Shall Overcome" that she was singing, the hymn of resistance, and the sentiments expressed maddened him, the simplicity of it and the assumptions.

He went upstairs. At last Zosie was awake. At the sight of him she gave an inarticulate cry and burst into tears, clinging to him, sobbing into his shoulder. It was strange and horrifying what had happened to him in those past twenty-four hours. He had lost his love for her. Overnight really it had gone. He had thought his feelings everlasting, profound, a reason for existence, as if he and she were all those things true lovers were supposed to be, one flesh, two halves of the one whole, all in all to each other and the world excluded. Twenty-four hours before he had wanted nothing so much as to live here at Ecalpemos with her, the others gone, the two of them in solitary bliss. She had been all sexuality to him but she had also been his high goddess. He was miserably aware now that it was a poor little frightened girl he held in his arms, an infantile creature, not very bright, not even very pretty.

"Stop crying," he said. "Please. Try and get yourself together."

She sobbed and shivered.

"Where's Catherine?"

"In our room. In the other room. She's to stay there, you're to leave her there, Zosie. Listen, we have to take her away from here today, we have to hide her somewhere. Yes, stop, please"—for she had begun to cry out in protest—"Zosie, she's dead. You know she's dead. She's not a baby anymore, she's not *there*. It wasn't our fault but we have to look after ourselves now. You don't want them to put you in prison, do you? You don't want us all to go to prison?"

He had meant to say that they would do what they had to do and then they must start to forget, come back here, just the two of them, and start forgetting. But he couldn't say it because he no longer wanted this. He didn't want to be here alone with her or anywhere with her. As for the two of them living together, having their own child . . .

Her face was swollen with tears, almost ugly. She smelled of sweat. He would have liked to shake her till her teeth chattered. It was your fault, he wanted to say to her, you brought all this on us, you with your crazy hunger for babies, your kleptomania, your lies. But he only set her upright on the bed, wiped her face on a corner of the sheet, handed her clothes to her item by item, helping her to dress.

"I'm not meant to have babies, Adam. Why are all my babies taken away from me?"

He was impatient with her.

"It wasn't yours. You'd no business with it."

"*She*. With *her*. She was a person." She pulled the gray sweater over her head, pushed her fingers through the fine pale hair. "Where are her things? Her clothes?"

"I burned them. I made a fire and burned everything."

As he looked again at the photograph, the skeleton of the house, its girders a blackened rib cage, he seemed to hear her wail again, her keening cry, fists clenched and shaken in the air. The shell of the portable crib had looked not unlike the burned bones of that house, reared up on a bed of smoldering ash with a soot-bleared wall behind.

Vivien was in the kitchen in her cream-colored dress, making tea in the big brown teapot Adam could remember his aunt Lilian using. And Shiva and Rufus sat on either side of the table, Rufus slicing up one of Vivien's smooth round loaves of brown bread topped with poppy seeds. It was like any other morning, any other day, only everything was happening much earlier. And outside, a little thin rain was blown in gusts against the windowpanes. He sat Zosie down at the table and put food in front of her, a mug of tea, a piece of bread with butter and honey. She began picking off the tiny blue poppy seeds and placing them on her tongue. She's mad, he thought, she's lost her mind.

Somewhere in the house a chiming began. A clock was striking. Adam started and shuddered. None of Hilbert's clocks had been set going since they came there.

"What the hell's that?"

"I wound up the grandfather clock," Rufus said. "On an impulse."

"Fuck you," Adam said, trembling. "Why can't you mind your own business?"

Ten times the clock struck. Last week he had hardly known there was such a time as ten in the morning. Vivien pushed a mug of tea over to him.

"Have a drink, Adam. It'll make you feel better."

Like a half-drowned kitten, Zosie looked, a rescued creature for whom there is yet no hope. She had her forefinger in her mouth, pulling down one corner of it. Vivien said, "Would one of you drive me to the village? I should like to phone Mr. Tatian."

Shiva looked angry. "You're still insisting on that? You realize how you are letting the poor man down, don't you? He is relying on you to come one and be nurse to his children. What will he do? Have you thought of that?"

"It's impossible," Vivien said. "I can't go there. Anything is better than my going there."

"I shall leave here without you then. I have my future to think of even if you haven't."

Adam could tell Vivien was waiting for him to say she could stay, that she would be welcome, but he wasn't going to say it. The bread they were eating she had made. Because of her the house was clean and everything smooth-running. By her house-keeping and her management she had probably saved him from denuding the place of furniture but he couldn't ask her to stay. Rufus hadn't looked at him since that outburst over the clock but now he did and Adam thought he could read a lot into that glance, especially when Rufus said, addressing himself to Vivien: "I'll take you back to London with me, if you like. If you want to go back to that squat you were living in, I don't mind taking you over to Hammersmith."

But Catherine Ryemark? What was Rufus indicating here? That he would take the tiny body with him or that he, Adam, left alone, was somehow to conceal it?

Rufus said, "Do you want to go into the village now?"

"The sooner the better, I suppose." Vivien looked troubled. She was making a decision to act quite against her personal desires, Adam could tell. She was doing this, as she did so many things, for an abstract principle. It mystified and mildly annoyed him. "I'll just go up and get my shawl," she said. "It's got quite cold. We've forgotten it gets cold but it does."

It was at this point that the post girl came. Shiva was the first to hear her. He sat quite still at the table, his head turned.

"What the hell's that?" Adam said.

They all thought it was the police, even Rufus. He got up and moved to a yard or two inside the window. The letterbox on the front door made its double rap and by that time Adam had been into the gun room and come back with Hilbert's shotgun. Shiva jumped up.

"My God!"

The red bicycle passed the window, a flash of red and silver only, as a bird might have flown by or a flag been pulled out by the wind. Rufus came in from the hall with an envelope in his hand.

"It was the mail," he said. "A bill. Are you crazy?"

"Jesus," said Adam, "I thought it was the fuzz."

"We all thought it was the fuzz. What were you going to do if it was? Kill them?"

"I don't know. Did they see you?"

"It was that girl again. How do I know if she saw me?" Rufus looked at the gun that Adam held pointing at the table. Limp, pale, wide-eyed, Zosie stared apathetically into the muzzle of it. "Put the bloody thing down. Christ, the sooner I get out of this madhouse the better."

From upstairs, a long way off, Vivien's voice came to them in a strange, drawn-out cry. Not a scream or a howl but a round O sound immensely protracted, a cry of sorrow.

They knew what had happened, what she had found. She had gone to look for her shawl. Adam, too late, remembered where that shawl was, that it had been used to cover the body in the tallboy drawer. Unable to find the shawl in her own room, Vivien had gone looking for it, recalling no doubt that she had lent it to Zosie for the baby.

They found themselves moving closer together, taking up a united stand along the back and the head of the table. Zosie got up and held on to Adam. There was silence in the kitchen but for Shiva clearing his throat, a nervous, muffled sound. Adam thought of the post girl, still not far off, no doubt having to push her bike up the drift. . . .

Vivien's footsteps sounded, running, along the passage, down the back stairs. Zosie began to whimper.

"Shut up," Adam said. "Shut up or I'll kill you."

Vivien opened the door and came in, her tanned face bleached as if she had jaundice. Her eyes had become big and staring, the whites showing all around the irises. She was goosefleshed and the down on her arms stood erect. He felt the hair rise on his own neck.

Incongruously Vivien said, "What are you doing with that gun?" And then, "Haven't you done enough damage?"

"It was cot death, Vivien." Rufus took a step toward her but she recoiled from him. "It was no one's fault. These things happen. It would probably have happened if the child had been in her own home."

"I don't believe you."

"Why should I tell lies about it? We're all in this together. There's no point throwing the shit around."

"You've lied to me once. You said you'd taken the baby back."

It was unanswerable. "Okay," Adam said. "We lied to you but we're not lying now." He wished he could keep his voice steady, he wished he could control the muscles of his mouth and throat. Rufus could. "D'you think Zosie would have hurt the baby? She loved her, you know that."

He had made a mistake in mentioning it. Zosie let out a wail, and rushing to the back door began pounding on it with her fists. If people are allowed to have guns, even in any sort of danger, people will use them. Adam had read this but never before put it to the test. He found himself raising the gun and pointing it at Zosie.

"Put that down," Rufus said.

It was brave of him not to be deterred by Adam's shout to mind his own business and keep out of this. He simply reached out and took the gun and laid it on the table. Vivien went over to Zosie and got hold of her arms, pulling her to her and holding her. She walked her back to the table, sat her down, sat beside her. Adam heard himself give a heavy sigh, a release of long-held breath.

"You must be brave, Zosie," Vivien said. "We're going to the police to tell them about this. I think you know that, don't you? The only thing now is to be open and honest about everything, tell them how you took the baby because you hadn't been well, because you'd lost your own baby. They won't be horrible to you and I'll be there. We'll all be there. We'll tell them how good you were to the baby, how you looked after her but she died just the same. Rufus will tell them it was cot death she died of and they'll listen to him because he knows about medical things."

"You have to be joking," said Rufus.

Vivien was measuring out drops from a little vial to give Zosie. They were her Bach rescue remedy. "There isn't anything else to be done, Rufus," she said gently. "We have to do it. We have to go to the village now and phone the police, or it might be better to drive to one of the towns. Yes, that might be best." Zosie was looking at her in fear. She smiled at her, gave her the cup with colorless liquid in it, the panacea that was supposed to be a restorative in any emergency. "They won't do anything bad to us, perhaps put us on probation at the worst. Zosie may have to have some sort of treatment, that's all they can do. You see, we didn't mean any harm, none of us did. The worst is that you three rather supported Zosie in keeping the baby, that's all."

Rufus had been watching Vivien's pouring of the rescue

remedy with contemptuous distaste. "They'd kick me out of medical school, that's *all*. I could say good-bye to all my prospects."

Shaking his head, swallowing, Shiva seemed to have difficulty in speaking, but he did speak, lifting his hands up to his neck in a curious gesture as if he were holding his head secure on his shoulders. "And what about me? My father? I am supposed to be getting to a teaching hospital."

"Do you really think those things important compared to what's happened here? This was someone's child, a precious child, and she's dead."

"They'd think we'd done something to her. We could go to jail for life," Adam said flatly.

Rufus shrugged. "Come on. Things are no different from what they were half an hour ago except that Vivien knows. So we go on as we planned. The first thing is for Shiva and Vivien to get ready and then I drive them to Colchester station. Right?"

She wouldn't have it. She stood firm. "No, it isn't right. I can't have anything to do with this, Rufus. I can't go in with you all. If the rest of you won't come with me, I shall go alone. There's a police house at Sindon."

"You're no driver, Vivien," Rufus said, and he came up to her and took her by the arm, a tall strong man, her weight and half as much again.

She shook him off. "I can walk."

"I'm afraid you can't. There are four of us to one of you. We can keep you here even if that means manhandling you."

One of the terrible things was that Vivien had said no more after that about going to the police, about telling anyone at all. She had declared her intention but had not repeated it after Rufus said that about manhandling her. Perhaps she had changed her mind and would not have gone. Adam could hardly bear to think this, even now. At the time, if he had thought coherently about anything at all, he had thought only that she must not be allowed to leave. But it was possible she never would have gone to the police. Though she hated what they had done, or what she believed they had done, she would not have shopped them, she would have been loyal. Alone, she would not have stood against them.

On the other hand, she had no bag with her. So in leaving the house she had not had the simple intention of escaping and making her way to London. Her clothes and her carpet bag were still upstairs, the box of flower remedies still on the table. But she prised off the hand Zosie had put out to clutch at her skirt and she pushed Rufus away. Her eyes lingered on Shiva, just looking at him without expression, but that blank gaze made him wince. She put up her hand and tore the Gestalt prayer down from the wall. Still holding the piece of paper, she opened the back door, but without a word, still not saying she would go to the police.

Somehow or other Shiva had got between her and Rufus, so that to reach her Rufus would have had to push him aside, and did not in fact reach her, did not come within feet of her. There was a rush of cold damp air into the kitchen and Vivien was running out across the flagstones. . . .

News from Wyvis Hall had disappeared underground. There had been nothing since Sunday. Adam thought he had observed this kind of thing before in the progress of a murder inquiry—or the progress that is made public knowledge—how day after day small paragraphs or a few lines would appear in newspapers to be followed by an ominous lull. A week might pass during which time guiltless readers would forget, dismiss the case completely from their minds. And then, suddenly, would come the short piece about the man helping police with their inquiries, succeeded the next day by the announcement of an arrest, a court hearing.

Rufus phoned to tell him the police had not come or been in touch. Adam was aghast to hear of the visit to Nunes. He felt he could never have dared approach it or that an invisible wall surrounded it and kept him out. As to the police, it was not worth their while to seek confirmation, for they had never believed his story. It was the coypu man they were interested in. He imagined Winder or Stretton or both of them closeted for long hours with the coypu man and the post girl and the farmer and Rufus's taxi driver while these people told them of the group of people living at Wyvis Hall, two girls among them, of the sounds of shotgun fire, of a baby heard crying, of a gardener peremptorily dismissed, of wine bottles, dozens of them, put out for the refuse collection each week, of a hasty departure, of new-cut turf in the clearing in the pinewood. . . .

There was nothing in the papers on Thursday. It was Anne's

birthday and they were going out to dinner. She had asked his parents to baby-sit because she couldn't find anyone else, she said, but Adam was annoyed by it. He didn't want to go out because he was afraid of coming in and finding the police waiting for him.

Lewis said, "Funny, that business at Wyvis Hall seems to have died a natural death." He sounded disappointed.

"Which is more than the people in the grave did," said his wife.

"Absolutely. You're right. I don't suppose we've heard the end of it." He said that Adam could offer him a small sherry if he liked, very dry if possible, but amontillado would do. The sherry glass did not have a Greek key design around its rim but Lewis asked just the same if this was "by any chance one of my poor old uncle's glasses."

Adam didn't answer.

"It's a bad business, all of it, I don't suppose that little cemetery will ever be restored. That little dog Blaze, a West Highland, you know, Anne—we had quite a funeral for him, do you remember, Beryl? I've a very strong notion you were there, too, Adam, but no more than a babe in arms. Your aunt Lilian read a piece of poetry, something of Whitman's about wanting to live with animals, and we laid the poor little fellow in the earth. Your aunt Lilian was a strange woman."

"Why do you call her my aunt? If she was anyone's aunt, she was yours."

Lewis went on as if he had not spoken. "Who would have imagined on that sentimental but rather charming occasion that the cemetery would be put to such a use?"

Adam said recklessly, "A girl I knew saw that dog's ghost on the back stairs."

Anne gave him a look of disgust. This time Lewis did reply. "Absolute rubbish. A load of twaddle. What girl?"

"Come on," Adam said to Anne. "We might as well go."

In the car she said to him, "Are you losing your mind or is there some purpose behind all this?"

A movement of his shoulders was all the answer she got.

"Why are we going out together like this? It's a farce."

"We're celebrating your birthday by quarreling in a restaurant instead of at home."

"I hate you," said Anne.

Those had been Zosie's words to him too. He had forgotten, or thought he had forgotten, but those words were the key that when touched gave entry to the last file of all.

"I hate you, I hate you . . ." as she tried to get hold of him, clutching at his clothes, tumbling over as he pushed her away.

He parked the car, the engine died. He sat at the wheel with his eyes closed. Then he made a great effort. He didn't want to remember any of this, he wanted to escape out of it to a blank screen. Anne had got out of the car and slammed the door. Adam also got out, lifting his face to the cold air, the thin sprinkling of rain.

It was the post girl on her bicycle he had been afraid of, that she had not gone, or not gone far enough, or was there waiting, her mercy to be thrown upon, her bicycle to be borrowed, her consent obtained to be a witness. . . .

But there was no one. He had seen no one. The drift was empty, windswept, under a gray tumbled sky. There was no one but the figure in the pale cotton dress running across the flagstones. And voices shouting and Zosie's voice raised in a thin wail. Following Anne across the pavement toward the doors of the restaurant, he found the escape key failing, the past inescapable, the present lost. He had raised the gun to his shoulder, braced himself for the kickback, and fired. She screamed and he fired again and this time she whirled around, shot full of arrows, fountaining blood, blood exploding from the little body, breaking in great scarlet splashes all over the cream cotton.

Now, as then, he stumbled, grabbing just in time the lintel of the door. In the dark entrance to the place he shook himself, opened his eyes wide, forced his mouth into a grin. Then after the third firing of the gun, he had fallen down, had lain spreadeagled on the stones, crying, "Stop, stop, stop, stop!"

20

When he came back from Nunes, or from his visit to his patient in a Colchester hospital, Rufus had found Marigold at home waiting unquestioningly for him. And he had not questioned her about her day either, though aware of how unnaturally they were behaving toward each other. It had been a precedent, he knew very well. Now she would never ask him and he would never ask her, they would get into the habit of doing separate secret things, bland and smiling and calling each other darling more often than could be sincere. But that evening, eating supper with friends who were another young married couple, he could not help feeling that her behavior with the husband was constrained. They behaved, he fancied, as if they intended to seem indifferent to each other while last time they had all been together there had been flirtatiousness. It was probably all in his imagination.

The days passed and he phoned Adam. He waited, as Adam waited, for more news from Wyvis Hall. As soon as he saw the name on the front page of the *Standard* he knew it was Shiva's. Manjusri. He remembered now. It was Shiva's house that had burned down and Shiva who had died trying to save his wife. A shop assistant, the newspaper called him, but it was the same one. Rufus, secret drink at hand, scoured the paper for what he had got into the habit of looking for every morning and every evening, and found nothing. But it was only a matter of time, he was sure of that now. Too many witnesses had been revealed for him to have much faith any longer in the possibility of escape. He had not begun making contingency plans, for there were none he could make, there were no options open to a doctor, a consultant, who had been concerned in murder and concealing deaths and concealing bodies. All he could do was psych himself up to behave with coolness and decorum when they came for him. But he was past feeling relief at the death or disappearance of witnesses, at the departure of Mary Gage, Bella's death and Evan's. For Shiva, looking once more at the photograph, he felt something almost alien to his nature, a kind of horrified pity. Yet in a way Shiva was better dead than facing what Rufus now saw as inevitable.

For Shiva had been even more deeply concerned than he. Shiva had thought up the ransom idea and his, too, was the idea of burying the bodies in the woodland cemetery. Sitting silent with the paper before him, Rufus thought of it now. He was too silent and Marigold's cheerful acceptance of his silence was almost unnerving. Weakening, Rufus had a vague absurd dream of being able to tell her, of weeping in her arms and of her weeping, too, and of love and commitment, but he steadied himself. That wasn't what he had ever wanted, certainly not what he would get. Almost better to contemplate poor Shiva than an alternative life he didn't have and never would. . . .

"We could put them up among the children—I mean the animals," Shiva had said. "No one would think of looking there, they'd be hidden there." And he had been pleased—*pleased* at that moment—because they had listened to him and agreed.

Or Rufus had and Zosie. Adam lay on the stones in the rain. He lay there till Rufus shook him and said, "Come on, get yourself together," and Rufus pulled him up and he covered his face with his hands. Shiva it was who carried the body into the house, covered it with one of those absurd heavy stiff monogrammed sheets. Already the rain was washing the blood off the stones. Rufus dragged Adam inside and stuck him at the table and gave him gin. Of course he had a secret bottle, a thick square bottle of Geneva he had bought with some of the gold chain money.

No one asked Adam why he had done it, then or later. He had done it, there was no point in asking. And the rest of them were already conniving, covering up, sticking together, planning how to survive. I never felt guilty, Rufus thought, only afraid of being found out. That's all I feel now. But Zosie, who took the baby, Shiva, who tried to get a ransom for it, Adam, who shot and fired that gun, how had they felt? Well, Shiva was dead.

Tears ran down Adam's face. He didn't try to stop them, nor did he seem ashamed of crying. How long had they just sat there in the kitchen, Adam and he and Shiva? Hours, minutes, half an hour? In retrospect it seemed a long time, it seemed as if they were waiting for something, and perhaps they were, perhaps they were waiting for Zosie to come down with the baby.

She took off her ring of gold plaited strands with the Z inside it and put it on the baby's finger. On the baby's thumb, rather, for it was too big for any of the tiny fingers but not too big for the thumb. In that curious way her own finger was stained black where that ring had been. It was a pointless act of sentiment, having no special relevance to the baby's situation or her relationship with it, whatever that might be. Rufus had been impatient.

"Let's get on with it."

The rain had eased up a little. In procession they went up into the pinewood, not yielding to the idea of using the heavy old wooden wheelbarrow that stood in the stables, but carrying the wrapped bodies, Rufus taking Vivien on his shoulders, and Zosie with the baby. Adam and Shiva each carried tools, the heavy spade and a fork, the lighter spade they had used to bury the coypu in the Little Wood being unaccountably missing. Or it had been unaccountable then. Now Rufus knew it had been taken by the gardener who came to Wyvis Hall at dawn and whose footsteps sent Adam to the gun room and the gun, who was in a way responsible for Adam's using the gun.

Adam woke very early on Friday morning, at about five. Waking had been preceded by a dream in which Hilbert and Lilian, with himself and Bridget and their parents in attendance, were burying the body of their only child in the cemetery in the pinewood. The body could not be seen, for it was sealed up in a tiny coffin of walnut veneered in a flame pattern. Lilian and

Hilbert looked less like themselves, or after a time began to look
less like themselves than like the parents in the picture. Adam
knew he had dreamed this because of what his father had said to
him the evening before about Blaze's funeral. He lay in the dark,
wondering if this was the day on which his world would end. He
had taken to wondering this every morning.

In the dream Hilbert and Lilian had been doing the digging
themselves, having selected the plot next to where Blaze was
buried, and they were digging deep. They dug deeper than their
own height, so that not even the tops of their heads showed above
the brink of the grave. When they had dug, Shiva and Rufus, and
then he had taken over from Shiva, they had not been so thorough,
and had gone down no more than three feet. If we had dug deeper,
thought Adam, if we had dug the statutory six feet down, none of
this would have happened. . . .

But it had been three feet, not six. Even so it took them a long
time and the worst part was putting the earth back, seeing the earth
trickle into the folds of cloth, the strands of hair. If the grave had
only been deep, deep enough for a man as tall as Rufus to stand in
and his head not show above ground level. They had been
oppressed with fear, and cold and wet, shivering in the rain,
wanting to get on with it and get it over. A Monday morning at the
end of summer and the end of the world . . .

Up there you could just hear the traffic, what there was of it, a
car or two passing, and once, horse's hooves. Shiva had cut the
turf back carefully before they began digging, cut it out in squares
with the spade. He had laid the squares on one side ready for
replacement when the grave was filled. Rain, which had been
falling intermittently all the time they worked, now came down in
a glassy sheet. Yet it was as if the rain were on their side, falling
swiftly on the grave to make the grass grow over it.

In the pinewood, among the dense growth of black tree trunks,
they took refuge. It was bone-dry in there, dark, scented and
close. You could hear the rain but not feel it. Hours seemed to
have passed since anyone had spoken, it was as if they had all
been stricken dumb, but inside the pinewood Adam spoke to
Zosie.

"Are you all right?"

She moved out of the circle of his arm. "Oh, yes."

They put the turf back and trod on it, pressing it down. The sky was all clouds, the treetops swinging. The cedar was doing its witchlike dance, clapping its branches in their black sleeves, when they came out of the wood and approached the house.

Shiva hung up the fork in the stable where the tools were kept but Adam held on to the spade. He went into the house, into the gun room where the turtle was and the fox came bursting out of the wall, and fetched the four-ten, the lady's gun, and then he and Zosie went down to the Little Wood and buried it near the spot where they had buried the coypu. He had meant to bury both guns, the lightweight shotgun and the heavier pump action, the one he had used, but when it came to the point he was afraid.

Up in the cemetery he had spoken only to remark on the rain falling, the rain being on their side. But Rufus had said: "We should all go our separate ways as soon as we can. We should pack up now and go."

"I haven't got a separate way," Zosie said.

Alone upstairs with Adam she said it as they bundled up their clothes into bags and Adam put the gun into Hilbert's golf bag. Zosie wrapped up the belt with studs in her pink T-shirt and put them and the rest of her clothes and the jeans she had made into shorts into her backpack.

"I shall go to my mother."

"But how will you? Where is your mother?"

She gave him a timid sidelong look, the small frightened cat, the hare that hears a stick break underfoot.

"Here," she said. "In Nunes."

"In *Nunes*?"

"They moved here from Ipswich a week before I came."

"Zosie, were you on your way to Nunes when Rufus picked you up?"

"Yes, of course. I did say to him to go to Nunes, though I didn't want to. I was scared. I knew they didn't want me. Well, they couldn't have. Look how they never searched for me."

Adam had had that feeling of faintness again that came from terror slipping out of control. He put his hand up to his head, pressing on the bone with cold fingertips. There was a cough, a knock, and Shiva came in. He was carrying Vivien's carpet bag.

"What am I to do with this?"

"I don't know. God knows."

"Can Rufus take me to my mother?" said Zosie.

Adam knew it was impossible. He tried to explain why. Their future safety lay in its not being known they knew one another or had been here. But Zosie would be bound to come out with it. Where would she say she had been? But even as he explained to her he felt that the responsibility for her should be his. Was he to abandon her? Where would she go? She had nowhere and no one. She had less than Vivien, who at least had had the squat and then the job with Tatian. . . .

Adam went downstairs, Shiva following him. He filled a glass with water and drank it, hoping it would stop his being sick. His stomach was empty and felt hollow but he knew that would not prevent him from vomiting.

Rufus sat at the table, his things ready, the van keys in front of him. He had emptied the fridge, packed the food into a box, switched the fridge off, and left the door open. Someone had washed and dried up the breakfast things. Shiva, presumably. And Shiva had put Vivien's flower remedies into the carpet bag. No one had eaten anything since breakfast. It would be a long time before any of them could eat, Adam thought.

He said, "Rufus, listen, what are we going to do about Tatian? He'll expect Vivien to come today. When she doesn't turn up he's going to wonder, isn't he? I mean, he's not just going to accept she's changed her mind."

"He's not going to tell the police either," said Rufus.

"He might tell them." Shiva had been a sick yellow color since the morning. He looked as if he were recovering from an illness or about to succumb to one. "It's his friends whose baby has disappeared. If Vivien doesn't come, they may connect her with that."

Adam sat down opposite Rufus. He felt weak, drained of all strength. The rain lashed the windows on a sudden gust and the start it made him give brought a sob up into his throat.

"Steady," said Rufus, quite kindly for him.

"I'm all right. I'll be all right."

"Sure you will. We're going to have to phone Tatian."

"Oh, God, no!"

"I'll do it," Rufus said quickly. "What else can we do? We're going to have to tell him Vivien's been taken ill or something like that. He knows where she lives, you see."

"He knows where she lives?"

"She told him Ecalpemos, Nunes, Suffolk. He's going to remember that when she doesn't come, and because the police will have interviewed him and asked him to let them know anything odd that has happened or does happen, he's going to tell them about her. And they'll be down here at every house. There aren't many houses in Nunes, so it won't take them long to find this one."

"That's what I said," said Shiva. "I said they'd question him."

Rufus's eyebrows went up. "So you did."

"Who's going to do the phoning?"

"Not you," said Adam. "You've got an accent. You sound Indian—or Welsh. He might be suspicious."

"Oh, I'll do it," said Rufus.

"And would you—I mean is it at all realistic to think of Zosie going home? She wants to go home to her parents in Nunes."

"In *Nunes*?"

"Yes, I know. She thought you might drive her home. I've told her it's impossible, but what alternative is there?"

She had provided it herself, coming quietly into the room and standing on the threshold wearing Vivien's blue dress.

The instant he heard Abigail, Adam got out of bed, went into her room and picked her up. He prepared orange juice for her, changed her napkin, loving to do these things, wondering how many more mornings he would be there to do them.

The paper came. He heard it fall on the doormat and the letterbox give a double slam. Like when the post girl brought the rates bill that time and then the electricity bill. The red flash of the bicycle past the window, the slam-slam of the letterbox.

Abigail sitting in the crook of his arm, he picked up the paper, stomach clutching, heart making it apparent to him that he possessed a heart in there in the cage of his ribs, sensations he had every morning now. He opened the paper and scanned the pages. Nothing, still nothing. There had been nothing since Sunday.

He wasn't interested in the post. He didn't receive many letters at home anyway. Bills would come and the occasional postcard and junk mail. This morning it was Anne who fetched the letters, wordlessly, cold-faced, putting the envelope down by his plate.

He was giving Abigail her breakfast and it was ten minutes before he opened it.

Rufus was shaking hands with Mrs. Shaw who was still enthusing over the success of her hormone replacement therapy when the special messenger arrived. His name was scrawled on the envelope and Rufus, though he hadn't seen it for ten years, recognized the handwriting as Adam's. It took all the nerve he had and all the resources to continue making amiable rejoinders, but he did continue, a paralyzed smile stuck on his face like a mask he had put on, and at last she was paying up and going and he could take the envelope—and its contents, whatever they might be—back into his room. With ten minutes to spare before the next patient.

You do not put off things because they threaten you, because you are afraid. It was a rule of life he had made his since before Ecalpemos. He opened the envelope with a paper knife, making himself breathe regularly. When he saw it was newsprint inside, he quailed but he unfolded it. Scrawled across the top of the sheet by a hand that had trembled were the words: *The Coypu Man.*

Instead of coming over to speak to him, Rufus had gone first to the bar. He saw Adam sitting in the corner and he raised his hand to him, went to the bar, and now approached, carrying two glasses. It was almost a week later. There was an intimacy in Rufus's manner that showed itself in the absence of any greeting or formal inquiries, and an extreme casualness too.

"I can drink them both if you don't want one," he said.

"Oh, I don't mind having a drink," said Adam.

Rufus lifted his glass. "Absent friends!"

That seemed to Adam in atrocious bad taste. He did not echo it. He said, "Most of it was in our own heads, wasn't it? There was never much in the papers, little paragraphs, a line here and there. Of course there was that bit on television while I was still away but nothing more. I suppose the police had an idea of the truth from the first. They never really suspected us or my great-uncle or Langan. They knew from the first it was the coypu man."

Rufus was looking strangely at him. "But it wasn't."

Shaking his head as if he were shaking off a delusion, Adam said, "I don't mean that. I mean all that questioning of me wasn't to find out about me but about the coypu man. Only I saw it back to front." He muttered softly, "My guilt made me see it back to front."

He looked terrible, Rufus thought, aware that he himself was looking particularly well. Only that morning a Mrs. Llewellyn (polyps and a partial prolapse) had told him he looked too young to be a consultant on Wimpole Street. Adam was gaunt and hollow-eyed, gray-skinned. And he couldn't keep still. Instead of relaxing now that all was over, he was fiddling with his glass, making those interlocking wet rings.

Rufus took the clipping from the *East Anglian Daily Times* out of his wallet, unfolded it, and laid it on the table. His glance picked out a few salient words, words he knew by heart anyway: "Zoe Jane Seagrove . . ." ". . . infant daughter . . ." ". . . stepfather Clifford William Pearson, died November 1976. An inquest verdict was recorded of suicide while the balance of his mind was disturbed. A police spokesman said that the Wyvis Hall case is closed and no further inquiries will be made."

"Do you want this back?"

"I shouldn't think so. I don't know who sent it to me, but it must have been someone who knew I'd—be interested is a bit of an understatement, isn't it? I suppose it was Shiva. There was nothing more, just the cutting in an envelope." Rufus said nothing, knowing it couldn't have been Shiva, suddenly averse to guessing who it might have been. "What do you think made her mother sure it was Zosie in that grave?" Adam said.

"The ring surely. She put her ring on the baby's hand."

"Yes."

"There would have been pellets of shot too mixed up with the gravel. Even if they had found it by sifting the gravel, those woods must be full of shot. Or perhaps they think Pearson shot her."

Adam said in a low voice, "She said to me once, 'He kills little things, he has no mercy.' All the time she must have known the man we called the coypu man was her stepfather. She must have been afraid he would come back and find her, hurt her as he had threatened to, put her mother against her. Had he been her—lover? The father of her child?"

"Who knows?" Rufus said dismissively. "It's an interesting

thing that the story didn't even make the national papers, it got no further than a provincial daily. It wasn't important enough."

Adam didn't seem to find it interesting. "All that about Zosima was lies too, wasn't it? She was called Zoe Jane."

"Was?" said Rufus.

Tasting the sweetish contents of his glass, cold, lemony, tingling, Adam wondered if it was gin or vodka Rufus had brought him. He was very ignorant about these things. Already the stuff was making his head swim. It was a good thing he had not brought the car, though he had thought of doing this, his parents' house being such a long way out. For a while, until he found a flat, he would be staying with his parents.

"In a sort of way," Adam said, "I suppose I forget that wasn't Zosie in the grave, but Vivien. I forget it wasn't Zosie who died. It makes you wonder what became of her."

"Didn't you wonder before?"

"Not much. I didn't want to know. I used to switch it all off, blank my mind."

"I think she wrote to her mother or more probably phoned her, told her she'd had the baby and could she come to see her. If you remember, she used to fret about her mother not caring much for her. But she didn't go. Perhaps she was afraid of Pearson or afraid of not having a baby to take with her. When she didn't come, her mother reported her as missing. We don't know anything about Pearson or his relations with Zosie, but the police do. They know his business was going wrong, he'd maybe threatened suicide, was perhaps a bit mad. He killed himself a couple of months later but when the bones were found and the ring . . ."

"Where do you suppose she is now?"

"She was a disaster person," said Rufus, thinking of Mrs. Harding and her daughter. "She wasn't a survivor. She's probably on hard drugs. Or in jail. Remember the camera and the bracelet? She tried to steal a little boy once too. Did you ever know that?"

Adam nodded. He pushed his empty glass away.

"Do you want the other half?"

"You can't say that about spirits," Adam protested. "I mean, about beer you can but not about spirits. The other half of what would it be?"

Rufus laughed. "Still the same old Verne-Smith. Remember the Greek verb 'to rub'? I'll remember that to my dying day."

"Yes, so you said before."

"That doesn't make it less true."

"No. No, it doesn't. I don't really want another drink."

"I should have expected you to be—well, euphoric, to say the least. Aren't you even relieved to be off the hook? I mean, you have realized, haven't you? This is the end of it. It's over. No punishment. This time society fails to take revenge?"

"Oh, I've realized. I've gotten away with it." Adam picked up their glasses. "I'll get you a drink, I ought to. I just never seem to think of it, that's all."

Rufus watched him make his way to the bar. What sort of curious nature would it be that never thought about drinking or that others might wish to drink? It seemed to him that Adam didn't know about Shiva, that he had not made the connection between the man burned to death in Walthamstow and the man they had known at Ecalpemos. There was perhaps no point in enlightening him. It might lead, Rufus thought with a hint of recoil, to quasi-philosophical speculations on the nature of retribution or even God not being mocked. No, he would say nothing.

Vodka and tonic was put down before him. Adam had bought himself something that looked suspiciously like neat Perrier.

"We drank a hell of a lot of wine at Ecalpemos," said Rufus. "Muck most of it. Plonk. It apparently did us no harm."

Adam looked up and said in an aggressive way, "Isak Dinesen said that life is no more than a process for turning healthy young puppies into mangy old dogs and man but an exquisite instrument for converting the red wine of Shiraz into urine."

Rufus gave a bark of laughter. "What brought that up, for God's sake?"

Adam muttered something about random access, so Rufus didn't pursue it but started talking about his plans to move, about a house far beyond their means really that Marigold had found in Flask Walk but which he supposed they would stretch themselves to the limit to buy. But euphoria was making Rufus enthusiastic and even expansive. He had been on what he called a high for five days now, doing his best to keep up there on it, too, because somewhere inside him a little tiny nasty voice was whispering that once he came down he would have to think about his wife, and his wife's friend's husband, and whether he was buying an astronomically priced house to please or even to *buy* his wife. So he said fulsomely to Adam: "We mustn't lose touch again. I mean, the point is we don't *have* to lose touch again. We can all meet up now. I'll get Marigold to give your wife a ring, shall I?"

At one point Adam had felt like explaining. He had felt like opening his heart to Rufus but the moment had passed or all that breezy insensitivity had made it impossible. So he nodded and said okay and because he didn't know what else to do, stuck out his hand and shook hands with Rufus. Rufus offered him a lift but Adam said no thanks, he would get the tube.

Marigold could call Anne, he thought as he walked toward Tottenham Court Road, and be told what would put an end to any possible cozy get-togethers: that Adam and Anne were no longer together. She had left him, or rather, had asked him to leave so that she might remain in Abigail's home with Abigail. It was the only possible way, anyone could see that. Adam was on his way to get the Northern Line up to Edgware, where his parents lived.

It was that remark of Rufus's about no punishment, about society not taking revenge, that had finished him. It was an irony, he thought, that all through the anxiety it had been his removal from Abigail that had worried him, never her removal from him. There was no doubt that they would be given joint custody and he would get to take her out on Sundays. . . .

21

A clearing in the pinewood was how you would have described it now, the turf as smooth and level as a croquet lawn. Meg Chipstead, standing on the green ride and looking at it from a little distance away—she still did not care to go too close— thought not for the first time that perhaps they should replace the monuments. It seemed a pity that something that was historic really, an interesting rural curiosity, should be destroyed because of that one horrifying act. The gravestones had been placed in two neat stacks in the stables: Pinto, Blaze, Sal, Alexander, and all. Of course she would have no idea where to re-site them, except in the case of Blaze. That could never be forgotten.

Meg called out, "Sam, Sam!" and the little dog, the Jack Russell, Fred's replacement, came running out of the deciduous wood. No dog would venture in among the pine trees—at least Fred never had. There was no point really in putting the gravestones back now that they had decided to leave the place. Let the new owners replace them if they chose. Meg and Alec had decided they must tell all to those new owners, whoever they might be. They would find out anyway.

It was May and the bluebells were out. Drifts of them gleamed between the trees like ground mist, like shreds of sky. The beech leaves were a pure pale green, each an unfolding cocoon of silk. A breeze moved the shafts of sunshine, or seemed to do so, making fluttering dapple patterns on the fallen leaves of last autumn. Last autumn . . . Whenever Meg thought of that she knew there was no use saying the place was beautiful and they would regret selling. She could never forget those days of disinterment and investigation, the spoliation of sanctuary and peace. They had made up their minds to go and would keep to this resolution.

She began to walk back to the house, the little dog running through the brakes of bramble, the uncurling green fern, chasing a squirrel across the drift. Meg called him, "Sam, Sam!" because she could hear a vehicle coming down. It would be the people with an order to view, the prospective buyers. A Range Rover in an olive green color, darker than the new leaves, came into sight under the arch of branches and lumbered down the tracks.

Meg waved to show they were expected, to show they had come to the right place, and got in return a hand raised in a salute. This unfamiliar presence started Sam off barking.

"Shut up," said Meg. "Come on, race you to the house."

She threw a stick to speed him on his way. Of course he was off in a streak of white and tan, boomeranging back to her with the stick in his mouth. This time he forgot the stick and went to yap at the people who were getting out of the car in front of the house. Meg came jogging down over the lawn, under the branches of the cedar tree. The front door opened and Alec came out, holding out his hand.

But what a lot of them there were! Meg was rather appalled. The old woman who lived in a shoe, she thought as from the rear doors of the Range Rover one child after another appeared. A stream of children, little steps, as her mother would have said. In fact there were five and the young woman, the wife, was pregnant. She looked a lot younger than her husband, close to twenty. He was tallish with gray curly hair, thin, a bit worn, as well he might be.

She hadn't quite caught their name on the phone, Lathom or Heysham or Patience or something, and she wasn't to learn it now, only to have her hand shaken and told, what a lovely house, really he had had no idea!

Rob, his wife called him. She was a little plump woman, in perhaps her sixth month of pregnancy. Her hair was streaked in rose pink and blond and she was still young enough to wear the fantastic loops and frizzes into which it had been tortured. The two older children, the girls, couldn't be hers. The elder of them was at least fifteen.

"Rob, we can leave this lot outside, can't we?" she said. "It's a lovely day. I mean, they could have a little look around the garden if Mr. and Mrs. Chipstead wouldn't mind."

"Oh, please," said Meg. "Whatever they like. I expect it would be boring for them inside anyway." She said to the children, the smaller ones staring at her, "Only you will be careful of the lake, won't you? You won't go near the lake?"

"I'll just take the baby in with me, if that's all right." A flicker of some indefinable emotion seemed to cross her face. "I don't like leaving him, not just yet."

The "baby" was a big boy of about eighteen months, able to walk but not steadily. His mother yanked him on to her hip, shaking her head when her husband tried to take him from her. They went into the house, where after the outer brightness, the gentle breezy warmth, it seemed as if a dark chill met them.

But this sensation lasted only a moment and the house unfolded itself in all its eighteenth-century elegance. They walked through the drawing room, where the pink marble was admired and the fireplace, and on into Alec's study that was more a library. The Chipsteads had had the room entirely lined with bookshelves and stuck to oak and leather for the furnishings. Meg was proud of the views across the garden from this room, the flint walls of the kitchen garden, the green slope down to the lake, where kingcups were in bloom and yellow flags. The two girls and the two little boys were squatting down at the water's edge trying to persuade a duck to approach them.

Their father tapped on the window and when the elder girl looked up, shook his head in an admonitory way. If they did decide to buy Wyvis Hall, he said to Alec, something would have to be done about that lake, fence it in perhaps.

"Or teach them to swim," said his wife. "And I could learn, too, in case I fell in."

He gave her an indulgent smile, tender, somehow sexual. It made Meg feel slightly embarrassed. To cover the faint confusion this glimpse into their private life had brought her, she asked him if they planned to move permanently to the country.

"Oh, no, we should keep our London house. My company is

there. I shouldn't fancy three hours commuting a day, though I know people do it."

On the stairs she handed the boy over to her husband, stood for a moment, getting her breath. She laid her hand on the swollen belly.

"It does lurch about so. It gave poor Dan an awful great kick just now. No wonder he wanted to go to you."

The master bedroom, the pink room, the lilac room, and the en suite bathrooms. Alec and Meg had had two new bathrooms put in soon after they came there. Just one for a house that size was ridiculous. An eye was kept on the children from the window of the turquoise room (green carpet, peacock feather wallpaper, green and blue striped duvet) and their father called out to the baby: "Take the little ones up into the wood, Nicola."

"And pick some bluebells if you like," said Meg.

"How kind of you! You are nice." Dimpled hands were pushed through the pink and yellow confection of hair, not very clean hands either, Meg noticed with surprise. The finger with the gold wedding ring on it was all streaked with black. They all stared at her when she said, "There's a staircase in that closet that goes up to the loft."

"Absolutely true," said Alec. "There is."

Meg opened the closet door. "More convenient than a trapdoor and a ladder. But how did you know?"

"My wife spent some time in this part of the world before we were married. You've never been in this house before though, have you, Viv?"

She looked with a kind of nervous wonderment, it seemed to Meg, at the pretty green silk curtains, the Klimt reproductions. "Not *this* house, no."

"Would you like some tea, shall I make a cup of tea? I think we have some lemonade for the children."

"Thank you very much but no, we must get back. Our nanny comes back from holiday today, thank God. We like the house. Actually we saw it advertised in the *East Anglian Daily Times*, we take it, my company has an office in Ipswich, but I suppose we shall have to go through the agent? I don't mind telling you we like the house very much."

"We *love* it," his wife said.

The children came running across the grass from the wood

with fistfuls of bluebells. The smaller boy gave a bunch to his mother.

"And we ought to tell you," she said, "we do know about all those grisly things up in the wood." She smiled, holding out her arms, her swollen body swinging under the full loose skirt, childlike no longer but powerful suddenly, a ruling force. "And we don't mind a bit."

ABOUT THE AUTHOR

Barbara Vine, as Ruth Rendell, has won three major awards: the Mystery Writers of America "Edgar Allen Poe" Award for **THE FALLEN CURTAIN**, the Crime Writers Association "Golden Dagger" for **A DEMON IN MY VIEW**, and **CURRENT CRIME** magazine's reader poll named **SHAKE HANDS FOR-EVER** as the best book of the year, over contenders such as Agatha Christie and Len Deighton. Her first book written under the pseudonym of Barbara Vine was the critically acclaimed **A DARK-ADAPTED EYE,** winner of the Mystery Writers of America Edgar Award for the best hardcover mystery of 1986.

Kinsey Millhone is . . .

"The best new private eye." —The Detroit News

"A tough-cookie with a soft center." —Newsweek

"A stand-out specimen of the new female operatives."
—Philadelphia Inquirer

Sue Grafton is . . .

The Shamus and Anthony Award-winning creator of Kinsey Millhone and quite simply one of the hottest new mystery writers around.

Bantam is . . .

The proud publisher of Sue Grafton's Kinsey Millhone mysteries: